Praise for Mercedes Lackey's novels of the *Elemental Masters*:

"Lackey's fantastical world of Elementals, plus her delightful Nan and Sarah, create an amusing contrast for Arthur Conan Doyle's Sherlock Holmes and John Watson.... The mix of humor, history, fantasy and mystery is balanced in a way that any reader could pick up the book and thoroughly enjoy it from beginning to end."   —*RT Reviews*

"This is Lackey at her best, mixing whimsy and magic with a fast-paced plot."   —*Publishers Weekly*

"Richly detailed historical backgrounds add flavor and richness to an already strong series that belongs in most fantasy collections. Highly recommended."
          —*Library Journal* (starred)

"Fans of light fantasy will be thrilled by Lackey's clever fairy-tale adventure."   —*Booklist*

"I find Ms. Lackey's *Elemental Masters* series a true frolic into fantasy."   —Fantasy Book Spot

"The [*Elemental Masters*] novels are beautiful, romantic adult fairy tales. Master magician Mercedes Lackey writes a charming fantasy."   —Worlds of Wonder

"All in fine fairy-tale tradition ... with some nice historical detail, and just a hint of romance to help lighten things."
          —*Locus*

A SCANDAL IN BATTERSEA

The Elemental Masters,
Book Twelve

Mercedes Lackey

DAW BOOKS, INC.
DONALD A. WOLLHEIM, FOUNDER
375 Hudson Street, New York, NY 10014

ELIZABETH R. WOLLHEIM
SHEILA E. GILBERT
PUBLISHERS
www.dawbooks.com

NAN Killian was surrounded by mayhem. Deafening pandemonium.

Darkness shrouded her and her companions; they were nothing but a handful of insignificant observers in the cavernous, shadow-wrapped room full of people.

And all of them were screaming.

"Look behind you!" Nan shrieked at the top of her lungs. Beside her, her ward, little Suki, screamed the same thing. So did Sarah Lyon-White, her dearest friend—and John and Mary Watson sitting on the other side of Suki. Even Lord Alderscroft!

Everyone else in the theater shouted the same words, together, in a thundering, raucous chorus.

"Look behind you!" they all screamed with delight, as Aladdin, resplendent in blue and gold satin, tiptoed his way across the stage, with the black-robed Evil Magician Abanazer right behind him, about to pounce and steal his lamp.

It was a week to Christmas, and that meant it was time for that hallowed and beloved Christmas tradition known throughout all of England, when theaters and music halls gave over their usual schedules to the Panto. The cherished, silly, absurd, childish Christmas Pantomime, that *everyone* went to, and probably enjoyed to the hilt even when they were pretending not to. It was a chance not just to feel like a child, but to *be* a child again. A chance to be dazzled by tinsel and stage magic, to enjoy a sugarcoated story where the hero and heroine would live happily forever and, for the adults, a chance to catch naughty double entendres that flew right over the children's heads.

And here in London, Christmas Panto time meant you were absolutely spoiled for choice. Every theater had a different show, but Suki, Nan and Sarah's "adopted" charge, had been very firm in her wish to see *Aladdin,* and only *Aladdin*, and only *this Aladdin*. When the papers began advertising the upcoming season, she had, it seemed, carefully perused the newspaper accounts of every production on offer, and she wanted this particular one, at the Britannia, which featured two stars this year, a ballet dancer (who was supposedly very famous) as the Princess, and a prominent Shakespearian actor as Widow Twanky, Aladdin's mother. Nan had never heard of either of them, but Sarah had assured her that they were both very highly regarded, which was good enough for her. So plans were made, and then put in motion.

But then the plans changed, for the better.

A few days ago, when Nan had begged off the lecture John Watson had proposed for this afternoon, and she had explained *why,* Mary had perked up so much even John had noticed.

"My love, are you actually—" he began.

"Proposing we go to the Panto?" she responded, before he could finish the sentence. "Oh yes, please! I haven't been since I was tiny—Father didn't really approve of theater in any form, and we lived very quiet lives. Can we? I should like to play at being a child again for an afternoon!"

John Watson had been very surprised at this side of his wife, but Nan could tell he rather liked it. "Very well, my dear, if it's all right with Nan, we'll *all* go, and we'll do the Christmas Treat properly. Luncheon at that tearoom you like so much, the matinee, then we'll look at store windows until Suki is tired, or we run out of windows, then dinner wherever takes your fancy, and home in a jolly old growler."

And the day had *almost* gone according to that programme—except that Lord Alderscroft had got wind of it, and nothing would do but he send his carriage and come along himself for the fun. So Alderscroft had picked them all up in his carriage, then luncheon had been in the tearoom. But dinner would be at his Lordship's townhouse, which he had opened for the Christmas season although he usually lived at his club. And here they all were, in the best seats in the house, a private box, no less, with his Lordship himself next to Sarah, bellowing with everyone else, *"Look behind you!"*

If anyone had told Nan as a child that the cold, forbidding Lord Alderscroft would be sitting next to her at the Panto yelling at the actors, she would have said, "You're barmy!"

This version of the Wizard of London was one she liked very much better than the one she had first been introduced to as a child. She was pretty certain *he* liked this version of himself very much better as well.

Mary and John appeared to be having the time of their lives. Mary was pink with pleasure, and John Watson had thrown off the least inkling of stuffiness and was catcalling and cheering like one of the little boys sitting below their box.

Suki was nearly beside herself with happiness. She had almost all of her favorite adults with her, and they were all acting just like children in the best possible ways—shouting for the hero and heroine, hissing and insulting the villain, and screaming at the stage at all the right moments.

Nan and Sarah were no strangers to the Christmas Panto tradition; the entire Harton School—barring the ones too small—went every year. But the expense of procuring tickets for dozens of children, not to mention the expense of transportation for so many, had meant that they'd only ever seen the stage from what Sahib Harton inelegantly called the "pigeon's seats," from which vantage the figures on the stage looked like brightly colored insects, and you couldn't properly see the magic tricks at all. Lord Alderscroft had taken over the expedition with his customary efficiency—or rather, his private secretary had—and so the private box was exceedingly comfortable, near enough to see everything clearly, but as his Lordship said, "Near enough to see the pips on the playing cards. Far enough away the tinsel looks like gold." It was a little bit of a squash getting all six of them in a box meant for four, but they managed.

In the interval between acts, much to Suki's joy, his Lordship bought them all refreshments, which were served to them by a girl in a black and white uniform, as elegant as Princes and Princesses. It all made Nan feel quite pampered, and Suki beamed.

And when Aladdin had triumphed, rescued his Princess (who had been given a *very* pretty selection of numbers to dance), and all the bows were taken, there was even a semi-private staircase down to where the carriage was waiting. But of course, since they were in a private box, with no need to clear the way for others, they stayed a little while longer, waiting for the crowds to make their way to the street before they took their leisurely way down.

When they left the theater it was snowing, which made the shelter of the carriage all the more welcome. From the dark gray of the sky, the snow wasn't going to end any time soon, either. When they had all piled into the carriage, and Nan had enclosed Suki in the shared warmth of her splendid sable cloak, the snow began to come down rather heavily. "Do you still want to look at shop windows, Suki?" Mary Watson asked the little girl with some concern. "That snow is getting deep."

Suki stuck her little feet in their smart, red boots out from under the shelter of Nan's sable cloak, and frowned thoughtfully. "I jes' got these boots," she observed. "I druther not ruint 'em."

"Well then," Alderscroft said, "I propose a nice drive through the Park instead of going directly there. And perhaps once we are at Harrod's, we can drive past the shop windows slowly enough to enjoy them without leaving the carriage. I very much doubt there will be many window-shoppers between us and the display today."

Nan moved so that Suki could sit next to the window to look out while the rest of the group chatted. Or rather they chatted, while Nan sat quietly, listening. She, Suki, and Sarah sat facing backward in the plush carriage, while his Lordship took one window seat and John Watson took the other, with Mary between them. While Suki gazed with great satisfaction at everything she could see from her window, Sarah, his Lordship, and the Watsons discussed rumblings and stirrings in both the occult and Elemental Magic circles of London. Once, when John Watson spotted a hot chestnut seller, his Lordship stopped the carriage and had the coachman get nuts for them all, including himself. Including the coachman in the warming treat would never have occurred to the old Lord Alderscroft—and probably wouldn't have occurred to one in a thousand other wealthy men.

Lord Alderscroft looked like exactly what he was—at least in part. A titled and very wealthy peer, with a seat in the House of Lords and more than one property at his disposal. Unlike many men of his wealth, he did not allow himself to run to fat; his elegant clothing fit well on the body of a vigorous man of late middle age, and if he wore his sandy hair a bit longer than was strictly conventional, well, he was a nobleman, and noblemen were allowed their little eccentricities. The cane he carried was a formidable weapon, with a weighted, solid silver pommel, and doubled as a wizard's staff of sorts—because he was, after all, the Wizard of London, in charge of the White Lodge of London Elemental Masters and Magicians, and held the magical safety of a great deal of Britain in his capable hands. Like the gentleman he was, he wore a modest top hat—not one of the towering pieces of parvenu vanity that made small, naughty boys ache to throw a snowball at it—and a long, soft black wool coat over his black suit. John Watson wore his gray coachman's bowler and, over his second-best suit, a dark gray coat that was equal in length but a good bit more worn than Lord Alderscroft's. Mary was enveloped in a sable

cloak like Nan's and Sarah's; all three were the gifts of a
grateful opera diva. Little Suki did not have a sable cloak,
but Lord Alderscroft had equipped her—over the girls'
objections—with a black astrakhan cloak of her very own—
much more practical for a little girl than fur.

Suki, having had little more than rags to wear before the
girls rescued her, was quite the little fashion plate now and
took a great deal of pride in looking like the illustration in
a Kate Greenaway book. Today she was wearing an ador-
able brand-new military-style polonaise and skirt, both in
red velvet and trimmed with gold braid, which went perfectly with her little red Hungarian boots. The outfit set off
her dusky complexion and shining, curly black hair to such
a good effect that she looked like a perfect little doll. This
outfit was also a gift from Lord Alderscroft, who was per-
petually amused at her innocent sartorial vanity and took
every chance Nan and Sarah would give him to indulge her
in it—and frequently "surprised" her with gifts before they
could object.

Nan and Sarah had each worn the Christmas gowns that
Lord Alderscroft presented them with every year. Nan's
was a deep garnet velvet, Sarah's a midnight blue. Both of
them were styled in the rather eclectic manner of the Aes-
thetic Movement, which borrowed liberally from nearly
every medieval and Renaissance fashion possible. Such
gowns would probably have raised eyebrows in more conventional circles. But given that they generally only wore
such things in the presence of his Lordship or within his
social group, such eccentricities were not only forgiven, but
expected. Nan thought that this year's gowns were very
likely the best ever. Sarah's sapphire gown complimented
her blond hair and blue eyes so well she looked like a
Christmas angel in a pageant. And while Nan was privately
of the opinion that nothing save an entire change of heads
would ever make *her* look beautiful, she rather fancied that
in this garnet-colored gown she looked a bit handsome.

"Coo!" said Suki, nose pressed against the carriage window. They had come out on the other side of the park and
were now just at Harrod's. The traffic was such that the car-

riage was able to travel very slowly indeed, and Suki was able to gaze on the shop windows to her heart's content without endangering her precious boots.

The adults exchanged indulgent smiles. "How long are you stopping with Nan and Sarah, Suki?" asked Mary Watson. "Does Memsa'b Harton give the usual Christmas holiday?"

"I go back t'the school a'ter—*after* the New Year," Suki replied, with her face still pressed to the window. "I *reely* loik—*like* bein' at school, on'y some of the lessons make m'head hurt." Now she turned her face toward the rest of them for a moment, her expression one of pained distaste. "It's so *hard* t'talk genteel-like! I druther talk Frenchy!"

They all laughed, and Nan dropped a kiss on Suki's forehead, remembering her own struggles with the Queen's English. "Believe me, I know exactly what you mean, darling. I know exactly what you mean."

This was turning out to be a lovely day. In deference to Suki's inability to stay awake, Lord Alderscroft had scheduled "supper" at the scandalously early (for him, anyway) hour of six. Under most circumstances, getting anything other than a late, hearty tea would have been impossible . . . but "impossible" was not a word often spoken around his Lordship. So they all settled into an elegant little dining room already warm and cheerful with a good fire, and, almost as soon as they were seated, staff entered with the first course.

Again, in deference to Suki, whose Christmas treat this really was, the courses presented them were nothing overly complicated, nor anything that required special utensils or etiquette. Nor were they covered in exotic sauces or anything likely to make a little girl turn up her nose. No oysters, for instance, and lobster arrived *out* of its shell, in the form of the first course, a lobster bisque. Otherwise, however, this was a quite grown-up dinner, with all the courses a full formal dinner required. Memsa'b Harton had been consulted, and had agreed that it was time for Suki to get her first exposure to such a thing—because given the circumstances that her life was likely to throw her into, even as young as she was, she might have to attend one. When one was a budding medium of great potential power and the protégé of the great Wizard of London himself, you were very apt to find yourself in extremely exalted company without much warning.

If the servants were astonished to find such a young child attending a dinner with her elders, they were well trained enough not to show it. The one serving her, however, very quietly advised her on things she might or might not like, and confined her drink options to water with just a little wine in it for flavor, and light cider. Suki listened to him gravely, generally accepted his suggestions, and then listened intently to the conversation going on about her.

Sarah had been dubious about whether Suki would remain interested and alert through such a long dinner, but she comported herself well, and was rewarded with her favorite dessert, Eton mess, at the end. Not the usual dessert for a formal dinner, but the smile on Suki's face put an answering smile on Lord Alderscroft's. It certainly would have been a relief to the kitchen staff to produce something this simple, rather than the usual dinner-party dessert. "Eton mess" was a mixture of whipped cream, broken meringues, and strawberries. In this case, strawberries being out of season, it had been made with strawberry preserve.

When the last dessert dishes had been taken away, leaving them with fruit, cheese, nuts, and wine, the servants departed. "Now," said his Lordship, "We can speak freely. I have a bit of a task I have often given John and Mary, ladies. I'd like to ask you to join them. When things are quiet, I send them to make visits to asylums for mentally afflicted."

Nan saw where that was going before Sarah did. "Oh! Because an inmate of such a place might *actually* be seeing things—like Elementals—and not be the victim of lunacy!"

"Exactly. And up until now, I haven't had anyone who could determine whether any of these poor creatures was the victim of his or her psychical gift, rather than insanity. Memsa'b and Sahib Harton have been called upon in the occasion that there was a strong likelihood of such a thing, but no one has been looking for it routinely. I should greatly appreciate it if *you* would, accompanying John, or perhaps John and Mary, as a party." His Lordship took a sip of his wine. "Do you think that would be possible?"

"I don't see why not," Sarah said, after a moment of thought. "It will probably be harder for Nan than me, of course, to tell if something of interest to us is going on—it will be immediately obvious to *me* if there are spirits plaguing someone. But if someone is unable to close out the thoughts of others and *that* is what is wrong with them . . . that might be harder to spot."

"I'll think of something," Nan declared, who already had a rather good idea of what she could do. "But what do we do if we find such a person?"

"Let me know immediately, and I will take steps," Alderscroft declared. He smiled thinly. "It has occurred to me that if said persons could be induced to place their talents at the disposal of the Crown. . . ."

Nan nodded. "You would probably have more luck in recruiting those who are full of gratitude on account of having been saved from a life in a lunatic asylum than those whose circumstances were more fortunate," she said dryly.

Sarah looked a little shocked at her cynicism, but his Lordship—and John Watson—both nodded. "I won't pretend that doesn't enter into our calculations," said John. "Because it certainly does. I'd like to be able to claim it is easy to persuade the more lofty members of the White Lodge to undertake unglamorous, dirty, or . . . 'common' tasks for the love of Queen and Country, but—" He shrugged. "And there isn't even a commission and a fine uniform to go with the service. I'm fortunate that during my tenure I've been able to bring in members who do not mind getting their boots and hands dirty, and it has been in no small part because of such rescues."

"I see no reason why we shouldn't," Nan agreed. "If nothing else, rescuing someone from one of those places that doesn't belong there is surely a task on the side of the angels."

At this point, Suki tried in vain to smother a yawn. "Beg pardon," she said, a little shamefaced.

"Not at all, Suki," Lord Alderscroft said with a smile. "It's definitely time for us to call an end to our evening. I confess I have an engagement I should be getting ready for. It is just that it will not be *nearly* as enjoyable as this afternoon was, and I have been putting it off." He rang for the butler, who appeared as quickly as Aladdin's Djinni had.

"The coach is already waiting, my Lord," the butler said, before Lord Alderscroft could say anything. "By the time your guests are ready to leave, it will be standing at the door."

"Thank you, Graves," Alderscroft said. "Very well done. Ladies? John?"

And indeed, within a very little time, they were all packed back into the carriage with the snow coming down out of the darkness and hot bricks at their feet. At this unfashionable hour—when most people in this neighborhood were *beginning* their dinners—the street was very nearly deserted.

There was a rapping at the little door in the ceiling of the carriage used to communicate with the coachman, and that worthy peeked down at them. "Beg pardon, ladies, sir—m'lord give me th' usual load of blankets an' 'taties for a night like this un—hev you got any objection to a stop or two along the way?"

"Good lord, man, no," John replied immediately. "In fact, when you spot an urchin, just let me pop out and you toss the goods down. That way you don't need to get off the box."

"Thenkee Doctor, that'd suit right well," the coachman replied, and closed the hatch. Nan heard him cluck to the horses, and off they went.

"Blankets? Taties?" she asked.

"Alderscroft has the cook bake potatoes on nights like this if he's having the coach go out of the neighborhood, and loads the top behind Brendan with blankets and a full basket. If Brendan sees a child or a woman out begging or trying to sell something in this weather, he's got orders to give out a hot potato and a blanket each," Mary Watson said warmly. "Perhaps it's a small thing—"

"But it might be the difference between keeping life in the body and freezing to death!" Sarah exclaimed.

"At the very least, it's the difference between going to bed hungry and cold, and going to bed warmer and with a full belly," Nan agreed, thinking that there had been *many* nights in her past where she would have greeted the gift of a hot potato and a blanket as if they were being granted by a ministering angel.

The coach made at least four stops to distribute comfort before they reached Nan and Sarah's lodgings. Twice it was for children, one trying to sell paper flowers, another a little match girl. Both those times, John came back with all they'd had to sell, as well. Once it was for a woman begging with two small children. Once it wasn't for a woman at all, but for a man, dressed in an old, worn Army uniform; he was particularly noteworthy for being out in the snow with a wooden leg and a crutch. That time when John got back into the coach, Mary gave him an inquiring look.

"Africa," John said shortly. "He's a pukka soldier, all right, not some faker. I gave him the address of someone that can put him on to a job. If he stays sober, this should be his last night of begging in the streets."

The coachman let Nan, Sarah and Suki down first, in their unfashionable, working-class neighborhood. Their landlady Mrs. Horace had probably just finished her own dinner and settled down to some mending or knitting before going to a virtuously early bed. The snow was calf-deep in front of their door, and to save Suki's precious boots, John Watson bravely carried her the few steps to the doorway, setting her down just inside, and was rewarded with a kiss. Nan and Sarah simply held their skirts up and waded through it, stamping their feet to clean them on the step before going inside.

"You are too good to us, John Watson," Sarah declared. The Doctor chuckled, and shooed them inside, turning to plow his way back to the carriage. They were not loath to follow his direction.

As Nan had more than half expected, Mrs. Horace popped her head out of her own door as they closed the outer one. "Well, you're in good time! How was the Panto?"

"Wunnerful!" Suki exclaimed, and looked ready to tell their landlady all about it right there on the spot.

But Mrs. Horace smiled with approval and forestalled her. "Then you can tell me all about it, ducks, while we make gingerbread and paper chains to decorate the Christmas trees with tomorrow."

Suki squealed with glee, and jumped a little. "I will!" she promised, and ran up the stairs.

"You spoil her," Nan said, mildly, as Sarah trotted up to unlock the door to their flat.

"She's easy to spoil, and it doesn't seem to do her any harm," their landlady replied fondly. "Good night to you, Miss Nan."

"Pleasant dreams to you, Mrs. Horace," Nan answered, and followed Sarah.

Sarah had already turned up the lights, poked up the fire, and was helping Suki out of her finery and into her nightdress, so Nan went to the birds' room to check on them.

In summer, the birds either slept on the headboards of Nan and Sarah's beds or on their perches, but in winter they shared a cage that had had the door taken off. It was shrouded in a nice, thick blanket, and had a hot brick wrapped in old flannel at the bottom of it. The raven Neville would have been fine without such a precaution, but with Grey being from Africa, Sarah and Nan preferred to take every precaution they could think of to keep her warm.

Neville seemed to feel the same, since Nan found them huddled together with Neville's wing over Grey's back.

They looked up at her footstep, and blinked sleepily at her. She checked the temperature of the brick with her hand, and decided to exchange it for the one on the hearth.

"Good fun," Grey said.

"Yes, it was a great deal of fun," Nan agreed. "I wish you could have come with us."

"Rrrr. Ginger nuts," suggested Neville.

"Providentially, Mrs. Horace has decided that tomorrow is going to be a baking day, so I think that can be arranged," Nan chuckled, putting the hot, newly wrapped brick in the bottom of the cage. "Good night, my loves."

She went to her own room and came out in a comfortable flannel wrapper over her own nightdress to find Sarah, who had done the same, waiting with chamomile tea. "Suki is already asleep," she said, handing Nan a cup and propping her feet up at the fire. "I'm surprised; I would have thought she'd be awake half the night."

"A very full stomach plus a nice warm bed probably did the trick," Nan observed. "And I would be feeling the same, were it not for Lord A's hints tonight."

Sarah sighed. "Christmas Eve *and* the dark of the moon coming together . . . he's right. We should be on our guard at this time of year. Or at least, John and Mary should. I don't know that *our* talents are going to be of any use when it is arcane perils that are most likely to walk the earth."

"Oh? I thought the Eve was when spirits crossed, too," Nan observed, sipping her tea. "That is quite firmly in *your* area of expertise."

"But moon-dark has absolutely no effect on that, at least not that I have ever seen." Sarah had set aside her empty teacup and toyed with the end of her golden braid like a cat with a bit of yarn. "It seems such a pity to spoil Christmas with having to worry about . . . that."

Nan thought about that for a moment. "Well," she observed. "There's nothing at all we can do to prevent trouble, true?"

"As far as I know, true," Sarah agreed.

"So whether we worry about it, or don't think about it and enjoy the holiday, trouble will happen, or not, regardless. True?"

"Also true." Sarah smiled at her friend. "I see where you are taking this. Yes, you're right. There is no point in worrying about it, as long as we are prepared for trouble to come."

"Which we *always* are," Nan pointed out triumphantly, and finished her tea. "So there is no point in troubling

ourselves about what *might* happen. Meanwhile I am going
to bed now, and I plan to enjoy the holiday to its fullest
from now until Boxing Day."

"I think I shall read for a bit by the fire," Sarah replied.
"It's too cold to read in bed."

"There, I agree with you." She gathered up the cups and
put them on the tray outside their door for Mrs. Horace to
collect in the morning. By the time she turned around,
Sarah was already deeply engrossed in her book, feet to the
fire. Chuckling, she sought out her bed, very grateful for the
flannel-wrapped brick Mrs. Horace had slipped into it. It
still had enough heat in it that she moved it down to the
foot of the bed to warm her toes. She was asleep in moments, and dreaming she was feasting on Eton mess with a
gaggle of Arab ballet dancers.

Sarah waited until she was sure that Nan was asleep and
exchanged her book for another. Not a romantic adventure,
this one was a volume from Memsa'b's library—one of the
very rare books on spirits and hauntings. Not that books
about spirits and hauntings were rare—if anything, there
were rather *too* many of them available in the shops. It was
accurate books that were a rarity.

This one, in particular, focused solely on vengeful or in-
imical spirits. She had believed that Puck's talisman would
protect her against such things. But thanks to this book . . .
she had come to realize it might not.

So far all the nasty spirits she had encountered had been
those of evil but perfectly ordinary people. The talisman
that Puck had given her as a child had been more than adequate protection against them, walling them off from her
so that they could do her no harm. But within the pages of
this book, she had found things that suggested that she had
merely been lucky thus far, in that she had never encountered the vengeful spirit of someone who, in life, had been
a magician, or worse, a Master. Such a spirit would not only
have the knowledge of magic it had wielded in life, it would

have access to whatever power was available in the spirit realm.

Tonight's discussion of Christmas Eve had brought her the sudden realization that if ever such a spirit was to strike, it would be then. She had not wanted to spoil Nan's evening, in no small part because there was nothing whatsoever Nan could actually do against such a creature, so she had kept her misgivings to herself. But as soon as Nan had gone to bed, she plunged back into the pages of the book, looking for answers.

Unfortunately, she found none, and closed the book wearing a frown of discontent. Finally, she stared into the dying fire, and sighed. *I'll just have to see if John and Mary know something, or if they fail me, Lord Alderscroft.*

But Nan was right about one thing. There really was *nothing* she could do about it, if there happened to be such a creature waiting for its moment to emerge from the spirit realm. She didn't know where it could manifest, nor what form it would take. She and the Watsons had already put every protection they could think of on their flat, the Watsons', and Holmes'. And Lord Alderscroft, of course, had so much magic layered on his various homes that to the inner eye they looked like impregnable fortresses. There was nothing more she could do, so she might as well stop fretting and enjoy the season.

Easier said than done, she sighed, as she put the book away on a shelf. No harm in rereading it later, after all. She might spot something she had missed if she came at it with fresh eyes.

She went to bed, grateful that Mrs. Horace had stowed a hot brick wrapped in flannel in it, and even more grateful for the featherbed and down comforter. She was sure she would have nightmares anyway, but instead, she found herself dreaming of Aladdin, who looked just like Puck, producing a series of amusing spirits out of a lamp.

2

ALEXANDRE Harcourt despised the Christmas season.

It was not merely that everyone around him—even occultists, artists and writers who should have been immune to such childish nonsense—became positively giddy in the presence of decorations, carols, and Christmas sweets. It was not just that everyone around him suddenly became mawkishly and sentimentally attached to their families, even when during the rest of the year they could barely stand to be in the same building.

It was that the season occasioned not just idiotic merriment, but upsets in everything. Christmas balls had an air of . . . desperation. Anxious mamas and equally anxious daughters were eying the deadline of New Year's Eve, still with no engagements announced, and were lowering their expectations and upping the pressure on any young man they considered a remotely acceptable catch. Parties were inclined to include children, at least for part of the festivities, and Alexandre loathed children.

But worst of all, the entertainments he could usually count on were supplanted by . . . other things.

Today, for instance. He had intended to spend the afternoon at his favorite music hall, one where the women danced the French Can-Can in the truly *French* manner, that is to say, *sans culottes*. He had been looking forward to a pleasant, dissipated afternoon, after which he would think about his dinner and his evening. But he arrived there only to discover the music hall was closed.

That is, he arrived at the hall to find there was a slouching fellow in an oversized coat and a soft hat standing outside the doors, turning people away. Alexandre ignored him and attempted to push his way in, but the fellow actually put an arm out, preventing him.

"'All's closed, guv," he said, pulling on the brim of his hat deferentially. Alexandre stared at him, stunned. He'd never heard of such a thing—a closed music hall is a music hall that isn't making any money, after all. The fellow nodded to confirm his statement and elaborated. "'Ole 'all's 'ired out till midnight," he stated. "Brother'ood uv 'Aulers an' Carters Christmas Ball."

Alexandre swallowed down rage, but enraged he surely was. How dared some dirty lot close this place for a whole day so they could swill cheap beer and cavort until midnight! "But surely—" he said, "The entertainers—"

"Part uv th' 'ire, guv," the man said, with a hint of sympathy. "Oi cain't letcher in, an yew wouldn' loik it, anyways. Gulls is dressed down t'their toesies an' up t'their necks, an' the singin's all carols an' senteemental ballads an' suchlike. No dancin', the jokes is all fer kiddies, an' nothin' sportin'. Come on back arter midnight, we got a midnight show. Or come back tomorrer."

No hope for it. He turned away, and just to complete his dissatisfaction, it began to snow. It was chancy enough to find a cab in this wretched part of town, but inclement weather made it nearly impossible. He had to trudge for blocks before he managed to catch one just as the driver was letting off his fare, before the man could whip up the horse and speed away to a more lucrative part of the city.

He gave the man the first address that popped into his head, which, on reflection, was the very *last* place he wanted to go to: Pandora's Tea Room in Chelsea, frequented by the

artistic, poetic, and esoteric sets. Not that he didn't frequent
Pandora's—just not at this hour, when the ... less adventur-
ous made it their haunt. But it would at least be warm and
dry there, and assuming that the snow would keep most of
the people he *didn't* want to see away, he could get something to eat while he decided on another destination.

Alas. The snow had only made the place more crowded
than usual. It seemed that every single member of the airy-
fairy-type artistic circles had decided to descend, and eat
tea cakes, and blather about Truth and Beauty.

Nearly every one of the mismatched tables was taken,
and there was no hope of getting a seat near the fire. Ciga-
rette smoke formed a haze up near the ceiling. And ... just
to add to the visual cacophony of mismatched furniture,
linens and crockery, the place had been bedecked in gar-
lands and scarlet bows and tinsel for Christmas, which further irritated him. Beatrice Leek was holding forth in her
usual corner but paused in one of her interminable stories
to give him a look that was one part contempt, one part
amusement and one part warning. And to his chagrin, he
spotted that new girl, another would-be poet he'd wanted to
introduce to *his* occult set, sitting right next to the Leek
woman. He would have *no* chance at her now.

He spotted a tiny table and chair in the coldest corner of
the room, right up against the windows, and made his way
there, feeling sour the entire time. He was slightly mollified
by the excellent ham sandwiches—unlike far too many
places patronized by either socialists or artists or both, the
food here was outstanding. But although he was not precisely being ostracized, it was quite clear that Beatrice had
poisoned her little clan against him, and the rest of the people here were too bound up in their own conversations and
interests to pay him any heed. He ate quickly, seeing no
chance for *any* opportunity here today, paid for his fare, then
went and stood ostentatiously at the fire, leaning up against
the mantelpiece and having a smoke himself to soothe his
injured temper. He was, by heaven, going to make sure he
was completely warmed before he went out into that
damned mess. And to the devil with the people who cast him

annoyed glances for soaking up the heat. He had paid, and he was entitled to it.

He kept one eye on the street, and as soon as he saw a cab pull up outside, he shoved his way to the door regardless of the objections of those he'd jostled. He barged into the middle of the three who had clambered out of a two-person hansom in order to engage the driver before he trotted off.

"I say there!" objected one of them, but he ignored them. The driver, who had not expected to get a fare this soon, ignored them as well.

"Where to, guv?" the man asked, as the three who had arrived sniffed with ostentatious contempt and made their way into the tearoom.

Alexandre had not even thought of a destination, at least, not consciously, but his subconscious must have been working on the combination of "warmth," "satisfaction," and "idle occupation," for his mouth opened and out came, "Treadman's Books. Thirty-three Store Street."

"That'd be Bloomsbury, ain't it?" the man said, but it was obviously a rhetorical question. "Right you are, guv."

Alexandre swung himself up into the cab, the man gave his horse a smart touch of the whip, and they were off.

The traffic was abominable, but the man made good time anyway, and soon enough had pulled up in front of the dark windows of Treadman's. Treadman's was always dark; the proprietor preferred to keep the lighting dim to save fading of his books. Yet Treadman's, so far as Alexandre had been able to tell, was always open. He paid the cabby and hurried inside.

Rather than a bell, Treadman had a curious little clockwork contraption over the door that wound up when the door was opened, allowing a couple of beaters on a small drum to beat out a rapid tattoo when the door closed. Treadman himself was not behind the counter at the front, but Alexandre had barely had time to look around and shake the snow off his coat and onto the mat when he appeared, seemingly out of nowhere.

"Ah, Master Harcourt," the tall, thin man with the perpetual stoop and squint of a scholar said, looking over his spectacles. "It has been some little while. I have several volumes I held aside for you. Would you care to take them to a reading room to look them over, or would you prefer to browse?"

Treadman was no ordinary book merchant. He specialized in the rare, the occult, the esoteric, the profane and the obscene. He treated all books equally. There had never once, in all the time Alexandre had known him, been a moment when so much as a flicker of disapproval passed over that thin, contemplative face, no matter *what* Alexandre bought.

"I judge the condition of books, I do not judge the content," he had said once, to someone else, but within Alexandre's hearing.

The first floor was devoted to rare books of . . . ordinary content. The third and fourth floors held literature that in other times would have gotten Treadman burned at the stake—and might these days have gotten him hauled into court for obscenity. Except that Treadman was clearly well connected enough to avoid that particular unpleasantness. Alexandre suspected he was supplying a long list of politicians, peers of the realm, and wealthy captains of the business world with those of their pleasures that could be contained within two covers.

The second floor was made up of a block of little "reading rooms." Each one had a lock, a good light, and a comfortable chair and reading desk. There, in complete security and privacy, a prospective customer could examine the wares he had selected—or Treadman had selected *for* him—at his leisure. There was no chance someone could, accidentally or purposefully, look over one's shoulder to see what one was perusing.

This was not the only use for these rooms. There were scholars that were too impoverished to buy some of the rare books Treadman offered. For a select, trusted few, Treadman would *rent* the books, allowing these scholars to study and even copy them so long as they never left the store.

There were also times when two people were in contention over the same book. If it was the contents of the book, rather than the rarity, that someone was after, Treadman would, for a higher rental fee, keep the wealthier party at bay while the poorer one copied what he wanted.

Thus, Treadman realized a great deal more money out of his second-floor reading rooms than if he'd kept his stock here. Not that he was altruistic. If you could not afford the rental he stipulated—then too bad. You would have to languish knowing that some knowledge was out of your reach, forever.

At the moment, being ensconced in a comfortable armchair with a good light over his shoulder and a stack of books was his best option for entertainment. *Well, there are worse things . . . sitting and listening to a gaggle of stupid women gossip and pretending to be interested, for instance.*

"I would very much like to peruse what you've held back for me, Treadman," he said, with a brief nod of approval. "And anything else that's come in that you think might be of interest to me."

"Then allow me to send up the boy with your selections, and while you wait for the room to be prepared, perhaps you may care to browse the shelves?" Treadman suggested.

"Fourth floor, I think. Send the boy when my room is ready," he replied, and made his leisurely way up to the fourth floor, where the vast collection of prurient material was housed, from erotica to outright obscenity.

He was leafing through a Japanese "pillow book" of woodcuts—not a particularly well-done volume, but amusing in its way—when the boy arrived with a key. He reshelved the volume, having given up on trying to determine if he was looking at a *ménage a trois,* or just an illustration accidentally created with too many limbs, and took the key from the lad. The boy, like Treadman, seemed utterly incurious. Perhaps having been around all this, any pubescent curiosity in erotica had long since been sated. Treadman had never said where the boy came from, but Alexandre fancied he had been plucked from the streets at a young enough age to have been mere putty in Treadman's hands. Certainly he was better off here than most of the urchins out there. He looked well fed, he was well clothed and clean, and presumably had a warm place to sleep here in the shop. That was more than the refuse of the streets had, however many hours in the day and night Treadman worked him. For as long as Alexandre had been coming here, there had been "the boy," this same, compact, dark-haired, dark-eyed boy, who looked at one with no interest whatsoever, and yet with the light of intelligence in his eyes. Was he kin to Treadman? It hardly seemed likely. Alexandre had seen women enter this shop, some quite beautiful, as many expensive mistresses frequented the place, and never had he seen Treadman show more interest in them than he did in any other customer.

The tag on the key only read "20." This suited him, and once again Treadman had anticipated his mood. The twentieth room was the one farthest from the stairs; he was unlikely to have any neighbors. It also shared a wall with one of the chimneys, so it would be quite cozy.

He took the three volumes he had found to be of some slight interest with him down to the second floor, and made his way to the door marked "20." When he opened it with the key, he found everything in readiness for him: a lamp, newly cleaned, chimney well-polished, fastened to the wall behind the chair, the chair itself dusted and supplied with a lap robe should he need it, and the gratifying pile of books on the reading desk next to the chair. He put the volumes he had brought with him on the desk and lifted the first of Treadman's choices from the stack.

There were several French novels, only one of which interested him; the others were copies of works he had obtained himself on the Continent. There was a *much* superior pillow book—one in which he was not left to guess whether the participants had too many limbs, or limbs with extra joints. It was not in particularly good shape, but the woodcuts themselves were fine and detailed. He put that in his "will buy" pile, once he satisfied himself it was worth Treadman's asking price.

There followed three occult books. One was errant nonsense—he had long ago worked out that Treadman himself could not tell wheat from chaff where the occult was concerned. One was a disfigured copy of a book he had in its entirety. And the third—

He almost discarded it. On first glancing through it, it looked like nonsense, and the book itself was in terrible shape. He almost put it aside—but hesitated. There was something about it—

He gave it a second chance, pursing his lips as he realized some of the loose pages were out of order. *There might be something worth looking at, here,* he thought, and looked inside the back cover for the discreet little note that would tell him Treadman's price.

The price was ridiculous. Ridiculously low. Low enough that if it turned out this thing was nothing but a farce, he could probably pass it off to one of the Leek woman's set for ten times the price. That decided him; he added it to the "will buy" stack and checked his pocket watch. He was gratified to see that several hours had passed, and if he had not experienced the pleasure he would have had at the music hall, well, he also hadn't experienced the usual tedium of being in the company of a lot of unwashed, half-drunk buffoons.

He left the room and descended the stairs to find Treadman behind his counter. A few moments later the boy came down with his "will buy" stack in a basket. Treadman tallied up the purchases and wrapped them tidily in discreet brown paper, then wrapped them again in waxed paper to keep off the snow. "One moment, Master Harcourt, I'll send the boy out to fetch you a cab," Treadman said, in his usual pleasantly neutral tone, as if the parcel contained essays and poetry, rather than some of the most eye-popping pornography in all of London. The boy wrapped himself in an enormous muffler and pulled on a hat and went out; within five minutes he was back, and a cab was pulling up to the front door.

Alexandre gave the cabby the address of his flat in Battersea; although he intended to dine at his club, he really did not want to take the chance, however slim, that the parcel should come apart and his purchases be exposed to the world's curious eyes.

But once safely home, and the books disposed of, a glance out the window showed the storm worsening. *If* he could get a cab, it would be a miserable ride, and for what? The dubious pleasure of a chop and some overcooked vegetables in the company of a lot of stuffy old bastards who had been friends with his father . . . there would be no one young or interesting there tonight, and knowing that the old gents were pretty indifferent to their food, the cooks tended to slack off on evenings like this. And after an indifferent dinner at the club, what then?

A quick perusal of his invitations left him with the impression of similar barrenness for the evening. They were all for "Christmas" this and "Christmas" that. He'd have accepted a decent musical evening, or a card party at which the stakes would be mere tokens at this point, but there wasn't even the promise of that. At least two of the invitations made him grimace; they were for "family" parties. Of course, neither of the men who had invited him had *any* idea of his interests and nature—and they were probably fishing for prospective husbands for their daughters. Still. The prospect of a deadly boring evening that would probably feature parlor games and the inexpert warblings or tinklings of (very) amateur musicians was enough to make him contemplate feigning a fit or flinging himself out a window rather than endure it.

He rang for his man. "Can you contrive something in the way of supper, or need I send you down to the 'Parrot'?" he asked.

"Oi reckoned we was in for a bad un, an' Oi took the liberty of sendin' t' the shops this arternoon, guv," the fellow said. He was rough-hewn, but he suited Alexandre. They shared similar tastes in food, drink, and women, he organized the flat well, he *never* forgot his place, and he was quite resourceful. And, within limits, he could cook. "If yew fancy a bite now, Oi can 'ave a nice Welsh rarebit, or cold roast beef."

"The rarebit will do nicely, Alf. And I believe I will have beer with it." The evening did not seem *quite* so bleak, with hot food in the offing.

"Good choice, guv," Alf touched one finger to his temple

by way of a salute, and disappeared in the direction of the flat's tiny kitchen. Alexandre had, curiously enough, "inherited" Alf from another occultist who had run afoul of the law and found it necessary to flee the country. Alf was utterly useless at many of the "normal" duties of a valet—he was hopeless at dressing his master, for instance. And there was no mistaking he was a direct import from the East End. But Alexandre was perfectly capable of dressing himself and running his own bath, and Alf more than made up for any deficiencies with his absolute discretion, his resourcefulness, and his cunning. It was he, for instance, who had gotten his former master out of the country one step ahead of the police. And on seeing his master safely on board a smuggling ketch and well underway, he had turned right around, gotten his own worldly goods packed up and presented himself to Alexandre, leaving the barren and stripped flat for the baffled Bobbies.

Alexandre, who knew Alf's valuable qualities from visits with his fellow magician, and who had been increasingly frustrated with his (then current) valet, fired the old one and hired Alf on the spot.

Alf was that rarest of *rarae aves* of the underclass. He knew what he wanted, and what he wanted was to be comfortable. He wanted to not have to work too hard for that comfort. He did not aspire to wealth. He knew better than to shear his sheep too often, or kill the proverbial golden goose. His former and current masters all had the same arrangement with him. He woke them after he woke. They shared a breakfast, a morning smoke, and papers. His master dressed himself and went on about his business, and Alf had the run of the flat and carte blanche to do what he wanted until his master returned. When the master returned, Alf might or might not cook dinner depending on whether he'd stocked the larder, gotten something at the pub on the corner that could keep, or his master intended to dine out. Alf might or might not procure women for himself and his master, might or might not slip a cosh in his pocket and follow his master off as a guard, either when venturing into the bowels of London in search of entertainment, or into other places for esoteric experiments. If his master went off unaccompanied, Alf put a hot brick in the bed but did not wait up. Alf was paid very well for these light duties, and this life suited him down to the bone. Very occasionally, his master needed something quasi-legal or outright against the law, and Alf would supply that thing for an extra consideration.

Alf, in short, suited his master, and his master suited Alf.

Alexandre retired to his bedroom and returned in soft trousers, slippers, and a warm smoking jacket at about the same time Alf appeared in the dining room with a laden tray. He set it down on the table, and as Alexandre took his seat, served him several triangles of toast, over which he spooned the cheese sauce, before making a plate for himself. He opened and poured his master's beer, and his own, and settled himself across from Alexandre with every sign of contentment. In that moment, Alexandre envied him.

"Wretched hall was closed," he said crossly, cutting himself a bite, then savoring it. Alf might not be a master cook, but he did make a masterful rarebit. "Some Brotherhood or other hired it for a Christmas party, if you please."

Alf *tsk'd*. "Them gels won't be well pleased," he opined. "Them lads'll all hev their famblies there, like as not, so them gels'll be workin' just as hard, with no chance fer a nice dinner or gennelmun what has the notion fer some company arterwards."

They ate a few more bites in silence. "Chrismus Eve's moon-dark," Alf observed. "Anythin' ye'll need?"

"I don't know yet," Alexandre admitted. "I've been researching, but I haven't come across anything that will advance *my* powers that calls for that specific combination."

That was not quite true. The actual truth was, Alexandre didn't exactly . . . research anything. He was more like a butterfly, flitting from one potentially attractive occult or magical flower to another, but never staying long at any of them.

But Alf just shrugged. "Early days yet. Happen ye'll run acrost somethin'. An' happen ye don't . . ." he lifted his beer glass in Alexandre's direction. ". . . then Chrismus Eve's a desperate thin noight fer workin' wenches. Eh?"

"There is that." Alexandre cheered up a trifle. The rest of the meal proceeded in silence; when they were done, Alexandre took his seat in his easy chair by the fire; Alf put the dishes on his tray and took them to the kitchen, where the housekeeper would deal with them in the morning. Unless Alexandre summoned him with the bell, he'd return to his room, and do whatever it was he did to amuse himself. One thing Alexandre knew he did from time to time was go out after his master had gone to his own bedroom and get a woman just for himself. Sometimes two. Alexandre admired his stamina. They were always gone long before morning, and nothing in the flat had ever gone missing, so as far as he was concerned, Alf could do as he liked.

As for Alexandre ... he had intended to leaf through that pillow-book, but that was only going to lead to a certain level of frustration—and he felt too burdened with ennui to send Alf out for a wench to relieve that frustration. He reached for one of the French novels, but his hand fell on that odd little occult book he had picked up instead.

Well, why not. He opened it, and looked at it more closely, and before long he realized that thanks to the ruined spine, it was more than a few pages that were out of order. Intrigued now by the puzzle, he plucked all the loose pages out and slowly began to piece the book together.

He startled himself with a yawn, and looked at the clock over the mantle, realizing with a start that a good two hours had passed. And his neck was feeling a bit stiff. He put the book down on top of the stack of pages that had yet to be inserted, weighed it down with another, heavier tome, and picked up the French novel, pouring himself a brandy from the bottle on the side table that held the books.

As he read, he was aware of a nagging discontent. This was not how he would have chosen to spend his evening, if he had had a choice. This was ... cloyingly domestic. Except for the subjects of his reading, it had been an evening even his *mother* would approve of, if she had a moment of sobriety in which to do so.

His father, thank the devil, had died while Alexandre was still at Oxford ... and thanks to careful management on

Alexandre's part, the *only* thing that the old Puritan had been aware of was that his son did not share his obsession with religion.

Then again, there probably wasn't anyone at the entire University, including the clergy, who could have been as obsessed with religion as the elder Harcourt had been.

Alexandre had, fortunately, been able to evade his father's eye because he was only the second, or "spare" son, a fact his father had often reminded him of. His older brother, the pride of the house, the ever-so-perfect Victor, was everything Andrew Harcourt desired in his son. Just as religious, impeccably obedient, never once, in all of Alexandre's life, had Victor ever done something for which he had been chided. Whereas Alexandre had seen the business end of a cane more times than he cared to think about, at least until he learned to be so sly and cunning in his misdeeds that, while there might be suspicion about him, he was never caught.

Eventually he became so good at deception he even evaded suspicion. When the odd half crown went missing, he made sure evidence pointed to someone who was already guilty of petty theft. And later, girls who might have looked for him to make good on his promises were always looking in the wrong town, for a young man of the wrong name at the wrong address. And later still . . . well his deceptions were aided by magic, so that even his face and voice were muddled in their minds, and they could, and often did, pass him on the street without recognizing him.

That was all while he was at Eton, following in the ever-perfect Victor's footsteps. A foray into a secondhand shop on one of his clandestine visits to the town had netted him a peculiar book that he was quite drawn to, even though he had been looking for something else entirely.

Handwritten, between two soft leather covers, it was nothing he would have picked up even to look at under ordinary circumstances. But he couldn't help himself, and he took it to the proprietor as if he was under a spell and paid the sixpence he was asked for without haggling.

He knew now of course that it *had* been a spell: a spell

designed to find someone exactly like him, and induce him to purchase the thing. The spell had been written on the inside of the leather cover, although he hadn't known that at the time. All he knew was that he *must* have this thing, and deciphering it became his obsession.

An obsession that had quickly paid off, as he learned things that allowed him to manipulate his fellow students, and even, occasionally, the masters. All small things at first, but as his mastery grew, so did his power. By the time he was ready to enter Oxford . . . he was ready for much more.

But first, there was a little matter he needed to attend to.

No one could understand it when the ever-perfect, ever-earnest, over-achieving Victor Harcourt one night in mid-winter rose from his bed, dressed carefully, and walked out of Magdalen College down into the Cherwell onto the ice. The ice broke under him, and despite the shallow water, he didn't seem to have struggled or attempted to save himself at all, but simply died of cold, or drowned, the coroner was unsure which.

Alexandre's parents were heartbroken, so much so that they paid no attention to Alexandre at all. His father put all of his business into a manager's hands (the manager, being unswayed by trivial matters of the piety of the investment, made a better job of it than Harcourt Senior had) and spent all his time pouring over Victor's papers, trying to find a reason why his beloved son should have done this. Within the year, his heart literally broke; he was found dead in his office, still with some of Victor's essays in his hands, and the doctor opined he had died of sorrow. And Alexandre's mother took to the comforting arms of some patent medicine that was half alcohol and half opium. Her maid managed her, the housekeeper managed the house, and the business manager managed the business and the household finances. Sometimes old friends attempted to draw her out of herself, but she was much happier in a half stupor in a sunlit window like a cat. Dreaming, perhaps, that her beloved son was still alive and would come home any day. Alexandre she barely acknowledged.

Which was exactly the way he wanted things.

He had cast that spell over his brother to send him out into the midwinter night. He'd intended for Victor to lie down to sleep in some remote place and freeze to death, but the fact that he went into the river was ever so much more convenient. It hadn't taken much occult nudging at all to turn his father's already-obsessive nature into an obsession with his dead son; late nights, poor sleep, and eating little had done for him without any other means necessary. And as for his mother, well, a mere suggestion that the tonic would "help," and the constant replenishing of full bottles, took care of her. And as long as she was content to dream away her days in the hands of her maid and housekeeper, Alexandre had no inclination to meddle with her further.

This left him in control of a very nice income—the business manager was a sharp, clever, calculating man, honest to a fault, with an entire law firm behind him. Alexandre knew better than to try to meddle with *him,* and really, there was no need for any of that. He was comfortable, he was let to do what he wanted as long as he didn't run through his allowance, and for the most part he was contented.

Except on nights like this one, where nothing had gone right. When he glanced out his window and saw people in expensive carriages making their way through the snow to the sort of parties and dances *he* would never be invited to. When he looked around his flat, he noted with discontent that while it was comfortable, and suited him very well, it was . . . slightly shabby, a bit shopworn. He would have no compunction in bringing people from the artistic set here, since most of them lived in far shabbier circumstances—but it was not the sort of place he'd have felt comfortable inviting anyone with a title to.

Not that he knew anyone with a title, except a few fellows from Oxford. And in all probability, if he brought himself to their attention (and he was wearing his school tie) they'd vaguely acknowledge him, issue an even vaguer invitation to "a drink sometime at my club" and fail to give him a card.

Not that he ever *would* know anyone with a title. Even the occult circles he moved in did not boast men with titles.

He knew what circle *did*—the famed White Lodge of Elemental Magicians and Masters, led by the redoubtable Lord Alderscroft. This, of course, was scarcely common knowledge even among those involved in magic and the occult, but one of the things he had mastered was the ability to see things from afar by way of crystals and bowls of water, and he had overseen and overheard enough to put all the pieces together. He himself would have been counted as a Water Magician, he supposed. Scrying by water...sending his brother to his death by water...even the nostrum he'd gotten his mother addicted to was a form of water...

He had been able to see and command—or rather coerce—the Elementals of Water as a child, though they avoided him in order to avoid being ordered about. But he preferred other magic, things that worked on other people, and made them do what he wanted them to. He was not a *Master,* but then...given the things he had done, he really did not want the attention he would have gotten if he'd been a Master.

Better to avoid the Elemental Magic altogether.

He stared out the window at the snowy street. It looked as if it was finally thinning out, so the toffs would have easier going coming home from their parties. It looked as if Alf had decided to stay in for the evening, however, which was probably wise. If he'd decided to go get a bit of skirt, he'd have come round to see if his master wanted a bit of his own—because with Alexandre's ready, he could go for a cut higher than he could on his own. With the snow this thick, girls would be trying to solicit from inside four walls, not out in the street, and Alf had probably taken refuge in sleep, gin, or both.

I need a better source of power.

The idea seemed to come into his head from out of nowhere, although now that he'd had the thought, it seemed so blindingly obvious he was amazed he hadn't thought of it before.

He knew all about using himself as a source of power, that was the first thing the book had taught him. The second thing it taught him was how to siphon power away from others. But the kind of people he could get drunk enough that they did not notice him performing incantations over them were not the sort that offered him a great deal of power, so mostly he had been limited to himself.

But what if there was a better way? He had not been paying a great deal of attention to the content of the pages he had been sorting through—just enough, really, to make sure he was getting them in order—but now that he thought about it, the obtaining of vast quantities of magical power had been a theme running through them.

For a moment he was galvanized by the thought. But his bed was warm and the sitting room was undoubtedly cold by now, and he could not quite muster the energy to go and look through it properly, peering at the crabbed writing in lamplight. It could wait until tomorrow. It wasn't as if the book would be gone in the morning.

But what if he had been drawn to this book, as he had been drawn to the first book that started him down the road to occult power? It made sense. He had always had the feeling that there was some greater destiny in store for him than anything his background would allow, and that he had to break free of it in order to achieve that destiny.

For a moment, it also occurred to him that this book, and even the first one, could have been some sort of baited trap—

But what would be the purpose of such a thing? It wasn't as if the authors were still alive to profit by trapping him.

Don't get your hopes too high, he reminded himself, as the urge to rise and try to make sense of the book took hold of him again. *Not everything old and handwritten is valuable.*

That was enough to send him back to his novel, and after a moment, a glass of whiskey he poured from the bottle he kept at his bedside. Eventually the whiskey did its work; he turned down the lamp and went to sleep—to dream of sitting on a throne-like chair with the Elemental Masters of the London White Lodge serving him like slaves.

3

NAN bundled herself into her sable cloak; Sarah was all ready to go. "I'm sorry to drag you out into the snow like this," John Watson said apologetically, as he held the door of their flat open for them. "But one of my medical colleagues who knows that I am not inclined to dismiss the *outré* as mere faradiddle sent me a message last night. He has a patient he thinks might be something other than mad, and last night she took a bad turn. He doesn't know what to make of it."

"And he thinks we might," Sarah stated, preceding him down the stairs to the front door. "Well, Mrs. Horace has Suki all day; Suki is going to learn how to make gingerbread and how to set a proper tea tray, serve, and pour, and they're making Christmas decorations as well. I'll just pop my head in her door and make sure it's all right if we leave for a few hours."

Nan made sure the birds were going to be warm and safe while they were gone; this did not seem to be the sort of situation where they were going to be needed. By the time she came down the stairs, it appeared that Sarah had already confirmed with their landlady that Suki could remain with her until their return. Sarah was waiting at the door, next to John Watson. "I hope you got a conveyance of some sort," she said to the doctor. "Getting anything big enough for all of us in this weather—"

"Mary is waiting in the growler outside," John replied reassuringly. "We'll be going almost all the way to Hampstead Heath. I've made sure the cabby will wait for us; I don't fancy trying to get another way back."

Sure enough, waiting outside the door was one of the larger cabs, a two-horse "growler" that could seat four in spread-out comfort—or more at a pinch. Nan had no idea how John had managed to get one in the first place; they were usually all pulled up at the railway stations or major hotels to convey passengers and baggage.

Mrs. Horace must have paid a street-sweeper to clean the snow off this morning; the street and sidewalk in front of the building were both clean. At least they could go dry-footed to the cab.

The girls took the rear-facing seats; neither of them had ever had any problem with riding backward. John got in beside his wife and banged on the roof of the cab with his walking stick, and the cab lurched into motion. "Here is what I have," John said, taking a small sheaf of paper from his pocket and unfolding it. "*This patient was consigned to our care by family. I was told, and the patient confirmed, that she had asked for consignment, due to increasing hallucinations. Patient appeared rational, and was intelligent, articulate, calm, and able to reason. Three days after consignment to our care, patient was struck with an apparent fit, during which she remained rigid and unresponsive, although she spoke during this fit, and described a scene of great tragedy in minute detail. I had the presence of mind to take down her words in shorthand. On recovering from this fit, she was in great distress, not only on account of her emotional reaction to the scene she had described, but because of succumbing to the fit itself. I had cause to be grateful I had taken down her words, because not two days later, an acquaintance of mine who happens to work as a London coroner described a pair of bodies brought in to him in a pitiable state that exactly matched the murders my patient had described. Nor could she have known of this from newspapers; the crime must have taken place even as she fell into her fit, at least according to my friend's judgment of the time of death. Over the succeeding months, this happened again and again; she would fall into one of these fits, describe an horrific crime, and I would later find she had described something that had actually taken place in London or its environs. I began to see a pattern; the victims were all innocent, often lower-class children, and the murders were unsolved and particularly heinous. No one had ever bothered to verify her visions before. I did my best to reassure the poor woman, and it did come as partial relief for her to discover she was not mad, but what could we do? We could not pass on pertinent information to the police for how would we explain where our information came from? At length, with her consent, I began experimenting with drugs to attempt to suppress these visions, since there was nothing we could do with them. I seemed to be having success until two days ago, when she was found in her room in a state of collapse and utter terror. She has not slept since. I then confessed what I had been doing to my friend the coroner, who listened with every evidence of belief, then suggested I contact you, with whom I have a speaking acquaintance. I pray if you can help, please come at once."*

"Well, clearly the poor woman is a clairvoyant," Sarah said immediately, a frown of annoyance on her face. "And it is a shame he didn't speak sooner instead of tinkering with drugs. Instead of making her less sensitive, it is likely he had the opposite effect."

Nan kept her thoughts to herself for now. But it seemed to her that parts of this story were not fitting up with others.

She also had some vivid memories of the time before she had been taken into the Harton School; people in the poorer parts of London would do anything to avoid hospitals and doctors; there were rumors of things they would do, experiments they would make on those who were too sick, injured and poor to object. . . .

Would the same thing happen if you'd been consigned to a madhouse?

"I thought as much myself," Watson agreed. "Do you think you can do anything for her?"

Sarah shook her head. "Not I. But Nan might be able to reach her."

Nan shrugged. "I can try," she offered. "But no promises. If this was caused by drugs . . . I'm not sure what I can do." She frowned. "If he'd said something to someone when he first realized he had a clairvoyant patient on his hands, he wouldn't be in this situation now."

I'd bloody well like to know why he kept all that to himself, if he could prove it all. . . .

Mary spoke the moment before her husband could. "This might seem like a case of physician's arrogance to you, and indeed, it might be that very thing—but it could also be simply because he was afraid of being accused of either knowing the criminal who was guilty of the crimes, or being involved somehow."

But Sarah frowned. "I know that you want to excuse him because he is a fellow physician, but this is not fitting together properly," she said, with some reluctance, echoing Nan's thoughts on the matter. "Sherlock has taught us all not to take anything at face value, not even the honesty of a physician. I believe we should tread cautiously. Things may not be what they seem."

For a moment John Watson looked offended . . . but then he took a deep breath, and let it out slowly. "You are correct, and I would be a poor example of an adductive reasoner if I did not follow your advice." He pondered a moment. "The truth is," he added, somewhat reluctantly, "I call this fellow a colleague, but it is only in the sense that we are both doctors. So I don't know anything about him. We've spoken at social occasions, but no more than that."

"It's hard, dear," Mary patted his knee with a gloved hand she slipped out from under her sable cloak for a moment. "You naturally want to think the best of him."

"Yet we all know there are bad physicians, unscrupulous ones, and physicians that take advantage of their patients." He nodded, as if making up his mind. "We must not forget that among the selfless, there are also the Thomas Creams, and the William Palmers."

Nan held her peace, but exchanged a speaking look with Sarah. It had occurred to her that they were placing a great deal of faith in not very much evidence, and all of it was the few notes written by a single man. She was very glad Sarah had managed to shake Doctor Watson out of his unthinking faith in a fellow doctor.

Mary Watson changed the subject before an awkward silence could grow. "And what is Suki planning for today? I would imagine that after the excitement of tea shops, Panto, and a full formal dinner, it might be hard to entertain her."

"You would be mistaken," Sarah said merrily, readily seizing on the opportunity to talk about their charge. "Suki has the admirable capability of being entertained by almost everything, equally. She takes a lively interest in everything around her, and today, she is especially excited to be learning how to make gingerbread, how to preside properly over a tea table, and to be making decorations for our Christmas trees."

Mary smiled, then her smile faltered. "I do not wish to spoil anyone's fun—but the practice of lighting candles on a tree—"

Nan held up a hand. "Mrs. Horace forbids it. And if she did not, we could not chance an accidental flap of a bird wing ending in tragedy. We have strings of cut German crystal beads, an entire hatbox full of bits of polished tin, and a great deal of tinsel. That will make the trees sparkle without courting a fire."

The practice of setting up Christmas trees had arrived with Queen Victoria's German husband, Prince Albert. Most people illuminated their trees with dozens of tiny candles set in holders on the ends of the branches. Memsa'b had never liked this practice, especially around two or three dozen excitable children, and she had passed her caution on to Nan and Sarah.

"You relieve me greatly," Mary replied, her smile returning.

"And me," John Watson agreed. "As a doctor . . . I have

seen the victims of far too many Christmas fires. So what else have you planned for Suki's school holiday with you?"

They were only too happy to describe what they were planning for the days leading up to Christmas, the extent to which Lord Alderscroft was "spoiling" her, and the presents they had planned for Suki. That filled the conversational void all the way to the establishment on Hampstead Heath.

Nan had not been sure what to expect—perhaps a large farmhouse, converted for use as a medical establishment— but it was quite clear as the growler passed the wrought iron gates in the substantial brick wall, discreetely marked by a small bronze plaque announcing that this was the "Hampstead Hospital and Sanitarium," that a great deal of money had gone into the building of this place, and that it had not been converted from anything. The enormous, four-storied, pale stone building at the end of the well-graveled drive had clearly been purpose-built, and was no more than twenty or thirty years old. From its state, this was one of those discreet private facilities that catered to the needs of the wealthy, those who, for whatever reason, could not be tended at their own homes. From an inconvenient and potentially scandalous pregnancy, to an equally scandalous addiction, to . . . well, just about any medical or physical condition that a family did not want bruited about, a place like this was where the unfortunate sufferer was sent.

Which immediately caused Nan to doubt the first assertion in the letter—that the patient *herself* had demanded she be sent here. Still . . . it was possible. A dutiful, obedient daughter, fearing she was going mad, *might* ask her parents to put her safely where she could live in comfort and spare her loved ones much distress.

The place was certainly well staffed; they were met at the front door by someone in a dark blue uniform who first summoned a boy to take the cabman to a stable at the back then led them in himself. There they found themselves in a sort of waiting room, furnished with stiff wooden chairs, papered with a pattern of pale green vines on pale blue, "enlivened" by three indifferent pastoral landscape paintings.

"We're expected," John told the uniformed attendant. "Doctor John Watson."

The other nodded briskly. "Indeed you are, sir. Let me show you directly to the doctor's office."

So . . . we are wanted badly enough not to be made to wait.

He led them through a double door to a set of stairs and up to the next story. There was an office directly off the landing, one with windows that gave a commanding view of the front of the building and the drive leading to it. The walls were lined with filled bookshelves, and the centerpiece of the room was a huge mahogany desk.

The man sitting behind the desk in front of those windows rose at their entrance. He was a little older than John Watson, wore the same sort of suit, though cut of much finer cloth, and it was obvious that he was used to moving in very exalted social circles. His abundant dark hair was liberally streaked with gray, and his beard and "muttonchop" sideburns were immaculate, probably having seen the attention of a professional barber or valet that morning.

"Doctor Watson!" he boomed. "Thank you for coming so promptly!" He held out his hand, and Watson shook it, as he glanced at the three women with Watson.

Watson took the hint. "Doctor Huntley, this is my wife, Mary, who acts as my assistant, and Miss Sarah Lyon-White and Miss Nancy Killian, who have a great deal of practical experience in the psychic sciences. Sherlock Holmes has relied on them in several cases."

"Several" cases is stretching the truth, Nan thought with amusement, *but it's probably better to exaggerate in this situation.*

"Splendid!" Dr. Huntley said, looking not at all dismayed. He glanced from Nan to Sarah and back again. "I don't suppose it is too much to ask if one of you can hear and speak in thoughts?"

Well . . . that's interesting. Whatever he thought before, he seems to have become a firm believer in psychism because of this experience.

"I can," Nan said promptly. "The scientific term is *telepathy.* Doctor Watson read us your notes, and I believe I might

be able to break your patient out of her hysterical state." She
waited to see what his reaction would be.

There was no doubt that the doctor looked relieved.
"Then let me conduct you to her immediately," he replied.
"If it will help, her given name is Amelia."

"It will," Nan said, noting with cynicism that her surname
was not offered—very much in keeping with her impression
that this was a place where surnames were eliminated or
obfuscated with the ever-useful "Smith."

"Please, come with me," Huntley told them, and led
them from his office, past another double door, and down a
long corridor with doors lining it. Nan could not tell if the
doors were locked, and truth to tell, she was not willing to
open herself enough to get a sense of what might lie on the
other side of those doors. Later, perhaps, but not now. And
for the same reason, she had not opened herself enough to
try to read Dr. Huntley's mind. To do so without touching
him would be to leave herself open to everyone else in this
place. And in her experience, when people lost their sanity,
their thoughts often gained in strength.

But the corridor was well lit, carpeted, and not unlike the
corridor of an expensive hotel. This outermost layer, at least,
was pleasant enough.

They turned a corner, and it became clear that the building was laid out either in an enormous U shape or a square.
Their goal was a door halfway along this second corridor,
and Nan's question about whether or not the doors were
locked was answered when Huntley removed a ring of keys
from his coat and used one of them in the door.

The room beyond could have been the bedroom of any
great country home, except for certain details. The walls
were papered in a darker version of the green-vines-on-
blue pattern of the waiting room. There were heavy green
curtains at the window. The furnishings were bolted to the
floor, through the dark green carpet. There were no ornaments, such as vases. There were no mirrors, and no pictures;
nothing anyone could use to hurt herself or others. There
were some books on a table by the window, and a comfortable, green upholstered chair beside it.

And huddled in the farthest corner of the bed was the patient, Amelia.

She was still dressed in a nightgown; her eyes were dark-ringed, as if she had not slept in days, her hair disheveled, and she sat with her back to the wall, knees pressed against her chest, bedclothes wrapped around her, arms wrapped around her legs. She stared through them from her corner as if she didn't see them at all.

Nan glanced at Sarah, who shook her head. So whatever was tormenting this young woman, it wasn't spirits. Resolutely, before Huntley could say anything, she marched to the bed, sat down on the edge of it, and fearlessly put one hand on Amelia's arm. No matter how much strength hysteria lent to this girl, Nan very much doubted that Amelia would be able to discommode her, much less hurt her, at least physically.

And as for mentally . . . well, Sarah could break her out of that.

She closed her eyes, and opened her mind, and saw what Amelia was seeing—and more importantly, felt what Amelia was feeling.

Absolute terror.

Nan was used to this game by this point, however, and she did not allow Amelia's terror to become her own. She walled it off, kept it at bay, and continued to observe.

London, but a London transformed into . . . not a hells-cape, because there were no flames, and no devils . . . but a place where no sane human would care to dwell. Dark, boiling clouds hung over the city. Lightning lashed the ruined buildings beneath them. Debris tumbled in empty streets, blown by an icy wind that carried with it the scent of decay; misshapen, shadowy creatures skulked just on the periphery of Amelia's vision, scuttling among overturned cabs and carriages, darting out of sight when Amelia tried to look squarely at them. As Nan watched, a man bolted from cover, trying to cross the street—he had not gotten more than halfway across before inky tentacles erupted out of a shattered shopfront, engulfed him, and before he could utter more than a strangled cry, pulled him into the ruined shop and out of sight.

"The Book," Nan heard Amelia whisper. "The Book—"

What *that* meant, Nan could not tell. There was no room for anything in Amelia's mind but fear, and certainly no sign in her thoughts of any books.

Although Nan viewed the vision as if it was at one remove, she could tell that Amelia was completely immersed in it—and afraid to move, lest some horror stretch out tentacles or claws, seize her next, and drag her away.

Amelia, Nan thought, firmly, making her thoughts a lance to pierce through Amelia's vision. *This isn't real.*

Nan felt a sort of mental jolt. The scene wavered for a moment, as if someone had passed a piece of flawed glass between her and it. Then it solidified again, but now she felt that Amelia was aware of her presence.

Who . . . are you? she heard.

My name is Nan Killian. I am here to help you. This isn't real.

The scene dimmed, and wavered again, then solidified, just as vivid as before. *Not . . . yet.*

I told you. I am here to help. But this is not yet real, and hopefully, will not ever become real. She interjected a feeling of warmth and humor. *It had better not. I shall be very cross if I cannot visit my shops.*

That broke through Amelia's terror, as Nan had hoped it would. The scene vanished, and the bed shook a little as Amelia started, then weakly laughed—and then as Nan opened her eyes, she burst into tears and threw herself on Nan's shoulder. The fear was still there, but it was no longer all-encompassing terror. Nan closed herself down again, now allowing herself to feel a bit shaken by the strength of the girl's emotion, and by what she had seen in Amelia's mind. Just at the moment, she didn't want to think about it too much. It would be better to try to analyze it after they knew the girl was not going to be caught in it again.

Nan put her arms around the distraught girl, and looked back at Huntley. "I believe she will be all right now. A nice strong pot of tea, I think, and something to eat. She's going to be very hungry when she stops crying, and then she will probably want to sleep."

And I am of two minds about telling him that I saw what she saw.

Huntley looked both stunned and unspeakably relieved. "I'll see to it myself," he replied, and hurried off.

"Good," Nan muttered under her breath. "Now we can learn what's really going on here."

It appeared that Huntley was impressed enough by how Nan had broken through to Amelia that he was willing to leave her and the rest of the group in charge of the girl while he took care of other business. There was a modern bathroom available on this floor, and the ladies took advantage of it, since Amelia was, to put it bluntly, a fright. Once she was clean, Mary, Nan, and Sarah helped her into a fresh nightgown, helped her comb out and braid her hair, and got tea, toast, and soft-boiled eggs into her from a tray brought up by an attendant.

That was *not* what Nan would have chosen, but at least it wasn't barley water, or beef tea, or something equally useless.

Amelia was mostly silent until still another of the blue-uniformed attendants—a woman, with a white, starched apron over her blue dress—came and took the tray away. John Watson took up a position by the window farthest from them. Mary sat in the bolted-down chair beside him. Amelia had tucked herself back into the bed, sitting up, with the covers pulled around her like armor, while Nan and Sarah sat on the edge, Nan closest to her. Finally, she actually *looked* at them, as if seeing them for the first time, and asked, "Who—are you?"

"My name is Nan Killian," Nan said, taking the lead. "These are my friends, Sarah Lyon-White, Doctor John and Mary Watson. Doctor Huntley asked us to come help you when he could not." She paused. "It seems you fell into a rather horrific vision that you could not be pulled out of. He says you have been awake and suffering for two days. That was me you heard, helping you find your way out of the vision. As you can see things happening at a distance, I can see what others are seeing and thinking, and speak to them in their thoughts. That was how I called you back. Would you like to talk about that?"

Amelia trembled, her eyes brimming with tears. "No," she replied. "I would not *like* to. But I feel I must." Her hands were shaking as she clenched them in the bedcovers. "I can accept that I can see things that are actually happening, terrible as they are—but that! London, in ruins and full of monstrous things! That was never real! Am I finally going mad?"

Nan considered that question for a long moment, because there certainly had not been anything particularly *sane* about that vision. "I don't think so," she said, finally. "Although it is clear that your vision was not of the real London of here and now, and personally I find it difficult to believe that what you saw was a reflection of some future reality."

At that, Amelia blinked, tears spilling down her cheeks. "Then I must be going mad. You—you were in my head, you saw what I saw! How can that be anything other than madness?"

Nan smiled reassuringly at her. "Yes I was in your head," she repeated. "That is what I do. I see and hear what others do, and I can read their thoughts. I am what is called a *telepath*. And you are what is called a *clairvoyant*."

The girl wiped her tears from her face and blinked at them. "There is a name for what happens to me?"

Nan considered her for a moment. She had been under the impression that Amelia must be of the age of majority, but looking at her now that she had been put to rights, Nan revised that downward. She could not be more than sixteen—possibly as young as fourteen.

This time Sarah answered. "Did you think you were the only one?"

"I—" Amelia hesitated. "I never heard of anyone doing such things except in ghost stories and the like. When it first started happening I was quite certain I was going mad, and I begged my family to send me here before I could do something to shame them all." Her eyes filled with tears again. "My sister is going to be coming out. I couldn't bear to spoil that for her. My family is going to tell people I have gone to Switzerland to a finishing school. Not even the servants know I am here."

All right, at least that part of the story is true.

"Then Doctor Huntley discovered that the horrible things I had been seeing were actually *true.*" She shuddered. "But I still didn't know what to do about them. They were happening miles from me. I wasn't seeing them ahead of time, so there was nothing I could do to stop them from happening, and he said the police would never believe me if I spoke to them and described the murderers."

And there's the first lie. Or at least, the shading of the truth.

"I couldn't make the visions stop. And I couldn't see anything but what was . . . imposed on me. I couldn't see pleasant things, no matter how hard I tried for Doctor Huntley." Tears spilled over her cheeks again. "I don't *want* to see these things! And I can't make them stop!"

Nan patted her hand. "That is why we are here. I am afraid Doctor Huntley is . . . far out of his area of expertise," she said, a little grimly. *He's a mere child playing with explosives, is what he is!* she thought, but did not say. "Would you object to coming away with us, to a school where there are children who also have these abilities? They would be very much younger than you," she added, as John Watson nodded significantly, and gave Mary his hand. "But you will be taught how to control this—and, if you truly do not want to make any use of it, how to shut it down."

John and Mary left, presumably in search of Huntley. Amelia wiped her eyes with the edge of the sheet, looking even younger than her years. "It would be . . . not so bad if I could see pleasant things," she answered after a moment, and managed a wavering smile. "Think of how jolly it would be if one could go to the theater from one's own bed!"

"And think of the money you'd save on tickets!" Sarah replied, with a broad grin.

Her smile faded. "But if what I saw was not real. . . ."

"I think it might have been a metaphor," Nan said

quickly. "You have been seeing horrid things for some time. You know now these things *were* real, and all were happening in London. Perhaps deep inside, you have come to think of London as a terrible, apocryphal place, full of monsters, and when another horrific vision began, instead of seeing that exact scene, your mind just created a scene out of that metaphor rather than subjecting you to another terrible murder. Just like when you dream of flying, it just means you want some freedom from some tedious task or other."

She didn't believe that, of course. Not in the least. She wasn't sure *what* she believed, but it wasn't that. And what had the child meant when she muttered "The Book!" over and over? Evidently Amelia didn't remember that part.

"I *do* always dream of flying right after I've had to do something dreadfully boring," Amelia replied, and the tight lines of her face relaxed, she sighed, and let go of her death grip on the covers.

Then she yawned, hugely, and her eyes began to flutter. "I'm dreadfully sorry," she began, and yawned again.

"You didn't sleep for two days," Nan reminded her. "Go on, put your head down. I doubt you'll have another such vision any time soon, and by that point, we'll have arranged for you to go to that school."

"I really shouldn't . . ." but Amelia's willpower had been exhausted by her struggle against that vision; helplessly, she slid down into her bed as her eyes closed, and in moments, she was fast asleep.

"Can you do anything to keep her from getting another vision?" Sarah asked anxiously.

"I think she's so overtired there isn't a chance of her having one until she's regained her strength," Nan replied. "Well, think about us. We couldn't do a thing with *our* abilities if we were tired. I just hope John and Mary can put the fear of retribution into that Huntley character. I don't think he was trying to help her turn her visions off at all. I think he was experimenting with drugs to strengthen her ability. I think he had some notion of profiting off it, and I think the last concoction he gave her is responsible for that fit she went into."

Sarah frowned. "I'd like to disagree with you, but I have the dreadful feeling you might be right. What do you think John and Mary will say?"

"I think they'll brandish the possibility of Sherlock Holmes turning up here at him," Nan replied, and chuckled. "If he's doing *anything* dubious, that will be the very last person he would want to see on these premises. It'll be subtle, I expect. Huntley isn't some common thug. But the implication will be very clear: release this child to Memsa'b, or be prepared to have every secret of this place revealed— possibly to the public."

"And if he actually has nothing to hide—" Sarah said thoughtfully, "—I suspect the next rabbit to be pulled from the hat will be Lord A."

"Very likely." Nan moved off the bed so the poor girl could spread out a little. Sarah followed her example and took the chair by the window. "I have to say, this *seems* to be a pleasant enough place. I find myself hoping Huntley is merely a man who yielded to temptation, and is about to learn his lesson."

"Or already has," Sarah suggested.

"Or that," Nan agreed. "And if that is the case, John and Mary can steer him gently into the path of righteousness, and we'll have a physician-believer who can keep alert for patients who *we* can help. Clearly, young Amelia made a believer out of him, if he wasn't one already."

Sarah picked up one of the books on the table, and examined it. "Well, she's a good reader, and a serious one." She held it up. *"The Sermons of John Donne."*

"Too deep for me," Nan chuckled and looked at the next volume. "I'll take the companion here—the *Poems of John Donne."*

"I like her very much already. I think Memsa'b will too."

Sarah moved to the arm of the chair where she, being smaller, could perch comfortably. Nan took the seat. They immersed themselves in their respective books, glancing up now and again at the girl to make sure she was still sleeping peacefully.

Amelia continued to sleep, and they continued to read.

Outside, the snow-covered landscape was peaceful, serene, without a single footprint to mar it. Inside, it was quiet, but not ominously so. There were distant sounds, of conversation, perhaps. Nan spared a hope that even those who were deranged were taken care of with kindness. Normally she had to put up mental defenses as strong as stone walls to get anywhere near an asylum.

Eventually, there was a tap on the door, and John cautiously stuck his head in the door, saw that Amelia was sleeping and the two young women were reading, and he and Mary entered quietly. "It's all arranged. I'll tell you in the cab."

They all went back downstairs, collected cloaks and coats from the attendant. By the time they were at the door, so was the cabby—who looked warm and fed and satisfied with his wait.

John waited until they were actually past the gate before speaking. "Well . . . Huntley is a bit of a humbug, but only a bit. As you might expect, he takes in . . . people who are inconvenient to their relatives. Most of 'em shouldn't be here, frankly, and I imagine that you have good ideas of why."

"He does have some genuine convalescents who need skilled nursing, and not a ham-handed chambermaid," Mary put in. "And some very aged people who need round the clock care. There may even be a few who genuinely *are* mad, but most of his 'patients' with that label have merely so displeased powerful and monied relations that they've been sent here—out of sight, out of mind."

"He's not a monster; once they're here, he treats them well . . . but . . . ." John made a face. "It's a very comfortable prison, but it's still a prison."

"But as long as the law is written the way it is, it's perfectly legal to declare a disobedient daughter or eccentric uncle insane and lock them up," Mary said with disgust. "Nevertheless, that gave us the chance to mention Holmes, which of course, is the very last person on the face of the earth he wants prowling about. So he's going to quietly transfer Amelia without telling her parents—who won't care, frankly, since they haven't written or made a call since she volunteered to be locked up here."

Nan sighed. "That's a relief. What was he *doing* with her, anyway? I began to very much doubt he was trying to help her repress her visions."

"Not with the drugs he was giving her, he wasn't," John said, his expression darkening. "And I wish I could *prove* he knew what he was about, but I can't. I *think* he was trying to turn her into his own little window into places he couldn't otherwise get to . . . collecting secrets. Again, I don't *think* he was intending to turn blackmailer—I fancy he was looking for business secrets he could use to increase his fortune by investing. But he was trying every line of drug that I know of that is reputed to open magical and psychical senses, and I think we're damned lucky he didn't kill the poor girl with them."

"Then she can't get to Memsa'b soon enough," Sarah exclaimed. "The poor child!"

"Child, indeed, she's barely fourteen," said Mary, confirming Nan's suspicions. "John made arrangements for Memsa'b herself to come collect the girl in two days, and believe me, Huntley will make no fuss about it." She held up a hand. "Don't worry, once he consented to it, John and I both sealed a geas on him, by Water and Air, to keep his word. No matter how badly he wants to change his mind, he'll still have to give her up, and smile about it. So no fear there." She finally smiled. "At least our magic has had *some* use in this situation."

"Now I'm curious, Nan, what exactly did you see in Amelia's mind?" John Watson asked, eying her speculatively.

She described everything she had seen; he had taken out his little notebook and was jotting things down as she spoke. When she finished, he shook his head.

"Well, all I can say is, this is nothing like the other visions she had," he said. "Huntley took very careful notes, and documented everything with newspaper clippings. I'll grant him this much, he has a first-class mind when it comes to science. Amelia did, indeed, witness several murders—

horrific, I am sure, to her, and to Huntley, who doesn't seem to have seen a cadaver outside the dissecting room. But fairly run-of-the-mill for London. Tragic, cold-blooded, absolutely, but nothing you young ladies or Mary or I would witness and fall into hysterics over. By Jove, even your little Suki has seen worse with her own two eyes."

"I wondered about that," Nan said, frowning. "That is what makes *this* vision so troubling to me. And I absolutely do not myself believe that Banbury tale I spun for her about it being a 'mental metaphor' for the very real horrors of London."

"But it certainly wasn't *reality,* since we just came from London, and it's not crawling with monsters," Mary objected, looking extremely skeptical.

"Nor can I imagine how London could end up that way," John agreed. "Why . . . on the face of it, that's impossible. Mary and I and every other Master and magician would have to be dead, first."

Nan kept her mouth shut. She remembered all too clearly how London had very nearly become a frozen wasteland many years ago, and how Robin Goodfellow himself had been willing to bring the terrifying powers of something not unlike a minor god against Lord Alderscroft to keep that from happening. So . . . on the face of it, it *wasn't* impossible.

"Report it all to Alderscroft anyway," she suggested. "He may have some ideas of what it all means."

John shrugged, a little skeptically, but agreed. "In any event, we've done a good day's work, ladies. And I suggest that since you want this reported to Alderscroft anyway, we go straight there and partake of his hospitality while he has the townhouse open. We should arrive just in time for luncheon."

"John!" Mary laughed.

"I believe there's a Bible verse about not binding the mouths of the cattle that thresh your corn," he countered. "And this old bull could do with a good feed."

4

ALEXANDRE frowned in concentration, bent over his writing desk, though not in a flurry of creation. His creative spates rarely lasted more than an hour or two at best, though of course, poetry did not require long periods of thought and hours and hours of writing the way prose did. But he had been at this task for hours, and expected to be at it for hours more. Days, actually. This was going to take days, even if he kept at it from the time he rose until the time he went to bed. Which he fully intended to do—not only did he feel a fever to get this accomplished, but it was an excellent way in which to avoid Christmas nonsense altogether.

The Book—he was starting to think about it with capital letters—had been handwritten, which made it problematic when it came to using it for actual ritual work. One minor mispronunciation, and all your hard work would go straight out the window—or worse. Although he himself had never had anything backfire, there were stories . . . and he had no intention of becoming another one of those stories. So he was copying The Book, word by word, taking great pains to make sure he clearly understood every word, in his own *printed* writing. Not script. While Eton had given him beautiful copperplate handwriting, even that was problematic when it came to reading something in a ritual. He had a dozen other books on the desk beside him, using them as references for words he was not sure he had made out clearly.

Mind, even that was not as much help as it might have been. There were many names in The Book that he not only was not familiar with, but could not find in his references. It was taking a great deal of concentration to compare letters in these names to similar letters in familiar words elsewhere on the page, verifying each unfamiliar word letter by letter.

He had finally abandoned this task last night about midnight when he no longer trusted the light and his tired eyes. He had begun it again as soon as he arose. It amused him to think, when he paused to rest for a moment, that he was taking more pains with this—and working harder at it— than he had for his *viva voce* exams at the University.

On the other hand, if this Book was going to give him what he *thought* it would—it would be worth a hundred times more than any University degree.

Every so often he had to rest his eyes and his cramping fingers. And were this any other task, he would have fortified himself with wine, whiskey, or even just beer. But . . . no. It would be monumentally foolish to have performed all this work only to have alcohol fuddle him at some critical point. So he directed Alf to keep him supplied with hot tea and soldiered on.

It was exacting and meticulous work. And while not exciting in and of itself, the potential was enthralling.

He was in the middle of his second day of it when, to his intense irritation, he was interrupted.

"Pardon, guv," Alf said from behind him, delicately timing his speech to make sure Alexandre's pen was not on the page. "The soli'ster's here."

There was only one "solicitor" who came here, and that was the administrator of his father's estate. And although he was, at this moment, the very last person in the world that Alexandre wanted to see, he was one who *should* be seen. There were certain inconvenient provisions in his father's will that meant that until Mother died (*and may she do so soon*, he thought), it was incumbent on him to at least put up the appearance of obeying.

"Send him in," Alexandre said with irritation, and carefully capped the inkwell, cleaned the pen, and set the page he was working on aside, making sure the marble "rule" he was using to mark the place in the page he was working on was firmly in place. By the time the solicitor was ushered into his study, he was on his feet and presenting every evidence of affable welcome.

He knew what the man would see; a room meant for work, with the writing desk at the window for the best light, a good fire in the fireplace, plenty of lamps. Lined with books the solicitor was utterly uninterested in, for aside from law, he did not read. Good, solid furniture, a decent carpet, nothing ostentatious. If the man had had even half a notion of what those books lining the walls held between their covers—but he didn't.

"Well, Master Fensworth, I presume this is just the usual tour of inspection before your firm deposits my quarterly allowance?" he said, with as charming a smile as he could muster, and holding out his hand to for the old man to shake.

"It is . . . although I could wish you would move to a more salubrious part of Battersea, if you are going to insist on living here," the solicitor replied, with a touch of irritation and apprehension combined.

"But the rents are ever so much cheaper here in the north," Alexandre said ingenuously. "Not to mention the services of my man, and my char. Good solid locks on the doors and windows ensure no one can break in. And my man and I are perfectly capable of terrifying any miscreant who thinks to accost us. I should think you would applaud my frugality."

"*I'm* terrified of that blackguard," he heard the old man mutter as he took a seat, but pretended not to have heard it. "Well, Alex, if I cannot persuade you, and since you do indeed seem perfectly capable of defending yourself and your property, I suppose I *should* applaud your frugality."

"I have a three-bedroom flat for the price of a miserable little bed-sitter elsewhere," Alexandre said, concealing the irritation he felt when addressed as "Alex." He took his own seat, and gave every evidence of being pleased to have the man's company. "So, what would you like to hear?"

"As you know, your father stipulated that you must be involved continuously in some form of *useful occupation* in order to keep receiving your stipend. When last we spoke, you were at work on a book of poetry. I should like a report on what you are engaged with." The solicitor steepled his fingers in front of his chest, as if expecting to hear that Alexandre was involved in no such thing as a *useful occupation*. It had only been Alexandre's pointing out that his father had allowed in his will that writing was a "useful occupation" as long as it resulted in a published book that had kept that quarter's stipend in the bank last time.

"I have gotten my hands on a most extraordinary book," Alexandre replied, smiling. "It appears to be one-of-a-kind, and handwritten. I am transcribing it—was doing so even as you arrived. I think the transcription will add something significant to religious history when I have finished with it." He pointedly did *not* mention *which* religion it would add to. Indeed, it was not likely to add to any religion with which the solicitor was familiar. It seemed to refer to a religion all its very own.

The solicitor blinked in surprise, and a thin, but approving smile stretched his lips. "Well, that is an improvement over your book of poetry. Was that ever published?"

"Not more than a month ago. It is too soon to tell how successful it will be," Alexandre replied, making an effort not to bristle. "I think this is a much more solid and substantial task. Indeed—" he forced a laugh, "—I do believe this transcription represents a great deal more work than anything I did at University."

"Well, I know nothing of religious history, so I shall not trouble you to show me any of it," the old man said, with a glance at the desk behind him and its stack of newly written pages. "But I can see you are certainly getting on with the work, and it is something of which I am certain your father would approve."

It was all that Alexandre could do to suppress a bark of laughter at that. *If Father knew what I was doing, he would be spinning in his grave like a windmill in a tempest.* He managed to turn his amusement into a fatuous smile. "Then I hope, aside from my frugal obstinacy in living here, I have satisfied you for this quarter."

"Oh, definitely." The old man rose. "Not that I doubted you. Your expenses show no signs of . . ." he waved his hands in the air ". . . excessive spending. You do not gamble, you do not keep loose women, and you do not drink to excess. Your allowance will be deposited as scheduled."

"Just in time for Christmas!" Alexandre said with false joviality. "And speaking of Christmas . . . does Mother wish my presence?"

"Your mother is still indisposed," the solicitor said, truthfully. "The house has not been decorated, and no one has mentioned the season to her. Her doctors think that reminding her of the holiday would do her more harm than good."

"Ah. I shall send her a floral tribute then, just to let her know she is in my thoughts. There is no reason why a loving son cannot send his mother flowers regardless of whether there is an occasion or not."

"That would be better than a visit, I believe." The solicitor moved toward the door. "Don't trouble yourself, Alex. I shall show myself out." And he suited his actions to his words.

Alexandre managed to not grind his teeth as he moved to the window and stood where he could make certain that the old busybody had gotten into the firm's carriage and actually left. *The cheek of him! What is he doing now, paying for information about my movements? Looking for gambling debts or a mistress somewhere?* He would not put it past the miserable old dotard. Fortunately, Alexandre's tastes did not demand expensive women who required apartments, furs, and jewelry, not when he could get exactly the same services out of a young and disposable whore. And gambling was for fools—unless you had the secrets to winning. He *did* gamble, but not often; not so often that people would start to remark on his extraordinary luck. He didn't need to cheat to win, after all. Not when he had magic. And he was very, very careful only to take money from those who could afford to lose it. Not out of any sense of pity—but because those who could afford to lose it generally took no notice of those who won it from them.

As the solicitor's coach pulled away, a small mob of boys pelted it with snowballs. Alexandre smiled, thinly, and sat down again to his task.

Not, of course, that he was abstaining from expensive mistresses, luxurious apartments, and all the wonderful things that money could buy voluntarily . . . he'd have been perfectly happy to finally be in control of the family's modest fortune. Without the need to conceal his gambling—and with the means to go to casinos on the Continent—he could build that modest fortune into an impressive one. As he had transcribed this book, dormant ambition had awakened in him. He would love to excite envy in the gazes of anyone who saw him. He could indulge all of his desires, and oh, he had a great many desires. But he was patient. Patience was, perhaps, his only virtue.

Except, perhaps, for the moments following one of these detestable interviews.

The old man had been a confidant of Father; if one of the other members of the firm had been put in charge of making sure the conditions of the will were followed, he doubted he'd ever see them. The business manager certainly did not care, and would not care, as long as Alexandre did not drain the principal and did not interfere with the management of the money. There would be no probing into his character, no quarterly interviews. As long as he kept his name out of the newspapers, the stipend would simply be deposited into his bank account.

But Fensworth took his obligations seriously, and seemed to regard himself *in loco parentis* to someone who was fully adult and certainly capable of handling his own affairs.

If only the old man would just *die*. Like Mother, he was a damned inconvenience. But not enough of one for Alexandre to undertake the kind of effort it would require to be rid of him. There were too many people around him who would prevent him from walking out into the middle of a winter storm to lie down and die—and Alexandre could not imagine how he would be able to get some personal item, like hair or blood, to set the spell in the first place. Victor had been easy; all Alexandre had needed to do was pay a visit to his brother's rooms at King's College on the pretext of borrowing something and stroll off with hair from his hairbrush. He had no such access to Fensworth's belongings.

Patience, he reminded himself. But he couldn't help brooding about it as he continued to work on The Book. *If only the old man would vanish. Life would be so much easier.*

Arthur Fensworth chided himself for the uncharitable thoughts that had crowded his mind on the way to pay his call on young Harcourt. Here he had been convinced the fellow was one of those idle fops, playing at being a poet, never really doing anything with his life—

And perhaps, at first, without the guiding hands of tutors and his father, he had been. But clearly he had found worthwhile work to do. Translating obscure religious works! He never would have thought it, but the fellow had clearly been hard at it when Fensworth arrived, and looked anxious to get back to it. And he'd gotten that book of poetry published as well! Old Harcourt would have been proud, of the translations at least.

He made his report to the head of the firm—who, as usual, seemed bored, and dismissed him with a wave of his hand. Fensworth was used to that. Old Abernathy would never have treated him and his report so flippantly, but Old Abernathy was dead and gone these three years, and his son didn't understand the need to see that a client was still a client even when he was dead, nor that it was the firm's obligation to make sure the client's wishes were fulfilled in perpetuity. Fensworth intended to keep an eye on young Harcourt and keep making those quarterly reports for as long as he lived.

With that dismissal, Fensworth returned to his tiny office, wrote out the release for the quarterly payment to young Harcourt's account, and went back to his regular duties. But, unusually, he couldn't quite keep his mind on them. Although he had a good fire going, the air was cold, and the light seemed dim no matter how much he turned up his lamps. He felt...drained. Dispirited. Finally, in mid-afternoon, he decided he must be sickening for something, and returned to Young Abernathy's office.

"Begging your pardon," he said politely, when Young Abernathy looked up impatiently. "But I don't entirely feel well. I was wondering if—"

"Good God, Fensworth," Young Abernathy said, his impatience turning to a sympathy that was entirely gratifying. "To my certain knowledge you haven't taken an hour off since I've been head of the firm. You're more than owed it. Go home. Bundle up. Get your housekeeper to make you a hot brandy or something. Don't come back until you feel better, you hear me? That's an order."

Young Abernathy's response warmed the cockles of his old heart. "Thank you, sir," he said with gratitude. "I appreciate it very much, sir."

"Appreciate it from the comfort of your bed," Young Abernathy replied, and taking that as the dismissal that it was, Fensworth took his leave.

But once he was bundled into a cab, that same oppression of spirits descended on him again, and he huddled inside his overcoat, feeling every one of his sixty years.

The cab let him out in front of the building where his flat lay, and he trudged his way wearily through the snow, his thoughts as gray as the sky. He put his hand on the door, and opened it.

And the darkness inside swallowed him.

By the time Alexandre was ready to stop again, he discovered to his surprise that it was dinnertime. "Alf?" he called, massaging his cramped fingers. They were very informal; he didn't bother with a bell, and he rather thought Alf might resent a bell anyway.

"Been down t'the pub, guv," Alf said. "Just settin' out a lovely bit of a pie."

Right now a steak and kidney pie sounded much more appealing than anything on offer at the club. Once again, Alexandre stoppered the ink, cleaned the pen, secured the pages he had finished, made sure the next line was marked, and weighed everything down before he joined Alf in the dining room. "Wine or beer, guv'nor?" Alf asked, serving a generous portion of pie on Alexandre's plate. "Lovely tinned peas, all hotted up, too." Alf approved of tinned goods. "No b'iling 'em to bits," he had commented when Alexandre asked why he liked them so much—which probably spoke volumes about Alf's mother's cooking, and why Alf himself had learned some basic cooking skills.

A generous pat of butter on the peas, plenty of bread and butter on the table, and Alf considered his duties discharged, save the drink.

"Red wine, Alf, and get a glass for yourself. Make it a red Number Seven." One of Alf's failings was that he never could be bothered to learn the care of wine, or indeed anything about it. He could distinguish between port and sherry, red wine and white, and that was his limit. So there was no use asking him for what was on the label; he'd scratch his head and take any old bottle of the right color. Alexandre had devised a system of simply pasting paper labels over the necks of the bottles when he bought them, and writing numbers on them before carefully racking them with the numbers facing up so Alf wouldn't be tempted to turn them and disturb the sediment. It was, all things considered a minor inconvenience—far outweighed by Alf's excellent taste in whores.

"Don't mind if Oi do," Alf said agreeably, and went out and returned, carefully carrying the bottle as he'd been shown, with two glasses. Alexandre poured for both of them, and they settled in to eat.

He caught a slightly unusual bit of movement out of the corner of his eye and looked up. Alf, contrary to his usual habits, looked as if he intended to make some conversation over dinner. Alexandre nodded to encourage him.

"Thet book," Alf said, with rare diffidence. "It's somethin' special?"

"I don't know yet," Alexandre admitted. "I think it may be. I'm making a good copy of it before I try anything out of it."

Alf nodded sagely. "Tha's all right, then. Was gonna warn ye, guv, t'do somet'in' of thet nature. My old master nearly lost a arm, not bein' careful in thet way." He took a bite of pie after that astonishing statement, and chewed thoughtfully. "*Did* lose th' book," he added.

Alexandre had known that Alf was in his master's confidences, but until now, he had not realized how far. "I'd rather not lose any part of me, thank you," he observed. "Have you any other advice?" After all, Alf had been with his previous master for more than a decade. And if he was *that* intimate with what the magician had been doing, it made sense to make use of his experience.

"Well, Oi seed you got a bunch of other books; yer checkin' names an' suchlike?" At Alexandre's nod his expression turned approving. "Can't be too careful. Wust that happens if ye miscall a cratchur, is 'e turns up, an' ye got no control on 'im."

They ate in silence for a little while longer. Then Alexandre spoke up. "The thing is . . . I don't recognize most of the names."

"Reely? Blimey!" Alf actually stopped chewing to stare at him. "Ever'thin' else tallies?"

"It seems to. I'll know better when I have a fair copy and I can look for humbugs." Alexandre had been taken in by faux manuscripts before this; he'd learned how to tell something truly original from something that had been deliberately created to deceive. There were usually subtle mistakes; mistakes that had the potential to get the magician killed.

"Huh." Alf cleaned his plate. Alf always cleaned his

plate—when he was done with a meal, it almost didn't need to be washed. Alexandre refilled his glass, hoping to coax more out of him. "Might be you got yersel' somethin' special. Them thin's . . . my old master said they was made to go lookin' fer magicians."

"My first grimoire was that way," Alexandre said. "It was how I first learned I was a magician."

"This un'll be more . . . hidden, like. It won't want to find just *any* old magician. It'll want someone as can ac'chully use it." Alf sat back in his chair with his wineglass in his hand, thinking, his brows creased. "That don't mean it's somethin' *you* wanta use, though."

Alexandre looked at him quizzically. "How do you mean?"

"Issa trap, guv." Alf winked. "What do you figger would be the best way for a canny old magician to cut down on competition?"

"Oh. . . ." For some reason, this had never occurred to him; perhaps because, aside from Alf's master, the only other magicians he knew of were those ever-so-lofty Elemental Masters and Mages. But now that Alf had brought it up, it made sense. Spread grimoires around that looked as if they held secrets, let the unwary get hold of them, and when they invoked the wrong creature . . . no more competition.

"An' accordin' to th' old man, there was some as would make deals . . . on'y, the payment come when some poor fool 'ud pick up one of them grimoires they left about an' used it. So they'd get rid of the competition *an'* make payment on their deal at the same time." Alf finished his wine and looked meaningfully at the bottle. Alexandre obliged him with the last of it.

"So how do you tell if a book is one of those?" he asked.

"By bein' careful. Ye check over ev'ry word. Ye look inside the cover fer hidden spells meant t'make ye careless. Ye check on ev'ry ward an' safeguard. No matter how temptin' this all looks, if somethin' don't add up, ferget it." Alf sipped the wine. "That's what th' old man said, anyway."

It all made sense. Perfect sense. "I get the feeling, Alf, you were a lot more to the old man than just his valet. . . ."

Alf laughed. "Oi ain't no magician, if thet's what ye mean. Oi jest paid attention. That stuff ain't fer me." He waved his hand, as if to shoo "that stuff" away from him, like an annoying fly. "But it wouldn't do *me* no good if the master was t'get et up, so Oi learnt what Oi needed to so's t'make sure he didn'. An' speakin' of et up, how'd the meetin' with Lawyer Skellington go?"

Alexandre snorted. "That's a good name for him," he replied, and his mood darkened. "Damned if I like being made to go through my paces like a schoolboy every quarter. But I told him I was working on transcribing obscure religious texts now, and that seemed to please the old sinner."

Alf barked a laugh. "Clever! Not a lie, neither."

"The best lies are always at least half truth. Care to join me by the fire for a brandy and a cigar?" His mood cleared again instantly at the thought of the way he'd bamboozled the old nosy parker.

"Don't mind if Oi do, guv. Jest let me clear all this away fer the char." Alf collected the plates, and Alexandre made his way into his little sitting room, his mind wandering back to The Book. He poured out two generous brandies, refreshed the fire, and took his favorite chair. In a few moments Alf joined him.

They sat, sipping the liquor, in silence for a while. *We're an odd pair,* Alexandre thought. As far as clothing went, Alf didn't *look* like the rough East Ender that he was; he dressed very properly, as any valet would, in a neat black suit, impeccably white shirt, tie, and immaculate waistcoat, although with his master's tacit permission, he had unbuttoned his waistcoat, loosened his tie and draped his jacket over the back of the chair. Alexandre could see why the solicitor had muttered what he had about Alf terrifying him, though. It was clear once the jacket was off that Alf was a bruiser and could probably win just about any fight with anyone other than a bare-knuckle professional pugilist. From the scars on his face and hands, he'd probably seen his share of fights, too. His short hair was about the same color as faded leather, and it was liberally sprinkled with gray hairs. He had deep-set, shrewd gray eyes that missed nothing.

But he held the brandy glass like a gentleman born; he ate and drank like one too. In all the time Alexandre had employed him, he'd never said much about his past, and Alexandre had never pressed him.

"Why'd you pick me, Alf?" he asked, finally.

"B'cause ye ain't stupid, guv," Alf replied promptly. "Ye might not be's serious 'bout magic as me old master, but ye ain't stupid. An' Oi reckoned 'ventually the not bein' serious 'ud wear off."

"I think it just did," Alexandre said slowly.

Alf nodded. "Thought so. Ye had that *look* when ye started on that book. Fact is, yer smarter'n my old master, Oi reckon. Don't drink too much, don't fiddle around with drugs, careful usin' magic when ye gamble, careful 'bout how ye live so ye don't get attention fer yerself. An' if somethin' needs t'be done quiet, well, thet's what ye got me fer."

Alexandre smiled to himself. He *was* careful. In fact, that, more than the low rent, was the reason he was living here on the north side of Battersea. Things that would be noticed and noted in a genteel, middle-class neighborhood would be ignored here. He could probably have women parading in and out of here every day at every hour of the day and no one would notice.

And as for the rest . . . well, the basement came with the ground floor flat. He and Alf had carefully sealed up all the windows so that you could light a thousand lamps down there and not a glimmer would show outside. And in the basement was a covered opening that led directly to the sewers—an opening large enough to drop almost anything down into it. And once something was down there, it wouldn't be seen again until it ended up in the Thames.

"Penny fer yer thoughts, guv," Alf said.

"I was just thinking that if this Book proves genuine . . . you and I could not be more perfectly situated to take advantage of it," Alexandre replied. And smiled. Alf smiled back.

"Fancy a bit of a skirt?" he suggested.

"I'm torn, Alf. I'm torn. I'm itching to get back to The Book—"

"Don't, not arter dark," Alf advised, and held up a finger. "Ye don't wanta make no mistakes, not if this book's what ye think it is." He held up a second. "An' if it *is* what ye think it is . . . daylight's some pertection 'gainst accidentally callin' somethin'."

"Those are both good points." He pondered a moment. "Yes, I think I could do with a little bedsport." He put down the brandy glass, went to the small safe in the wall behind a picture of a dead pheasant, and unlocked it, extracting a couple of banknotes.

"Here you are, Alf," he said, handing the valet the money then locking the safe. "You know what I like."

"'Deedy do, guv," Alf said genially. Then his voice took on a tone of warning. "An . . . lissen. Don't go back to that book t'night. Lookit one uv yer pitcher books t'get in the mood. Oi got a feelin' 'bout that book. Oi got a feelin' it's the gen-u-wine article. But that jest makes it dangerous."

Alexandre raised an eyebrow at the valet. He had never, in all the time he'd employed Alf, heard him speak this way.

But that was all the more reason to pay attention, now that he had.

"Very well, Alf. I will take your advice," he promised. Alf got up, donned his jacket, and went in search of his coat.

When the flat door closed behind him, Alexandre suddenly felt it. The lure. The siren call. The Book wanted him to work on it.

But Alexandre was determined to prove that Alf was right. He *was* smart, and the fact that he felt this inexplicable pull to do what was quite difficult work, even after a full day of it, only proved that Alf knew what he was talking about.

"You might as well give up for tonight," he called into the study, not feeling in the least foolish about talking to a book. "I'm taking Alf's advice. I'm not working on you except during daylight hours. You'll just have to wait."

Was it his imagination, or did he feel a faint sense of . . . disappointment?

5

"I HAVE had many occasions to be grateful that Lord Alderscroft is our patron," Sarah said to Nan, as they rolled through the suburbs of London on their way to the Harton School. "But I have to say that I am more grateful than usual today." She snuggled in her cape and thick, warm lap robe, and felt the gentle warmth from the brick in the foot warmer permeating her boots.

On the bench seat across from her, Suki knelt, little nose pressed up against the window with interest. There was a great deal to see, and she drank in every bit of it. It was only two days to Christmas, and London was still covered in snow, but the snow had not put any damper on Christmas spirits. Shop windows had all been decorated to at least some extent for the holiday. There seemed to be carolers of various sorts at nearly every corner, from the Salvation Army brass bands to ordinary buskers turning their hands to festal music in hopes of pennies falling into their hats. Entire blocks had been decorated by the joint efforts of shopkeepers or residents, with wreaths on the lampposts, on the front doors, and on front gates.

They had been picked up at the door of their lodging by

It was not his imagination that the tugging on him to go into the study lessened. It didn't stop . . . but it did lessen.

Smiling a little, he turned to the preparations for more carnal pursuits. That had been a good idea, too. No man was capable of thinking of a Book, no matter how important, with a naked girl under him.

Lord A's private carriage. There had been luxurious quilted lap robes waiting for them and hot bricks in cast-iron foot heaters on the floor. The top of the carriage was piled high with presents for the children of the school—not individual presents, but things they could share. If past gifts were anything to go by, there would probably be a flood of new recruits to the blue and red armies of tin soldiers, additions to the wardrobes of the school dolls, possibly a new rocking horse or two (since Dobbin and Blackie, the current horses, were getting a bit shabby, loose in the joints, and in need of an overhaul), but other than that, Nan and Sarah would be as surprised as the children would be. These presents, by Lord A's decree, were to be opened today, after supper, at the Christmas Party. That way there would be new things to occupy the youngsters until Christmas Day and the opening of their own personal presents. The Christmas Party brought together such "old students" as still lived in London with the "current crop," and was a good chance for the youngsters to meet with adults who shared their psychical talents.

"I wouldn't miss the party for the world, but I was not looking forward to the journey we usually make to the school in this weather," Nan agreed, glanced out the window at the snow, and shivered. "Agansing is the only one of all of us who is rejoicing at this cold."

She couldn't help but think of how she'd have fared if she was still on the street. Winter was the killing season for the poor, the season when even such a small thing as a hot potato and a blanket sometimes meant the difference between life and death. She often felt guilty that she was doing so little for the enormous problem out there in the shambles, but . . . she and Sarah only had so much money and so much time, and the problem was so . . . vast. *We do what we can,* she reminded herself. *And we remind people like Alderscroft, who have fortunes, that they can do more.*

"Cor, look!" Suki exclaimed, pointing. She and Sarah craned their necks to see there was a winter bridal procession coming out of a church, the bride wrapped in a white velvet cloak, with a white velvet dress, carrying a bouquet of holly, the rest of the wedding party in their very best gear.

"Oi ain't niver seen a widdin' afore!" She pressed her nose even harder against the window, trying to take it all in before they got out of sight.

Neville and Grey poked their heads out of their sable muffs at her exclamation, but on discovering there was nothing that interested either of them, they pulled their heads back in again, leaving nothing but their black beaks showing. The muffs were in their carriers for extra safety in case of jounces or accident, but in this weather it was unlikely either of them would stir from the warmth of those shelters. Grey could not take the cold, and even though Neville *could,* he made it very clear he didn't *want* to.

Suki was afire with excitement and anticipation. She was about to see her schoolmates again after a vacation of a week, and to a little girl her age, a week was nearly a century. There were going to be presents involved, and a feast of all the foreign foods she had come to enjoy—biryani, and chole bhature, rajma and pani puri, tandoori chicken and rogan josh, naan and gajar halwa. The children at the Harton School, created for the children of expatriate parents, had mostly been born in India, and had been raised on native foods. Isabella Harton understood very well how "food" meant "comfort and home," and her Indian cooks served the kinds of spiced things *most* English boarding schools would look upon with horror. No bread-and-butter and milky tea for these children; they got the things they were used to. Suki, having come from the streets, would eat anything that didn't run away fast enough to escape, and had taken to the spicy fare with relish. When she stayed on the holidays with Nan and Sarah, she ate what they ate, and what they ate were the solid—sometimes stolid—plain English dishes Mrs. Horace cooked. She never complained, but Nan knew for a fact she got tired of such plain food after having had her palate educated in the spices of India.

If they'd been making the trip without the convenience of the carriage, they'd have gotten up in the dark, gotten a hansom to the station, and taken the train, to be picked up with some of the other former schoolchildren in the school cart. It would have been very cold, and they wouldn't have wanted to expose the birds to all the jostling, the curious, and of course, the cold itself. But with Lord A supplying his lovely carriage, they could travel in great comfort and the birds could come along too.

Sarah had brought a book to read aloud in case Suki got bored. She should have known better, Nan thought with amusement. Suki *never* got bored. If they were in any kind of conveyance, Suki found endless entertainment in the streets at this time of year. If there had been nothing going on, she would make up stories about the people or things they were passing by.

So Sarah silently read the book to herself, and Nan listened to Suki's excited running commentary, and in a much shorter time than if they had been going by train, the carriage was pulling in through the gates of what once had been Lord Alderscroft's manor, and now was the home of the Harton School.

The children had been waiting for them, because, of course, they already knew there were presents coming; they swarmed the carriage, and the coachman, laughing until he cried, got the presents down off the top and into their hands to be carried away. Suki got carried off with the horde, one of the (few) school servants got their overnight bags to take to their rooms, and Memsa'b appropriated Nan and Sarah and the birds. In no time at all they were enjoying hot tea and cakes in Memsa'b's cozy little sitting room.

"Well, you certainly uncovered a pretty piece of work in that poor child you rescued from the asylum," were the first words she said as soon as they were all settled and the birds had bits of cake of their own, in saucers on the floor.

"Is Amelia a problem?" Sarah asked, looking anxious.

"No—yes—well, not a problem because of *who* she is, but rather *what* she is." Memsa'b shook her head. "She's a very powerful . . . whatever. I am not yet certain if she is a clairvoyant or a precognitive. Or both! And absolutely no control, poor thing." She frowned. "A year in the care of that meddling quack and she *would* have been mad."

Memsa'b Harton was not a pretty woman, and never had been—but she was striking, with very defined and sculpted features, a long and graceful neck and a pair of wonderful gray eyes. Her dark hair, put up in a heavy chignon, was liberally streaked with silver now, but she seemed to Nan not to have lost a bit of her energy and vigor. Just now she wore an expression of concern.

"Has she had any more visions since she came to you?" Nan asked.

"One. And I have asked Alderscroft to have one of his London agents pursue details on the other visions. You see, that doctor she was with was not as careful about exact details as he could have been. He only made certain that there was no way in which she could have learned of the murders by some ordinary means; he did not trouble himself to find out if she had seen the murders during their commission, or before. This is why I am not certain if she is clairvoyant or precognitive. Actually I am just as glad he was so careless; he might have worked harder to force her to see things that he could have profited by." Memsa'b sighed. "I haven't told her that her initial visions might be precognitive, and I probably won't. The poor child would blame herself for not preventing them. But I digress. She had another of those visions of a London in ruins, inhabited by monsters."

The fire popped and crackled as Nan and Sarah both considered that. The birds stopped eating for a moment, then flew up to the back of the sofa and sat watching and listening.

"And you don't think this is just her mind supplying her with a metaphor for the reality of the dark side of the city," Sarah stated.

"No, I don't," Memsa'b replied. "I think it's a warning. I'm just not sure how literal a warning it is. I would have thought that if London were likely to be taken over by monsters, more clairvoyants than just Amelia would be sounding the alarm. I'd like to consult with Alderscroft about this as soon as possible; this seems more of a task for a magician than one of us, if what she saw is any indication." She sipped her tea. "The trouble is, I would *think* that if there were a magician working in London who was powerful enough to make that come to pass, Alderscroft would already know about him."

"If these visions are anything to go by, perhaps it's a case of someone who is all right *now,* but who is going to go to the bad, or himself go insane, or something of the sort," Nan said after a moment. She frowned. "I don't know how we would identify someone like that. Not without knowing who it might be. . . ."

"I don't know how we would *stop* someone like that," Memsa'b said frankly. "Although if it came to that, psychical talents might be more effective than magical ones. The miscreant would not know we had them, would not be prepared for them, and would not know how to defend against them."

"But we wouldn't know how to defend against magic, either," Nan pointed out.

"True. And yet . . . so far, you girls have done very well in dealing with magicians." Memsa'b gave them approving smiles, then sobered again. "Well, the first thing to do is contact Alderscroft and consult with him directly. I never thought I would say I find Christmas tiresome, but it *is* tiresome that he is tied down with all the to-do of the season and can't come when I call!" Memsa'b sniffed theatrically, and Nan laughed.

"So I suppose you're not concerned this is an imminent danger?" Sarah asked.

"I think if we were, the two precognitive students I have would be having nightmares." Memsa'b put down her teacup. "Although . . . Nan, do you think you and Sarah might be able to stir up your old friend by going out in the conservatory and calling him? I won't ask you to trudge out into the grounds in this weather, and the conservatory is as good as any place outdoors, only near at hand."

"I think we'd be fools not to try," Nan replied, setting her cup aside, and rising. "He was the only thing that stood between England and disaster when Alderscroft himself was corrupted by that wretched woman; I should at least warn him there may be something in the wind, if he doesn't already know." She made a face. "That's the disadvantage of living in the city; it's very difficult to contact him."

"I have my talisman," Sarah said, and looked at the birds

as she rose. "You two keep Memsa'b company, and don't get into mischief while we're gone."

Neville looked affronted; Grey laughed.

"I'll take that as saying that you'll be good, so don't start poking your beaks into things you shouldn't get into," Sarah replied, then fished Puck's talisman out of her reticule, and she and Nan headed across the manor to the conservatory.

There were two parts to the conservatory, as there were in many manor houses that could afford to keep such things heated in the winter. The larger part supplied some flowers and out-of-season fruits to the kitchen; once the School took over, the flowers had been replaced by herbs, and the fruits had been joined by vegetables. The smaller part, in this case, had been designed as a sort of pocket wilderness; short of going out into the wilder parts of the grounds—which was impractical without saddling up a couple of the working horses and riding there—this would be the best place to try and summon Puck.

They held hands with the talisman between them, and began reciting lines from *A Midsummer Night's Dream*, which seemed to be the most reliable way to get his attention.

This time, however, he was either involved with something elsewhere, didn't want to venture so close to a human habitation, or was not inclined to answer. They waited a good fifteen minutes after speaking the line that gave Puck his cue to enter, and nothing happened.

They looked at each other. "Well. . . bother," Sarah sighed.

Nan shrugged. "There's another way, you know. We can ask John or Mary to pass on word that we'd like to speak to him via their Elementals. We can always meet him at Hampton Court Palace."

"Or possibly Kensington Garden or Kew Garden. That *might* be wild enough." Sarah sighed. "I would like to have talked to him now, though. If there is something in the wind . . . something bad enough to ruin *London* . . . I don't know how we'd ever be able to do anything about it."

"You and I wouldn't, not alone, because we don't have to do this alone," Nan reminded her. "We have Alderscroft's White Lodge. We have Memsa'b's circle of psychical friends and students. And we have—*oh!*" She made a fist and struck her forehead with it. "I am a complete idiot. Beatrice!"

"Beatrice Leek?" Sarah looked puzzled. "But she's not a Master—"

Nan snorted, and gestured to her friend to follow her back into the manor. "She might not be a Master, but I would bet my favorite hat that she can do more with Earth Elementals than most Earth Masters can. And I'd trust her knowledge of all things occult in London over just about anyone else's, and that includes Alderscroft. I'll try and talk to her when we get back, although I might not be able to until after Christmas. If she's as much of a witch as she claims, she probably has some ceremonies to do."

"Bother Christmas! Why did it have to come at such a *bloody* inconvenient time?" Sarah asked crossly.

"We've got that backward," Nan said, as the significance dawned on her. "Christmas is the *cause* of all this, not just something that's getting in the way of us contacting people. It's what we were afraid of."

"Oh . . ." Sarah replied, putting her hand to her lips in alarm. "It has to be. You're right. It's moon-dark and Christmas Eve."

Nan, Sarah and Memsa'b managed to keep cheerful faces for the children, who ripped into Lord Alderscroft's presents with unholy glee after a sumptuous Christmas party dinner. Lord A had gifted the school with many dolls over the years, most of which had survived even from Nan and Sarah's day. Each little girl was allowed to pick one that was hers and hers alone until she decided she had outgrown dolls, the rest were common property. Lord A—or, more like, his secretary, who had an uncanny knack for such things—had made certain these dolls were all the same size, and made sure there was a nice variety in the various hair and eye colors and face-molds, and even that there were a few boys among the girls. So when the big box of brand new doll clothing was opened, *all* the special darlings got new clothing out of it, with plenty of frocks and underthings and sailor suits to spare. And of course, that was just the beginning of the bounty. There were, in fact, two new rocking horses and a pleasing assortment of hobbyhorses, all of them with magnificent manes and tails. The expected reinforcements for the tin army were there. There was a big box of games, another of various sized balls, and a dazzling box of marbles and another of jacks. And to cap it all off, enough new paints and pencils and crayons to replace all the old ones. The children all went to bed thoroughly tired out. Even Amelia decided she was not too old to join the fun, politely accepted a doll from among the "unclaimed" and saw her garbed in a brand new gown, and romped with the rest. Nan was relieved to see her finally get some color in her cheeks, and to wear herself out with jumping rope, dancing, and blindman's bluff.

Although the other "old students" went back to their respective homes, Suki, Nan, and Sarah were expected to stay the night; Nan and Sarah had overnight bags, and of course most of Suki's belongings were already here. Alderscroft's coachman would return for them in the morning.

Which meant a message to Aldersoft could go with him, when the adults had had their conference.

Memsa'b gathered them all in the library, fortified with ginger tea, since they were going to need clear heads. Sahib delegated himself to take the notes. They all settled on the couches in front of the fire—Memsa'b, Sahib, and Sarah on one, Nan with Karamjit and Agansing on either side of her on the second, and Selim and Gupta on the third. The four Indians wore modified versions of their native dress—Gurkha, Sikh, Moslem, and Hindu, all wool rather than cotton, mostly—and they all sported proper stout leather boots.

Sahib Harton had streaks of gray at each temple, wider now than when Nan had first met him. The stiff way that he walked, was due to an injury in military service. Most striking about him was the odd expression in his eyes, which seemed to Nan to be the eyes of a man who had seen so much that nothing surprised him anymore.

"Let's start with what we know," Sahib suggested.

Nan described the vision she had seen in Amelia's mind; Memsa'b the one *she* had seen two days ago. Once laid side by side, it was evident that there were some differences. In Nan's vision, it had been a man who was swallowed up; in Memsa'b's, a young woman. In Nan's vision, something with tentacles had dragged him into darkness—in Memsa'b's the earth had opened under the woman and engulfed her. Nan had heard nothing except the wind, Memsa'b had heard what she described as "chittering noises, a little like the sounds monkeys make, but more metallic."

Sahib tapped the end of his pencil against his lips. "I don't think this is random," he said, finally. "Can you two share the visions with each other, so you can get a better comparison?"

"I don't see why not," Memsa'b replied. "That is an excellent idea, my love. Nan?"

"I am ready when you are, Memsa'b," Nan replied easily. She closed her eyes and reached for Memsa'b's mind as Memsa'b reached for hers.

Yours first, please, Memsa'b requested, and Nan obliged. When she had let it "play" through both their minds, she waited to see Memsa'b's.

And immediately, there were some obvious differences. In Nan's vision, it had been very difficult to make details out; it was as dark as a moonless night. In Memsa'b's, things were a little bit brighter—as if there was a half-moon in the sky, although there was no moon evident. The extent of the damage to the street and buildings was clearer. And in Nan's vision, the man had appeared from out of the shadows, as if he had emerged from a hidden doorway that was now visible. In Memsa'b's, the woman appeared right in the middle of the street, out of nowhere.

They broke the contact and their eyes met. Nan nodded. "I believe something changed between the first vision and the second," Memsa'b said. "It is as if the second one was stronger, perhaps."

"Or nearer to the real world?" The words came out of Nan's mouth before she actually thought of them, but they seemed right to her.

"That's a nasty thought," Sahib murmured. "I am beginning

to get some vague notions . . . but as they are based on hints in certain fiction, rather than fact, I believe I will keep them to myself until after I can speak with Alderscroft."

"Do any of you recognize the glimpses of creature we described?" Nan asked, looking at her four friends from four very different parts of the Indian subcontinent. Agansing was a Gurkha, and had taught her the use of the wicked knives his people were famous for. Selim was a Muslim from the center of the country. Karamjit was a Sikh from the North, and Gupta a Hindu from the South. All of them were as expert in the mythology and magic of their respective regions as Memsa'b and Sahib were of the mythology of Britain and the powers of psychics. All of them shook their heads.

"The closest *I* can come is that . . . whatever it was that nearly killed us as children," Nan said thoughtfully. "But that was confined to a single house. This thing, in the vision at least, seems to have taken over all of London."

"That's possible, if an entity is fed enough power," said Sahib. "Which is not at all comforting, considering what is almost upon us."

They all contemplated that, glumly.

"We have two days," Selim pointed out. "You can send a message to the great Lord Alderscroft, who can in turn gather as many of his White Lodge as possible to interfere with dark powers on Christmas Eve. The four of us can perform certain rites, separately, I am sure."

"I can get hold of Beatrice Leek, and she can organize *her* circle, or circles," Nan offered. "I'll do that directly as we are back in London."

"I think that's all we can do, until and unless we can find out more—" Sahib was clearly not happy about saying that.

"Or if we discover this is some sort of psychic attack on Amelia," Memsa'b said, as if that had suddenly occurred to her. "I don't know *why* someone would do that to a mere child, but that's one possibility we almost overlooked." She clasped Sahib's hand. "I can look into that."

"I would be overjoyed to discover it was that, and not some damned magical apocalypse that is bearing down on us," he said. "Because right at this moment, we are woefully undermanned for a magical apocalypse."

"You have our swords, Sahib," Selim said, bringing his head up proudly. "We are not inconsiderable."

"No, you are not, and there are not four people in the world I would rather stand against the darkness beside," Sahib replied emphatically. He looked around the group. "I think we have done everything that we might for now. Try to get sleep. In the morning, we will all get to work."

Nan had thought she wouldn't sleep a bit, but instead, it was as if being back in the old room she shared with Sarah worked some sort of spell, because she fell asleep as soon as her head touched the pillow. And in the morning, right after an early breakfast, they gathered up birds, Suki, and their belongings, and mounted the carriage for the ride back to London.

And Nan decided that this was nothing to be kept from Suki; there might be danger that would include *her,* and she deserved to be forewarned.

"Suki," she said, in the "very serious" tone that always got the little girl's attention. "There may be some frightening times coming."

Suki immediately took her focus off of what was happening outside the carriage window, and sat with her hands folded inside her little muff and all her attention on Nan while her guardian explained carefully what was going on.

She considered that for several moments when Nan had finished. "I ain't gonna be able t'do much," she stated.

"That's true," Sarah agreed.

"Quork," Neville said from his muff.

"So . . . best would be fer me t'practice hidin'," she stated.

"That would be a great deal of help," Nan told her. "If we know you can keep yourself safe, we can concentrate on what we need to do."

Although in a way it broke her heart, it also was a great

relief to know that Suki, unlike most children her age, was very well aware that adults could not, and often *would* not, protect children, and in some cases the best way for a child to stay safe was to make sure she knew how to protect herself.

"If we know danger is coming in advance, we will send you to Memsa'b," Sarah promised. "And you'll be going back there after Boxing Day at any rate. If there is any place in all this world that will be safe, it will be with Memsa'b."

Suki's troubled brow cleared a little. "Ol roight then," she said. "An' ye'll hev Neville an' Grey to pertect *you*, so I won't need t'worry none neither."

Well, we have gone up against terrible things together, Nan thought. *And we have bested those things. We can do this again.*

When they arrived at their lodgings, only Sarah, Suki and the birds alighted. Nan directed the driver to leave her at Pandora's Tea Room in Chelsea, perfectly determined to stay there for the rest of the day if that was what it took to contact Beatrice Leek.

But fortune for once was with her. Beatrice was already at her usual table in the back, partaking of an early luncheon, and for once was alone. Despite the fact that the tearoom was already half-full, they made eye contact as soon as Nan opened the door. Nan made her way through the crowded tables and chairs, but as soon as she reached Beatrice, that worthy ate the last bite and stood up. All the black glass beading and jet ornaments on her person danced, as if showing an agitation that Beatrice herself refused to display.

"I've been expecting you, dearie," she said. "There's something nasty in the wind, and we need to talk about it. Come along, then."

She led Nan out into the snowy street again and trotted along at a brisker pace than Nan had ever seen her make before. That might have been due to the cold, but Nan fancied that it was more than likely due to the fact that Beatrice wanted to have this conversation as much as Nan did.

Nan would not have been at all surprised had Beatrice

led her to a little witchy cottage nestled among enormous trees—Chelsea still had such things after all, for despite a great deal of building, it had not been turned entirely into row houses, terraced houses, and elegant homes. But instead, she found herself waiting for Beatrice to unlock the front door of a perfectly ordinary white terraced house, which stood in its row with all the other white terraced houses, one solid block of building broken up by windows, doors, and black iron fences. She could not have imagined anything *more* unlike Beatrice Leek.

But once they stepped inside, well, she might very well have been in a witchy little cottage off on the moors or the wild lands of Ireland.

The hall was not fashionably papered; it had been hand-painted, possibly by one of Beatrice's artist friends, in an imitation of a medieval tapestry. The scene was of a forest meadow, dotted with flowers and full of animals and birds both real and mythical, the centerpiece of which was a unicorn. There were three coat racks, all of them burdened by shawls, coats, and hats. There were two umbrella stands, full of walking sticks and staffs, all of them fancifully carved. Some of the staffs were surmounted by glass globes or odd little sculptures. They were met at the door by the biggest black cat Nan had ever seen, which meowed at his mistress, then jumped up into her arms.

"And who's my handsome man, then?" Beatrice cooed to her—pet? familiar?—and handed him unceremoniously to Nan. "You go along into the parlor, first door on the right, and I'll make some tea. His name's Caprice. I call him Cappy."

Cappy weighed every bit of eighteen pounds if he weighed an ounce, but he gave no objection to Nan holding him. In fact, he purred so loudly he sounded like clockwork being wound up.

She went into the parlor, and discovered that the theme of the walls was more of the same as in the hall. Here, tall, elegant women in flowing gowns danced, disported, or dozed amid the flowers and the animals. There were no framed pictures on the walls, but they would have been superfluous.

The parlor was small, just big enough for three comfortable chairs and a couple of tables. There was a good fire in the grate, and Nan took the chair that showed the least wear, assuming the one with the most wear was Beatrice's favorite.

Cappy draped himself over her lap with every sign of pleasure and continued to purr. A few moments later, Beatrice arrived with tea in mismatched crockery.

"Now," she said, when she had poured for both of them. "Tell me what brings you here, with worry in your face."

Nan explained; it didn't take long, because there really wasn't much of anything that they knew. Beatrice listened without interruption, and when Nan had finished, Cappy jumped down off her lap and moved to his mistress's.

"Well," Beatrice said at last. "There is *something* making the little Earth creatures uneasy . . . but not frantic, not uneasy enough to correspond with something as terrible as that vision. I would say, if I were to hazard a guess, that this is one of two things. A psychical or magical attack against that child, or, rather than a definite problem, this represents the possibility that something very bad could happen, and the seeds of it will most likely be planted on Christmas Eve."

"I wanted to contact the Oldest Old One, if I could, but I haven't been able to get his attention," Nan said. "At the very least, he should be warned *something* might happen. Could you ask one of the little ones to carry a message for me?"

Beatrice pursed her lips, thinking. "Well, a body would think that the Oldest Old One would already know about such a thing . . . but we both know he gets distracted. He won't take offense if he already knows, and if he don't, well, then he will." She nodded. "And lucky for us, I've got a brownie in the house."

"A . . . what?" Nan asked.

" 'Tis a little Earth creature—but a rare one that shares a house with you." Beatrice put Cappy down, and got up from her chair. "They're not very common anymore, more's the pity, and even so, they're rare in cities. Let me trot along to the kitchen and fetch what I need."

Beatrice came back with a flat, dished stone, a tiny cup of milk, and a scone topped with double cream and jam. She moved one of the chairs aside, and that was when Nan realized that there was a faint circle woven into the rug there, and that those weren't flowers—they were symbols. Beatrice moved a stool to the center of the circle, and sat down on it. "When I was younger, I'd sit on the rug," she sighed. "But if I did that now, you'd have to fetch a neighbor to help me get up. Aging is not for the faint of heart!"

"I wish that were less true," Nan acknowledged.

Beatrice set the scone in the middle of the stone, the little cup beside it. Then she closed her eyes, and Nan waited patiently. After a moment, a little creature . . . grew, or emerged, right out of thin air. If Beatrice had been standing, he'd have barely come up to her knee.

It looked like a wizened old man in a country-style smock and buff trousers, wearing a pointed cap. He looked at Nan warily for a moment, then at Beatrice.

"Mistress Leek, you call me, with a feast for a favor?" he said.

Beatrice's eyes opened. "I did, Hobson, and it is a very large favor. This young lady and I need you to carry a message to the Oldest Old One."

The poor little man paled. "Oh . . . oh lady . . . speaking to *him* is not for the likes of me!"

"Look at her, Hobson. Look deep," Beatrice said, in a coaxing tone, not as an order.

The brownie half turned and stared at Nan. After a moment, his eyes grew huge. "Oh . . . oh!" he gasped. "Oh, and she has *his* favor and grace all over her!"

"And I'll tease a bit of it off her and put it on you. *He'll* know who you come from, and you and the word you bring will be respected." Beatrice smiled slightly, and the little man flushed at the last word.

"Respected?" he asked. "The likes of me, by *him?*" He drew in a long, careful breath. "Ah well, then . . ." He made a little grasping gesture with his hands, and the milk and scone vanished. "A feast for a favor, done." He looked at them both, expectantly.

Nan sucked on her lower lip. Could Robin Goodfellow *read?* She'd have to chance it.

"Let me write a note," she said, feeling in her reticule for some paper and a pencil.

"Oh, that would be a grand thing, mistress," the brownie replied, looking relieved. "Better if I don't have to remember. Because . . . if I do go standing before *him,* I think all my memories will drain right out my ears, I truly do."

She was getting so used to this story she was able to condense it down into two pages of closely written notepaper, which she folded and sealed with a blob of candle-wax, and handed to the little man. He stowed the packet inside his smock and waited patiently again.

While Nan had been writing, Beatrice had been making little motions with what could only be a *wand.* Nan had never seen anyone use a wand before . . . the Elemental Masters she'd seen in action all used their hands, not wands.

Beatrice was making tiny circles with the tip of the wand pointed at Nan, eyes narrowed in concentration. Nan *thought* she saw little transparent, glowing wisps of something collecting on the end of it, but she couldn't be sure.

Eventually, she held out the tip of her wand to the brownie who cupped his hands around it and apparently pulled an invisible ball of something off it. "There you go, pet," Beatrice said easily. "That will show *him* who you're from. Favor for a feast. Tell him Miss Nan will meet him, if he can come, in Kensington Garden the day after the Eve." She looked at Nan. "Don't worry about finding him, he'll find you."

That was a good choice, Nan realized. On Christmas Day Kensington Garden would be practically empty.

"Thenkee, mistress," said the little man, who bobbed an awkward bow, then faded away.

"Well," Nan said after a long pause. "That's done."

"'Tis," Beatrice replied. "And I would take it kindly if you'd help me up and back to my chair!"

6

THE coal fire on the grate kept the sitting room warm, and supplied most of the light. Alexandre waited, somewhat impatiently, for Alf to return with the last component of the magic work he was about to attempt. He had spent the last two days carefully going over the ritual he had copied from The Book, making sure he clearly understood each and every word of the incantations, and that, barring mistakes in The Book itself, he could pronounce everything perfectly. He didn't want to take a chance on this going wrong, because if it did, he couldn't try again for another year. And even then . . . this would be the most effective Eve for quite some time. Everything would be perfect *right now,* but only if Alf could get him that one final, and all-important, thing.

But if anyone could, Alf could.

He paced the floor of his sitting room, eager to start, even though midnight was three hours away. He planned to take his time and move slowly and methodically, but the longer it took for Alf to get back here was less time for him to use. Time wasn't critical . . . yet. But if Alf took much longer, it would be.

He thought he knew now why The Book had found its

way into *his* hands. Most of the people who frequented the bookstore were interested in the erotica, not the esoterica, and the few who had any interest at all in the occult had not, at least to his eyes, shown any signs of real power. Like the proprietor, they could not tell trash from treasure. And he was certain now that, like many such items of power, The Book had a certain level of sentience, and had deliberately bent the mind of the owner to show it to him.

Or . . . no, that was not quite correct. It was not The Book itself that was sentient. It was that there was a power behind The Book that had been seeking for the proper person to find The Book. Now, its ability to interact with the material world was thin and feeble, and the best it could do was dimly influence minds to get The Book to someone that could use it. Once he set it free . . .

That would take some time; six months and as many moon-dark major rituals, in fact, with additional minor rituals as he got the components and time to do them.

The clock on the mantle ticked loudly, one second for every step he took. It was exactly eight steps across his sitting room in front of the fireplace. He thought by now he must have measured out several miles. What could be keeping the man?

But then he heard footfalls on the steps, and ran to open the door. "Did you—"

Alf held up a basket. Alexandre frowned. "But that—"

"Ye said a virgin, an' Oi thought, on'y way to be *sure* is t'get one too young t'hev been interfered with." Alf pushed past him and headed for the cellar stairs. "Le's get down afore it wakes up and starts cryin'. Oi give it some whiskey-milk t'shut it up, but Oi dunno how long thet'll last."

Alf hurried down the stairs ahead of him; Alexandre made sure the heavy cellar door was firmly closed. Now he was worried. It wasn't that he objected to sacrificing a baby—but would the entity *accept* a baby?

By the time he got downstairs, Alf had already put the baby, closed basket and all, on the altar stone in the middle of the basement floor. Fortunately the altar stone he was already using had been acceptable according to The Book. It was just a good thing he knew so many artists. It hadn't been that difficult for him to get hold of a proper sized piece of black marble, and the way he kept enthusing about the bust of Prince Albert he was going to make it into had kept the workmen who brought it here properly incurious. Getting the top polished had been the hardest work he'd ever done in his life.

"It's awfully quiet in that basket," he said, doubtfully, as he descended the last couple of stairs. "Is it even still alive?"

Alf looked in the basket. "Jes' sleepin'." He turned to his master. "Look, ye tol' me it was most important fer it t'be a virgin. There hain't a lot of virgins on the market, not ones with gar-an-tees, an' Oi figgered if it was thet important for it t'be a virgin, there was a damn good reason. We didn' 'ave a lot uv time t'get one, neither. Them as goes about buyin' virgins gets attention, an' Oi reckoned ye didn' want that."

Well, all that was true. That just hadn't occurred to him, and it probably should have; *would* have, if he hadn't been concentrating so hard on The Book. Still . . .

The Book didn't specify age, or even sex, he reminded himself. *Just that it be a virgin.*

But that brought up another question. How on earth had Alf gotten a baby? Had he bought it? Wasn't buying a baby likely to bring questions? A new set of anxieties assailed him, "Where did you get it?" he asked.

Alf chuckled. "Roight orf th' steps uv a Foundlin' 'Ome. Oi'd reckoned t'see if I could slip in an' take one, but there was a girl leavin' one jest as Oi gets there. Oi nips in an' snatches the basket an Oi'm 'round th' corner afore anyone comes t'answer th'bell." He sniffed and rubbed his nose with the back of his hand. "Oi dunno if ye've iver seed th' inside uv one uv them 'Omes, guv. Nobody minds th' back door, 'cause there ain't nothin' t'steal. Babies is all in one big room, loik, all wrapped up like sausages, six, eight uv 'em to a bed. Nobody comes if they cries, so they gets useta not cryin', cause it don't get 'em nothin'. Mebbe one nurse t'the room, an she's likely drunk. If babies die i' th' night, they jest put 'em in a shed 'til ground thaws, an' buries 'em wholesale. Ain't nobody gonna notice if one goes missin'. If this works, I c'n get more, easy-peasy."

Alexandre nodded, mollified. "Damn good work, Alf," he said, and fished out the gold sovereigns he'd put in his vest pocket. "Here," he said, tossing all three of them to Alf, who caught them out of the air, deftly. "Get us some girls so we can celebrate after, and keep the rest for yourself. Is there anything I should do about—" he nodded at the basket.

Alf looked in again, and shook his head. "Nay. 'S warm enuff, sleepin' hard, an' Oi reckon th' whiskey'll keep it quiet till midnight. Anythin' more, guv?"

Alexandre shook his head. Alf grinned.

"Oi'll get me somethin' t'eat then, an' get them girls. Ye ain't gonna need 'em till arter midnight?"

"I'm sure you can find something to keep you, and them, occupied until then," he replied dryly. Alf grinned again, tugged at his cap, and went back up the stairs, closing the door firmly behind him.

And Alexandre got to work.

He'd removed every trace of magical work he had done here before, scouring the room down to the stone floor and walls. For now, he needed light, and plenty of it, so he lit the lamps he had hung from the beams of the ceiling and got his paint and brush and, of course, The Book.

Using a stiff, fine brush, he painted a circle around the altar stone, then a larger one outside of that. With The Book in one hand and the brush in the other, using the paint that had been made of very specific ingredients—none of them, oddly, blood—he wrote words in a language he had been completely unable to identify. When they were painted, starting in the north, he walked three times counterclockwise, slowly, intoning a sequence of syllables that had been *very* carefully denoted in The Book.

When he ended, chanting and walking both, he got back down on his hands and knees and painted another pair of circles, and another set of words, and repeated the walking and chanting.

He did this for a total of nine circles. And when he was

finished, with tiny dots of paint, he marked north, northeast, east, south east, south, southwest, west, and northwest, with absolute precision. And in each of these positions he left an object. In the north, a piece of meteorite. In the northeast, a small fossil. In the east, a piece of fulgurite, the glass formed when lightning strikes sand. In the southeast, a tiny cube of electrum. In the south, a pyramid of black jade. In the southwest, a saucer of mercury. In the west, a dodecahedron of obsidian. And in the northwest, a crystal skull. That last, he had found as the pommel of an expensive walking stick.

He set incense of dragon's blood burning and placed lit black candles behind each of the objects. The incense fumed and filled the air with its pungent and peculiar aroma. He licked his lips, and tasted it, lingering resinously on his tongue.

Then, with his watch out in one hand, The Book in the other, and a lantern behind him to illuminate the words clearly, he began a long, sonorous chant, of which he only understood about half the words. As nearly as he could tell, it included the names of gods so old they were ancient even to the Egyptians, but what the sense of it was, he could not tell.

And he ended the chant precisely as the bells in the churches around him and the watch in his hand chimed midnight.

For a moment, nothing happened.

Then, slowly, all the light drained out of the room, and the lamps hanging from the ceiling went out, leaving only the eight candles on the floor, flickering with dim, blue flames.

The temperature in the room dropped until it was so cold his face hurt. And then, all the darkness was sucked toward the altar stone, shrouding it and the basket atop it, a pillar of darkness he could not see into. He shivered all over and his teeth chattered . . . but not just because of the cold. There was something about that pillar of darkness that sent all the hair on his head standing straight up, and evoked a primal and bone-deep fear.

"The offering is inadequate."

The voice did not seem to come from anywhere. Rather,

it seemed to echo within his own mind. Alexandre went rigid all over, his words freezing in his throat. Even his teeth stopped chattering. What was he supposed to do now? The Book hadn't said anything about "inadequate" offerings, only "acceptable" and "unacceptable" ones. "Acceptable" meant he . . . well, would have anything he wanted. "Unacceptable" would mean the door would slam and he'd have to wait until next year to try again. But . . . "inadequate"?

"The offering is inadequate," the voice repeated; emotionless, expressionless, as dead as Alexandre's father. *"But the offering is accepted."* He sighed in relief.

Too soon.

"You must do more. You must bring Us more."

"Now?" he bleated, frantic, unable to imagine where he was going to find a virgin *anything* on Christmas Eve, or — maybe Alf hadn't left yet, maybe they could go back to the Foundling Home and steal more babies. How many babies would equal a virgin girl? Four? Six? How soon could they do that?

And now his mind was running in frantic circles as question after question about how to do this impossible task made him dizzy. How would they steal six babies at once? How would they carry them all? They couldn't get a cab! How would they explain toting around six babies on Christmas Eve? Alf had used a basket . . . could they use baskets? Could they fit three babies each to a basket? What if they woke up? What if they cried?

"The offering has opened the door, but We are not strengthened. You will strengthen Us. Come in three days time, and We will instruct you. Now go."

The pillar of darkness collapsed into a pool of darkness on the floor. There was no sign of the altar stone, or the basket that had been on it. A wind out of that pool swept around the room, blowing out the candles — and, somehow, the lamps, all but the one behind Alexandre.

He shivered in every limb as he stared into the darkness, and felt the darkness staring back at him, reaching into his soul. He had to get out of here before whatever he had called changed its mind and decided it wanted him. He finally made his arm reach for the lantern without taking his eyes off the pool of blackness; his body seemed to move with glacial slowness.

Is that thing in the floor the door? Alexandre wondered, as he took the lantern and backed slowly away from what looked like a bottomless hole in the floor. He wanted to run away, screaming, and it was all he could do to move slowly, cautiously, trying not to attract that . . . thing's . . . attention any further. He inched his way up the steps, and only when the cellar door was shut and his back was to it did he finally breathe, wiping his sweating face with his handkerchief. His body flushed, went cold again, flushed and went cold. Nervous sweat plastered his hair to his skull.

Mustn't let Alf see me like this, he thought, dazedly after a moment, only now remembering Alf had promised to bring back girls. He made his way to his bedroom, still carrying the lantern, and poured himself a tumbler of whiskey from the decanter there, and when that seemed inadequate, another. Then he stripped off coat, vest, and shirt, put on a clean shirt, toweled his hair dry with the old shirt. He sat on the edge of the bed, and waited for the whiskey to soothe his nerves.

After a moment he realized he was still clutching his copy of The Book. He must have put it down to change . . . but he didn't remember picking it back up again. In fact . . . he didn't remember putting it down, either. He stared at it. So innocuous, just a plain copybook with cloth covers, the kind anyone could buy at a stationers.

It's not too late to end all this now, whispered a voice in his mind. *You know people who know Lord Alderscroft. You could go to them in the morning. You could tell them you were trying out something and it went wrong and you need their help. One look at what's in the cellar, and they'll go straight to Alderscroft and he'll summon his whole damn White Lodge to deal with it. The worst you'll get is a tongue-lashing for dabbling in things you don't understand. They won't think you sacrificed anything more than a cat or a dog. No one knows about the baby, and it's gone now, without a trace. Alf certainly won't tell them. If you never show them*

The Book, if you never mention the baby, no one will ever know what you were really up to. This can all be over in a day, perhaps two, long *before that thing in the darkness can . . . instruct you.*

But that would mean giving up everything The Book promised. . . .

These things never end well, the voice whispered. *These things always end in the sorcerer screaming, and blood spattered all over the ceiling, and neighbors saying afterward, "But he was so quiet and well-mannered . . ."*

He listened to that voice for a moment, then violently shook his head. That wasn't the voice of reason, that was the voice of cowardice, the same voice that had told him to be a good boy, go to church, obey his father like a little mindless slave. That voice had led him to undergo years of misery before he'd found his *first* magic book. He knew better. That voice wanted him to be weak, not strong. *These are tales told to keep the bold from triumphing,* he told the voice, and downed a third tumbler of whiskey. All those stories of "deals with the devil" never ending well had been written by people who had a vested interest in making sure things stayed exactly the way they were—that no "unauthorized" individuals dared to reach for power. People like his father! People who wanted to keep people like him under their thumb. It was always that way! People like Alderscroft and his precious Lodge would rather that everyone believed that if you took an unorthodox approach to magic, terrible things happened to you.

Courage rose in him once again. Look what he'd accomplished! Even the entity that he had summoned had recognized boldness and greatness in him! It had said the offering was "inadequate," and yet—It had still taken the offering. It must know he was ready for the kind of power It could offer him.

Nothing terrible had happened in the cellar. In fact, the outcome had almost been better than if he'd had the "proper" sacrifice; in three days he would know exactly what the entity wanted, rather than guessing. He took a long, deep breath. *In every single one of those "cautionary*

*tales," when an offering was not exactly what the entity de-
manded, it was the summoner who paid.* But all the entity *he*
had called had said was that he would have to strengthen it.
Things were good. In fact, tonight was a triumph.

He realized he was still holding The Book, and carefully
put it away in the locked drawer of his dresser. Not that he
actually needed to lock it up, but it made him feel better to
know it, and the original, were under lock and key.

That niggling little voice telling him to go be a good boy
and confess to the Elemental Masters now nicely squashed,
he left his bedroom and headed for the kitchen. That was
where Alf usually brought girls, and this time was no excep-
tion. Alf had gotten out a bottle of gin, there were three
glasses on the table, and the bottle was mostly empty.

There were three girls this time—so Alf was going to
perform another of his superhuman feats of sexual athletics.
*Maybe the first thing I'll ask for is to be able to perform in
bed like Alf,* he thought with amusement, as he surveyed his
man and the three strumpets. Alf, as usual, was nearly as
sober as a judge. The man had a head for liquor like nothing
Alexandre had ever seen before. The girls, however, were
tipsy and giggly.

One was a redhead, almost, but not quite, past her prime,
dressed in red satin with black lace, a gown that showed her
cleavage down to her nipples. That one would be for Alf.
One was an athletic looking blond, in a black-and-tan
striped dress with a slightly higher neckline. And she looked
familiar . . . in fact, now that he thought about it, he had the
notion that they were two of the can-can dancers from his
favorite music hall. That one would be for Alf too. The blond
sat on his knee, the redhead beside him, leaning on him.

The third was a waifish brunette, sitting by herself, in a
slightly childish looking gown that might have been red
once, but had faded to dusty pink, the kind of gown a girl
who wasn't "out" yet would wear. That one would be for
him. He liked his girls either young, or looking young, and
obedient.

"Where's yer friend, Alfie-walfie?" giggled the redhead.
"Wot's 'e doin' thet's so 'portant?"

"Alf's friend is right here, madam," said Alexandre, emerging from the shadows into the brightly lit kitchen. "As for what I was doing, it was just a bit of very necessary work, that is now thankfully concluded."

"Cor, a toff!" said the blond, fluttering her eyelashes at him.

"Nothing of the sort, madam," Alexandre replied, with a little bow. "Just a man who appreciates beautiful ladies."

That was probably the whiskey talking. But it made the blond and the redhead smile and giggle some more. And before they could express any preference for *him,* Alf swept them both up and hustled them off to his room. "Time t' get the party started, gels," he was saying as he vanished through the door. "There's more gin where we're goin'."

Alexandre offered the brunette his hand. Silently she took it, and let herself be led away.

Maisie found herself propelled out of the toff's front door by the toff's foot on her arse, and landed facedown in the snow. A moment later her dress came flying out of the same door, and landed on top of her. She hadn't even got so far as taking off her shoes when he'd—Oh! The filthy bastard! What he'd wanted!

She'd whirled and told him where he could stick his wants, and the next thing she discovered, he had picked her up, carried her to the door, and kicked her out. *Literally* kicked her out. Into the snow. Without getting paid.

The door slammed, and there was the decided *clack* of the lock being turned.

She scrambled to her feet, so furious she didn't even feel the cold. "Yer roight *barstard!*" she screamed, and unleashed a stream of profanity learned from a short lifetime of walking the streets. She continued to shriek curses as she pulled her dress on, wondering—hoping even—that a copper would come along and take notice of the row, or the neighbors would start looking out their windows. She might be helpless to do anything else against him, but embarrassing him in front of his neighbors would be partial revenge. She could just picture their avid, hypocritical faces. *Cor, luv-vie! Toff brought 'ome a trollop! On* Christmas, *if yew can believe!*

But nobody came along. And not a single light appeared at any of the windows.

Her fury redoubled. *All* the way from the East End, and for what? *Nothing!* It had been a wretched night—she should have known better than to go out on Christmas Bloody Eve—and she'd thought her luck had turned when Alf pulled up in a hansom with two girls she knew vaguely from around the pubs. They'd had a jolly old ride out to . . . wherever this was. She was sorry now she hadn't paid attention, but Alf had had a bottle of gin with him and a girl needed to keep warm, right? Then there'd been the pleasant surprise of the cozy, posh flat, and the second waiting bottle, and when that toff had shown up at the door, she'd thought, *cor, this'll be an easy night!*

The ones that wanted girls that looked like her, usually they wanted her to at least play at being an innocent . . . maybe they'd like a little struggle, a bit of make-believe rape. Faint calls for help, and lots of "oh, no, sir, no, I bain't loike that." She'd feigned reluctance as he ordered her to undress, watching her avidly, hungrily. But then he'd grabbed her bum and whispered in her ear what he wanted and how she was supposed to—

"Yer roight pervert! At least gimme back me coat!"

The door opened long enough for her coat to smack her in the face. It slammed again. She screamed some more.

Nothing. No coppers. No neighbors. Not even the lights from the flat upstairs came on.

There was *no* sign of outrage or even disturbance from the buildings around. And now she realized that the faint cooking smells still lingering around here were fish and cabbage . . .

So the neighborhood wasn't nearly as posh as the flat had been, and probably people were used to the bloody bastard kicking his whores out in the middle of the night when they wouldn't—

Another stream of invective poured out of her mouth in an incoherent scream and she gathered herself and prepared to charge up the stairs to the door, planning to beat on it until he *had* to pay attention and he'd at least pay her off to go away.

Now engulfed in a white-hot rage, she charged through the snow to the dark rectangle that was at the top of the stairs, intending to hit it full force, maybe with luck break it in, and if not, pound on it with every bit of her strength.

She barely had a chance to gasp in shock as her arms disappeared into a black void . . . and her body followed.

And then there was silence.

Alexandre rose late Christmas morning, mollified by the fact that Alf had sent the much-more-compliant blond to him when his first choice had turned into a harridan at the mere mention of what he wanted from her. *Harpy. She's a whore, she'd better get used to doing what the customer wants, or she'll find herself starving,* he thought, still more than a bit irritated at her attitude. She'd screamed all the way out of the house and probably had stood there half-naked in the snow screaming for a good long while before she gave up and went away. She'd probably still be there screaming if it had been spring or summer. Well, he figured the snow would cool her temper pretty damn quickly.

Serve her right if her feet freeze and fall off, he thought vindictively. Fortunately the bedrooms were at the back of the flat, and once the blond had turned up, he wasn't listening to anything anyway. The other two were sane, sane enough he'd let them stay the rest of the night. Girls who pleased him got that special treatment. Alf knew to feed them as well as pay them in the morning, and come dawn, they could make their way back to wherever he'd found them.

Though he did his best never to be a repeat customer. That was on Alf's advice. "Ye treats 'em noice once, they're obligin' an' don' make no fuss. But come to 'em agin, they 'spect better the second time. An' th' third! Loik queens, they think they be! Nivir be a whore's reg'lar, guv, unless yer got a arrangement w' a brothel." And Alf was probably right. When it came to strumpets, he generally was.

He had awakened alone, which meant the girl was already gone, or—*hmm*. He listened, and thought he heard laughter.

He pulled on a shirt, pants, and a dressing gown, and ambled into the kitchen. There was Alf, presiding over the stove and dishing out bacon and eggs, while the two girls put together a tray, giggling.

"Well," he drawled, leaning on the doorframe. "This is a nice domestic little scene."

Alf turned and winked. "Iss Chrissmuss, an' ye give the char the day orf. So she wuzn't gonna be 'ere t' be outraged. Figgered we'd give ye breakfuss in bed, an' we'd be orf oursel's."

"I'll take the tray myself," he said, and did so. The blond gave him a saucy wink as she passed it to him, then sat down to her own breakfast. Alf followed him out for a moment.

"Lissen, guv, Oi'm roight sorry about thet liddle bitch—" He shook his head. "Iff'n Oi'd'a knowd—"

"She's gone, right?" he asked.

"Not 'ide nor 'air," Alf confirmed, frowning fiercely. "Dunno where she went, and don' care. 'Ope she turned inter a icicle or fell in th' bloody Thames, Oi do."

Anger flared in him, but he let it die down. "That makes two of us. But you made it up to me, so all's even." In fact, now that he was fully awake, the pleasant smell of well-cooked eggs and beans and bacon were wafting up to his nose, and knowing he had triumphed in his magic last night—all things considered, last night's little dust-up was a mere trifle. The blond had been . . . very satisfactory. Even imaginative. "It's all right. And . . . my business last night went well enough. When the house is empty again, I'll show you."

"Roight." Alf hesitated. "Ye moind if I keeps 'em around a liddle longer?"

Dear god. If such a thing is possible, I really am going to ask for his sexual stamina, I swear. "Suit yourself, Alf," he replied. "As long as they don't get too comfortable. *You* are the one who told me about not letting whores stay too long."

"Roight ye are, guv." Alf gave him a two-fingered salute, and headed back to the kitchen. Peals of giggles greeted his arrival.

With an amused snort, Alexandre took his tray to the sitting room. This might be a good chance to peruse The Book, and determine exactly what first to ask of the entity in exchange for his services in . . . strengthening it.

7

KENSINGTON Garden on Christmas Day, late morning was, as predicted, deserted. Those who had assembled to see the Swimming Club swim the hundred-yard "Peter Pan Cup" race in the freezing water of the Serpentine were long gone, and winner and losers alike were probably on their third or fourth "medicinal" brandy. The Park was dotted with snowmen and snow forts, all deserted. An overcast day promised more snow later. Suki romped on the path ahead of them, bags of breadcrumbs stuffed in both pockets to feed the birds, eyes bright as she looked everywhere for Robin.

They had both decided to bring Suki along. After the excitement of opening presents was over, and breakfast was eaten, when the time came for the (hoped-for) rendezvous with Robin Goodfellow, Nan and Sarah just couldn't leave Suki behind. She adored Robin, and he for his part seemed to have a soft spot for children. And they didn't like to ask Mrs. Horace to either take Suki with her to church, or stay behind and watch her. So when Mrs. Horace went off to her midday church service, the three of them walked until they could summon a cab and drove the rest of the way here.

"Where do you think he might choose to meet us?" Sarah asked, shading her eyes to peer ahead.

Nan was going to answer with her best guess—when a sprightly voice spoke up from practically in her ear.

"Look behind you!"

Her heart jumped into her throat and she and Sarah both whirled to find Robin standing behind her, grinning.

Today he looked just like any sort of ordinary adolescent boy you might find in the Garden on a late Christmas morning; cap pulled down on his head, muffler tied around it and wrapped around his neck, mittens, stout coat, corduroy trousers and waterproof Wellington boots. But Sarah and Nan would have known him anywhere, for surely there was not a single living soul on this earth that had those brilliant, emerald-green eyes.

Suki must have heard him too, for they heard her scream, *"Robin!"* in delight, and a moment later, she hit Robin like a little cannonball. He caught her effortlessly, and just as effortlessly swung her around several times before putting her down.

"Did you bring crumbs for the birds and sweeties for my friends?" he asked her, for the moment paying no attention to the adults. When she nodded vigorously, he turned her around and pointed over her shoulder at a congregation of wild birds (strangely, none of them pigeons, which was unheard of in this park), some rabbits and squirrels, and two creatures of the sort that had appeared in Beatrice Leek's house. "Go play!" he ordered, and with a squeal, Suki pelted toward them.

"Are those brownies?" Nan asked, incredulously.

"Hobs," Robin corrected. "brownies won't leave housen if they can help it, except t'move. Mistress Leek's brownie brought the note to her hob, and her hob brought 'em both to me. She don't know she got a hob; he minds her garden and her dovecote." He eyed them both gravely. "You were right to be troubled. Something dark's on the move. Dunno what it is, neither, but I can *feel* it, pushing to come through."

"What do you mean, 'pushing to come through?' Pushing on what?" Nan asked, bewildered.

"There's worlds and worlds, lying right up against this one," he replied. "One of 'em's where the Fey creatures go, when your Cold Iron and crowding get too much for 'em. But there's others, worlds that I don't know, and I don't want to know. What's trying to get here is from one of those worlds. I'm the Oldest Old Thing in England . . . but there's Older Old Things in those other worlds, and most of them are none too nice."

His eyes were grave as he said that, and Nan swallowed. Robin had a habit of understatement, and when he said "most of them are none too nice," she knew these things were probably terrible indeed. "Can you help us?" she asked.

"Gonna try," he replied. "But this isn't a ghostie, that Sarah and I can send onward, or I can wish the Wild Hunt on, at least not while it's on its own ground. And 'tisn't a thing of the Fey, that I can command. Like I said, I can *feel* it pushing, but I can't tell where it is, or even if it's in a where at all. It's kind of a general feeling, y'see—like I feel it seeking for thin spots, sometimes finding them, but not that it's come all the way through." He shook his head. " 'Tis mortal hard to describe, and that's probably because it is what it is, and I am what I am. I'm rooted deep in this world, and this thing's . . . not." His chin firmed with determination. "But I'm the Oldest Old Thing in all England, and this is *my* place to defend, and defend it I will!"

His tone was brave, and there was no doubt he meant what he said—but would he have the power to make them a reality? If *he* was afraid of this thing. . . .

. . . then maybe it *did* have the ability to lay waste to all of London.

"So, we're still where we were before we asked to speak with you," Nan replied, wishing she felt more relieved. "Though at least *you* have been warned, and through you, all creatures of the four Elements. I just wish we knew more."

"Don't despair! It hasn't come through yet, and it may never. Unless it has help on this side, the barriers between the worlds are mortal hard to breach. Them as has the Second Sight will be of aid, I reckon," Robin said confidently.

"Their Sight is tied to things being as they should be. It's when things go awry that the visions come."

Well, that certainly sounded like what was happening to young Amelia. Nan glanced over at Suki, who was practically covered in birds and being aided by the hobs. "I suppose we're done here for now . . . how can I quickly contact you if we find out something, Robin?"

Robin smiled slightly again. "Well, that's why I brought yon hobs. They don't mind housen, they don't mind Cold Iron, and they like the company of Big Folks. If you need me, you tell one of them, and I can be with you quick as you can say *knife*. I reckoned one could live in your dwelling, and one can go to Memsa'b's School with Suki. They'll make themselves handy, too, it's what they like to do, to pay for their keep. Tidying up, things of that nature. Tending gardens and crops. Fixing things."

Nan blinked at him, and Sarah looked amused. "And how do you think Grey and Neville will feel about this?"

"Same way the other birds yonder feel about it," Robin said promptly. "Birds like hobs. Hobs like birds."

"I think it would be lovely if the hob could keep the toys at the school in good repair," Sarah told him. "The children are mostly very good about trying not to break things . . . but they *are* children."

"That'll suit a hob down to the bone." Robin cast another look in Suki's direction. Nan followed his gaze. It appeared that the breadcrumbs had been exhausted, for the birds had all taken to the trees, where they sat preening themselves in contentment. Robin waved a hand as one of the hobs happened to look at him, and a moment later, both hobs and Suki were trudging happily through the snow toward them, like something out of a Snow White panto.

"So," Robin began, when all three stood before them. "I'm sure the lads have already introduced themselves to *you*, Suki, but Grown Folk need proper introductions." He cleared his throat, and waved at the two hobs. "Mistresses Nan and Sarah, I make known to you Durwin and Roan."

Each hob made a little half bow when his name was spoken. Both came about as tall as Nan's waist and were wearing stout boots, heavy, gray canvas trousers, heavy oatmeal-colored woolen tunics, and the sort of soft felt hats that farmers wore in winter. Both were bearded. Durwin had a shorter beard than Roan, and Roan's hair and beard were a dark red, as opposed to Durwin's straw-color, but otherwise they were so very much alike Nan was afraid she'd never have been able to tell them apart if it hadn't been for hair color. Both had heavy, bushy eyebrows, and at the moment, both had slightly anxious expressions, as if they were hoping to please.

"I'm very pleased to make your acquaintance, Master Durwin, Master Roan," Nan said as gravely as she could. *It's just a good thing there's no one in the Gardens right now, or we'd look like right lunatics, standing about and talking to the air. I'm pretty sure no one can see Robin or the hobs but us.*

"As am I," said Sarah. Both little men blushed shyly. "Our friend Robin has suggested you might be willing to come live, one with us, and one at the school where Suki will be in a few days."

"Oh aye, Mistress!" said Roan quickly. "Us hobs like you Big Folk, allus have! All we need is a corner to oursel'n to tuck into out of sight."

"And a bit of somethin' now and again . . ." said Durwin wistfully. "We can feed ours'l's, 'deed we can, but Big Folk food be . . ." Roan elbowed him hard, and he fell silent, blushing harder, this time with embarrassment.

"If you're *sure,*" Nan said. "We'd love to have one of you, and . . . someone . . . can introduce you to Memsa'b who runs the School, and she'll see to it that whichever of you goes with Suki is settled happily." She glanced at Sarah. "How . . . exactly would that work?"

Robin chuckled. "You leave that to me, Daughter of Eve. I'll have a word with Memsa'b myself, tell her what's what, and get Roan settled."

And I'll send a note to make sure Memsa'b knows to have someone in the kitchen leave out food for him. "I hope you like Indian food, Roan," she cautioned. "That's almost all that's served at the School."

"We hobs aren't par-tic-u-lar," Roan replied, but from the way his face lit up for a moment, she rather fancied he

did. *And* where *would he have tasted Indian food, I wonder?*
Another mystery. Did hobs serve English folk exclusively,
or were they inclined to move into any household where
they were welcome? Was there an Indian version of a hob?

"Meanwhile, would you both like to stay with us until
Suki goes back?" Sarah asked—impulsively, Nan thought,
although she didn't dislike the idea. These two little men did
not seem disposed to mischief.

Now the faces of both little men lit up like the sun. "Oh,
yes, Mistress, please!" Roan spoke for both of them. "That
would be excellent for us. Thank you!" And then, they vanished. Between one blink of the eye and another, they simply disappeared. Now, Nan was quite used to seeing
Elementals fading from view, or whisking out of sight, but
just vanishing into thin air was not something she would
have expected.

Nan blinked in astonishment. "Do they do that a great
deal?" she asked. "Just pop out of existence, I mean."

"It's a hob's way." Robin shrugged. "They like to get out
of sight as quickly as they can. They're shy. They don't much
care for being seen at all, and then only when it's only likely
to be by one or two Big People. And it's not as if they
needed to come home with you in a hansom; they know
how to find where you live. In fact, they're probably already
there."

Nan and Sarah exchanged a wry look. So . . . now strange
little Elementals could appear in their flat whenever they
chose! Nan turned back to Robin. "I have to say," she said,
"It is distinctly *unfair* how your kind can just flit wherever
you choose."

Robin shook his head mockingly. "And when, Daughter
of Eve," he replied, "Has life ever been *fair?*"

Sure enough, when Nan unlocked the door to the flat, she
could hear deep chuckles, the lighter laughter of Grey imi-
tating Sarah, and the distinct chortles of the raven. So,
Robin had been right. The hobs had managed to get to the

flat long before the girls could, and must have spent the time since making the acquaintance of the birds. Suki squeezed into the flat before Nan could fully get the door open and made a beeline for the bird's room.

Once there, she broke into peals of laughter. Curious now to discover just what was so funny, Nan tossed her cloak and hat aside on the nearest chair, and hurried into the room herself.

There she found Roan and Durwin, each with a bird balanced somewhat precariously on the top of his head, performing a sort of pavane to music that was coming out of thin air. Suki bounced on her toes with delight. The birds were clearly enjoying themselves. And Nan's worst fear—that the birds would somehow resent or even dislike the hobs—was assuaged. In fact, from the look of things, the birds found the two hobs to be the most entertaining things to come into their lives in a long time.

When the music stopped, the birds flapped into the air and went to their perches, and the hobs looked with alarm at Nan, as if they were afraid they had somehow offended her. It even looked as if they were going to vanish.

"Don't go just yet," Nan told them, as they were poised to flee. "You said you needed a little space to make your own. Let's find that corner for you. How much room do you need?"

The hobs relaxed slightly. "Just enough to curl up in, Mistress," said Roan. "Out of the way where we won't be a bother to you by day."

"With a book?" Durwin added hopefully. Roan elbowed him hard again. Nan did her best not to laugh. This was certainly a distraction from worrying about Amelia's visions.

"Then I have just the thing, and Roan, for now, and later if you come visit Durwin, there is room enough to share." Sarah flung open the doors to the huge old linen cabinet in which the bird's toys, their traveling carriers, and their extra dishes were kept. "Look," she said, pointing to the bottom, where there were two shelves, completely empty, that probably had been meant to store very bulky things like pillows, blankets or heavy coverlets. There was about as much space for the hobs as there would have been for a sailor in his bunk. "There's plenty of space for both of you down there, we never use it, and I'm sure we have pillows and shawls to make it comfortable for you."

"There's no need Mistress—" Roan began, but Nan had already gone in search of pillows that had gone flat that would serve the hobs for mattresses, and something for blankets. She returned with a "mattress" for each of them, a couple of cushions Suki had made when learning to sew that would serve them very well as pillows, and a number of shawls that she and Sarah had been given as presents that . . . well . . . the giver meant well, but the colors were so garish that they'd been relegated to the back of the wardrobe. She thought that spare pillowcases would probably serve well enough as sheets, and had brought two of them as well.

"Here you are, gentlemen," she said cheerfully, dropping her burden at their feet. "And do feel free to help yourselves from the bookshelves. All that I ask is that you not borrow a book one of us is already reading."

The two little men were clearly torn; they were delighted at this hospitality, but also embarrassed by it. "Really, Mistress . . ." Roan said, and trailed off. "You're very generous. We hobs do with little. It's not our way to be so . . ." he appeared to be searching for a word. ". . . luxurious."

"Really, Master Roan, we're going to be working Durwin rather unmercifully," Sarah replied, a look in her eye telling Nan that evidently *she* understood this situation better than Nan did. "This isn't a gift, nor is it charity. We hope we can rely on him to stand guard at night when we are asleep, and whenever we are gone, so that the birds are safe and nothing catches on fire. It's been a constant concern for us when we've needed to leave them alone. So many things can go horribly wrong. He'll be taking a terrible burden of worry off of us."

Roan's face cleared, and so did Durwin's. "Well, then . . ."

Durwin whispered in Roan's ear. It was a very loud whisper and Nan could hear it. *"I can clean up after the winged ones too."*

"And the one thing that no one can keep up with at the school is the repair of the toys!" she continued. "They're *good* children, but they are children, and they play very hard. Why, there are two whole rocking horses that are in the school workshop to be extensively repaired now, and I really don't know when anyone is going to be able to get to them!"

Now Roan's face lit up. "Toys, indeed." He rubbed his hands together. "Now, the making and fixing of toys is something I am a bit of an expert in. Happens, I once lived in a toymaker's shop . . ."

"And of course, we'll need your presence around the clock to take messages to Robin," Sarah concluded, and sighed theatrically. "And now I am afraid that is so much work you are going to regret saying you'll live with us. I cannot conceive of any hob ever doing as much work as we will need doing."

Roan marched up to Sarah, reached up, and patted her hand. "There, there, now Mistress. Don't you worry your pretty head about that. Hobs are tough! Hobs are resourceful! Do much with little, that's what I always say!"

Durwin bobbed his head. "That he does, Mistress," the sandy-bearded hob concurred. "Do much with little! He says it a lot." Durwin glanced sideways at his compatriot. "Says it a *whole* lot."

Roan elbowed him again.

Sarah sighed with exaggerated relief. "All right then, if you're sure. We'll leave you to get comfortable. Suki, it's time for your lesson."

Suki opened her mouth to object, because, after all, it was Christmas Day, and there *weren't* any lessons, but then she exchanged a look with Nan. *We should let them settle to suit themselves, Suki,* Nan thought at her. *They're shy, and very much not used to being around Big Folk who can see them.*

Suki's eyes widened, and she nodded. With the birds to supervise, they left the hobs to work out who was to get which shelf. "I call the top!" "Rubbish! I'm eldest, I get the top." "Rubbish yourself! I'm smaller, I get the top!" "Then I'll be having this red blanket." "Oh, you will, will you?"

Nan had to stuff her hand in her mouth to keep from laughing. It was like listening to a couple of siblings argue over a room. *It's a good thing it's a cupboard. They can't draw a line down the center of the room and forbid each other to set foot across it.*

They retreated into the sitting room. "If they're not brothers, they're the next thing to it," Sarah giggled. "Well, how are we to feed them? I assume they'd be horrified if we asked them to sit at table with us."

"I think there's something in one of the books Mary Watson lent me," Nan replied, and went to the shelf on which she was keeping the borrowed books on Elemental Creatures separate from the rest, to avoid mixing them up. She found the book on Earth Elementals she wanted—like most such books, it was a handwritten tome, with empty pages at the back for the next Master to own it to use for his or her own observations. Unfortunately, it was not indexed or alphabetized in any way, which made looking for anything specific a bit of a chore. While she looked, Sarah laid out food—not much, just some bread and butter and cheese, as Mrs. Horace was making everyone a lovely Christmas dinner when she returned from church, and indeed, the aroma of chestnut-stuffed goose had begun to fill the building. Nan absently nibbled as she searched the book, while Suki, who never turned down food, sat with a piece of cheese in one hand and a thick slice of bread-and-butter in the other.

"Ah, here we are. We should simply leave it by the hearth when we go to bed. They like anything dairy, anything baked, and anything sweet."

"That sounds like the kind of diet that would give Memsa'b the horrors," Sarah chuckled. "There are always leftovers from our dinners. We can make up a plate and leave it covered at the hearth."

"It appears," Nan continued, still reading, "That Durwin and Roan are bending the hob rules considerably for Robin. They're supposed to work secretly, and humans are never to offer anything as 'payment.' In fact, if they are given anything as 'payment,' especially clothing, they are supposed to leave. We rather implied that, and they deliberately did not take offense."

"Any more rules we should know about?" Sarah asked, as the quarreling in the bird room ceased.

"Well, we should never make it appear we take them or their work for granted, and get lazy." Nan looked up from the book directly at Suki. "Which means, my love, putting away your clothing and toys is still *your* responsibility. Roan is your friend, not your personal servant. If he *happens* to help you out on a day when you are terribly busy, then just be quietly thankful."

Suki heaved an exaggerated sigh of regret, and stuffed the last of her bread-and-butter into her mouth.

"We should try not to take any notice of Durwin . . . although to be fair, I think it's in his nature to be not as secretive as Roan. Perhaps he's not so much a traditionalist. At any rate, it seems that the proper etiquette is to announce whatever is pertinent to the emp   , or your companion. Such as, if we were going out, something like, 'Well, since we are going out, I hope the birds and the flat stay safe.' That lets the hob know something particular needs doing." Nan looked at Suki again. "I think the rules can be bent for children. So I think if we go out and leave you, you can play with them."

Suki's face was wreathed in smiles at that.

"What about at the school?" she asked.

"Memsa'b will probably have Roan stay in the workshop, so you probably won't see him. And it's not as if you don't have plenty of friends to play with at the school. You can't expect magical creatures to be popping in all the time just to play with you." Nan put a tiny touch of chiding into her tone, as a reminder that Roan was to be there mostly so that Memsa'b could call on Robin directly.

Suki sighed again. "Well, orl right," she agreed.

"It also says here that *Robin* is a kind of hob," Nan concluded, shutting the book. "I think someone was very much mistaken if they think that."

"Well, technically he is one of the Great Elementals, so I suppose, if you stretched a point . . ." Sarah said, but doubtfully.

"That's stretching it until it snaps back on you and leaves a welt on your chin," Nan chuckled. "And I think I hear Mrs. Horace now! Let's go down; the more we can help, the sooner we can feast!"

They returned to their flat laden with a tray and two baskets of good things, having told Mrs. Horace that they would attend to their *own* tea and supper from the leftovers. And still they had left Mrs. Horace with things to store in the pantry and the cold pantry, and wondering aloud why she had cooked so much and where she was going to put it all. It was a very good thing that Christmas was at the end of December, and that this was a cold Christmas at that. In the cold pantry, you could see your breath, and nothing was going to spoil.

They stowed their own goodies in their own, much smaller pantry, and went to bring the birds their share of the feast and look in on the hobs. The birds were overjoyed to see the food—Grey went immediately to work on one of the goose's thighbones, cracking it open and eating the marrow with almost ghoulish relish.

"You know that's cannibalism, right?" Sarah said, teasingly.

Grey looked at her. "That's a bird. I'm a bird. I want some," Grey retorted, and went back to her bone as Neville chortled. Then he set to on his chopped giblets.

Nan eased the door of the cupboard open, just a little. There were two shawl-covered lumps on the shelves, backs to the door, looking entirely comfortable, and easing Nan's fears that the arrangement would be less than desirable, at least by hob standards.

She closed the door again. "They're sleeping like a couple of stones," she said. "The book implies we should just go about our business as normal, and they'll be fine."

The birds flew to their shoulders, and they moved back into the sitting room. Suki decided she would go and play with her Christmas toys, leaving them alone.

"Then that's what we'll do." Sarah frowned a little. "And the one thing that we have *not* done is to try and figure out if there is any way our two particular talents would be of use in this uncertain case."

She took her favorite chair on the hearth, and Grey went to the back of it. Neville elected to hop to the back of Nan's chair before she could sit.

"Mine, probably not, unless this Old Thing decides to try and manifest somewhere near me," Nan admitted. "And even then, it probably won't be my telepathy that warns us, but having the Celtic Warrior manifest. I have the notion that this Old Thing may be related in some way to the creature in Berkeley Square that we finally trapped. The Warrior reacted strongly to that, and I think she would react even more strongly to this. But *you*—spirits might be able to tell you something, if you can find one that isn't tied down to a place."

"Oh it might be easier than that," Sarah replied after a moment. "Something like this is going to upset the spirits. All I have to do, really, is ask them if there are rumors of something matching that description. Tonight would be a good night for that."

"And meanwhile. . . ." Nan looked at the bookshelf she had taken the Earth Elemental book from. "This might be a good time for some more research."

Suki emerged for tea and supper, but otherwise she had found *something* very engrossing in her room. Nan didn't enquire as to what it was. Suki would tell them later, probably. At this point, she was a very self-sufficient little person; she washed up by herself, and appeared in her nightdress to hug and kiss them goodnight, but no longer required tucking in, nor wanted to be *told* a bedtime story, as she preferred to read one on her own. Nan did check on her when silence had reigned over the flat for about an hour, and she was sound asleep, book on the bedside table, all lamps extinguished.

She came back out to find Sarah already disposed on the sofa, Robin's talisman in one hand, Grey at her shoulder. "Should we warn the hobs?" she wondered aloud. "They should probably know that I am about to try to call in a ghost."

"A ghost is it, then?" said Durwin, softly, peeking through the door to the bird room. "Lummy! I've never seen no Big Folk spirits! OW!"

Oh dear. I think Roan must have stamped on his foot this time. Nan and Sarah both politely ignored the questioner, though not the question. "Time to extinguish all the lights," Sarah said. "Just leave the one burning on the table."

Nan went around turning off the gaslights and blowing out the candles on the mantelpiece. Sarah made herself very comfortable on the couch in front of the fire, while Nan took her usual chair.

Under most circumstances, Sarah maintained something rather like Nan's mental shield. Nan's shield was meant to protect her from intrusive thoughts—and from having her own thoughts read by another telepath. Sarah's shield, however, was meant to keep the fact that she could communicate with spirits hidden. If she didn't do that, it was entirely possible that she'd never get a wink of sleep some nights.

They had long since cleared the immediate vicinity of Mrs. Horace's house of any restless ghosts, but, well, people were always dying, and if there *were* any new spirits about, Sarah would be like a lighthouse beacon to them.

Nan knew that there were generally reasons why spirits lingered and did not pass on to whatever came next for them. The very wicked were *afraid,* as well they should be, and would resist being sent on their way to the last of their strength. Those would avoid Sarah like the poison she was to them, for she could force them on. Some who were not necessarily wicked, but also afraid, might very well come to her, because they would have come to understand how dreadful and empty the "life" of a spirit still bound to earth was. Some simply did not know they were dead, and they would also come to her as the only person they could communicate with in what was to them a nightmare existence. And some had unfinished business; they would *flock* to her, in order to find someone living who could help them finish it.

Nan was hoping for one of the last of these. They tended to have the most motivation to help in exchange for being helped.

The hardest part of this is the waiting, Nan thought. This wasn't the sort of thing where you could just sit down with a nice book until a ghost showed up. They didn't like light; it "interfered" with them, Sarah said.

Nan was prepared for a long, boring night, at least until Sarah got tired of waiting and went to bed.

She was not prepared for an immediate answer.

Or one *she* could see.

She heard Sarah's swift intake of breath. She saw—well it could have been a cloud of steam, or a wisp of fog, but it condensed somehow, and grew brighter, and then, well, it was something like one of those "fake ghosts" made with a magic lantern, a kind of sketch of white-on-black hanging in midair.

Except this one was moving slightly, and it was someone she knew.

Not well, but it *was* an elderly lady a few houses down the street, who had been fading this last six months. Mrs. Horace had sent them with soup several times; the old lady was being well tended by one of over a dozen granddaughters.

"Well, if it isn't little Sarah!" the voice was as much in Nan's mind as it was in her ears. *"I had no idea you were mediumistic, my dear!"* She chuckled. *"Still waters do run deep! I heard your call as I was on my way, so I thought,* Maudie, they were so kind about visiting you, well you should return the favor. *What can I do for you?"*

Sarah explained as best she could, keeping her explanation to Amelia's visions and not going into what Puck had said.

Maud listened intently. *"I don't know of anything myself, but I'll ask that word be spread. I hope that will help you?"*

"It will, Mrs. Maud," Sarah said gratefully. "And thank you for taking the time to talk to me."

The spirit smiled. *"My guide is getting a tiny bit impatient, so I'll be on my way. I hope this is all just something that will blow over, my dear."* Her smile faltered. *"But . . . I fear it is not."*

ALEXANDRE had not done more than peek into the basement from the door during the three days between Christmas Eve and when the entity had told him to return. Each time he did, he saw that nothing had changed. The bottomless pool of shadow was still in the middle of the floor. It had not gotten larger, or smaller—but it was still there, so what had happened to him that night was no dream, and no hallucination.

On the other hand, there was no imperious voice ordering him about, so the entity was living up to its word and leaving him alone for now.

That was a very good thing, and he didn't feel very much like tempting fate by venturing any nearer to it.

He spent most of the time during those three days reading and rereading the book, trying to anticipate what might come next. He didn't even leave the flat; he sent Alf out for more brandy, and ate whatever Alf cooked or brought him from the pub or the fried fish shop. This scenario of the offering being "inadequate" but also "accepted" just wasn't in The Book at all. There was no roadmap for him here. So he spent half the time terrified, and half trying to calculate what the entity might want and what he might, possibly, be able to extract from it.

But now . . . now the moment had come. The three days had passed. He was going to have to face whatever lived in that shadow and find out what it wanted from him. Because he had the feeling . . . if he didn't give it what it wanted, it had no intention of going away, and it might find *him* to be an "adequate" offering.

Leaving Alf upstairs, he waited until after darkness fell and made his way down the solid wooden staircase, carrying a lantern. There was no other light source but the one he carried in his hand. And it was utterly, utterly silent; in fact, the silence made his ears ring. When he had rented this place, he had hired a carpenter to make sure the steps didn't creak; now he wished he hadn't. At least that would have been *some* sound. He hesitated when he reached the bottom step, then, after a long pause, put one foot on the flagstone floor.

Nothing happened.

Feeling a little less terrified, he made his way to the place he had stood when he had invoked this . . . thing . . . in the first place.

There was still no sign of life from the pool of darkness on the floor.

He hung the lantern on the hook in the beams of the floor above him, and waited.

That was when he realized that it was very, very cold here in the basement. Colder by far than it should have been; unnaturally cold, he would have said. He could see his breath puffing out in clouds, and the silence . . . was unnatural too! It wasn't just that the basement was silent, he couldn't hear anything in the house above him. Surely he should have been able to hear *something*, but . . . there was only silence and the cold, and that unnerving pool of inky black in the middle of the flagstone floor. It seemed to drink in the light. It had no texture, it reflected nothing, and he could not see into it. It might have been just lying on the surface of the stones. Or it might go all the way to the center of the earth.

Or it might go somewhere else, not *of* this earth.

His chest was tight; the hair on the back of his neck was surely standing straight up. He wanted desperately to run away, and at the same time felt paralyzed, too frightened to move.

He spent a very long, terrified time trying to get the courage to speak, to break that silence. All of the bold plans he had made had flown right out of his head. And all he could really think of was how badly he wanted to bolt right back up those stairs. That, and the growing certainty that if he *tried* to do any such thing, that black pool would rise and engulf him as the altar stone and the basket had been engulfed. He wavered between wanting to flee and not daring to until he vibrated like a harp string.

Then there was no chance to do anything.

Suddenly, between one second and the next, there was not a pool of blackness on the floor. It was a *pillar* of blackness, looming over him.

He bit back a yelp of terror, as his flesh shrunk away from that inky blackness. *You are here,* he heard in his mind as well as his ears.

"Yes," he squeaked.

You will bring me adequate offerings, the entity said. *I will show you what I want.*

He felt something, then. Something . . . intruding into his thoughts. Pushing what he was thinking to one side and inserting what it wanted him to see. And into his mind came images of people, a vast crowd of people. There was nothing really alike about them, other than that they fit into a certain age group. No younger than, say, ten or eleven. No older than mid-twenties. The faces were blurry, so it was clear that looks did not matter to this thing. Short, tall, male, female, handsome, hideous, fat, or thin, none of that mattered to the entity. *You will bring me two,* it ordered. *They must be healthy. Unpolluted is preferable.*

"Unpolluted? You mean virgin?" he managed to gasp.

He actually felt the thing rummaging in his head to understand what he had asked. Felt more of his thoughts pushed aside, rearranged, picked up and examined, with no regard for how private they were. He felt it going through his memories; felt it stop and examine one where the girl Alf had brought him actually *had* been a virgin. Felt it consider that.

It was . . . singularly horrid. Like putting one's hand in one's underwear drawer and feeling it full of slugs climbing all over and through one's most intimate things. He gagged a little.

Yes. Virgin. Two. One to strengthen me. The second to serve me in your world. The second, you will put back where it can be cared for.

Dear god, what in *hell* did that mean? All he could figure was that he'd have to risk snatching someone that had family that would be looking for her, and would care for her when this thing let go of her. That would mean taking someone out of a better neighborhood, one where people who went missing were hunted for. Which meant, conversely, that it was a neighborhood where people would *notice* if you took someone, and if they were too timid to try and stop you themselves, they'd call the police.

And *how* was he going to manage that without getting caught himself? And when the second victim was let go again, what was to stop her from identifying him or Alf or both? Nothing, that was what!

He felt that horrid rummaging in his head again. *Do not concern yourself. When I am done with the servant, she will say nothing.*

Which didn't address how he was supposed to snatch such a person in the first place!

As it happened, that very frustration was what managed to push some of his fear into the background. He was able to think again. He was still terrified, but he—and his brain—weren't paralyzed.

Finally he managed to dredge up just enough courage to ask . . . not for anything specific, but surely he wasn't expected to do this for nothing!

"What's to be my reward?" he managed.

He sensed a dreadful amusement. That amusement was more than enough to push him over the edge again, and if his legs hadn't been shaking so hard he would have fled. *You have opposition to disposing of your goods as you will. You no longer have that opposition.*

He could not for the life of him imagine what that was supposed to mean, but at this point he was so close to soiling himself with terror that all he wanted was to conclude this interview and get out of there. "When do you want these two?" he stammered.

Between now and seven days from now. No later than that . . . or we will be displeased.

And the pillar collapsed down into a pool—and he snatched up the lantern and ran for the stairs. He didn't actually know what he did next—when his mind was working again, he found himself huddled up in front of the fire, swathed in blankets, half-frozen with fear and physical cold. It felt as if he was never going to get warm again, and it took him an hour, sitting on the mat in front of the hearth, before he could feel his hands and feet.

Alf left him alone until he was ready to talk, just bringing him a couple of brandies while he shivered with cold that seemed a part of his very skeleton. After about an hour had passed, and he was finally beginning to feel less than terrified, Alf sat down across from him and handed him a third brandy. "So, guv. Wot's it want, then?"

"Two sacrifices. Male or female, doesn't seem to matter, between about ten and twenty-ish. Doesn't have to be virgins, but the thing prefers them. But one is supposed to be special; the thing wants us to snatch someone that has family that will look after her, and we're supposed to return her to them, or at least put her where they'll find her. We've got a week."

Alf made some discontented noises. "Guv, I don' loik this, but I reckon we hain't got no choice. Oi'll hev t' get some help."

"Help?" Alexandre repeated with alarm. "That's not a good idea!"

"No, it hain't," Alf agreed, sitting on his heels beside him on the hearthrug. "It's a reel bad idear. But if we're snatchin' people loik that, we gotta 'ave a cart or somethin' t'put 'em

in. Hain't a good idear t'be draggin' 'em about the street. *Oi*
hain't got a cart, an' Oi dunno how t'drive. *You* hain't got a
cart . . . ye know how t'drive?"

"I do, actually," he said, Alf's words setting his mind slug-
gishly to working. "I could *buy* a cart and horse. We'd have
to have a place to put them . . . I could drive. . . ."

"Bit uv an expense, guv," Alf replied skeptically.

"Not as big an expense as if we hire someone who turns
around and threatens to expose us unless we pay him," Alexandre replied. "What I need is a stable somewhere
around here where I can keep a cart and a horse, or even a
donkey." He was still thinking. "We'd need an excuse for
why we were using it late."

"Leave thet t'me, guv," Alf replied. "Oi'll find yer a place
wut don't care wut ye do. On'y goin' out a couple times a
week, an' jest carryin' a couple gels . . . reckon thet 'orse's
gonna think 'e's in clover."

"Which means I can buy some old nag no one will look
twice at." Alexandre was liking this idea more and more.
"And all we need for a cart is something sturdy, with high
sides. And clean. We won't want something that can leave
telltale mud smears on the one we put back."

"Roight then, we got a plan." Alf stood up. "Oi'll find
wut we need. Stable fust, reckon stable lads'll know where
Oi c'n git a hanimal an' a cart. Oi'll git all thet set up, then
come t'ye fer the ready."

Alexandre felt limp with relief. It wasn't impossible after
all. In fact, it probably wouldn't be that hard. *Twilight, supper-*
time, will be about the best time. Most people will be home.
The streets will be uncrowded, with a few people hurrying
home or running an errand, but an old man driving a cart
won't be anything anyone will note. Alf can get the target.
We'll be off the street and gone before anyone notices that
our target is missing.

As his fears ebbed, and his anxiety went with it, he found
himself wondering what on earth the entity had been
talking about when it had said it was "removing opposition." The only "opposition" he could think of was that
damned meddling solicitor who kept coming around every

quarter. And how would something with no agency of its own be able to stop the officious old goat from insisting on his quarterly "inspection"?

But that reminded him of possible interference from that particular quarter. *I'll have to think of a way to hide a cart, horse and stabling in my accounts,* he realized, and frowned sourly. *Damn that man. Now there is some "opposition" I would love to see removed.*

The next morning, Alexandre was scribbling down some notes on places where he had noticed girls and young women out alone and unsupervised when someone rang the bell and startled him so much that he thought his heart was going to stop. It was such an unusual sound at this time of the morning that he actually froze, trying to work out who it could be, or if it had somehow been a mistake, when the bell rang again—this time as if someone had pulled the chain with a bit more force.

Why hasn't Alf answered that?

"Alf!" he called—then realized that Alf was out on his transportation errand and, with a grimace, got up to answer the damned door himself. *Probably some wretched urchin wanting to sweep the snow from my step for a penny, or some damned impertinent salesman, or worse, some religious fanatic wanting to save my soul. . . .*

The man standing on the front step was not any of these. There was a carriage waiting for him out in the road, a modest, sober-looking affair that Alexandre glanced at with concealed envy, because a carriage like that would have been ever so much more convenient than a cart. In fact, his thoughts raced with how easy it would be to pull alongside a girl, entice her in or snatch her, hold a sponge full of chloroform to her nose, and be off with no one the wiser.

He quickly snatched his wandering thoughts back to the present and this unexpected visitor. The man himself was dressed in an excellent dark overcoat and wearing a handsome derby hat; he was perhaps ten years older than

Alexandre, with hair and moustache suitable for a professional of some sort. This was distinctly . . . odd. People who looked like *that* generally sent notes around, asking if the person they wished to see would be at home at such-and-such a time. Could this be a mistake? Could this man be looking for someone else?

But who in *this* neighborhood would someone who looked like a prosperous man of business be looking for?

"Is—ah. Excuse me, am I addressing Master Alexandre Harcourt?" the man asked, with punctilious politeness. The sort of politeness Alexandre was accustomed to hearing only from doctors and solicitors.

"You are," Alexandre replied. "I beg your pardon for leaving you on the step so long. My man is out. How can I help you?"

"I have come—please, may we conduct our business inside, sir? It is not the sort of thing to be bandied about in public." The man appeared . . . anxious, as if there really *was* something that was of a delicate nature to be discussed. This was not the sort of anxiety that came when someone was about to deliver a paternity suit on behalf of a strumpet, and in any case, a strumpet would not be able to afford someone dressed like this. This was more like the anxiety of someone about to deliver bad news. Alexandre's heart sank.

"Yes, yes, of course, certainly." Alexandre moved aside and waved the man in, then conducted him to the sitting room. "Please, have a seat, Mister—"

"Abernathy. Of Abernathy, Abernathy, and Owen, your solicitors and the administrators of your trust."

The man took a seat as Alexandre suddenly felt faint. He sat down himself, and clutched at the arms of his chair. There was only one reason why Abernathy would be here. *Oh god. The trust's gone bust. I'm penniless. I'm—*

"Master Harcourt, there is no easy way to say this," Abernathy said, taking off his hat and holding it in his lap, gloved hands resting on the brim, his face a mask of polite concern, with just a touch of professional sympathy. "Mrs. Emily Harcourt, your mother, passed to her reward last night. She was found this morning in her bed. We are deeply sorry for your loss. You have our every sympathy."

Alexandre had been so braced for the horrible news that he was dead broke that the words did not at first register with him. And when they did, he stared at Abernathy in open-mouthed astonishment. "My—mother?" he stammered. "She's dead?" The words made no sense. No sense at all.

"If it is of any consolation to you, it appears she departed from this mortal world in her sleep," Harcourt said ... with the air of someone who is withholding information, if Alexandre was reading him correctly. "The doctor has been called, and there is no need for an inquest. There is no foul play suspected, nor does it appear that she somehow, accidentally poisoned herself with her medicine. Of late, her maid has kept that locked up and administered measured, safe doses herself. No, the death is certainly ... er ... natural."

There is something he is certainly not telling me. Oh dear, I should present some sort of semblance grief ...

He buried his face in his hands. "Oh mother ... poor mother...." he forced his voice to break as if he was sobbing. He imagined himself if he *had* lost the trust fund, penniless, and in the street, and managed to produce real tears of self-pity. "I would have come at Christmas, but the doctor said not to ... I *should* have gone, and I didn't, and now I shall never see her again." This ended in a real sob, as he pictured himself huddling for warmth against the chimney of his own house, hoping no one chased him away.

"Now, Master Harcourt," Abernathy said uncomfortably. "You must brace up. This was not unexpected. We both know she has not been well for a very long time, and has been pining for your late father since he died."

He wiped his eyes, pleased to have produced some genuine tears. "Yes ... yes of course you are right. And now she is with him, where she longed to be, both safe in the arms of Jesus." He rather thought that was a nice touch. "Tell me, Mister Abernathy, what must I do? What must be done now? I am sure there are many tasks but—I don't know where to start."

Now more comfortable with his role, Abernathy straightened, and his expression smoothed into one of professional sympathy. "According to the terms of our agreement with your late father, the firm will undertake all the necessary arrangements for you. We assumed it would be a modest funeral—?"

"Yes, of course, just myself, and mother's servants," he replied, trying to sound just heartbroken enough to be bereaved, but not unmanly. "Any friends she once had fell by the wayside when she became . . . ill."

"Quite right, quite right." Abernathy removed a notebook from inside his coat and consulted it. "Fortunately she can be interred in the family vault beside your father immediately, and there will be no need to wait. Would Wednesday do?"

It can't be soon enough. "Yes . . . yes of course," he replied. "Just send me the details, and anything I might need to sign. I rarely leave the house; my work, you know. I will be here, certainly until at least ~~~~ ~~~~time every evening." He started to get up to show Abernathy out, but the man remained seated. "Is there something more?" he asked, and sat back down again.

"One small matter, of your trust," Abernathy replied, and coughed. "As you know, the trust specified that you were to have your affairs overseen by a member of the firm." He flushed a little. "However, Arthur Fensworth, who undertook that task, seems to have taken leave without notice. This leaves us shorthanded, and the other members of the firm have suggested that your mother's sad demise effectively breaks that trust, leaving you the sole heir and us with no obligation to continue what must have been somewhat distasteful, since you are a grown man in perfect command of his senses." The very slight lift of Abernathy's eyebrow conveyed to Alexandre, without words, that only the insistence of Fensworth had led them to continue the practice of the quarterly visits and the minute examination of his accounts. Precisely as he had suspected. *Only that old goat knew my father, and knew how little my father trusted me to handle my own affairs.*

"The firm hopes you will allow us to continue to administer the estate, but from henceforth, you need only drop us a message to have whatever you like transferred from the account of the estate into your own," Abernathy concluded. "We will, of course, under this arrangement, arrange for all the final expenses and death duties without needing to trouble you."

"Of course," Alexandre said, numbly, unable to believe his good fortune. No more penny-pinching! No more having to account for the least little expense! No more busybody Fensworth! "That would be . . . admirable. Thank you. My father was right to put his trust in you."

"Have you any suggestions as to the disposition of your mother's servants?" Abernathy asked delicately.

"Six months pay, and letters of recommendation from the firm?" Alexandre replied. "I . . . don't think I can bear to even look at the house. I think it must be closed up. Possibly sold. So much death . . . I am the only one left . . . I could not bear to be alone in so much familiar, empty space."

"Quite, quite," Abernathy rose, uncomfortable again now that there might be a second display of emotion. He probably put all that down to Alexandre's being a poet. "We'll see the house is closed up, and revisit the disposition of it, and your mother's personal effects, in three or four months, shall we? And your suggestion for the servants is perfect—generous, without being effusive. We will see to that as well. Now, I really should go. There is much to do."

"Yes, yes of course," Alexandre replied, rising himself. "Thank you, Mister Abernathy. Thank you."

He saw the man out, and closed the door only when Abernathy was inside his carriage and pulling away. Then he went to his sitting room and poured himself the largest brandy he thought he could drink at one sitting without being fuddled by it.

Dead! he thought with glee. *The bitch is dead at last! And that meddling old dotard is missing! And I, I, I have control of every damned penny, at last!*

He tossed down the brandy, scarcely able to believe in his luck.

Or . . . was it luck?

Having his mother die, just after the entity had told him that "opposition" was going to be removed could have been coincidence. But having Fensworth *vanish?* At the same time?

No. That was not coincidence, could not have been coincidence. Fensworth vanishing alone would not have broken the trust. His mother's death would not have removed Fensworth. As long as his mother lived, Abernathy would have felt duty bound to make sure Alexandre did not misuse the funds that were supplying income for both of them. And the tyranny of Fensworth would never have ended until the old dotard died himself.

But *both* of them going? And the firm deciding that he could handle his own funds? No, that could not possibly be coincidence. Somehow that thing in the basement had exercised its influence, and given him the one thing he wanted *and needed* above all others at this moment—financial freedom. Financial freedom to make sure the entity got what it had demanded.

He would not even have to buy a horse and cart now. There was one elderly horse, and an even more modest carriage than Abernathy had used at the house. He could send for it now, if he chose, claiming he needed it to go to the funeral, and would keep it for his convenience. All perfectly proper, and it would allow Abernathy to dismiss the stablehand along with the rest of the servants, and would not leave him trying to be rid of a horse only useful for occasional service.

Perfect. It could not have been more perfect. All that was needed was for Alf to return with stabling arrangements, and everything would be set in motion. He went to the study to write out that note to Abernathy about the horse and carriage. Alf could take it over when he returned, get the stableman to drive it to the stabling, and with any luck the entire issue would be taken care of tonight.

An old coat, a coachman's hat, and no one will look twice at me.

No, this could not possibly be coincidence. He repressed

the urge to dance with glee. If *this* was how his life was going to be conducted from now on, well. . . .

. . . that thing in the basement can have anything it likes!

After consultation and scouting, Alexandre and Alf had decided on West Ham as their initial hunting grounds. At sundown, dusk, and twilight, the streets still had *some* people on them, but not many. It was a part of London where most people were prosperous enough to rent entire homes, but generally not prosperous enough to have servants. The folk who lived in West Ham were well off enough that they had the freedom to be concerned about their daughters' virtue—rather than scolding her for losing her position because she wouldn't let her master do as he pleased with her. And the area was well off enough that the streets were considered safe. Girls were not afraid when strangers spoke to them.

So it was trivial for Alexandre, in his disguise as an elderly coachman, to drive his old horse alongside a girl who looked to be about fourteen and call to her from the box, in an ingratiating voice, "Miss . . . could you tell me how to get to 124 Portway Road? This isn't my part of London and I'm fair lost, I am."

And despite the fact that in the gathering gloom between the streetlamps you couldn't see across the street, the girl quite trustingly came right up to him to tell him the directions. Alexandre knew she would be perfect as soon as he laid eyes on her. She was a pretty little thing, in a black and white dress, white stockings, black boots, and a little black coat and wool hat with brown curls escaping out from underneath it. Just as neat and clean as you could wish. It was clear her parents thought a great deal of her. "I'd be happy to," she said, smiling up at him. "It's no trouble at all."

Which was when Alf crept up to her from behind the coach, clapped that chloroform-laden sponge over her mouth and nose and had her inside the coach and on the floor before she even had an inkling there was a second person behind her.

Alexandre started the coach moving as soon as Alf got the door shut, to cover any sounds that might be coming from inside it, and any swaying the girl's struggles might cause. But he really needn't have worried. Alf, it seemed, was very good at this. *I wonder if he did a bit of abduction for his previous master?* It wouldn't have surprised him. There had been rumors . . . and Alexandre never had found out why the police were interested in him.

The double *thud* on the coach roof that told him Alf had the girl secure, silent, and probably sleeping was the signal for him to take the next two turns to head back to Battersea. It had all gone so smoothly that he was very careful to keep the horse to an amble so as not to attract any interest. And he was careful not to tempt fate by thinking they had this job locked up and finished. It wouldn't be finished until the entity in the basement said *"offering acceptable"* and turned one of the two girls they needed to snatch back over to them. Actually, it wouldn't be finished until they figured out what to *do* with that second girl, and got her safely away from them.

And they would have called it a good night's hunting, except that on the way home, they spotted a girl sitting on the curb beneath a streetlamp and crying. This one was dressed like a servant, in a plain, dark dress and white apron, with nothing but a shawl pinned around her shoulders for warmth, and had a tatty old carpetbag and a scarf done up around a bundle next to her. *Her* tale was as plain to read as if it had been written out; she was a servant who had done something wrong, or at least something her employer didn't like. Hopefully, it wasn't being caught in bed with another servant or the master's son. She'd been turned out on the spot, with no references, and she was either afraid to go home and confess she'd lost her place, or she had no home to go to. If the first girl matched the description of someone who would be missed . . . well this one was clearly someone who wouldn't be. At least, not for a good long while. And there was absolutely no one in sight, on either side of the street, for as far as Alexandre could see in either direction. Even the building she sat in front of was dark; either no one was home, they were early sleepers, or it was vacant. Alexandre gave the triple rap on the roof of the coach that signaled to Alf that he had spotted another target.

Alf must have been astonished, but Alf never stayed surprised for long. As Alexandre stopped the coach right at the girl's feet, and she gaped up at him in shock and surprise, Alf already had the door open and was leaning out. She had no time to react before he had her. This time he clapped his hand around his victim's mouth to prevent her screaming, and dragged her, kicking and thrashing inside. There was some bumping about until he overpowered her, then silence — presumably as he applied the chloroformed sponge. Meanwhile Alexandre had leapt down off the box, picked up the girl's belongings, and tossed them inside the coach with Alf and his captives. Then he was back up on the box and urging the horse forward, taking a quick glance all around to make sure that no one had spotted them. The street was still deserted, and there was no sign of life in the house.

All was soon quiet in the coach. The horse ambled its way back to Battersea. Once in a while they met a coach not unlike theirs; in the universal fraternity of men who must be outside in wretched weather, the other coachman invariably nodded and touched his hat to Alexandre in sympathy, and Alexandre echoed the gesture. *What would they think if they knew what I carried?* he asked himself, and felt a thrill of excitement at getting away, literally, with murder.

And that was that. By the time he usually had a late supper, they were back home. Alf carried the girls under the cover of darkness into the house, and Alexandre took the second girl's belongings up beside him on the box. Halfway to the stable, he pitched the carpetbag into the backyard of a place dilapidated enough that he knew whoever found it would take whatever was in it, and the bag itself, with no questions asked. A little farther along, he dropped the scarf-bundle at a crossing where, again, the first person to come along would snatch it up and carry it off. Alf's stabling solution had been a good one; it was a place for both vehicles and draft animals of men who did all sorts of odd jobs. The care and feeding of the animals could be done by the customer or by the stablehands, if you paid a little extra, which Alexandre was happy to do. There were long, covered sheds with spots for wagons, carts, and old cabs and coaches. Alexandre's story was genius; he gave the name and history of his mother's now-dismissed coachman and stableman, except that in this version, he'd been given the horse and vehicle in her will, and he reckoned to pad out his savings by hiring himself out now and again. No one batted an eye at the story.

He backed the coach into its shed, unhitched the horse, and took it to its stall. He'd learned to do all of these things at his father's insistence, as the price of having his own pony and cart as a boy. The old skinflint had even made him do all the feeding and mucking out, no doubt to spare himself the expense of a stablehand. He had burned with resentment as a boy whenever he'd been forced to do such menial work, but now, the skills were literally his salvation. *The old man is probably spinning in his grave, knowing* he *is responsible for my carrying all this off so successfully.* When the horse was unharnessed, the harness hung on a peg in the stall, and the horse put up under a blanket, he made his way to the front of the place. There were vehicles coming and going here at all hours of the day and night, and it was no trouble to catch a ride for a penny most of the way back to his flat with a carter on his way to collect night soil. By the time he returned, Alf had everything in readiness in the kitchen.

The girls were awake now, but tied up, with balls of cloth stuffed in their mouths and gags tied in place for good measure. The most they could manage were muffled grunts. Alf had them sat down in two of the kitchen chairs. Alexandre surveyed them with pleasure. He knew what they were expecting. He chuckled to himself.

"Good night's work, guv," Alf observed, rubbing his bristly chin. "Bit uv luck, that second one."

"When fortune was so obliging as to provide her, I couldn't see any reason to pass her by," Alexandre smiled, as the girls shrank as far away from him as they could manage, their eyes huge and terrified above the gags. He regretted that the entity had specified it preferred virgins; that first girl was really quite pretty, and it was a pity he wouldn't get to enjoy her and her terror. The very few times he'd paid for the privilege of "breaking in" a new girl at a brothel, the experience had been exhilarating.

"Shame t'waste 'em," Alf observed, echoing his thoughts.

"More where they came from," Alexandre replied. "And I don't fancy the risk if you-know-what objects to us enjoying ourselves. Let's give our *guest* what it wants. We're both just lucky it was temporarily satisfied with that baby, Christmas Eve."

"Roight ye are, guv," Alf agreed. "Oi'll take th' feet. They're kickers, they are. Yew take th' 'ead."

The girls did, indeed, kick, but Alf was far stronger than he looked, and he wasn't even thrown off balance as they carried the girls, one at a time, down the stairs. Alf eyed the eerie pool of blackness in the center of the floor as they brought down the second one. "Oi'll jest wait upstairs an' make supper," he said hastily, and made his way up, taking the steps two at a time.

Leaving Alexandre alone with the girls, now lying on the stone flagging of the floor, panting with fear, illuminated by a single lantern. Aside from that pool of shadow, the basement was strangely normal, just a cold, but not unnaturally cold, room, smelling slightly of damp.

All right, then, I have them here as it wanted . . . I wonder, should I repeat the invo—

The pool of darkness became a pillar of darkness, and the temperature in the basement plummeted abruptly. Muffled, strangled screams came from both girls—scarcely loud enough in the sudden silence to qualify as squeaks.

The basement had turned from a prosaic room to a freezing, silent, portico of Hell—not the Hell of the Christians, all fire and demons, but the silent, cold Hel of the Norse. Was that a clue? Was this thing Nordic? But what about—

The offerings are acceptable, said the voice in his head. And the darkness erupted into tentacles that seized both writhing, horrified girls and dragged them inside it within a second or two. It all happened so fast it took his breath away, and he was left gasping, cold fear closing around his heart. *Remain,* it commanded, when he started to back away.

He swallowed hard, all his earlier exuberance gone. Time seemed to stand utterly still—but he was afraid to move. The pillar of darkness remained motionless, neither shrinking nor growing. The silence was absolute. Alexandre couldn't even hear Alf moving around upstairs.

Then, with no warning whatsoever, the first girl stumbled out of the pillar and collapsed facedown on the basement floor.

Take her away, said the voice, and the pillar once again became a pool.

The silence vanished; in its place were the sounds of Alf shuffling around overhead and the girl breathing. The air warmed, and the scent of damp returned.

The girl was no longer tied and gagged, but she wasn't moving except for breathing. Cautiously, Alexandre went to her, and turned her over.

Her eyes stared fixedly into nothingness, the pupils so dilated that he couldn't see any iris at all. He touched her face; she was cold, almost corpse-cold, even though she was clearly still breathing. At the touch of her clammy, chill skin, all thoughts of enjoying her before turning her loose on the street vanished out of his mind.

Bloody hell . . . am I going to have to carry her? He decided to see if he could get her to her feet first, before trying to carry her. Taking one hand, he tugged on it, saying "Stand up." She obeyed him like some sort of automaton, getting easily to her feet and standing on her own. Encouraged by this, he turned her so that she faced the stairs.

"Go over there, climb the stairs, open the door at the top, and go into the kitchen," he ordered. And just like a clock-work toy, she lifted her feet, one after the other, and did as she had been told. He followed behind her, both of them surprising Alf as he laid out a cold supper on a tray in the kitchen.

"Bloody Jesus!" he choked, catching himself on the back of a chair. "The *'ell!* Did—is—"

"Our guest got what it wanted," Alexandre informed him. "This is what it left."

Alf left his task and prowled around the girl like a nervous cat investigating something it was not at all sure of. The girl paid him no more attention than she had anything else.

"I can order her about, and she'll do what I say," Alexandre continued, as Alf peered into her black eyes and shook his head. "My thought was to take her to the street and set her on her way. I think she'll just keep going until someone stops her."

Alf pulled a handkerchief out of his back pocket and mopped his face with it; Alexandre saw he was sweating nervously. "Sooner ye do thet, guv, th' better Oi'll loik it. Thet thing . . . Oi dunno wut 'tis, but 'tain't 'ooman no more."

Alexandre blinked, a little surprised at Alf's perceptivity. "I think you might be right," he said. "But at least our *guest* left her with enough that we'll have no trouble disposing of her—and there's not a chance in the world she'll betray us."

After making sure there were no potential witnesses, he steered the girl-husk out the front door and down to the street. He pointed her in the direction he wanted her to go; she evidenced no more will nor personality than a giant wax doll. But she *did* manage to navigate all the hummocks and ruts in the snow, which solved the question of whether or not she was actually going to be able to walk far enough away to erase any connections between them and her.

"Walk forward, move quickly, keep on this street, and don't stop until someone tells you to," he ordered, and exactly as if he had wound up a clockwork toy and set it in motion, she began walking. She was able to maintain quite a good pace; he waited, shivering in the cold, until she was three blocks away before going back inside.

He and Alf looked at each other. Alf mopped his face

again. "Oi've seen a lotta thin's, guv," he said finally. "But Oi hain't never seen anythin' thet give me th' shivers loik— thet. There weren't nobody in there, guv, Oi swear it."

Alexandre thought that over. It was as good an explanation as anything. "How about a brandy?" he suggested.

"'Ow 'bout a bottle?" Alf countered.

Alexandre thought about the moment that pillar had erupted into grasping tentacles and engulfed both girls, hauling them into its blackness.

"I think that's a capital idea," he said fervently, and went to get the bottle himself.

9

THE flat was much quieter. Suki was back at school, and Roan had followed her there; Memsa'b said both had arrived and were settled safely. From what Durwin said, Roan was as happy as could be with a workshop full of broken and worn-out toys to repair. Durwin himself was a cheerful *absence* rather than a presence in the house. They seldom saw him, but his satisfaction at being here was palpable, and demonstrated in the way that the flat was always in spotless order—and they had fancied themselves to be good house-keepers! Not that they shirked—Nan, for one, was determined to give Durwin no chance to think they were taking him for granted—but no matter how clean and tidy things were before they went to bed, they were somehow cleaner and more tidy when they woke.

For their part, despite Amelia's prescient dreams and their own forebodings, it appeared that life had elected to grant them a temporary holiday, for until three days after Suki left for school, nothing came up that required their talents and attention.

Which was just as well, really, since while Suki had been with them, they had not had a moment when the three of them weren't doing something—generally a lesson disguised as an outing, like the entire day they spent at the British Museum. With Suki gone, and their time to themselves, they got the chance to put their spring and summer wardrobes in order, doing all the mending and retrimming they'd put off after cleaning the garments and putting them away. The trimming was the enjoyable part—making old gowns, waists and skirts look new with new lace, ribbons, and other trims. The mending part . . . not so much. They even got a chance to mend what needed mending in their winter clothing before a message came from Sherlock Holmes.

They had just started on the incredibly dull task of darning stockings when there was the sound of the bell at the front door of the house. They looked at each other with hope; a moment later, there were footsteps on their stairs, and a knock at their door.

Nan opened it to find one of the Irregulars on the doorstep, with a note. He presented it to her with a flourish and a grin. *Doctor Watson has a patient that needs your talent, Nan, who has given me a satisfying puzzle to solve. Please take the cab Billy brings to Baker Street.*

Nan looked at Sarah. Sarah's eyes were alight. "Thank *God*," she said. "If I'd had to darn another sock, I think I would have thrown them all out the window."

Nan smiled. "All right, then," she agreed. "The game's afoot! Let us get our cloaks, Billy, and we'll be right down."

The sable cloaks were so warm—and so very welcome with the weather so cold—that they'd long since got over the faint embarrassment of swanning about in something so ostentatious. As Nan tossed hers over her shoulders, she wondered where Sarah had gone—until her friend came out of the bird room, already swathed in sable, with a carrier in either hand. "You think?" Nan asked, raising an eyebrow.

"They haven't been out of the flat since before Christmas," Sarah pointed out. "And if we need their help and don't have them with us, we'll feel the fool. Or worse! It would be horrid to have something go wrong because we hadn't brought them."

"Point taken, and besides, Sherlock likes Neville," said Nan, and took Neville's carrier from her friend. Inside it, she spotted Neville's black beak just sticking out of his sable muff. Nan locked the door of the flat behind them, and they both ran down the stairs and out to the waiting cab, with the Irregular right behind them.

"Cor," said Billy, when he was sandwiched in between them, up to his chin in black fur. "This's more like!"

Nan grinned. "Toasty, are you?"

"The toastiest!" the boy replied, and closed his eyes in pure, luxurious bliss. He stayed that way all the way to Baker Street, even dozing a little, rousing with regret when they got to their destination.

Nan paid the cabby as Billy, his errand complete, ran off, and Sarah preceded her into 221 B.

When she trotted up the stairs to join her friend, however, there was no one there except Holmes himself. "Where's the mystery patient?" she asked.

"At the good doctor's surgery," Holmes explained. "I have just finished interviewing her parents and I wanted to have some words with you before you looked at her."

Seeing that Holmes was dressed to go out, except for his overcoat, Nan settled on the arm of Watson's usual chair, and Sarah took the seat, while Holmes strode up and down as he generally did when he was excited. From the look of things, it was probably just as well this new case had turned up. There were new bullet-holes in the woodwork above the mantle, the room smelled as if Holmes had been smoking continuously for days, and there was a certain small leather case on one of the tables, although Holmes showed no sign of having used it recently.

"Our clients are the Penwicks," Holmes said, crossing his sitting room in a few strides, turning, and coming back. "They live in West Ham. Last night their daughter Elizabeth vanished on her way to the fish shop to purchase fried fish for the family supper. The neighborhood was scoured for her. She had not arrived at the shop, and no one remembered seeing her on the street. She is, by all repute, a sweet and slightly simple girl, of good temper, who was still enamored of dolls and tea parties and tended to play with girls three or four years younger than she—so they almost immediately ruled out that there might be a possible boyfriend she had run off to join. As you may imagine, by morning they were distraught, when a police officer from Battersea came to inform them that their daughter had been found there, wandering about, apparently witless."

Nan looked at him in astonishment. "Battersea? How did she get from—" She stopped herself. "Well, obviously someone took her there."

"The question is *why*. She doesn't seem to have been . . ." he cleared his throat with embarrassment. ". . . ah . . ."

"Raped," Sarah said crisply. "You can say the word, Sherlock. You should know by now we aren't wilting lilies. Good heavens, we traveled to Africa and back on our own, and defended ourselves very well too, thank you."

Holmes recovered himself quickly. "Yes, well . . . the only thing that seems to have been interfered with is her mind. Even the money with which she was to buy the fish was still in her pocket. She was *definitely* abducted; there are abrasions on her ankles, wrists, face, and neck corresponding to being bound and gagged. But she sits or stands as she has been arranged, doesn't react to anything except direct orders, and is oblivious to any attempt to question her or converse with her."

"Right," Sarah said, nodding. "So I assume you want Nan to try and read her mind?"

"Exactly," Sherlock replied. "I will undertake to discover who abducted her and why, but Watson needs you to see if this is merely shock or if there is something more complicated going on with her, and I need to see if you can glean any information from her thoughts."

"Let's go, then," Nan said, jumping up and getting a grumbling *quork* from Neville. Sarah got up with a little less vigor, as Sherlock threw on his Inverness coat and preceded them out the door.

The surgery was not that far away; it seemed ridiculous to take a cab so short a distance. This, of course was necessary for the ruse that John and Mary lived over the surgery, rather than above Sherlock in 221C. It was much easier to slip over two streets on foot without being observed than it would have been if cabs had been involved. Holmes had many enemies, and he was well aware that if they could not get to him, they would try to use his friends against him. It was safer for the Watsons to be close at hand—and safer for Holmes to have help directly upstairs if he needed it.

Sherlock led the way; a bell over the door, like that over a shop door, rang as they entered, but the detective went down the narrow hall, papered in pale green stripes, straight through the first door on the right into the tiny but comfortably appointed reception room, and through that to the examination room.

"Ah, good, Holmes, you brought them," Watson said, looking up from his patient as they all crowded into the chamber. Watson had a girl sitting in an examination chair, rather than lying on a table, and from where they stood, they couldn't really see very much past Watson. It was a bit of a squeeze and there was some fumbling as they all got out of outerwear and got themselves sorted out. Nan finally freed Neville from his carrier, and Sarah did the same with Grey. Once cloaks and carriers were disposed of, they joined Watson around Elizabeth Penwick.

Nan's initial impression was of nothing so much as a giant wax doll, and frankly, the way the girl looked made her skin crawl. Elizabeth Penwick sat rigidly upright in the examination chair, hands folded in her lap, staring straight ahead. The only proof that she was alive lay in her breathing. She would have been a pretty thing, with a round face, curly, light brown hair, and a slight figure, if she had not been so uncannily without expression. That was not at all helped by her eyes. She had brown eyes . . . but you could only tell they were brown by the thinnest of rim of iris; her pupils seemed to be dilated to their fullest extent.

"John, is she under the influence of a drug?" Nan asked doubtfully. Not that she was at all familiar with the effects of drugs, but some foolish women used belladonna to dilate their pupils to make their eyes look bigger, didn't they?

"Not so far as I have been able to determine," John Watson

replied. "It was the first thing I thought of to account for her state, of course. But any drug I am familiar with would have interfered with her balance and other automatic reactions, and I found no such interference — and a drug would surely have begun to wear off by now; she's been in police custody since ten in the evening yesterday. She is exactly the same now as when she was found."

"If she was found yesterday evening, why did it take so long for her parents to be informed?" Sarah asked sharply.

"I am sad to say that the police initially thought she was an opium-eater, and merely locked her in a cell to wait for the effects of the opium to wear off," Watson replied. "I find it hard to fault them for that; in the ordinary run of things, if this had been a girl having a 'thrill,' they could have questioned her and turned her over to her parents or guardian by morning. It was only when the descriptions of the missing girl from West Ham began to circulate by messenger to the other precincts that they realized this was Elizabeth."

Sarah shook her head. "It's a shame there is no telegraphy office in every precinct," she observed, as Grey leaned down off her shoulder to peer into Elizabeth's eyes. "You would think in these modern times people would be clamoring for such a thing." After a moment the parrot went bolt upright with an alarmed growl. "What's wrong, Grey?" Sarah asked, as all attention turned to the bird.

"Careful!" Grey replied. "Danger!"

John Watson stroked his moustache. "I . . . did not expect *that* reaction. I am having second thoughts about you using your talent on her, Nan."

"That's why I have Neville," she pointed out, with determination. "And if any sense is going to be made of this, I don't think you have a choice except to allow me to proceed."

"Well said, Miss Nan," Holmes approved. With a nod to him, she flexed her hands to limber them, stripped off her gloves, and put her fingers on the girl's temples, closing her eyes to better concentrate.

There was . . . silence.

For a moment, she feared her telepathic talent had suddenly deserted her, for there was ... nothing there, nothing there at all. She had *been* inside minds in shock; there was generally something like a great wall of terror, behind which were the memories of what caused the shock, and behind *that* a second wall of protection, behind which the self cowered. She was a powerful and well-trained telepath; unless someone was just as good as she was, it would be impossible for anyone to keep her from penetrating their barriers and reading their thoughts.

Yet she sensed Neville's thoughts, and Sarah's, and Grey's—and a little distant from that, Watson's warm compassion and Sherlock's calculation and blinding intellect. No, her talent was in perfect working order.

Here there was ... nothing. No emotions. No memories. No "self." This was an empty, echoing, soulless hulk, which moved, and lived, and breathed, but with nothing animating it.

Nothing within this girl but a void. A void where a personality, a soul, had once been, but was there no more.

Impossible.

Nevertheless, it was the truth.

Unable to bear this travesty of life a moment longer, Nan withdrew, and dropped her hands—and quickly thought of an adequate way to describe what she had found to Holmes. "Sherlock, it's not that she's in shock, not at all. It's that there is nothing *there* anymore, as if her mind has been wiped clean of every memory, every fragment of *self.* I've never encountered anything like that. There's nothing for me to read, because there is nothing there. Nothing but the basic instincts that keep her breathing. I honestly don't even know how she obeys commands, because for all intents and purposes, there's nothing in there to recognize commands."

"A *tabula rasa,*" Holmes muttered. "By Jove ... this becomes more interesting by the moment! If you all will excuse me, I need to go to the British Library—"

And he snatched up his coat and sped off, without so much as another word.

Now Nan turned to John Watson. "Her soul's gone," she

said, flatly. "Oh, her mind's been wiped as well, but her soul is *gone*. I'm not sure why this thing in front of us is still breathing, but . . . everything that once made it a young girl isn't there anymore."

"Good God," Watson murmured, shaking his head sadly. "In that case—there really isn't anything any of us can do, is there?"

"You should consult Memsa'b, but not to my knowledge, no, not unless you know some way of calling the soul back to the body," replied Sarah, looking ill. "I *might* be able to do such a thing if her soul was anywhere near, but it's not. I would have sensed it, if it was. Or, recognizing me as someone who could communicate with it, the soul would have appeared to me. John . . . I can't help but think this might be linked to Amelia's prescient visions in some way. It seems just as unlikely, and just as, well, *evil* as her visions, and I can't think that the two coming so closely together in time is a coincidence."

"I think we would be foolish to discard that idea," Watson agreed, and sighed. "I fear that I must speak to the Penwicks and tell them there is no hope of bringing Elizabeth back to herself, and advise them to find an institution in which to place her, unless they can care for her themselves. Shall I meet you at the Harton School this afternoon?"

"Yes, please," Sarah agreed. "And bring Mary."

Memsa'b's parlor seemed a better place for the meeting than Sahib's study. It was warm and bright with sunlight; Sahib's study had few windows, and Nan wanted a lot of sunlight just now. Trying to read Elizabeth Penwick's mind had left her feeling chilled to the bone. Only now, after drinking two cups of good, strong hot tea and sitting in the chair closest to the fire, was she starting to feel warm again. Mentally touching that empty shell had been so profoundly *wrong* that she was still unsettled from it. She was not religious at all, and despite having had many encounters, directly and indirectly, with spirits and creatures of the supernatural, she did not often think in religious terms. But at that moment, she had found herself wondering how God could have allowed such an abomination. She could only fall back on something Memsa'b had told her when, as a child, she had asked why God allowed evil.

"Because we are not children, and God does not treat us as children, to be given orders and forced to obey them, or punished if we do not. But that also means we are not rescued from evil things, nor from the consequences of our own folly."

It was not comfortable thinking. But then, as she very well knew, the world was anything but "comfortable."

She had finished describing what she had found, and now Memsa'b and Agansing were muttering to each other. Finally they seemed to come to some conclusion, and Memsa'b gestured to Agansing, the Gurkha, to speak first.

"It is said that among the holy men, and among those who seek to master mystic arts without aspiring to holiness, there are those who can send their spirits out of their bodies," he said, as Watson listened, showing no signs of skepticism. "I am sure that you have heard of these things, Doctor. It is also said that those who attempt this feat before they are properly skilled can become lost, swept away on the winds of the spirit world, and if the link to their body is broken, they leave behind a thing much like you describe."

Watson nodded. "But this is a young English girl," he objected mildly. "How would she have come by this knowledge?"

"That is the difficulty," Agansing agreed. "If she had had a high fever . . . that has been known to drive the spirit out. Also the action of certain drugs." He pondered for a moment. "Also life-threatening danger, such as being caught in a fire."

"She *was* abducted," Sarah pointed out. "Could that alone have frightened her enough?"

"I do not know," Agansing admitted. "Perhaps? If she was frightened enough? She was, by all accounts, a gently treated girl."

"If she suddenly fell senseless . . . I suppose her captor might have discarded her because she was no longer of use to him?" Watson said doubtfully. "—whatever it was he wanted her for."

"I should think a giant, soulless doll that does exactly what you tell it to without fuss would be *exactly* what someone who abducts young girls off the street would want," Memsa'b said dryly. Nan nodded, agreeing entirely.

The fire crackled, punctuating the silence. Nan sipped her tea.

"Well, where would her spirit *be,* then?" Sarah wanted to know. "It's not anywhere near her."

"I do not know that, either," Agansing replied. "If the tales I have heard are true, it should have been hovering about the body, trying to find a way back. No matter where the body was moved, the spirit would have followed. The very first thing that should have happened when you entered that room, Missy Sarah, is that it should have made itself known to you so you could help it back into the body. This is a very great puzzlement."

"Which is further compounded by the question of what Grey meant when she told you there was 'danger,' Sarah," Memsa'b continued. "Has she been able to make herself clearer?"

"Only that she could sense that something had actively done this to Elizabeth, and that it was dangerous." Sarah chewed on her lower lip. "Honestly, I didn't sense anything. I don't doubt that Grey did, but I can't verify what she felt." She was quiet for a very long moment. "We really should consider if . . . if her spirit has actually been destroyed."

"Is that even possible?" Mary Watson asked, going a little pale.

Sarah shrugged. "I don't know, though I have heard of such things. It is difficult to determine what is pure myth and what reflects a level of reality, when you do what we do. There are things that *eat* souls in African beliefs, but if Elizabeth's soul had been taken by one of those, her body would have turned to dust."

"There are other things that eat souls . . . Ammit, in Egyptian lore . . . but Ammit only eats the souls of the wicked dead, to prevent them from ascending." Memsa'b frowned. "Elizabeth's body is not dead, so Ammit seems unlikely."

"Wanyūdō," Sahib suggested.

"I should think that if a flaming cartwheel with the head of a man in the center of it had been rolling down the streets of West Ham, someone would have noticed," Memsa'b pointed out. "And I rather doubt Elizabeth would have gone running toward such a thing. She'd have been more likely to run back home in terror. And that does not address the marks of her abduction. We must somehow arrive at possibilities that address both that abduction, which surely took place *before* she was rendered into what she is now, and that current condition."

"Nalusa Chito, then." Sahib looked at Watson. "Find out if the girl showed signs of depression—"

"None, according to her parents" Watson interrupted. "She was, if anything, rather too childish and playful. And what is that creature, anyway? Where is it from?"

"Choctaw, dear," Mary Watson murmured, and raised an eyebrow at Sahib. "If you have any explanation for how a Choctaw forest spirit should have come to be transplanted to West Ham, I should truly like to hear it. That makes no more sense than a Japanese demon."

"It does seem unlikely," Sahib admitted. His brows creased as he pummeled his prodigious memory for supernatural lore. "I can think of nothing," he said, finally.

"And none of these supernatural beings would account for the signs of abduction," Watson pointed out. Then blinked, as something occurred to him. "Unless, of course, the girl was abducted *specifically* to feed this creature, and turned loose the moment it was sated."

"In Battersea?" Mary Watson said, sounding incredulous. "I would be hard put to think of an area less inclined to the supernatural. The banal, the mundane, certainly, but not the supernatural."

"Evil can be anywhere," Memsa'b pointed out. "There are many sailors and former sailors living in Battersea. *That* would account for something not native to this soil being here, if a sailor had acquired some sort of object such a thing was associated with." She turned to Sahib. "We need access to the White Lodge library."

"I'll see to that," Sahib replied. "Since there are specific creatures we are researching, it should take me no more than a day to find out if they can become associated with objects. Or if they are inclined to grant favors for being fed, or can coerce someone into feeding them."

"Holmes seemed to be inspired to look into something," Watson mused. "It would be ironic if it turned out Elizabeth's state had something to do with a purely physical cause."

"I don't believe that, not for a moment," Nan said flatly. "You weren't in her head. *I* was. There cannot possibly be a natural explanation for what was—or rather, wasn't—in there."

"Has Amelia had any more visions?" Sarah asked, before Nan could wax any more vehement. "I find it . . . unlikely that her visions began not that long before Elizabeth was found in her pitiable state. It's my experience that there are very few coincidences when it comes to the supernatural."

Memsa'b hesitated. "I . . . have had her taking a concoction designed to suppress visions," she said at last. "I wanted her to have a rest from them, and get back to being a normal girl. Her nerves were nearly wrecked by being plagued by such disturbing things, and it seemed only right to quell them and allow her health to return."

"Very kind of you, I am sure, Mrs. Harton, but what if she were to see something pertinent to this case?" asked Watson. "At least give her the information and let *her* make the choice whether to refuse the medication and resume seeing the visions. She's certainly old enough to be able to make a judgment for herself, and I think she has the right— either to agree or refuse."

Memsa'b flushed a little, as if a trifle ashamed. "You're right, of course. *I am doing it for her own good* is a terrible excuse when there are other things in play. I have no right to impose my will on her at this point."

She looked at Agansing, who said, before she could ask, "I shall bring the young lady, myself," and left the room.

"I have one more thing to add," Sarah said. "We shouldn't be so sure whoever took Elizabeth lives in Battersea." She turned to Watson. "If someone just set her somewhere and told her to walk, would she have?"

"As far as I can tell, yes," he admitted. "The streets were clear of snow, and she was bundled up in her coat. She wouldn't feel any tiredness. So she could have been walking for hours."

"So, we should not eliminate Battersea, but we should not confine ourselves to it, either," Sahib said.

At this point Agansing returned with Amelia.

Sahib motioned her to a chair; she sat down, and looked at the gathered group with a nod of recognition for the Watsons, Nan and Sarah. "Amelia," Memsa'b said, "You know I have been giving you medicine that prevents you from having visions since you arrived here."

"Yes, Mrs. Harton," Amelia said, but with enthusiasm that had been lacking the last time they saw her. Nan eyed her critically; the rest from those horrific visions had done her good. Her complexion was pink again. Her hair was smooth and tended. She looked rested, well, and contented. Happy, even. "And it has been such a relief! I can never thank you enough!"

"Well . . . it may not be a relief for much longer," Memsa'b said reluctantly, and described everything they knew or had surmised about Elizabeth Penwick. Amelia's eyes widened and she glanced at Nan, aghast, when Memsa'b described what Nan *hadn't* found inside Elizabeth's head.

"And we have no idea what has done this to her," Memsa'b concluded. "And it isn't just that we wish to discover this. It is that, if some of our guesses are right, there may be *more* girls that become victims. Sarah thinks it is no coincidence that your visions began not that long ago."

"Sarah thinks that there are probably victims we'll never know about because they don't have loving parents to go frantic with worry," Sarah said, darkly. "Actually, I am wondering if those strange visions weren't triggered by an abduction of which we know nothing. Girls go missing in London all the time, as I am sure the police told the Penwicks. And no one ever hears about them, because either no one cares to look for them, or it is assumed they ran off with lovers or to escape uncomfortable or intolerable conditions."

Nan nodded; back when she had been with her late unlamented mother, that had been exactly the case for *her*. "For all we know, if there's a human agency behind this, he only moved to abducting girls because he couldn't find anyone to sell him one at the time," she said with a grimace. "The Good Lord knows my mother tried hard enough to sell *me.*"

Amelia's eyes grew large, and Nan could tell she was bravely holding back tears. But she nodded. "You are right, of course. If there is *anything* my visions can tell us that will help us find this fiend, then I would be the sinfullest person in London if I didn't put my own ease aside and help." She straightened her back and held her head up high. "I will certainly do without the medicine tonight, and as many nights as you think best, until I see something," she said.

"Well done, Amelia," Sahib congratulated her warmly. "Don't worry. We won't leave you alone with them."

"We'll stay here overnight, even a few nights," Nan offered. "We've got the birds with us, after all, and we can send a note to Mrs. Horace to let her know we'll be stopping away for a visit here."

And Roan can tell Durwin.

Now Amelia's eyes did brim over with tears. "Oh, Miss Nan, if you would stay with me in my room, that would make every difference!"

"Then it's settled," Nan said firmly. "Why, we've even got clothing here that we keep for that very purpose, in case we need to make an unexpected stay."

"And what you don't have, I can certainly supply," added Memsa'b. She looked at the birds, Neville perched on Nan's chair, and Grey on Sarah's shoulder. "I assume you two approve as well?"

Grey bobbed—but slowly, rather than enthusiastically as

she normally did. Neville uttered a meditative *quork* followed by a quite clear "We stay."

Watson added his own approval. "That settles that, then." Doctor Watson and Mary rose. "Let us know if something turns up. We'll tell Sherlock where you are. Meanwhile, I'll see what Elizabeth's parents want to do about her." He shook his head. "It's a heartbreaking situation. They'll want to think she'll somehow get better, of course. Every time she obeys a command they'll take that as evidence that she is improving. And while there is no doubt they'll take better care of her than an asylum—is it right to ask them to devote their lives to a . . . a . . ."

"Soulless husk," Nan said bluntly, and shuddered. "It would be kinder if that . . . thing . . . died."

"But we have no evidence she can't be restored," Sarah pointed out. "Let them hope for a while, at least."

Is it right to let them have hope when it's false? Nan thought, as the group broke up and Memsa'b made arrangements for a second bed in Amelia's room. *I'm glad it's not my decision to make.*

Amelia's room was the same size as the one Nan shared with Sarah, and even had a second bed in it already, since most rooms at the school were meant to be shared by two or more children. All she had to do was move one of Neville's portable perches in, and all was in readiness. Of course, as an adult, she came to bed somewhat later than Amelia, but the girl was waiting up for her, reading in bed, when she eased the door open and sent Neville to his perch.

"Oh good, I was afraid I would wake you," she said, and made quick business of slipping out of her clothing and into a nightdress. "Don't be afraid, Amelia. This time, when you have one of those visions, the moment it begins, if I don't awake by myself, Neville will awaken me, and I will be *with* you the entire time."

Amelia had been eying Neville with curiosity and just a

touch of nerves. "He's . . . very big. Does he stay with you all the time? I've never seen a raven for a pet."

"Neville is my partner, not my pet." Nan smiled. "I sometimes think I am Neville's pet, actually."

Neville made a chuckling sound. "You are, pet," he said insolently.

Amelia started. "Oh! He talks!"

"I can talk," Neville said cheekily. "Can you fly?"

"And he speaks his mind. Do go make friends, you limb of Satan," she said to her bird, who chortled again, then hopped down off the perch, walked with immense dignity to Amelia's bed, jumped up onto the foot of it with a couple of wingflaps, and sauntered up to her.

He put his head down, offering her the nape of his neck. "Give pets, pretty," he said with great politeness for Neville, and Amelia gingerly stroked his head.

"He's soft!" she exclaimed, and ventured a little scratch. Neville purred. When she stopped, he walked down to the foot of her bed, and flew back to his perch.

"Neville is my partner, just as Grey is Sarah's," Nan explained. "He's quicker at sensing some things than I am, and he's quite able to defend me. He'll do the same for you, now that you are friends."

"What if I don't have a dream?" Amelia asked anxiously.

"I don't think you will, actually; not tonight anyway," Nan told her. "The medicine will need time to wear off, and you'll probably sleep very lightly because you have a stranger and a bird in your room. But we'll stay until we know for certain whether or not you'll see visions again, and that's a promise."

"Promise," Neville echoed.

"And now—" Nan blew out the lamp on her side of the room. "Lights out. And we'll see what we will see."

Amelia obediently blew hers out as well. "I hope I do," she said into the darkness, though her voice quavered a little. "I want to help you, as you helped me."

"And you will," Nan promised, closing her eyes. *Brave girl. She reminds me of Sarah. I think we'll do, I really think we'll do.*

10

ALEXANDRE woke in a cold sweat, the voice of that entity in the basement ringing in his head. It had woken him out of a profound sleep, and his heart was pounding both from the icy fear the thing induced and from shock at being so suddenly awakened.

The damned thing could reach him *here* now! In his bed, in his own bedroom.

It didn't seem to care that it had awakened him, which honestly should not have surprised him in the least.

The offerings were acceptable. I need more. If anything, its tone was even more arrogant, and he hadn't thought that was possible.

But it wasn't finished. *And better,* it added.

Better? What the hell is that supposed to mean? he thought, unable to control his reaction. He hadn't meant the damned thing to overhear . . . but it had.

Better. The ones who serve must be . . . he thought the entity was struggling with concepts that were utterly foreign to it in order to express what it wanted from him. *They must be better cared for. Cherished. Finer.*

Bloody hell. Is it asking for what I think *it's asking for?*

What he thought it was asking for was upper-class girls! Panicked, he couldn't keep himself from thinking about all those girls—sisters, cousins, sweethearts—that he'd seen surrounding his classmates at University when visitors paid calls on the students. Images sprang into his mind without prompting, memories of well-bred young women, pampered, cosseted, protected. Young women who were *never* without protectors of some sort.

Yes! came the emphatic reply. *When the witnesses return, they must assemble. The first witness is being kept. This is not acceptable.*

What did the thing mean—"kept"? And "assemble"?

He didn't have any privacy even in his own damn head. No sooner had he formed the thought than the thing reacted to it.

Vague pictures were shoved into his mind, roughly. Girl-shaped creatures all together in a single room. *Acceptable.* One girl by herself, with two other shapes tending her. *Not acceptable.*

Did that mean the girl he'd abducted and sent off down the street had been found, and that she was being tended to by her parents? He shuddered at the thought. He couldn't imagine any task more repulsive than to have to tend to that lifeless, soulless simulacrum of a human being. So, the entity didn't like that. . . .

Had it somehow intuited that well-bred girls reduced to that state were more likely to be hurried off into an institution, hidden away, out of sight, under the pretense that they had consumption or some other acceptable disease? Because the damned thing was right; that was *exactly* what a rich parent would do. Get her out of the way, lest rumors of insanity creep out and taint the rest of the family, ruining the chances for marriage of the rest of the brood. Well-bred girls might be cosseted, but they were, in many families, a commodity—useful in business negotiations, in making alliances, and in the case of the *nouveau riche,* useful in giving the family entrance into social circles they could never aspire to, otherwise. And once a commodity is spoiled, the best thing to do with it is destroy it—impractical in the case of one's daughter—or hide it.

And the number of such institutions, where inconvenient girls could be hidden away, discreetly, and given decent care, was of necessity rather small. And . . . available only to the rich. That was probably why the parents of the first girl were tending her themselves. That inanimate body wouldn't last a month in the asylums they could afford. She'd be left in a bed, and there she would stay, to slowly starve to death, or fall sick and die, given the indifferent attention attendants would give her.

Yes, the entity said, with overtones of satisfaction. *The consumed may be anything, so long as they are pure. The witnesses must be gathered.* The mental presence loomed over him, as the pillar of darkness had loomed over him, and he shrank into himself, although there was nowhere he could turn to hide from the thing in his mind. *You will do this.*

"Yes!" he blurted, though he had no idea *how* he was going to accomplish such a thing. Abduct an upper-class girl? *How?* It wasn't as if girls like that were sent off on errands. Oh, *maybe* he could find one shopping, or seeing sights, but that would be in the company of dozens of other people. He couldn't exactly clap a chloroform sponge over her face and drag her away!

Well, the entity had an answer for that, it seemed. *You will find a witness, away from her guardians. You will speak to her. If she speaks to you, I will work through you, and she will obey you and come with you.*

This both angered and terrified him. Angered him, because why hadn't the entity done this *before,* rather than put him and Alf to such risk? Why had it forced them to abduct girls, instead of helping them lead their victims away?

And terrified him, because . . . maybe it hadn't been able to reach out in that way until he'd fed it. But now that it had been fed once. . . .

Now that it had been fed once, it could not only reach him outside of the basement, it could work some form of mesmerization *wherever* he was. With a single feeding, it had strengthened exponentially.

What would it be like when it had fed three times? And four? Because it had said *"the witnesses will be gathered,"* which implied there were going to be at least three more abductions to go through with, and maybe more.

"How—" he quavered, and was not even able to come out with "—soon?" when it answered him.

No more than seven days.

Then he felt the thing leave his head, and he lay in his bed sweating and ice-cold. *Bloody hell. Bloody, bloody hell. I can't wait to hear what Alf has to say about all this. I wouldn't be surprised if he quits my service over it.*

But Alf, surprisingly, was philosophical. "We got two choices 'ere, guv," he pointed out over breakfast. "We does wut it says, an' it says it'll 'elp thin's go all smooth. An' mebbe it'll toss summat we kin use when it tosses out th' witness, by way of reward, loike. Or we run, mebbe go move inter yer mum's 'ouse, or even futher, crost th' Channel, an' 'ope it cain't reach us from 'ere." He stabbed meditatively at a sausage. "If me old guv'ner learnt me anythin', though, it's *niver go back on yer bargain wi' a devil-thin'.* Mebbe it cain't reach us. But moir loike, it can."

He thought about that. Thought once more about sending a letter to Alderscroft—anonymously this time—before fleeing.

But—"It's in my head, Alf," he said plaintively. "And it seems to be saying it can stay in my head no matter where in London I am."

Alf nodded. "So, on'y one choice then. Make th' best uv a bad bizness." He ate his eggs; obviously nothing about this was hurting *his* appetite. "'Bout them gels," he continued. "Concerts. Leck-chures. Opry. Thet's where ye'll find 'em. Ex-hibits. Mooseums. If thet thing c'n work through ye, we hain't gonna need t'work by night. We c'n work by day, or arternoon, anyroad. Find a likely gel. Talk to 'er, an' let th' thin' get inter 'er 'ead an control 'er. Bring 'er round t'where I'm wi' coach. Keep 'er in coach till dark, so's no one sees us comin' in'ere with a fancy kinda gel, then go out, get t'other kind. Easy-peasy. 'Specially if th' thin' is gonna 'elp us with both."

He felt some of his panic ebbing, now that Alf had put it all so sensibly. Well . . . of course, if the thing really *could* do what it claimed, Alf was right. And . . . if it couldn't, well, he'd dress the part, and all it would look like would be a rather good-looking young man in possession of wealth chatting up a pretty girl. If he was accosted by a parent, he could present a card and ask if he might be permitted to call some time. And if he couldn't get the ideal candidate within seven days, well, the thing would just have to make do with what he *could* abduct for it.

"Now . . . we hain't goin' out on this ternight," Alf said, emphatically. "Cuz thet thing'll jest say *get me more* an' give ye th' same seven days. No, yew an' me, we're gonna take our time. Yew go t'them places I tol' ye, hev a look around. Plan thin's. An' teach me t'drive. Oi'll look better on th' box than yew."

"We can start that today," he decided. "There's a new exhibit at the Grosvenor Gallery. I'll teach you how to drive wearing my shabby coat, then change into my good one when we get there. People see coachmen training stable-hands all the time."

"An' Oi'll chat up t'other drivers, so's they gets used t'seein' me an' the coach." Alf seemed to have a good answer for everything. "Oi'm reddy now."

"And I will be shortly." He rose and went to his room to get completely dressed. He had to admit he'd feel a lot better being *away* from this house. It was a very good thing that there was no one living in the upstairs flat—

—*Hmm. I should speak to the landlord and arrange to rent that flat as well, now that I won't have to answer for the extra expense to my ex-keeper.*

When he joined Alf some minutes later, he was dressed in his shabbiest overcoat and battered coachman's hat, with his good hat and coat over his arm. It was a bit of a walk to the stable, but the streets were clear, and the walk gave him a chance to get a good, solid grip on himself.

It took almost no time before they were on the road, and now the benefit of having a really *old* horse became apparent. The beast was very tolerant of Alf's initial fumbling. Its reaction to getting mixed signals was to slow down from an amble to a crawl. It didn't misbehave, or take advantage of having a novice on the box. Alexandre remembered only too well how his pony had done just that—including running away with him, a terrifying incident that had ended in a crash, a damaged pony cart, and a scolding from his father—as if it had somehow been *his* fault!

By the time they reached Kensington Gardens, Alf was feeling fairly confident in his ability to keep the horse going where he wanted it to go, so they stopped a block short of the place for Alexandre to get inside, change his coat and hat, and emerge at the Gallery as if he had been in there all along.

The exhibit was fairly crowded; fortunately the artist in question was *not* one of the sets that frequented Pandora's Tea Room, since Alexandre really did not want to be associated with the artistic crowd. He was here to simulate being a potential buyer, not an artist himself. He circulated among the groups examining the paintings in detail and reading their catalogs, though of course he was paying very little attention to the paintings and a very great deal of attention to the patrons.

Most young women here seemed to be in family groups, or with friends, which was disappointing. But he persisted in his quest, circulating through the crowd for the better part of three hours, until he began to get a sense of what to look for.

Especially when it occurred to him that he had been looking for women who appealed to *him*. But the entity in the basement did not really care about a pretty face, or a slim figure. And when he stopped looking for choice specimens . . . he discovered that there was a bit more available than he had thought.

The bluestocking with spectacles perched on her nose and her face set in a nearsighted frown, for instance. She seemed to be here completely on her own, and while she might be a trifle outside the age limit the thing had specified, he doubted that the entity would care. The mannish one in tweeds better suited to a stroll on a country estate than a visit to a gallery was here with a friend, but that friend went off to talk to the artist, leaving her alone. He probably could get a conversation going based on horses, and if the entity could work its mesmerism on her, then everything would be set. The ill-dressed creature who was clearly too fond of sweets with the bad complexion (and the too-tight corsetry making her pant for air) trailed behind a party of prettier girls, clearly along because she had to be there, not because she was wanted. All he had to do was separate her from the rest, and he'd probably be able to lure her off to a meeting later, even *without* the entity helping.

In fact . . . he was spoiled for choice, and he might well have tried his hand at one or more of them, if the gallery had been less crowded. There were too many potential witnesses who would be able to see him clearly right now.

When he had satisfied himself with his scouting expedition, he made a graceful exit out to where the private coaches waited and answered Alf's interrogative raised eyebrow with a nod of satisfaction. "We'll run a few errands, then return home," he told Alf quietly, before he got into the coach. "Let's see how you manage without me."

Alf managed very well without him; the old horse was utterly indifferent to crowded streets, noise, even urchins running right under its nose, just as long as Alf didn't ask it to move faster than that amble. One of the errands was to stop at the solicitors; he emerged from that meeting feeling fully satisfied. It had taken very little persuasion to convince the man that as a modest bachelor he really did not need the huge old house . . . the merest suggestion that the firm collect a commission from the sale was enough to clinch the bargain. He suggested that instead, he might rent—or better still, buy—the house he was in now, also for a commission, should the solicitor manage to buy. And after that, the transfer of additional money from the trust to his personal account was a mere bagatelle.

So the last few errands were stops at a wine merchant, Fortnum and Mason, and Harrod's, and the loading of the coach with several highly satisfactory hampers and bales and boxes. Pub meals and things put together by Alf had sufficed in the past, but eating and drinking well *were* some of the finer pleasures of life, and he and Alf deserved to enjoy them.

So at dinner, Alf got his first taste of several things he'd only heard of, and some he hadn't . . . and professed himself pleased and amazed. "That 'am, guv," he said afterward in wonder. "Oi niver knew 'am could taste loike thet."

Alexandre didn't bother to correct his calling *Prosciutto di Parma* by the vulgar name of "ham." "I'm very glad to discover you can appreciate such things, Alf," he replied, leaning back in his chair and savoring his after-dinner brandy. "As you pointed out, if we're going to be working hard for our guest, we deserve some luxuries. Now, I'd like you to apply your clever mind to what I observed at the gallery, and see if you come up with the same conclusions I did."

Alf listened carefully, brows furrowed, and when Alexandre was done, he nodded approvingly. "Yer learnin' t'find marks, guv. Oi'd'a picked them same ones. Oi'd'a gone fer th' ones what was alone, fust, an' if they didn' work, I'd'a gone fer the one trailin' the gaggle."

"Really?" Alexandre was surprised. "Why?"

"Cuz odds are, gel loike thet reads romantical books i' secret, loike. She's dreamin' 'bout some 'andsome bloke hack-chully *seein'* 'er, seein' 'ow she's nicer'n 'er sisters an' their friends. You oughter pick up a couple'a them kinda books; ye'll know jest what t'say t' a gel loike thet, then."

Alexandre felt fairly rocked back in his chair. "Alf . . . I knew you were clever, but I will be *damned,* man, if I had any idea you were that sharp!"

Alf snorted. "Learnt all thet off me old guv'ner. 'E was a one t'gull the gels, on'y 'e was arter somethin' other than them. Niver knew wut 'twas, but thet's wut got 'im in law trouble, I 'spect." He shook his head. "Rum old goat, was the guv'nor. 'E weren't 'arf as clever as 'e thought 'e were. Or ack-chully, mebbe 'e were as clever, but 'e weren't near careful enough. Clever is as clever does, but careful, thet'll go yew a lot futher than clever."

"Well, I think that I will wait one more day before trying the Gallery in earnest," he said after some thought. "I don't want the crowds to thin *too* much, but I don't want them as thick as they were today. That will give me a chance to pick up some of those silly novels and do my due diligence." He toyed with his brandy a moment. "And, I shall have to keep being careful in mind at all times. I don't know if that thing in the basement has any understanding of how many ways we can fail in this endeavor—and I don't know what it would do if we did."

Alf nodded. "A foine plan," he agreed. He cast a covetous eye on the wicker hamper with *F&M* emblazoned on the label. "A very foine plan. Naow, weren't there some sorta fancy puddin' in thet 'amper?"

Alexandre ambled up to stand beside another bespectacled bluestocking. This young woman had her hair scraped severely back and balled into a tight, hard knot at the nape of her neck. She did not acknowledge his presence. Together they gazed at a painting of the Downs. It was, he supposed, very fine. Everyone else who had gazed upon it had said so. For his part, he could not imagine why anyone would want a painting of grass and hills. "Have you ever been there?" he said aloud to the young woman beside him. It was an innocent enough remark.

"The Downs? No," she said, her tone cold.

"I suppose it is very fine, for its type, but this doesn't do the scene justice," he persisted. "The light—"

"I daresay," she replied, her words one step above freezing, and moved off briskly. She clearly wanted nothing to do with him, and there was no sign that the entity had made her more susceptible to him.

So much for the entity helping, he thought, with irritation. *It had better do a more competent job of helping me if it expects to get the sort of "witnesses" it wants.*

But he remained in front of the painting of grass, as if he had not just been rebuffed. It was in a good, central spot, about halfway through the Gallery. This was where people who were trailing behind their groups tended to get out of sight of them. And where people who wished others to think them "artistic" or "romantic" usually paused to gaze critically, or heave great sighs of admiration. Someone else would be along shortly. He had only to be patient.

And sure enough, after a few single males and two couples, along came a gaggle of girls—beautifully dressed, and obviously here not to view, but to *be* viewed. And they were trailed at a few steps distance by a wallflower, who was exactly the sort of thing he was looking for. Someone's cousin, perhaps; painfully plain to the point of being ugly, with a sallow, muddy complexion, untidy hair, with a hat pinned on anyhow. Her dress must have been borrowed; it hung on her skeletal frame, so poorly fitted she was managing to make a very expensive gown look dowdy. She was acutely embarrassed; perhaps by some of the nudes, perhaps by what the other girls were saying, perhaps by the fact that she was here at all, alternately blushing and going pale.

But, to his acute annoyance, as soon as they spotted him, he was surrounded by the butterflies, who begged to know his opinion of the painting of the Downs, and *were* the Downs like that, and *did* he know the artist? He realized at that moment he had made himself rather too good a target for girls like that, who were lagging behind their more fortunate sisters in the marriage market. Handsome, young, and without a sign of a wife or a fiancée, well dressed, he was exactly what *they* were here to find . . . it remained only for them to find out if he was titled or not, approximately how much money he had, and where it came from.

He was momentarily annoyed . . . but then decided to make the best of things, and allowed himself to be carried off with them as they continued to pretend to tour the Gallery. He had the feeling that if he let it slip, ever so slowly, that he was *not* in possession of a title, and his fortunes were modest, and, in fact, were due to being in trade. . . .

And within ten pictures, he managed to do just that, finishing with, ". . . and I rather fancy if you ever ventured into the kitchen, you'd see my bottles . . ." going on to describe how the lowly pressed-glass bottles and jars were made. He had never had occasion to be grateful for the many forced tours of the glass-works his father had made him take—but he was now. By the time he was finished, all the others had left him in front of a still life of slightly dyspeptic-looking vegetables crowned with a dead rabbit, with only the plain one (who he now knew was named Cynthia) still listening to him. He smiled down into her eyes, making it rather clear that he was perfectly happy with her company.

"I never knew all that, Christian," she said (he'd used a false name, of course). "I always thought bottles were blown by people." When she gazed up at him like that, she resembled a sad-faced hound with a pronounced overbite. Her teeth were appalling, and her chin a mere suggestion.

"Those that are for decorative use, like perfume bottles are," he told her. "And of course, those that are artworks in and of themselves are hand-blown by master craftsmen. But good, common, practical bottles, meant to last and be used, are pressed glass, mechanically blown into molds. I'm very proud that we make things people can depend on. People so rarely value virtues like dependability, don't you think, Miss Cynthia?"

She flushed, and gazed up into his eyes, mouth open a little. "Oh yes," she agreed fervently. "They so seldom . . . do. . . ."

And at that moment, he had the sensation of icy, cold hands reaching *through* him, and taking the girl's head between them. Her eyes glazed over, her mouth fell completely open, and it looked as if she was drunk or drugged.

"Why don't you come along with me, my dear," he said, taking her hand and tucking it into the crook of his arm. "Drop your head and look at the ground, so you don't trip." She didn't resist and obeyed him. With her head down, and her face hidden by the brim of her hat, she couldn't be recognized. And she didn't resist when he drew her along with him at a brisk walk, retracing his footsteps so they wouldn't run into that herd of inconvenient girls, heading for the entrance where Alf waited with the coach. The group she had been with probably would not miss her until they exited the Gallery, and maybe not even then.

As soon as they stepped outside the doors, Alf saw them coming and moved the coach along the line of waiting vehicles to meet them. Alexandre moved with deliberation and care, neither too fast nor too slowly, so that it looked as if he was aiding an elderly woman rather than a younger one. Under the guise of giving simple, courteous help, he practically lifted the girl into the coach. He followed her quickly and pulled the curtains down over the windows as Alf clucked to the horse and moved off.

The girl hadn't seated herself; evidently the entity couldn't control her *that* well. Instead, she was in a heap on the floor, which was just fine with Alexandre. As she lay there, unmoving, he bound her wrists and ankles, gagged her, and applied chloroform as Alf had instructed him, just in case. Then he rapped on the ceiling of the coach to let Alf know everything had proceeded according to plan.

Then he raised the curtains. The girl was out of sight, and they planned to amble along, doing nothing to excite any attention, until dusk, when they would head again to West Ham. Alf was convinced that it was a superior hunting spot, and Alexandre was inclined to agree with him.

He waited to see if the girl was going to awaken, and if she did, if the entity was still going to be in control. It was safe enough to allow her to regain consciousness now that she was gagged and restrained; even if she had been a trained fighter, the way he had her trussed up, she'd never be able to inflict the slightest amount of damage on him nor free so much as a single finger. And he was, he flattered himself, rather an expert at gagging someone so that nothing they uttered would be heard outside the confines of the coach. He'd taught Alf the right way to go about it, and neither of the first two girls they'd taken had been able to do more than utter a muffled squeak.

He did have quite a bit of practice in that sort of thing—although usually it was so that sound didn't penetrate room walls, not coach walls.

Eventually her eyes fluttered open. And he was enormously gratified to see, first, sense, then terror in them.

She wiggled uselessly, and vague, smothered sounds emerged from her, rather than the screams she undoubtedly wanted to produce. He leaned over in the dim gloom of the coach and put a finger to his lips.

"Hush," he said, as her eyes filled with tears and she began to cry. "You won't be alone for long. You're about to have a companion. And then I'm going to introduce you to an experience unlike anything you have ever imagined in all your life."

She shrank away from him, and he laughed at her. *You pathetic bint. Now I can have my revenge on you for being forced to stare at your repulsive face and pretend that I liked you.* "Oh, don't worry. I'm not the least interested in your pitiful virginity. An ugly little stick like you—I wouldn't want you if you were served to me on a golden platter and came with a knighthood and a manor."

Oh that did it, now she was terrified *and* humiliated, and began to weep. Excellent. In four sentences, he had utterly broken her. He leaned back in his seat and laughed quietly. Now this . . . if only he could have his enemies at his feet like this. People who had humiliated him, who had snubbed him, who had stood in his way. *This* was real power . . . the power to break the spirit, the power to break the heart.

Well, girls like this would do, for now. But . . . it was possible, given the reach the entity had now, that he could ask for revenge by way of reward.

He and Alf shared a sort of picnic while they waited for the sun to go down, parking the coach in a deserted yard by the river and giving the horse a bag of feed to keep it quiet. The girl continued to sob brokenly. It was delicious—both the meal and the girl they were resting their feet on. In fact, this was probably one of the most entertaining meals he had ever eaten.

Then, once the sun was below the horizon, they went on the hunt again, heading for West Ham. Not the same street—that would be too risky. He left the selection of the street and the selection of the girl up to Alf. He had pulled the curtains down so nothing could be seen of the interior of the coach, and had applied chloroform to Cynthia again, so she wouldn't be making any noises to disturb or alert their quarry.

He heard the sound of a girl's voice in the distance but growing nearer, calling a name. "Jackie! Jackie! Oh where *are* you?" He felt the coach slow and stop; heard Alf tap on the left-hand door with his whip. He opened that door, made sure he had the chloroform sponge in his right hand, and slipped around the back of the coach, crouching in wait.

" 'Ere, miss? Yew lookin' fer a liddle lad?" Alf called.

"Oh aye!" he heard—the girl sounded much more irritated than worried. "Jackie run off with his friends, and Mum wants him back right now! Did you see him?"

"Well Oi moighta," Alf replied. "I seen some lads down by riverbank. C'n yew come over 'ere an' tell me wut 'e looks loik?"

As the girl prattled details of her brother's clothing and appearance, Alexandre waited for the signal. And finally, it came.

"Well blimey," Alf heaved a huge sigh. "Hain't seed 'im."

Alexandre leapt from out of cover. The girl was *exactly* where she should have been, standing right below Alf where he sat on the coach box. His sudden movement, or perhaps the sound of him coming around the back of the coach, even though it was getting quite dark, caught her attention. She turned quickly, spotted him, and opened her mouth to scream.

That was when he clapped the sponge over her nose and mouth, and the involuntary intake of a huge breath, meant to power a shriek, instead sucked the sleep-inducing fumes deep into her lungs. She struggled, but only a little, and went limp. In moments she was in the coach too, and he with her. He shut the doors of the coach carefully, so as not to arouse any interest with a noise of slamming, and rapped on the roof. As Alf pulled away, he gagged and trussed her up as well, so adept at this that he could easily do it in full darkness.

And then, he leaned back into his seat, breathless, almost

giddy with relief and glee. They'd done it! They'd done it again!

It was full dark when they got back home, and it was child's play to carry the two girls into the flat and down into the basement without anyone seeing. At this time of night, everyone in this neighborhood was busy with supper. Alexandre suspected you would have to set a cannon off in the street to get their attention. This time he and Alf did not linger; since the entity didn't need their help, they just put the girls down beside the pool of darkness and got back up the stairs as quickly as they could. *He* didn't want to see the entity take its prey a second time, and, he suspected, neither did Alf.

Alf hurried out, to take the coach back to the stable, while he waited in the kitchen for the entity to summon him.

Finally, it did.

Come and take the witness, it ordered. Then nothing more. Even that short a contact made his skin crawl. He hurried back down the stairs to find what was left of Cynthia lying facedown on the stones. Once again, he ordered the empty husk up the stairs, out the door, and out into the street. Once again, he told it to keep walking until someone stopped it.

And once again, the thing walked mechanically off. He hurried back to his own door, after a quick glance around to make sure no one was snooping—but no one was. He watched the girl—or whatever it was, now—until it was long out of sight.

As he closed the door and waited for Alf, he wondered just how long the girl would walk this time. And was the entity going to hold him to blame if something happened to her—if she got run over by a cab or a cart, or someone with fewer scruples than he snatched her off the street to have his way with her?

No one will, he heard in his mind, and shuddered at the touch, at the cold of those words. *She is under my protection.*

He had no hope, of course, that this would be the last—
I need more, came the answer before the thought was complete. *Many more. More to strengthen. More to witness. You have seven days.*

Seven days.

11

NAN woke straight up from a sound sleep immediately when Neville *quorked* a quiet alarm call above her head.

As she had expected, it had taken several days for the last of Memsa'b's "medicine" to purge itself from Amelia's system. Amelia had looked . . . on edge tonight at dinner, as if she sensed there was something looming over her, and Nan had expected that tonight would be the night she fell into a vision. As a consequence, she had kept a single lamp burning low, just in case.

She was up out of bed and across the room to Amelia's bedside in moments, Neville fluttering in the soft half-dark to land on Amelia's headboard. Amelia lay in her bed, rigid, every muscle tense. Nan sat on the edge of the bed, reached out to cup Amelia's face in her hands, and she didn't even have to close her eyes; the moment she made mental contact with Amelia's sleeping mind, she found herself pulled immediately into Amelia's vision.

Literally pulled into the vision. Instead of being a mere observer, she found herself standing beside a rigid, statue-like Amelia in a horrific nightmare-scape of a ruined London, and she reached out and took Amelia's right hand without saying a word.

That broke the spell holding Amelia paralyzed; she jerked her head around to face Nan, eyes wide with shocked surprise. Her terrified expression eased, just a little, as Nan smiled reassuringly at her. Her hand clutched Nan's convulsively.

I'm here. And Neville is anchoring us. If anything threatens us, he can pull us out of this, she said into Amelia's mind. *You're not alone.*

Amelia did not answer in words, but her hand squeezed Nan's tightly as they both turned their attention to the scene in front of them.

The sky swirled with ever-moving clouds, low and ominous. Lightning lit them from within, but there was no thunder. If Nan were to make a guess about the time of day, she would have said "twilight," but there were no clues as to the actual time. It was not completely dark; there was a dim, apparently sourceless light. Shreds of mist moved among the ruined buildings around them, but how those wisps moved had little or nothing to do with the wind.

Nan could not tell what part of London they were in; once you got into the "newer" areas, places that had sprung up or gotten built up over the last half century, they all tended to look alike—streets of terraced houses, all built as a single block-long building, streets of houses set narrowly side-by-side, streets of blocks of flats, streets of shops with living quarters above them. She knew it was London because . . . she *knew* it was London. There was no doubt in her mind that it was anyplace else; the feeling was as certain in her as it was that the earth was round. This happened to be a street of terraced houses; a street that presented a single, block-long face, with identical doors all along it—but what appeared to be a single building was, in fact, broken up into separate homes, each of those doors leading into one of those homes. They were set very near the street, with only a narrow strip of lawn or garden between them and the thoroughfare.

But there were gaps in the row of terraced houses in front of them, like missing teeth. The rest of the houses were in various stages of decrepitude and overgrown with some evil cousin of ivy. The ivy swayed and rustled—again, like the mist, in a way that seemed to have nothing to do with the wind moaning through the ruins.

She felt the urge to walk up the street; in the middle, avoiding that ivy. She looked at Amelia and she could see Amelia felt the urge to move too. The girl was torn between wanting to flee and feeling impelled to move forward.

Remember, nothing can hurt us here. Neville can pull us out. And I . . . with an effort, she summoned the Celtic Warrior she had once been centuries ago, her bronze sword in her right hand, Amelia's hand still in her left. *I am not exactly unarmed.*

Amelia's eyes widened with startlement. But the sight of Nan in her bronze corselet, made from the armor of Roman soldiers she'd killed back then, seemed to put more heart in her. Together they walked down the center of the street, Nan staying wary, ready to fend off anything that threatened them.

But there was nothing this time, no tentacles reaching out of the shadows, no hint of other humans. Nothing but the moaning of a cold, bitter wind and the swaying of the barren trees and that evil ivy.

They came to the end of the row of terraced houses and entered into a section of houses and shops that were set a little apart from each other, with bits of yard in front and more walled backyards behind. These were in no better repair than the ones they had left behind them.

But one, at least, was in good repair. And it showed something like signs of life, although there was nothing about it that made Nan want to go knock on the door.

The house itself was faintly luminescent, a sickly blue ghostlight. There was a dim red light coming from the windows, and as they watched, a terrified girl burst out of the door, ran into the street and looked frantically up and down it before breaking into a run in their direction. From the little Nan could see of her, she looked to be fifteen or sixteen years old, dressed in a coat and woolen hat and decent frock of some dark color. She looked exhausted as well as terrified, and she stumbled as she ran.

But she hadn't gotten more than a few feet before the street opened up beneath her, and with a shriek, she dropped into darkness. And as soon as she was gone, the gaping hole closed.

The dim light faded, and shadows closed in around them. The vines seemed to reach out toward them, and Amelia gasped with fear.

That's enough. Neville!

There was a rush of enormous wings. Amelia screamed as something as big as a house swooped down out of the sky and a claw closed around her waist, another around Nan's. Before Amelia could do more than cry out, the gigantic raven thundered into the sky, aiming for a single bright light above them, which grew, and grew, and grew, until they flew into it and—

Nan opened her eyes to find Amelia clutching the hand that had been held against her cheek.

"I told you Neville would get us out," she said, matter-of-factly.

Amelia smiled weakly at her. "You did," she said softly.

"I think some warm milk with honey in it is in order," Nan replied, making an effort to sound calm and ordinary. "Will you be all right if I leave Neville with you?"

"Oh yes," came the heartening answer. "I do think he is my hero tonight!"

Neville pulled himself up and preened. "Thank you, pretty," he said, looking immensely pleased with himself.

Nan padded down to the kitchen in her wrapper and slippers, made some warm milk with honey and a touch of cinnamon, and brought up two glasses full—plus some sugarplums for Neville. He had certainly earned them. She returned to Amelia's room to find the girl with her arms full of purring raven, his head down against her chest as she gently scratched the back of his neck. She smiled a little as one eyebrow rose. "I brought the milk, and a treat for you, my pirate," she said, as Neville looked up, his eyes half-closed in pleasure.

She handed one of the glasses of milk to Amelia and put

the saucer of sugarplums on the floor for Neville, who hopped down off the bed and proceeded to stuff himself.

Amelia sipped the milk, color coming back into her pale face. Nan sat at the foot of her bed and picked up a shawl draped over the footboard to hand to her. She wrapped it around her shoulders with one hand.

"I think we should talk about what we saw while it's still fresh in our minds," Nan said calmly.

Amelia looked very much as if she would really rather not do anything of the sort, but nodded. "This felt like . . . now," she said. "Like the visions I had of those murders, as if it was happening right *now.*"

"I had the same impression. Did you recognize the area?" Nan asked.

"Only that it was the same area as the other vision. It didn't look like any place I've been before—well, except that it looks like a lot of places in London." Amelia sipped her milk with both hands wrapped around the glass like a child. "I didn't recognize the girl."

"I didn't think you would." Nan privately thought the girl had looked to be about the same class as the soulless creature Doctor Watson had had her examine. Was that significant?

"I think the plants were alive," Amelia said into the silence. "I mean, I think they were *thinking,* in a way. They hadn't noticed us at first, but when we got to that house, they had started to."

"I think whatever was in that house made the ground open up under that girl, and dragged her back inside," Nan replied, thoughtfully. Amelia shuddered, but nodded.

"I could feel that. I could feel it wanting to *eat* her." Amelia started to shake.

"I think we both got the same impressions," Nan replied, as Neville hopped back up on the bed and cuddled up to her, poking his head under her arm so she could put it around him. "And I think that is about all that is useful that we are going to decide tonight. Would you like me to stay here until you sleep?"

"Yes, please." Amelia drained the glass and gave it to Nan, hugged Neville, and slid back down under the covers. "But I don't think I'm going to be able to . . ."

Neville snuggled up next to her in the crook of her arm, laying his head along her shoulder. And Nan gave Amelia's mind a little, gentle *push* . . .

And her eyes fluttered closed, and in moments, she was asleep.

"Excellent. I am glad to see that trick works on her. You want to stay with her until we're sure she's not going to be pulled into another vision?" Nan asked Neville, who turned his head slightly to look at her with one bright, black eye.

"Yisss," the raven breathed, barely opening his beak.

Knowing Neville was now "on duty," and would wake her if she was needed, Nan got up, put both glasses on the bedside table, and sought her own bed.

But not to sleep. At least, not yet.

She closed her eyes and pored through her own memories, trying to find something in the landscape she might be able to identify precisely. If she could find something she could recognize later, she should be able to identify which borough of the real London the one in the vision corresponded to. She wasn't entirely sure why she was doing this, except that she had the vague feeling that if she could identify the place in the real world, they might find something there giving it a physical link to the world of the visions.

And if they could do *that,* they might be able to find out just what was happening to those poor girls.

Because she had the other, much stronger feeling that Robin had correctly identified the place in the visions as *another world,* one that paralleled the one she knew, and one that, somehow, was affecting people in the world she knew. This was not some horrific future . . . at least, it was not *yet* some horrific future.

One step at a time, she told herself.

But she wanted very much to ask Robin about this. And the Watsons. Both of them had spoken of other worlds. Both of them might be able to tell her if her feeling had any basis in reality.

So, chilling and horrific as it was, she kept working at the vision until exhaustion caught up with her, and eventually she fell asleep, and as far as she was aware, there was nothing in her dreams but the usual muddle of mismatched images she always had.

Fortunately, Amelia, too, slept undisturbed through the night.

Now that Sahib had turned over his import business to the management of a younger protégé—a former military man himself, with a knack for business and an eye for the sort of ornaments likely to be popular with the middle and monied classes alike—he had become an instructor at the school himself. As a result, he and Memsa'b took it in turns to eat meals with the students, in order to keep at least a semblance of decorum at mealtime. And it was Memsa'b's turn this morning. So this morning Nan and Sarah and the birds were having breakfast with him, instead of his wife. He listened with interest to Nan's detailed recitation of Amelia's vision last night.

"Well . . ." he said, when she had finished. "I prefer to keep unpleasantness until *after* eating, but this telegram arrived this morning for us." He reached into the breast pocket of his coat, pulled out a folded piece of paper, and read the contents aloud. "'*Second girl found Battersea. Coming afternoon. Watson.*' So, given what you saw last night, it seems that your impression that this was happening in the present was absolutely correct, Nan. And your initial conclusion, that Amelia's visions had a concrete reflection of reality rather than a symbolic one, was also true. However, I do not think we should jump to the conclusion that the girls are being pulled into this world of the vision. I think it more likely that the vision reflects the horrific effects that something from that world is having on them in the real world. I would suggest a convocation in the greenhouse this afternoon."

"So you also think we should summon Robin," Sarah stated. "I agree. This *has* to concern him, if something from another world is reaching into this one."

Nan kept her own opinions to herself, although Sahib's

idea was probably more likely than hers. That ruined London—well it *could* reflect the last thoughts of the victims as their souls were being torn from their bodies.

Which begged the question, of course . . . if that was true, what did this thing want with souls in the first place?

"I will confess I cannot imagine what possible use Memsa'b and I will be," he added, "But I think we should be there, if only to have another set of brains to work on the problem."

"We'll go talk to Roan and have him take a message to Robin," said Nan, pushing away from the breakfast table. Then she paused. "I would like one other thing on the agenda for this convocation. Whether or not we should continue to use Amelia like this. It seems . . . unfair."

"In that case, I think we should include Amelia in the discussion," Sahib replied. "As has been rightly pointed out, she is more than old enough to make her own decisions about when and how her abilities are to be used."

With a nod of agreement, Nan and Sarah left the breakfast room and went down to the workshop, which was just off the stable. Roan was nowhere in sight, but they didn't expect him to be. He seemed to have a much more "traditional" view of how a hob should behave than Durwin did.

The signs of Roan's presence were quite pronounced however. The workshop was a hundred times tidier than it had ever been when Nan and Sarah had been at the school. Every tool was in its proper place. Paintbrushes were cleaned and neatly arranged. Paint cans were tightly capped and arrayed according to color. There was an actual painting *station*, an area with its own workbench away from where all the sawdust was. Instead of half-mended toys being distributed haphazardly about, there were toys in a logical progression of repair, with repainting being the last of the stages. The air was full of scents: the sharp, oily smell of paint and lacquer, the pleasant smell of sawdust, the tang of drying glue. One of the rocking horses that they had last seen in sorry shape, mane and tail gone, paint chipped and faded, one of the rockers splitting, now stood on the workbench in splendor. It had a brand-new horsehair mane and tail of shining, silky black and a real leather saddle, bridle, and reins. Both rockers were sound, and it was in the very last stages of painting, lacking only the fine details of the eyes, nose, ears, and hooves. In fact, to Nan's eyes, the grand chestnut steed would have looked finished, and she only knew Roan was going to add details because of the array of small paint cans and fine brushes beside it on the workbench.

"This is amazing," Sarah said, echoing her thoughts. "The craftsmanship is. . . ."

"Spectacular," Nan finished for her. "I hope there is time enough this morning with all this work going on to let Robin know that we urgently need to meet him in the greenhouse around teatime." If Roan was going to keep to the traditional ways of his people, she would certainly do him the courtesy of the same and pretend he didn't exist.

She waited for an acknowledgement—not sure what she was waiting for—when a bell behind her rang twice. Or at least, it sounded like a bell. She had not seen any bells at all in the workshop.

"I'll take that as a yes," said Sarah. Nan nodded, and the two of them left the workshop so that Roan could get on with both his work and carrying their message to the Great Elemental that called himself Robin Goodfellow.

The Watsons arrived a little after luncheon—to Nan's surprise, they appeared on the doorstep in a coach, a small one suitable for two or three, with Alderscroft's crest painted discreetly on the door. This coach was a good bit more old-fashioned than Alderscroft's usual coach, and nowhere near as ostentatious. She ran out to meet them as the coachman opened the door for them.

"Where on earth did that come from?" she asked. "I mean, other than from Lord A?"

"Apparently his Lordship has more than one vehicle, as I should have known all along," Mary Watson replied as John handed her out. "His servants at the Hall use this one, along with the estate wagon, several carts, and for all I know, a traveling coach. He's given us the loan of this one for the duration, since it has mostly been used only for conveying the butler, housekeeper, and his valet to church on Sundays, and ordered us to telegraph if we need the larger one."

"What does Holmes think of all this?" Nan asked, as they brought the Watsons to Sahib's study, "And do you need luncheon?"

"He's utterly intrigued, and yes, please," John replied, seating Mary first, before taking a spot himself. "I've prevailed on Dr. Huntley at Hampstead Heath Hospital to take in the first girl, even though her family cannot possibly afford his services. I pointed out that having two such patients doubled our chances of finding a cure." He smiled thinly. "I will not pretend that I did not exert the gentle threat of Sherlock paying a visit, then followed it with the inducement of Lord Alderscroft being interested in the case."

Mary gave him an admonishing look. "I think he was persuaded without that, dear. Underneath it, Dr. Huntley *is* a good doctor and he saw the advantages of having two such girls there. After all, this means he can try different treatments on them at the same time."

Nan held her peace; she had a very good idea which of the two girls was going to get the "benefit" of the more drastic treatments. Which would possibly have made a moral difference, had there been anything like a human spirit in either of them. As it was . . .

As it is he might just as well be experimenting on a pair of sausages.

Selim himself arrived at just that moment with a tray. He had begun to open his mouth, probably to apologize for the scant luncheon, when Watson forestalled him. "Ah Selim, excellent, thank you. How thoughtful of you! A couple of plates of curry are exactly what we need after that cold drive. You must share Memsa'b's mind reading talents!"

"Not at all, Doctor, I am glad the selection pleases you," Selim replied, with great dignity. He left the tray on a small table between the Watsons, and took his usual spot, standing behind Sahib's desk.

The man himself arrived a moment later with his wife. When everyone was settled, John Watson began the full story, interrupted only by spoonfuls of curry and rice or sips of good hot tea.

"This girl was found very near where the other was, by the local constabulary again. Having had one girl wandering witlessly about already, they immediately took her to a hospital instead of the police station—although," he added a little sourly, "I imagine the fact that she was dressed expensively and extremely well didn't hurt. And they sent around to the rest of London to see if there was a missing girl matching her description. There was. Cynthia Denniston, a niece of Lord Denniston, had been missing since a group led by Lord Denniston's oldest daughter went on a visit to the Grosvenor Gallery. She was last seen in the company of a well-dressed young man, whose name the other girls did not remember, but they thought he made money in some manufacturing trade. Lord Denniston was quite adamant that Cynthia would never have gone off with a stranger of any sort, much less a strange man. The girls were adamant that no man, especially not one as good-looking as this one had been, would ever be interested in Cynthia."

"But that's a couple of assumptions that don't hold up, if we assume this man wanted her for—for whatever occult purpose is leading to these girls ending up as prey," Sarah pointed out. "He could have overpowered her, after all."

"And yet, the guards at the Gallery and the various coachmen and cabmen waiting outside are absolutely certain that no man of any description carried off a girl who was struggling, or fainting, or anything suggesting foul play." Watson held up his hand, as Memsa'b looked about to speak. "Yes, Memsa'b, I know you are about to point out that someone with *your* talents could easily overpower the girl's mind and get her to go with him. Someone with the more mundane ability at mesmerism could do the same—as could virtually any Master and many magicians. This is merely information so we can eliminate outright abduction-by-force."

"Of course," Memsa'b replied. "Do continue, Doctor."

"Naturally I said nothing of this to the police, nor to Lord Denniston." He shrugged. "It's really of no use to suggest anything in the way of the mystical to the police, it would only make them think I'd taken leave of my senses."

"Did Dr. Hunter call on you again?" Sarah asked.

"No, actually," John told her. "It was Sherlock who brought me in this time, and Sherlock who was brought on the case first, instead of the other way around. Denniston sent for him as soon as he learned the girl had been found, and I came with him. Sherlock suggested mesmerism, which . . . honestly, is not out of the question, and the police did not disagree with that notion, which is broad-minded of them." He made a face. "Then again, Lord Denniston jumped on the notion like a cat on a fat mouse, and the police are eager to please him."

"So we are looking for a Svengali?" Memsa'b hazarded.

"One who is also some manner of magician," Watson reminded her, and frowned. "To return to the narrative, none of the cabmen remembered driving away with a girl and a young man, so he would have had to walk or come by private coach."

"You said Sherlock has some notion—one that does not correspond to the girls' fate as soulless husks," Nan prompted him.

"Well . . . that is not entirely true. Sherlock's theory actually *might* explain their condition," Watson admitted. "He mentioned something called *zombies.* Haitian sorcerers are supposed to create them out of the dead. Of course, Sherlock scorns the notion that they are actually reanimated corpses. Holmes posits that those sorcerers actually poison their prey ahead of time and 'resurrect' the corpse after it's buried. Their behavior, which he believes is caused by severe brain damage due to the poison, is alleged to be very like that of the girls we have in custody—nearly mindless, they will do exactly what they are told to do until they are told to stop. They can't perform complicated tasks, but simple ones, like plowing, fetching water and wood, simple cleaning tasks, they can. And whether Holmes is wrong and the sorcerer actually makes a corpse rise, or whether he is right and the sorcerer administers a drug that essentially wipes the mind blank — perhaps even stops the heart for a time — the process would give us something that is virtually identical to these girls." He put his plate aside and drank the last of his tea. "To be honest . . . I think he might be on to something."

"But *why* would someone in London go about abducting girls, turning them into these creatures, then turn them loose again?" Sarah demanded. "I can see many reasons, most of them heinous, for the first two — but why set them free to wander the streets? And if an immoral and unscrupulous person had such creatures at his mercy, why were they not interfered with in any other way?"

"Well, that's the sticking point," Watson admitted. "And if the intention was to have helpless women that would satisfy one's carnal desires, poor Cynthia is a terrible selection for that purpose. She is . . . exceedingly plain."

"Perhaps she was the only one he could separate from the herd," Nan pointed out. "And where I come from, it isn't a woman's *face* that men care about when they intend pleasuring themselves. I've often heard them tell each other *Don' matter if she looks loik a monkey. Jest put a bag over 'er 'ead.*"

Sahib and Memsa'b were used to Nan's occasionally earthy and utterly honest pronouncements, but Selim coughed, Mary blushed, and Watson grew quite red in the face. Nevertheless he acknowledged the truth of her words. "Fair enough, Nan — but Sarah is right. Remember that neither girl was outraged, and the first one was quite a pretty young woman."

"And at some point his power over them faded, and he needed to restrain them conventionally before he rendered them into what they became," Mary reminded him.

"Ah, yes, that's correct," John agreed. "Both had ligature marks on their wrists and ankles, and the signs that they had been forcefully gagged."

"So at the moment, it looks as if the same man took them both," Sahib concluded.

"Exactly. And since he did nothing physical to them that we could discover, one can only conclude that either he is performing some sort of occult or chemical experiments on them, or—" John paused. "Well, I am at a loss for the *or*. Sherlock is going to explore the *zombie* theory; he's looking for young men—since the last person Cynthia was seen with was a young man—who have recently been to Haiti, Jamaica, or the Bahamian Islands. He is also making enquiries about mesmerists, but that will be a great deal more difficult to track down. We, of course, will explore the theory that they have had some sort of dreadful encounter with the occult."

"If this man has his own carriage . . . it would have made the first abduction that much easier, not to mention the second," Nan mused.

Sarah's expression darkened. "You do realize that these two girls may only be the ones we *found,* don't you?" she asked. "He could have abducted more—girls vanish from the streets of London every day, and in places like West Ham and Battersea the police assume they have run off with lovers—and in worse places, the police don't look hard for them at all."

Mary nodded. "He could still have other girls—or he could have told them to walk into the Thames."

"He deserves the death of a thousand cuts," Selim said, a growl in his voice. "Whoever he is, even if he were my brother. I would deliver him to his destiny with my own hand."

"We have to catch him first," Sarah reminded him.

"We have to prove it's a *him,* first," Nan pointed out. "Cabmen were only asked about a young man with a girl. They weren't asked about a *woman* with a girl. And Cynthia wouldn't have many qualms about going off with a woman who struck up a friendship with her, especially if she'd been subjected to snubs all day by her cousin and her cousin's friends."

"By Jove . . . you're right about that," John Watson said, looking stricken. "That never occurred to me."

All four of the women exchanged a telling look. *I'll bet*

Sherlock has already thought of that, Nan thought to herself. *I don't think he will ever underestimate a woman. Not these days, anyway.*

They all dove into the school's occult library—paying particular attention to the "restricted" books kept in Sahib's study. They didn't find anything by the time teatime came around and they needed to move to the greenhouse to meet with Robin.

Then again, they hadn't really expected to. The Hartons had already gone over those books, and they generally dealt with the occult in the East, India specifically, or in Britain, Ireland, Scotland, Wales, Cornwall, and the Isle of Man. There was nothing about the Caribbean Islands at all. And not a hint of anything in any of the others that could leave someone mindless . . . or soulless.

Robin was already waiting for them in the greenhouse, very sober, very adult, with no trace of his regular humor. In fact, he looked and acted like the Great Elemental that he was, a prince among his kind, even though he was wearing a quite simple tunic, trousers and boots. When each of them had finished expounding what he or she knew to him, he shook his head.

"The City confounds my magic," he said. "I can't watch over it as I can a stretch of woods or fields. I've not sensed anything, because there's *too much* to sense, and I have tried, oh, I have tried. I fear I'll be of more use to you when you find the cause, not in finding the cause itself." He looked into their faces, mournfully—Nan had never seen him sad. Angry, yes, furious in fact. Somber. But never sad. "I feel as if I am failing you, and failing England."

"Well, have you got any notion as to whether any of our theories is the right one?" Mary Watson asked, finally. "Because that would at least give us somewhere to start."

He licked his lips thoughtfully. "If I were to say anything, it is that I think Nan has the right of it. But . . . that could be because I am what I am, and I see things directly."

He shrugged. "The hospital is at Hampstead Heath, aye? That's an easy place for me to go." He fished in a pocket and pulled out a talisman of twigs tied together with red thread and handed it to John Watson. "When next you go to have a look at those girls, put this someplace in their room where it won't be cleaned away. I'll come and look in on them myself and see what I can see." He tapped his temple with his finger. "After all, I can see farther into a millstone than most."

"So you can," Watson agreed, and pocketed the talisman. "If you would do that, I could at least be certain we'd left no stone unturned."

Robin made a little half bow. "Then I'll do my best." He straightened. "And for now, since there's little enough I can do, I'll be gone. I'll be having a word with those creatures that can still dwell in Londinium; especially the ones in the places where the girls were lost and the girls were found. We'll at least have a few more eyes about, and ears to the ground."

And before they could thank him, he faded into the grapevines and was gone.

Mary Watson sighed. "I wish our Elementals were of more use. My sylphs would be willing enough, but I doubt they would be able to remember what it was they were to watch for for more than a day. I could put a compulsion on them to remember—but that would be a *compulsion,* and they'd rebel, as rightly they should."

"Well, I will be the last person to tell you to violate their trust with such a thing," Sahib told her. "You have a covenant with them; breaking such a contract is a terrible thing to do."

"And my water creatures are fundamentally useless in this case," John admitted. Then he got a thoughtful look on his face. "I could try scrying—but into the past. I know where the girls were last seen—I could see if I can find them at that point, and follow them."

"Have you ever done that?" Nan asked him.

He shook his head. "No, but I know it can be done, and I can at least try."

Sahib looked at each of them in turn, thoughtfully. "All right, then. Let's try that first, in controlled conditions, with all of us guarding you. If you can't manage this, we'll know. And if you can—you'll be well protected."

"To your study, then?" Watson asked.

Sahib nodded. "Indeed. And if nothing happens, we'll try to think of something else."

We're going to have to think of a great many "something elses" Nan thought as they all headed back to the study. *Because so far we have a history of running into a great many brick walls. . . .*

12

As expected, the entity—whose voice had become disturbingly strong, although it was still laconic—gave Alexandre another seven days to produce two more victims. But now that he knew just how easy it was to get what the thing wanted (at least with the entity's help), Alexandre intended two things. The first was to take his time about it. There was no point in rushing right out and obeying the damned thing when it always gave him the same seven days. He'd worked hard, and by Jove he deserved some time to enjoy himself.

The second was that from now on, he needed to be especially careful. By this point the police had certainly taken notice. Four abducted girls in the course of two weeks, two still missing and two turning up witless—that was certainly going to wake up even the sleepiest police. And that gaggle of idiot girls in the gallery would *certainly* have told their papas that the ugly wench had last been seen in his company. He doubted they remembered the false name he'd given—they seemed to have more hair than wits—but the authorities would be looking for someone like him at the Grosvenor Gallery by now. And given how rapacious that lot had been, the one thing they *would* remember was that he had said he was in trade.

So, he should definitely change his hunting ground, and possibly his style. Alf had suggested the opera, and it occurred to him that although young ladies were unlikely to be allowed to attend the theater at night unchaperoned, they were very likely to be permitted to attend a matinee, which were usually Thursdays and Saturdays. Armed with that, the day after the second hunt, he perused the theatrical advertisements.

There were, on offer, only two productions he thought likely to attract the sort of prey he was hunting: the latest Gilbert and Sullivan production, and a production of *Hamlet*. Of the two . . . he rather thought *Hamlet* was the better choice. For one thing, it was likely to attract Very Serious People, and judging by the favorable reception the entity had given the odious Cynthia, the hunting would probably be very good there. The entity had so far preferred a hideous wench with pretensions to intellect over a pretty girl of ordinary intelligence. For another, having passed himself off as a man in the trades on the last hunt, it was time to put on a different guise, and he was, after all, an actual *poet* with a published book. He just had to remember not to mention the name of the book to anyone but the potential victim.

And to clinch things, there were plenty of tickets still available for the Shakespeare; not so many for the operetta.

So, now he had a hunting ground and part of a plan. Things were going very well.

The second day after the last hunt, he got a note from the solicitor that he opened over breakfast, thinking it was some trifle about his mother's estate.

Instead, it was a note congratulating him. The solicitor had caught Alexandre's landlord in a moment of weakness. The note informed Alexandre of the speedy purchase of the house entire, and at an exceptionally good bargain. The key to the flat upstairs was enclosed.

He now owned the property. He would never again need to fear a landlord's inspection, or someone spying on him from the flat above. Potentially . . . potentially if he was able to round up more than two victims, he could store them in the flat above. Or . . . he could outfit the flat above to suit his particular fantasies, and never again concern himself that a casual visitor to his flat might stumble over something incriminating.

Alexandre stared at the note in astonishment. Alf noticed his slightly stunned gaze after a moment. "Wuts that, guv?" Alf asked at last.

He uttered a shocked laugh. "It's the key to the upstairs flat. I own the entire house!" He reread the short note, shaking his head. "This is . . . well frankly hard to believe. I didn't even know it was possible to purchase a house in so short a time. It seems—"

"Loik magic?" Alf asked shrewdly. "Moight be. Thet ald toad wut use'ta come check up on yew's gone. An yer old mum popped off. Ever think hit moight be—" Alf nodded at the floor, and emphasized the nod with the poke of his fork downward. "Ye niver know."

"I . . . suppose it could be . . ." If so, the entity was granting what he needed even before he could ask for it, which, on the one hand, was extremely gratifying, and on the other . . . a bit worrisome. *How* had the thing been able to influence his mother, or that solicitor, or the landlord? It couldn't physically move beyond the basement—and as far as he knew, it couldn't exert any mental control if he wasn't the medium for it.

"Or, could be co-inky-dink," Alf continued with a wink. "Landlord ain't bin hable t'rent thet flat fer over a year naow, an' we both know 'e's got a weakness fer gin, 'orses and 'ores. Yer mum coulda popped off any time, wut with all the patent medi-cines. Them things is 'alf poison. An thet old toad coulda been robbed an' rolled inter Thames. All perfukly normal, aye?"

"True enough." He shook off his feelings of vague alarm. "Alf, I want you to scout out the Palace Theater for me for the next couple of days. That will be our next hunting ground. I want you to find a place to park the coach where it won't be out of place but also won't be easy to see. We'll be hunting at the afternoon matinee, so like the gallery, we can't count on shadows to conceal what we're doing."

"Sure 'nough, guv," Alf said agreeably. "What say to I bring back a couple girls?"

Alexandre grinned, all concerns about the entity forgotten. "I'd say you were reading my mind."

Alexandre had carefully dressed in his best "poetic" clothing; a velvet brown jacket, shirt with a soft, floppy collar rather than the stiff, starched object so *de rigueur* for a businessman, a soft garnet-colored silk scarf instead of a tie, brown corduroy trousers, and a hat with a wide brim, as Tennyson was known to wear. Over it all, instead of a coat, he flung a beaver-lined cape. And off he went to the theater.

He had Alf let him out about a block from the theater and strolled the rest of the way, making sure he looked unhurried. It occurred to him, as he attempted to survey the faces of his fellow theatergoers without looking as if he was staring, that it would not be a bad idea to invest in some false moustaches and beards. Perhaps even a wig or two. The more he changed his appearance, the easier it would be to elude scrutiny. And of course, there were several starving young actors among the habitués of Pandora's Tea Room; it would not be hard at all to get them to talk about roles, lead that into a discussion of preparing for the role, then laughingly ask them where they *found* such things as moustaches and wigs, as if one were more likely to find a roc egg or a phoenix feather than false hair in this city.

He dragged his attention back to the task at hand. He had decided that he would take his ticket up in the first or second balcony; he was just as likely to find a bookish girl up there as down in the more expensive seats, and far more likely to find one that was here by herself.

The one thing he didn't want was another bohemian. He was under absolutely no illusions as to the probable state of their "purity." But it was vanishingly unlikely that

a musician, painter, or writer would turn up at a Shakespearian matinee performance in a normal gown. Half of
the fun the bohemian set got out of turning up in public was
in scandalizing people with their wild, unfashionable garb.

So he took a seat at the back of the first balcony, the end
of the middle row, where he got a good view of everyone
else in it—and since he had arrived as early as possible, he
could observe them as they came in and took their seats.

There was a party of half a dozen schoolchildren with
what he assumed was a teacher. They were wildly excited
and at the same time on painful best behavior—he assumed
this must be a treat for good behavior or good marks in
their literature studies. They took the middle of the first row
and draped themselves over the balcony rail, absorbing
everything.

I shall have to be careful of them, he decided. *I should do
nothing to attract their attention. If police track my victim
back to this theater, and come to find out about a gaggle of
children, they might remember me better than an adult would.*

After that came a fairly steady parade of the usual sort
of theatergoers for a Saturday matinee: one or both parents
with child or children, older couples without children,
young couples without children, old men alone, old ladies
alone, a handful of Serious Young Men by themselves, and
to his relief, a handful of Serious Young Ladies who also
arrived on their own. He concentrated his attention on
these, considering what (if anything) of their personality
was on display.

Finally, just as the house lights dimmed, he made his selection. Getting up silently, he paused at the back of the balcony for a moment, then made his way down to his victim,
who was sitting on the aisle of the right-hand row, halfway
down the section. Tapping her on the shoulder, he whispered, "I beg your pardon, but I believe I have a seat just
past you, miss. If you would like, I can switch with you to
avoid any inconvenience."

She got up, all aflutter, but moved down two seats. He
took the one she had vacated. And there they sat, all through
the first act.

The Hamlet was an understudy, and apparently he was under the impression that a good Shakespearian actor chewed as much scenery as he could, because his overacting was—at least to Alexandre's practiced eye—appalling. He rolled his eyes so wildly in the Ghost scenes that they could even see the whites of his eyes in the balcony. And while it was certainly easy to hear his lines, he bellowed them so, he had so much vibrato at the ends of his words that he sounded more like an opera singer than an actor.

He knew he had a hook with which to catch this little fish when he heard her stifling giggles after the first ten minutes or so. When the house lights came up at the end of the first act, and she didn't immediately rise, he leaned back in his seat and groaned.

"If I had known this was the Christmas Panto version of *Hamlet*, I wouldn't have come," he said aloud, but in a voice just loud enough to carry to her seat and no further. "They should be paying *us* to sit through this atrocity."

She glanced over at him, and smiled. "He really *is* dreadful, isn't he?" she said. "But the others are rather good and the Ophelia is quite fine, so I am determined to suffer through this Hamlet."

"Even though my ticket was a gift, I would flee this place, but it is warmer here than in my garret, and in the face of your bravery, I shall keep you company." He made a little half bow. "Alexandre Harcourt, at your service, milady. We shall whisper rude things to one another under his howls."

"Katherine Dalton," said his victim, with a wry smile. "Are you a poet, an artist—no you cannot be an artist, there is no paint under your fingernails—"

A clever one, this. I won't cozen her with words. It will have to be the entity. "A poet, with a single slim volume to my name. You won't have heard of it," he said.

And he didn't expect that she would answer otherwise, but it still stung when she replied, frankly, "No, I'm afraid I don't recognize your name. But I shall order it at the bookseller, on the strength of our mutual detestation of bad acting."

She could have pretended she knew it. That would have been polite and ladylike. Just out of pure spite, he was about to prod the entity to exert its power over her and get her under his control right then and there—

—but just as he thought of that, he heard the thing's cold voice in his head. *There is danger. Convince her to go outside.*

And at that point it was too late to go outside. The bell rang for the second act, and people began filing back in to take their places. So he was reduced to trading whispered quips with her every time Hamlet spoke a line. He *almost* had second thoughts when she said at one point, "I do believe Ophelia drowns herself to get rid of his voice in her ears," but reminded himself that he had no more business getting fond of his chosen target than a wolf had in getting friendly with a lamb. *She's just a girl with pretensions of intellect.*

When the lights came up after the second act and she showed no signs of moving, he said, "I really cannot bear this any longer. I must flee, before I begin hurling my boots at the stage. Would you consent to join me for tea? My pockets may not be deep, but they will extend to tea and cakes for two."

And when he rose, so did she. "I'm really just here because my mother and her bridesmaids are having their fittings, and I was told I was in the way," she said frankly. "Tea sounds lovely."

He offered her his arm, and she took it, and they made their way down to the lobby, weaving a path through the people who had gathered at the refreshment counter for lemon squash for the children, and for the adults, something much stronger. They claimed their cloaks at the cloakroom and left through the nearest exit. "Why were you in the way?" he asked holding the door open for her. "Aren't you in the bridal party?"

She made a face. Now that she was in daylight he saw she had brown hair, brown eyes, and a face that resembled a very eager rabbit. He fancied she was trifle shortsighted, as there was a line between her brows that made him think she squinted a lot. But there was nothing timid or rabbit-like about her answer. "My mother would rather people not be reminded that she is old enough to have a daughter who came out last year," Katherine said frankly, and with more than a touch of acid in her tone. "I have been told to sit in the back of the church and not draw attention to myself. For this, I am being rewarded with the liberty to do anything I care to between waking and sundown, every day until the wedding. And, possibly after. If women were allowed to attend University, I'd be perfectly contented." The implication was that she considered attending theater matinees and browsing bookshops to be very thin fare compared to a University education. *Oh, one of* those. *She probably wants women to have the vote as well.*

It was snowing again, and the fat, white flakes starred her beaver cloak and his woolen one. "Hence, *Hamlet?*" he responded.

"I should have chosen *Iolanthe,*" she admitted. "I — "

They were about half a block from the theater, and that was when he felt the entity moving through him. His hands and his insides went as cold as the street pavement. He felt the thing brush up against his mind, and felt his gorge rise in response. Katherine's face lost all animation, and she stopped speaking in mid-sentence. He smiled to himself, even though the entity's touch chilled him worse than the winter wind. "Put your head down, Katherine," he said. "Walk normally with me."

She obeyed, and he led her down the street, taking care to keep out of the way of others to avoid attracting their attention. But the snow was in his favor; people hurried along, eager to get into shelter, and not paying any attention at all to what was at first glance a perfectly ordinary, well-dressed, if a trifle bohemian, couple.

Alf had parked the coach down an alley, precisely where he said he would be. Together they lifted Katherine inside, and Alexandre followed. He closed the doors and pulled the shades — then, taking no chances, administered the chloroform and bound and gagged her. Alf had done some work on the coach seats, adding stout straps under the cushions and bolted to the floor so that their prizes could be strapped in for added security. When Katherine was nicely trussed up to his liking, he laid her on the seat opposite his and buckled her in, around her chest, waist and legs. Then he tucked a rug around her, to make her look like a bundle of goods he had just bought. Just in case, for some unknown reason, someone got a glance inside the coach.

Alf stopped once, and after an interval, tapped on the door and opened it, handing him a paper of hot chestnuts, a meat pie that was also still warm, and a bottle of beer. "If you've got the same, and we're parked out of the way, you might as well join me," he told his man, and moved over on the seat to give him room. Alf was nothing loath.

"Snow moight make it 'ard t'catch our second coney t'night, guv," he said, taking a huge bite of his pie and following it with half the beer. "Oi 'ad me a ideer. Could go out alone an' snatch a beggar-brat."

Alexandre followed his example. He had to hand it to Alf; the man knew the best places to get ready-made food in all of London. This was a good meaty pie, with just enough gravy to keep it from being dry. "Let's give West Ham a try anyway," Alexandre advised. "If we haven't got one by full dark, we can take this one back to the house and I'll guard her while you look for another option."

But Alf was right. The snow kept everyone inside. By the time they got to West Ham in the dusk, there was no sign of anyone on the street—and Alexandre soon realized that if they drove the coach through the borough for much longer, it was going to be conspicuous. With not a single other vehicle out, the coach stood out like a fish in a flowerbed. After they'd traversed up one street and down another, and he'd given Katherine another dose of chloroform, he tapped on the roof. Alf opened the roof hatch to peer down. In the last light, he was little more than a black silhouette against the charcoal sky.

"We oughter—" Alf began.

"Go home, or people will start to notice us, I know," Alexandre completed for him. "You were right. We'll try something else. Maybe something will turn up on the way home."

With a grunt of agreement, Alf closed the hatch and clucked to the horse, who resumed his plodding pace. Alexandre sat back in his seat and pondered several things.

First . . . how many of these "witnesses" did the thing need? He *hoped* it was three; three was the first number generally associated with magic. Three wishes, misfortune comes in threes, Death knocks three times . . . somehow, though, he doubted it. Five would be more likely. Or seven. He hoped fervently it wasn't nine; five would be hard, seven harder still, and nine? The police would be frantic, the papers would have got hold of it somewhere between five and seven, and there would be guards and police everywhere that one of the girls had disappeared from. He'd have to leave London entirely in order to find victims.

And most important of all, no female of any age of a good family would be out alone. If a girl couldn't get a male escort, she'd go with a gaggle of friends. Could he handle more than one, even with the entity's help? He didn't think so.

Suddenly the coach stopped, and he heard Alf fling himself off the box. He made sure Katherine was still sleeping, then flung open the door of the coach just in time to see Alf pull down a fleeing street urchin into a snowbank. He rushed to Alf's assistance; Alf had the brat by the ankles, and the little wretch was flinging chunks of snow at Alf's face. Alexandre flung himself bodily over the boy's torso and was rewarded by several vicious elbow-blows to his ribs. He gritted his teeth on the pain, and awkwardly beat one-handed at the boy's head; Alf let go of the brat's ankles, scrambled to his feet, slipping in the snow, and administered a scientific blow to the boy's head with his favorite cosh. The brat went limp.

Alexandre got to his feet, looking warily up and down the street to see if the ruckus had attracted any attention. They were still inside the bounds of Battersea, in one of the areas of waterfront warehouses. There wasn't a sign of anyone coming to the boy's assistance, much less any police.

"Liddle barstard wuz tryin' t'rob the boot," Alf explained as Alexandre dusted himself off and rolled the boy over with his toe. "Snuck outer th' lane, 'e did. 'Opped up there quiet's a mouse, I waited till 'e wuz thinkin' 'bout wut wuz i' the boot an' not me." He kicked the boy vengefully in the ribs. "Reckon 'e'll do?"

Alexandre huffed in surprise at the thought. True, the entity had not *specified* females. True, the entity *had* specified "pure," but the brat couldn't be more than twelve, and it wasn't all that likely he'd had any sexual experience yet. Although with these street Arabs, you never knew . . .

Still. "Never turn down a gift horse," Alexandre stated, to Alf's approval. "Let's get him sorted out and secured. I've half a mind to stick him in the boot, once he's secured."

Alf laughed. "I don' want 'im crushin' nothin', guv." Together they heaved him onto the floor of the coach; Alf got back up on the box and Alexandre trussed the brat up and gagged him, taking revenge for his bruised ribs by tying the wrists and ankles extra-tight, and not only tying the boy's hands behind his back, but tying him at the elbows as well, wrenching his shoulders back in what would be a very painful position once he woke up.

Then he strapped the boy down on the floor and took his place on the seat, putting his feet up on the bench as well. This was going to be interesting.

Sooner than he would have thought, he heard changes in the boy's breathing that indicated he was conscious again. A moment after that, he heard sounds indicating the brat was testing his bonds. Of course, it was pitch dark inside the coach, so the little bastard didn't know he was there. He listened to the muffled grunts and futile kicks for a while, before speaking out into the darkness.

"I wouldn't bother," he said, as the sounds immediately ceased. "I'm very, very good at tying people up."

After he spoke, there was nothing in the coach but the boy's labored breathing, Katherine's drugged breathing, and the creaks and rattles of the coach itself.

"You probably think I'm taking you to the police," he continued, after what he considered to be a suitable length of silence. "I'm not."

He let the silence lengthen again. When he judged enough

tension had built, he continued. "Your next guess would be that I am taking you to a ship, to be used as labor. Or straight to one of the penal ships, to be taken to Australia. I'm not doing that, either."

He was enjoying this . . . this was almost as much fun as tormenting that ugly, ugly girl had been. He sensed he probably wouldn't be able to break this brat's spirit, not in the short period of time he had before he left the little bastard in the basement. But he could certainly terrify him.

"Now, I want you to bestir what few wits you have, and try to think of every terrible thing that could befall a boy like you at the hands of a man like me," he said softly, allowing menace to creep into his tone. "A man with no morals, no Christian virtues. A man who enjoys inflicting pain. A man who thinks creatures like you should be exterminated like cockroaches. A man who does not know mercy or pity. Just think about everything I could do to you. I have a house with a deep basement. No one will hear your screams. And I have a drop straight into the sewers. No one will find your body until it washes up somewhere downstream. Why, it might even get as far as the Channel."

A moan of terror escaped from behind the gag. The boy began to pant with terror. Alexandre let the silence linger one last time.

Then he leaned over where he knew the boy's head was, and whispered, "Whatever you are imagining . . . it's going to be a hundred times worse."

Then he laughed.

About that time, the coach came to a halt, and he knew they must be in the lane behind the house. The coach rocked as Alf climbed down off the box. The door opened, and Alexandre leaned down to unbuckle the straps holding the boy down. It was nearly as black outside as it was inside the coach, but Alf had put out the coach lamps. They didn't dare chance one of the neighbors looking out at the wrong time. "Yew got 'im trussed up good, guv?" Alf asked.

"Ankles, knees, hands, elbows," Alexandre replied. "I think he's probably a kicker, so be careful when you take him up. Or no, wait—" He felt for the sponge and the chloroform, and gave the brat a good dose. When he went limp, he grunted with satisfaction. "He won't give you any trouble now."

"Proper," Alf said with satisfaction, and heaved the boy up and over his shoulder.

Alexandre gave a more measured dose to the girl; when Alf came back they took her up between them and carried her down to the basement. The boy was already lying beside the pool of darkness; they put the girl down beside him. Alf went out and came back with the bag with the sponge and chloroform, materials for gags, and the extra rope. For one thing, it was just a good idea not to leave anything in the coach that could be stolen. For another, it was a good idea not to leave anything in the coach that could be connected with abductions. When they had begun this, Alf had laid out a set of what he called "sensible rules," and they had been just that, eminently sensible, and Alexandre had not a single quibble with any of them.

Alf clearly had done this before.

Lastly, Alf came and went with the things that had been in the boot, purchases they had made earlier in the day, and the excuse they would use if anyone noticed activity out in the lane. Finally he heard Alf shout from the kitchen, "I'm orf, guv!" and the kitchen door closed for the last time. When Alf returned, he would use the front door.

The entity had not yet made a move. Nor had it spoken in Alexandre's head. *Now* he was planning what he would do if the entity rejected the boy. Try to bargain, of course. Promise to come back with something more suitable tomorrow. If the victims simply had to be presented in pairs, he could hide the girl in the empty flat upstairs and—

The girl was waking up; he could see her eyelids fluttering. A moment later, her eyes opened, and she looked about herself in confusion and terror.

She couldn't see Alexandre; he sat with the light behind him so she wouldn't be able to see his face. The gag kept her from talking. He didn't say a word.

Her eyes went from the unconscious boy beside her to the apparently bottomless pool of blackness to him and back again. None of this made any sense, of course . . . unless she was the kind given to reading sensational novels, like *The Monk* or *Varney the Vampire.* He didn't think she was; she had sounded like a proper bluestocking.

The boy's face was black and blue, one eye swollen. Alexandre smiled a little to see that; it made up for the condition of his ribs.

The girl *did* look like a terrified rabbit now. *See, now, if you'd just stayed at home where you belong, you wouldn't be in my basement about to be devoured by an eldritch horror,* he thought spitefully at her. *It's your own fault you're here.*

He kept silent, however. He was waiting for the entity to "speak," or at least put in its appear—

—the void in the center of the basement suddenly thrust up into a pillar of darkness. The temperature dropped so quickly that between one breath and the next, frost rimed on all the exposed surfaces. The girl tried to scream, but through the gag, it came out like the pathetic squeal of the rabbit she so resembled. The boy woke up in that same instant, and stared, petrified, at the thing looming over him.

It pondered them both, for so long that Alexandre went from anxious, to uncomfortable, to terrified. Surely the entity wouldn't take *him* instead? He was anything but "pure!"

The offerings are . . . unusual, but acceptable, the entity said finally. And the pillar swelled preparing to engulf its victims.

"Wait a moment," Alexandre croaked. "How many more are you going to need?"

Four pairs, it said shortly, and enveloped its prey.

"And what do you do with them?" he bleated, although he was trying very hard to sound forceful.

One I make into my witness. The other I hunt on my own ground. I feed on their terror and despair. And when they are too weak to despair, I feed. You have seven days.

Alexandre waited for the inevitable. And within ten minutes the pillar disgorged the rabbit-girl, her face an utter blank.

He untied her bonds and removed her gag and ordered

her upstairs, out into the street and on her way. Then he went back into the house and stood in front of the stove in the kitchen, trying to warm up.

Perhaps ten minutes after that, he heard the key in the lock, and the sound of feet stamping on the mat. Alf, of course; and moments later, Alf came into the kitchen, looking for him.

"All's well?" he asked, turning his grizzled head to one side in inquiry.

"It took both of them. It did seem to study them for a while, but it was pleased enough," Alexandre told him. "It told me we'll need four more pairs."

"So . . . magic seven." Alf pondered that. "Oi t'ink we'll need t' change our pattern, aye? Perlice are gonna go crazy. This's nummer three, and lummy, even if Ma an' Pa try t'keep it quiet . . ."

Alexandre nodded. "The papers will be on to it soon. I was thinking the same thing earlier today. But the thing is absolutely *firm* that we take girls that are going to be kept together, and that means girls whose families have money or rank, and I don't know how we're going to manage that for much longer."

"Lemme poke about fer a couple days, see wut I c'n learn," Alf replied. "Yer missed somethin'. Wut the thin' said, or wut hit kinda said."

"What do you mean?" Now Alexandre was mystified.

"Hit said, hit wanted four more pairs, which's seven, which's good solid magic. *But* th' last time, hit said hit wanted fancy girls, so's they'd be kept t'gether. Roight?"

"Right," Alexandre replied dubiously, then it struck him. "Oh! With this one, there would only be *two* kept together, which would mean we'd need *five* more pairs, not four!"

"Roight. So fer some reason, they went an' moved th' fust girl." Alf nodded. "Thet means we c'n 'unt fer somethin' a bit less risky from naow on."

"Well . . . well spotted, Alf!"

Alf laughed, and touched two fingers to his temple by way of a salute. "Thenkee guv. I jest wanter find out 'o 'ad th' fust girl moved, an' *why*. Then we'll figger where next t' 'unt."

"Meanwhile . . . peckish?" he asked, getting up and fetching the brandy, intending to raid the larder. It occurred to him at that moment that lately he'd been doing a fair amount of waiting on Alf, rather than the other way around.

He shrugged mentally. Alf wasn't getting above his place—and in a sense they were partners now, with Alf contributing as much or more to the situation as he was. *I certainly couldn't do this without Alf.*

"Fair starvin', guv," Alf replied. "But arter all that ridin' around i' th' snow, Oi want somethin' 'ot. Yew jest sit, an' Oi'll make up a rarebit."

There, see, he knows his place. He set the brandy aside and got bottled beer for each of them. The brandy could wait until later.

He had the feeling that after that "conversation" with the entity . . . he was going to need it to sleep.

13

"I THINK we should go to the theater," Sarah said suddenly, over breakfast.

"What, now? Today? Why?" Nan looked up from her eggs, and Neville took the opportunity to steal the bite off her fork. He flapped off with it, cackling. She sighed. She'd *given* him eggs . . . but evidently stolen food tasted better.

"Because we've been working our minds into a froth, trying to get even a glimmer of an idea about these abductions," Sarah replied, giving Grey a piece of buttered toast before the parrot could follow Neville's example and steal something. "We've been eating, drinking, breathing, and even dreaming about this problem, and we need to give our minds a rest. *Hamlet* is playing, and I've never seen it on the stage, I've only read it."

Nan rubbed her temple as she considered the idea. It had merit. She'd been thinking in circles for at least two days. There was no news from Sherlock, none from John and Mary, and Memsa'b's visit to the hospital had only led to the same conclusion that Nan had come to—that the two girls were completely soulless, which was absolutely of no use whatsoever. The only references to being unensouled any of them had found thus far were in folk and fairy tales and fanciful theatrical productions. None of these were in the least helpful, since people without souls in such things were perfectly able to think and act—they just did so with no morals whatsoever.

"Well, I hate to admit it, but we're getting nowhere," she said. "All we know for certain is where and when the girls were taken, and where and when they were found. The fact that they were found in Battersea suggests their abductor took them somewhere about there, but *we* can't search five boroughs for a magician. It would be like asking a blind man to search for a red marble in a bowl full of white marbles."

"I'm certain Sherlock is doing something clever about that," Sarah replied. "Really, when it comes to searching the non-magical aspects of this case, it should be left up to him. *He* is the detective, he has the practice, the skills, and most of all the knowledge of what clues to look for. Robin is looking for the magician, and he and John and Mary are best suited to that. What we need to do is to figure out what we, and we alone, can do. We already know what we *can't.* And for that, we need to give our minds a rest. And I think the theater is the best way to do that. If we try to read, we'll just keep interrupting ourselves, fretting, and losing track of the story we're reading. At least, I know I will. And if we listen to a concert, I am certain I won't be able to concentrate on it. We need a complete distraction."

"All right," Nan agreed. "The theater it is."

After no more visions from Amelia—and time for Amelia to get better acquainted with Memsa'b—they had returned to their flat for a few days. Amelia was feeling braver, and more confident, after that last foray into— wherever it was the visions had taken her. And she had agreed to let Memsa'b accompany her the next time it happened. Her room was already next to Memsa'b's, and thus far, the visions had all occurred shortly after her usual bedtime. So, it had been decided that Memsa'b would simply stay up a little while longer, reading, and if nothing happened by midnight, go to bed. Sahib had agreed to let her sleep late and take over any of her morning duties.

Nan looked over her shoulder at Neville, who had finished his stolen beakful of egg and was now eating his *own* food. "Do you two have any objection to us going to the theater this afternoon?" she asked.

Neville looked up, and shook his head side to side. Grey swallowed what she had just picked out of her bowl and said, "Go play."

"I believe we have permission," Sarah said wryly, with one raised eyebrow.

It struck Nan then that before all this started, Sarah would have chuckled at that—and that neither of them had laughed since . . . well, since they'd seen the first victims. *But how can we laugh when we know there is someone, something, out there that can rip the soul out of someone's body? Knowing that . . . gets between me and everything else going on. It feels wrong doing anything except concentrating on the problem.* It was probably just as well that Sarah's choice of play was *Hamlet,* a tragedy. It wouldn't have felt right, going to see Gilbert and Sullivan or something of the sort.

Feeling as if she needed to *earn* her brief respite from thinking about the problem, she applied herself grimly to it after breakfast and the usual chores, plowing through several desperately dreary tomes sent over by Lord Alderscroft from the White Lodge library; these were mostly dry and erudite treatises on obscure religions. They didn't help either.

The two of them set off with a word to Mrs. Horace that they were going out and would be back by supper. Snow threatened, but so far was holding off. As they walked far enough to a 'bus stop and caught an omnibus, Nan found her spirits lifting a little at the prospect of getting away for a few hours. And immediately felt mingled relief and shame. Relief, that they were at least leaving the insoluble problem for one wretched afternoon . . . and shame that she was feeling relief.

Blast it, she thought, pulling her cloak tightly around her in the unheated 'bus. *It's not as if we're going there with the intent to get pleasure out of it! We're going to stop our heads from going in circles for a little while! There's no shame in that!*

She wished she had a mind like Sherlock's in that moment—a mind that actually enjoyed teasing apart impossible things until he got to a solution, a mind that found the apparently insoluble to be stimulating. There didn't seem to be any challenge so great that Holmes didn't welcome it. But then . . . *then my mind would be buzzing in aimless circles like his does when he* doesn't *have a problem to solve, and his solution for that is cocaine . . . no, perhaps that is more of a curse than a blessing.*

At matinee prices they could afford to splurge on good tickets, and so they did. They had arrived just as the box office opened, and so they were in good time to settle into very good seats in the dress circle before anyone else was in that row. The seats weren't as plush as the ones in the boxes, of course, but they were a lot better than the ones in the balcony, and Nan felt a glimmer of pleasant anticipation. They both examined their programmes critically.

"Oh dear," Sarah said, her brows creased as she encountered something in the programme.

"What?" Nan wanted to know. *Surely there isn't anything in an innocuous booklet to cause her to make that face.*

"Well . . . we've got a very good Ophelia and Horatio, and quite sound actors for the other roles—but the Hamlet is an understudy. Not just that, but the third understudy." Sarah's mouth twisted wryly. "I fear the worst."

"Well, he can't be *that* bad, can he?" Nan replied, and clapped her hand to her mouth the moment the words came out of it. Because of course, now that she'd challenged Fate, fickle Fate would certainly take notice and prove her wrong. "I shouldn't have said that."

Sarah sighed. "No. You shouldn't."

"Do you know *anything* about him?" Nan asked with trepidation. Perhaps Fate hadn't noticed her blunder yet.

"No," Sarah replied, a little grimly. "Well, the very worst that will happen is that either this will turn into a farce, or the producer will pull him and put the Ghost into his costume.

I'd almost rather see a septuagenarian Hamlet than a terrible Hamlet." Then her grim expression turned a little lighter. "If it turns into a farce, we can whisper rude things to each other and laugh at what are supposed to be the most serious parts. That should be ample punishment for him."

It appeared, as the seats filled in around them, from the murmurings of their fellow audience members, that the rest of the audience, at least those down here in the dress circle, shared Sarah's trepidations. And when the curtain came up—

—the Hamlet was every bit as dreadful as they'd feared.

Halfway through the first act, Nan decided that she had seen better acting at the Panto before Christmas than that man was producing in what was ostensibly a serious production. It was past belief. It was well past farce. In fact, Nan finally decided that since the tickets were paid for, she would just sit back and marvel at just how terrible it was— and, as Sarah had suggested, giggle at the places where he was overacting the worst. Perhaps she could get other audience members to share in her laughter. There was a certain sardonic pleasure in it—and it *certainly* was a distraction from their problem.

When the first interval came, and people began moving to the lobby for refreshment, she was about to ask Sarah about doing the same when—

She felt it. A familiar brush of cold, calculating *evil*. A flash of a cold, bleak London, where the trees were barren, but there were living things that ached with hatred, and behind it all was a savage, arrogant intelligence with a hunger great enough to devour a world. This was *certainly* the same ominous presence she had sensed in Amelia's visions!

Her head snapped up like a hound that has caught a scent, but in the next moment, it was gone, leaving no trace of itself behind. As if the thing *knew* she had sensed it, and vanished out of her world and back into its own.

"What?" Sarah asked urgently, as Nan cursed under her breath and sent her mind skimming through all the others in the theater, hoping to find a glimmer of what had summoned the thing.

"I thought I felt that . . . intelligence behind Amelia's visions," she whispered back. "It's gone now, but . . . I wonder if I felt it hunting?"

"The places it has hunted before were a mostly deserted decent street, a gallery . . . all places where a girl should feel perfectly safe. So a theater matinee *would* be another place a respectable young woman could go without a second thought," Sarah replied, now sounding quite as concerned as Nan felt. "I don't think you're being alarmist. Did you get any sense of direction, where it was, or who it was looking at?"

Nan shook her head, regretfully. "No, nothing. But if it's hunting, I might get another brush of it, if I keep my inner eye open. And I will," she added grimly, and settled down in her seat, closing her eyes. *So much for* Hamlet.

Indeed, she was so intent on sniffing out the least little hint of that *presence* that she was scarcely aware of a word of the second or third act. *If* that thing was still lurking about, she didn't want to leave her own mind open to it, so she had to skulk behind her shields. Which made her able to sense things only obliquely, and see nothing of the thoughts of those beyond her immediate area. Certainly she couldn't read the thoughts of anyone in the first balcony, much less the second. But then, it was nothing human she was looking for; the icy *alienness* of it should shout out to her without her needing to be able to read thoughts.

The audience responded only tepidly when the curtain came down, so there was only one curtain call, during which Nan made a last scan for the cold aura of the hunter and found nothing. She was both frustrated and angry as they made their way to the street. Frustrated, because of her lack of success. Angry—well at herself. If that *had* been a hint of whatever had been preying on those girls, she had let it get away. *I should have found a way to track it! Damn and blast it all!*

They fetched their cloaks and shuffled out with the rest of the crowd into the late afternoon gloom—it was overcast, and the snow that had been threatening was coming down in earnest. If it kept up like this, there'd be several inches on the ground by morning.

Sarah hailed a cab, and Nan was not disposed to object, both because snow was coming down quite thickly, and because there would be no chance to talk in private in a 'bus. Despite the crush of other people wanting to get out of the snow as well, Sarah managed to catch the eye of a young fellow, who grinned at her and beckoned them over, waving off several other would-be riders.

When they were both tucked into the hansom and the doors were closed, Sarah turned to her with concern. "I know that look on your face, Nan, and you are *not* to blame yourself!"

"And why not?" she said, tightly. "I *sensed* the damn thing, and now we know it's out there hunting, if it hasn't already found a victim. I sensed it, and I wasn't fast enough; I couldn't keep track of it!" she snapped.

"Because it's *magic.* I'm sure of it! And what do we know of magic, really?" Sarah countered forcefully. "Only what we've seen others doing! Frankly I think you're lucky you sensed it at all. It probably wasn't aware that you—or anyone—could. It either withdrew quickly, or hid itself in a way you couldn't possibly hope to penetrate. Being angry at yourself for losing it makes as much sense as being angry that you can't track a tiger like Karamjit can. We can't do *everything,* Nan, no one can."

For once, Sarah's admonishments got to her. She nodded.

Seeing that her words were having an impact, Sarah's tone softened. "Now what we *can* do is what we're *going* to do. We're going to stop at John and Mary's and leave a message for them, then we're going home and tell Durwin to tell Robin we think the thing was on the hunt today and may have already found a victim. Nan, be sensible! Would you try wrestling with a fire hose if you saw a house on fire and there were already firemen about? The smart thing, the only thing to do is make sure people who *can* do something are on the alert."

Nan sighed, and some more of the anger at herself ran out. Though not the frustration. "When you put it that way . . . no."

"Then see if you have a pencil in your purse. I know I

have paper, but I didn't bring a pencil with me," Sarah said, with great practicality.

Nan hunted among the pennies and odd buttons and a peppermint or two at the bottom of her purse and did come up with the stub of a pencil. Armed with these, when the cab reached 221 Baker Street, Sarah popped out of the cab and ran in. She was gone longer than it would have taken to write a note, so Nan surmised she'd found one or both of the Elemental Masters in.

When she finally emerged, she paused long enough to give some instructions to the cabby and flung herself into the cab precipitously. She didn't even have a chance to get the door shut before the cab lurched off. She and Nan both had to lean out together and pull the door shut with a slam.

"I told him there was a florin in it if he got us home as fast as the traffic and his horse could take us," she told Nan, as they both settled back into the seat. "John is at his surgery, Mary was in. I explained what you had sensed to her. She agrees there is great cause for alarm. She's going to get John and they are going straight to Lord Alderscroft. They are going to convene as many of the White Lodge tonight as they can, in hopes of finding something, or even stopping this thing."

It was evident that this cabby knew every backstreet in London like the lines of his own hand. He didn't send the horse into a careening gallop—that would be bad for the horse in these conditions, not to mention foolhardy with regards to pedestrians—but he kept the beast at a brisk trot and occasionally broke into a canter when he cut down a particularly quiet lane. It was an agony, every moment that passed in which she hadn't been able to tell Robin or Memsa'b that the monster was abroad made her more frantic to get home. She kept reflexively checking the pendant watch around her neck. Florin or not, Nan hadn't really had much hope for speed, but this young man pulled the cab up in front of their door in roughly half the time she had expected. Nan flung herself out of the cab and let Sarah pay the driver; she ran in the front door and up the stairs, pausing only to unlock the door and throwing herself through the door as soon as she got it open. "Durwin!" she cried as soon as she got inside. "It's an emergency!"

Durwin darted out of the bird room, skidded to a halt at her feet, and saluted. "Yes, milady!" he replied. "I be ready! Gi' me yer orders!"

"Get to Robin Goodfellow immediately. I felt that—that presence that Amelia and I felt in her visions—hunting in the real world when we were in the theater. It vanished as soon as I sensed it, and I think it felt me and knew I had identified it. But I am sure it didn't stop hunting for a little thing like that; I'm positive it just went somewhere else to hunt. Once you've informed Robin, tell Memsa'b the same, and that I am sure Amelia will need her tonight and that she must glean whatever information she can when Amelia has a vision. Then come back, quickly, especially if you have any messages." Nan paused for breath, and before she could say anything else, Durwin saluted again.

"Tell the Great One the monster is a-hunt in Londinium. Tell the Lady the same. Come back with messages," he replied, as brisk as any Army messenger.

"Yes!" she exclaimed, and before she could say anything else, he vanished. She collapsed into a chair, feeling breathless and drained. A few moments later, Sarah came running up the stairs.

"Durwin?" she asked, looking around as if she expected to see him still there.

"Is gone. He's . . ." Nan cast her hands in the air. ". . . amazing. One would think he'd been a messenger all his life. Now . . . I suppose we wait."

"That's the hardest part," Sarah replied and motioned to her to get up. "We might as well get out of our things and hang them up to dry."

Just as they'd done so, there was a tapping on the door, and Mrs. Horace called, "I've got your supper, if you've a mind to it. I 'eard you running up the stairs. Is everything all right?"

Nan opened the door, and their landlady bought in a tray laden with covered dishes. "We just wanted to get in out of that snow and into the warmth, Mrs. Horace," she lied. "We practically perished of cold in the cab. The play was terrible," she added, by way of a distraction.

"Oh, it's no night fit for man nor beast," Mrs. Horace agreed, setting the tray down. "I've more than half a mind to go to bed early where it's warm and cozy, so I thought I'd bring up your supper as soon as I heard you come in."

"That was lovely of you, thank you," Sarah told her. Somehow—Nan was not sure how—Sarah managed to chitchat with their landlady in an absolutely natural manner until Mrs. Horace was quite sure they were all right. When she had satisfied herself, Mrs. Horace beamed at them and took herself briskly out. Nan closed the door behind her with relief.

"I don't think I can eat a bite," she fretted. "I—"

"Durwin, reporting with messages, milady!" said a voice coming from behind her at about the level of her knee.

She whirled. There he was, solemn-faced and earnest. She could have kissed him. To have him back—at least *now* she could be certain that anyone who could do anything about the situation was on alert.

"What have you got for us, Durwin?" Sarah asked, before Nan could gather her wits.

"The Great One's been told, milady, and he's rousing those who can bear Londinium to make search tonight. And the Lady of the Manor's been told, and Roan as well. There's more, that the Great One told me to tell ye. Just in case the thing might come a-calling, on account of the Seer being able to get a look into its realm and all, the Great One's setting a guard on the Manor. All Four Elements are on the watch." He peered up at Nan anxiously. "Do ye think it might come here? My sword's yours, milady." And to prove his point, he pulled a sword that was probably the size of a letter-opener out of a sheath at his belt.

Nan shook her head. "I think it was anxious to escape notice," she replied. "It's powerful in its own realm, I don't think it's all that strong in ours yet. And in any case, it would be looking for me where I sensed it—at the theater. We're quite far from there."

Durwin's face wrinkled in an expression of deepest concern.

"All the same, milady, if ye'll take the word of a hob what's seen a thing or two, ye shouldn't attract its attention. It's a magic thing, according to the Great One, and ye've got no magic. My sword's yers, and I can call on more to help us at need."

Sarah gave Nan a look, as if to say *And what did I tell you?* Nan thought about objecting that they could take care of themselves, given that she and Neville could invoke the Celtic Warrior and her Protector . . . then remembered the horrid creature in the long-abandoned house in Berkeley Square. If it hadn't been for the fact that *everyone,* John and Mary, Memsa'b and Sahib, Karamjit and Agansing and Selim as well as she, Sarah, Neville, and Grey, had all been working together, they would never have trapped it. What's more, they hadn't actually *defeated* it, they had only trapped it, and sent the trap to the Water Elementals to be buried in the deepest part of the ocean.

The five of us have about as much chance of defeating this thing without the help of magicians as we have of flying to the moon and back. We'd better concentrate on making sure that if this thing decides to look for us, it can't find us.

"You're right, Durwin," she sighed as the birds came flying into the room to take their places on their stands. She gestured helplessly. "I *hate* this, but you're right. It's maddening to know something horrible is going to happen to some poor girl tonight and not be able to do anything about it."

Durwin sheathed his sword and took off his soft, pointed hat, scrunching it in his hands. "I know what you mean, milady. But this's Londinium. There's terrible things happening to girls all over this city tonight, there were terrible things happening last night, and there will be terrible things happening on the morrow. And to men, and little chillern, too. And ye can't do anything about those, either. We can only do what's in our strenth, don't ye see? We just have to make sure we *do* what's in our strenth."

"He's got you there," Sarah pointed out. "Come and eat, you're not going to do anyone any good if you're weak and irritable from hunger."

Her friend went over to the table and took the lid off the

largest dish—a bowl, really—and the heavenly scent of Mrs. Horace's Irish stew filled the room. Nan's stomach growled involuntarily.

And Durwin licked his lips, and looked longingly in the direction of the table. He was too small to see what was on the table, but he could certainly smell it as well as either of them.

"Would it be against the rules for you to eat with us, Durwin?" Nan asked on impulse. "Just this once. Seeing as we have a sort of emergency and you might need to carry messages again, or help us in some other way."

Durwin's face screwed up with concern for a moment, but then he relaxed. "Seeing as ye might need me. And seeing as ye're special to the Great One. Why, ye're honorary Folk, ye are! Haven't ye been given leave to *come and go and look and know?*"

"Yes we have," Nan assured him. "Let me get some books for you to sit on."

She piled those huge, dull tomes that had proven so useless onto the seat of the chair Suki usually used when she was home, making a second seat for him so he could reach the table. *At least now they're of* some *use,* she thought. Mrs. Horace had, of course, only brought plates for two, but with a bit of juggling and some creative use of what they had, everyone had something to eat out of. And even though moments before Nan had been certain she couldn't eat a bite, by the time supper was over, everything was gone, and Durwin was contentedly sopping up the last of the gravy with the last of Mrs. Horace's good fresh bread.

Sarah went to the window while Nan gathered everything up on the tray and set it on the stand outside their door for the girl that helped Mrs. Horace to fetch in the morning. "The snow isn't as bad as I thought it would be, but it's going to be no treat to be out in it tonight," she observed.

"Maybe the snow will keep that thing from finding a victim," she said, but without much hope. The first girl had been taken at around dusk, but the second had been taken in broad daylight. . . .

". . . and was last seen with a *man,*" she said aloud, wanting to slap herself for being so stupid.

"What?" Sarah asked, as Durwin stared at her in bewilderment.

"The second victim was last seen with a *man,* a completely ordinary man," Nan groaned. "What if this thing has a human partner? It would make sense. The thing picks out its victim, the human lures her away. Or the two overpower her in some way. I was hunting for a . . . a monster, when what I should have been looking for was the human that was working with it! *I'm an idiot!*"

"Granny, don't yew stay up all night watchin' at th' winder agin," the querulous voice of Granny Toscin's granddaughter Jilly followed her to the room she shared with the "baby," who was now old enough to sleep through the night, as well as the baby's three-year-old sister. "I won't hev yew fallin' asleep whin yer s'pposed t'be watchin' baby. What if she goes off and pulls somethin' down on herself?"

Granny didn't answer. Ungrateful chit. *Didn' I raise yew when my Caro died? Yew oughter be raisin' yer own babbies, that's what, an' let me henjoy me old age. An' if thet means I be lookin' out winders at night, then thet's none o'yer business.*

She wrapped herself up in three shawls and a blanket and sat herself right down beside the window that overlooked the street. She'd never liked that feller across the way. Him with his airs and his hoors. Oh, she'd seen the hoors goin' in and outa that house, she had! And hadn't he tossed one of 'em *on Christmas Eve,* no less, comin' in, and gettin' tossed out inter the snow! *And* he'd let her back in again! At least, she *thought* he'd let her back in; she'd gone to beat on the door, and gone through it instead. A *hoor!* He was *fornicatin'! On Christmas Eve!*

She was watchin' 'im, she was. 'E was up to no good, no good at all.

She hadn't seen him nor his "man" since nuncheon—such

airs! "His man," indeed. Their flat had been dark when she'd gone to get the bit of warm milk with a little rum in it that Jilly begrudged her, but now it wasn't. There was light showing through gaps in the curtains. Granny had a feeling. He was up to no good again. This was a night she had best watch.

Besides, it wasn't that late. No more than an hour past full dark. The babbies wouldn't be up till it was light anyways. Granny watched the flat, narrowing her eyes when the occasional shadow passed in front of a light, but as usual, unable to make anything out through the curtains. He had mortal thick curtains, he did. No one had curtains *that* thick unless they had something to hide.

Snow . . . oh, snow was coming down so thick now. And frost-flowers were creeping up the window, and she had to keep breathing on a spot to melt them, rubbing a clear spot with the corner of a shawl so she could continue to watch. And still, nothing.

She was about to give up and go to bed after all, when the front door opened, and out *he* came. *And* with a girl!

Another of his hoors, no doubt! She rubbed the spot in the frost clear again and watched avidly as he led her down to the street, and right into the *middle* of the street, turned her so she was facing up it, and gave her a little push.

Oooo, 'e's gi'en 'er opium! I knewed it! I knewed it! She walked like a sleepwalker, paying no heed to anything around her, taking one plodding, mechanical step after another through the snow. *'E's gi'en 'er opium, so's 'e won't haveta pay 'er!* And, more likely than not, the poor hoor would fall down in the snow and die of the cold. And he *knew* that, and he was *counting* on it, and that was pure, cold-blooded *murder! I knewed 'e weren't up to no good!*

Jilly did for two or three bachelors along this street, which was why Granny had to watch her babbies, and she always brought home the papers from two days before, faithful as faithful. Granny knew how to read and write, and proud she was of it, and never mind that Jilly and her foolish man saw no need of anything of the sort. She'd be watching the papers for a girl froze to death in Battersea, oh, she would, and as soon as she saw it, she'd go *straight* to the perlice, and give her evidence, and there *he'd* go, with his high and mighty ways, and his *man,* and his fornicatin' on Christmas Eve!

She watched the girl until she was out of sight in the distance and the snow. *He* had gone back in almost immediately of course. When she could see nothing else, she got up—

—and squinted a little in surprise. Had Jilly left the wardrobe door open? There was a black rectangle where the pale painted wood of the door should have been. That door needed to be kept closed, or the older babby would pull all the clothes down and make a nest in them.

She detoured the three steps it took to get to the wardrobe and fumbled around, trying to find the edge of the door.

She was still trying when black tentacles seized her, wrapping around her face and smothering her screams, and pulled her into the black void where the wardrobe door should have been.

14

ALF stopped shoving eggs and bacon into his mouth for a moment and looked at Alexandre from across the kitchen table. Alexandre's mother and father would have dropped dead of shock if they had seen him eating in the kitchen like a servant—but Alexandre saw no reason not to. The food was piping hot, right off the stove or out of the oven, the kitchen was clean and tidy, and much more cheerful than the dining room. "Guv, Oi got an hideer," Alf said, looking expectant.

Alexandre looked blearily up from his newspaper. He'd had a restless night. He *should* have been relieved that the unpleasant task of rounding up the weekly pair of virgins was over, and he had been until he'd gone to bed. Yet somehow that relief had not translated over into sleep. He'd tossed and turned, and the eight-day clock had struck midnight before he'd been able to drop off.

And even *then,* he hadn't slept well, not well at all. He'd had disturbing dreams, and still remembered parts of them. It had put him in a bad mood, on which the fragrance of breakfast had not had its usual positive effect.

He really wasn't in the mood to listen to Alf's suggestions for whores, a feast, or a visit to the music hall, the three things that Alf usually proposed over breakfast. Often, all three at once.

But when he looked up at Alf's expression—it didn't *look* as if Alf was going to suggest any of those things. "Let's hear it," he said, instead of telling Alf he wasn't feeling well (which was true) and that he was going to go back to bed with a sick headache (which was near enough to the truth).

"Wut if we c'n git three'r more girls at once?" Alf asked. "Oi mean ter say, ye said the thing tol' ye we got t'get four more pairs. But wut if we c'n get three or four at a time, 'stead'a two? Ye think th' thing'll be set? Give us wut we wants and go 'bout its bizness?"

"I . . . don't know," he replied, struck by the question. "But how *would* we manage to acquire more than a pair at a time?"

Alf grinned. "Oi 'appens t' 'ave found out th' 'irin' 'all where yer fav'rite madame gits 'er virgins," he said in triumph. "She gits country girls; she checks 'erself t'make sure they're virgins. An' 'ell, Oi c'n git as many boys as ye want. An' we *know,* now, thet the thing'll take boys fer feedin'. Hit'll take money fer the girls," he added, warningly. "Virgins ain't cheap."

For a moment, the idea seemed a sound one. But then he remembered. . . .

And he had to shake his head. "That won't work," he sighed. "I wish it would, but the entity told me that the girls all have to go to the same place. It seems the three we already took went to some private hospital, and without wealthy parents, anyone you got at a hiring hall would just be sent off to Bedlam."

"Mebbe. Lemme look inter hit, guv," Alf urged. "Meantime, Oi c'n git boys easier'n girls from 'iring 'all. Oi c'n git a boy fer each girl we git, we c'n keep 'im nice'n'snug, till we needs 'im, then we c'n concentrate on them girls. But we needs t'be extree careful naow. Tha's three girls we took, an' coppers gonna take notice."

"I was thinking the same thing." Although this was the *last* thing he wanted to contemplate this morning—well, they were on the subject, and it was clear Alf was actively looking for solutions for him. And for all his lack of education, Alf was smart and clever. And while he himself was not a magician, as far as Alexandre was aware, he had a lot of practical experience in what a magician needed, and how a magician worked. "We can't do another gallery. We can't do the theater again." He briefly thought about the bookstore ... but no. Of all things, he should not take a victim from *anywhere* he himself was known to go. That would leave him open to being recognized and remembered with the victim in tow. He'd taken enough of a chance at the gallery; it was entirely likely he could have run into some of the people who knew him from artistic circles—although he had done his best to minimize that chance by picking a time and day that set was unlikely to come.

"Church?" Alf asked, suddenly. "Lotsa good girls in church. An' the thing don't care wut they look loik."

"Too many people, most of whom know each other." That would not be true for the vast majority of the parishioners in a London church, of course, but the anonymous herd would all be unsuitable—not wealthy enough. The wealthy patrons of any church in question would *all* know each other, and so would the resident clergy, and a wealthy newcomer would be spotted immediately, and more to the point, remembered. He'd have to keep going in order to throw suspicion off himself—

"Too bad yew cain't drive a cab," Alf observed. "Yew'd hev yer pick, an' they'd jest walk right inter yer open harms."

Now, that was true. Impossible, of course, since all the cabbies knew each other, and a newcomer would be watched like a hawk by all the other cabdrivers. Not even in the rush at a train station would he be able to get away with impersonating a cabbie.

Nowadays only the very rich, the kind who could still afford stabling or carriage houses behind their townhouses, kept private carriages in London. Even many of the merely well-to-do used cabs instead of relying on their private carriages these days. Especially those who were staying in their clubs, or hotels—

"Hotels!" he exclaimed aloud. "Americans!"

Alf looked at him oddly, puzzled by his outburst. "Wutcher mean, 'Muricans, guv?"

"Wealthy Americans stay in hotels. Their daughters are very . . . bold," he explained. "The girls are accustomed to being allowed to go where they want without chaperonage to a far greater extent than English girls are. They'll be ever so much easier to acquire than English girls. And when the girl turns up witless, the parents will want 'the best care in London,' and the best care in London is *exactly* where we want her to go." He pondered this again. "If we work fast, and we have good luck, we might be able to get two or even three in a single day."

"Oi c'n get eight boys in a single day, guv, betwixt takin' 'em off street an gettin' 'em at 'iring 'all," Alf chuckled. "Oi think we got a plan."

"Not quite. We need to be precise about this," he cautioned. "This will have to be by daylight, and we'll have to be fast. We need a very detailed map of the area around each of the best hotels. We'll need to have a secure spot for the coach near each hotel where you won't be bothered, and where no one will see us putting the girls into it. And we'll need one more thing." Because while *getting* the girls was a difficult proposition . . .

"Wut's thet, guv?"

"We'll need to find a secure place to get rid of them *from out of the coach*. Once the entity spits them out, we'll need to load them back *into* the coach, and take them somewhere else to drop them. I can't just turn three girls out into the street in front of the flat all at once, and I can't turn them out an hour apart, either. Someone is almost certainly going to be able to backtrack them if I do that. And it will have to be a *safe* place for them." It did him no good at all with regards to the entity's demands if some enterprising fellow reabducted them to use as prostitutes.

"Roight. Yew c'n leave thet part t'me. An' th' mappin'. But yew need ter talk t'thet thing in basement, an' foind out if it c'n 'andle more'n a pair, an if it loike's th' ideer." Alf tapped the side of his nose with a finger. "Be jest our luck fer us t'nobble three girls an' three boys, an' hev it turn up its nose, eh?"

Although going down into the basement this morning was the very last thing he wanted to do, Alexandre sighed, and nodded. "Let me get dressed, first," he told his man. "I don't fancy shuffling down there in slippers and a dressing gown." He had no more appetite for breakfast, so he got up from the table and went to his room.

Rather than lingering over his morning preparations, he hurried them, skipping shaving, doing little more than a splash of water over his face, and putting on yesterday's clothing. The sense of dread he felt at facing that thing only grew in him as he dressed; he wanted to get it all over with as soon as he could.

A mere half an hour later saw him treading the basement stairs, lantern in hand, peering anxiously at the void in the middle of the floor. He was pretty certain he knew what it was, now. It was a passageway to some other . . . existence. Like a door into a world populated by nightmares. Some of the magic books in his collection—and a great deal of fantastic fiction—hinted at, or outright described such things. And it was the only thing that made sense; how else could half the victims have been spit back out again? The entity wasn't "eating" them as such; it was pulling them into its world, keeping one, stripping the mind of the other, and throwing that one back into this world. Whatever had happened to them over there, it had rendered the ones that returned mindless and malleable—and the thing had created some sort of mystical link to them, or it wouldn't be able to use them once they were back here.

Though, of course, he still didn't know what the thing was going to use them for. He only knew it wanted them all together to do it.

He hung the lantern up and stood as far away from the void in the floor as he could. He *thought* he was out of tentacle reach, but . . . how could he know for sure? In the silence of the basement he cleared his throat, hoping the entity would notice him if he made a slight noise.

Nothing. Tension grew in him. And so did dread.

"Ah, oh Great One? I have a question?" He realized he was trembling at this point, and he wasn't in the least ashamed of doing so. Anyone who wouldn't have been quaking in his boots in this situation would have been an oblivious blithering idiot, and deserved to be eaten.

He stood there uncertainly for what seemed like hours. He could hear a very few sounds from the flat above—the creak of floorboards as Alf moved about, a faint clink of china and silver. And then, just as he was getting ready to leave, the temperature plummeted; one moment, he was mildly uncomfortable; normal in a basement in winter. The next, he was *freezing,* he could see his own breath, and it had gone completely silent. Not a single sound penetrated from outside the room.

What do you want? The void remained the same. *Thank God.* If it had suddenly reared up into the pillar-shape, he might have gone too witless to ask his question.

He swallowed. "I was wondering if it would be acceptable to bring more than one pair of offerings at the same time," he said, clenching his teeth to keep them from chattering.

Acceptable, said the entity.

And the next moment, the temperature in the basement abruptly rose and he could hear the sounds in his flat again.

He grabbed the lantern, rushed up the stairs two at a time, and nearly ran into Alf, who had been waiting at the basement door. "Jeezus, guv!" the man exclaimed in shock. "Yer white's that snow out there!" He took the lantern from Alexandre's nerveless fingers. "An' yer 'bout as cold!" He all but shoved Alexandre into the study, the warmest room in the flat, hurried out, and came back with a blanket folded in two, which he wrapped around Alexandre's shoulders before pushing him down into a chair in front of the fire.

"It said we can bring more than one pair at a time," he got out around his still-clenched teeth, holding his hands out to the fire. It felt as if he was never going to get warm again.

Alf nodded with satisfaction. "Well, tha's good, hain't it? We c'n get this thin' satisfied, an' get on wi' henjoyin' oursel's."

Maybe. And maybe it's only going to demand more *of us.*

"Yes, but . . . now I can't help wondering what this thing wants all these girls for," Alexandre said slowly. "It called them *witnesses,* but what it is they are supposed to witness, I have no idea, since they're presumably locked up in a London hospital and not witnessing anything but the four walls of their room. And it wants seven of them, which suggests it has some manner of magic planned to use them for."

Alf shrugged, incurious. "Don't matter to us, do it? If they be locked up in 'ospital, that'll be far 'way from 'ere, so whatever it's up to, it hain't gonna 'appen 'ere."

"I suppose not." Once again, Alexandre thought about going to Lord Alderscroft and his White Lodge. But he was in too deep now. There was no way he'd escape punishment for the girls he had sacrificed to this thing's needs. And there was no way he could play ignorant; they'd have it out of him, or they'd smell the thing's dark power on him. No, the only way out of this was through.

Alf didn't go so far as to slap his shoulder like a boon companion, nor tell him to "buck up," but it was clear that now that they knew the thing could and would take multiples of the victims, he wanted to get it all over with as quickly as possible. "Look, guv, once yew warm up, yew get yersel' outside'a th' best part uv a bottle an' go t'bed. Oi'll go nose about. Foind th' 'otels with 'Muricans in 'em. Foind places fer th' coach. Thet'll take me one, mebbe two days. Soon's Oi can, Oi'll get us three lads, an' 'ide 'em in th' upstairs flat."

"How do you propose to keep them quiet?" That concerned him. If he knew anything about boys . . . keeping them tied up for more than a few hours was going to be a problem. They'd have to eat, eliminate . . . and there was only himself and Alf to keep watch over them. You couldn't leave them alone, they'd find a way to get out of their bonds. . . .

But Alf laughed. "Fust, Oi'm pickin' skinny, meek'uns, all bone. Second, Oi'm tellin' 'em th' Marster's away, an' wants 'em fit t'work when 'e comes 'ome, an' they has leave t'eat an' drink an' rest so's they are. Third, Oi leave 'em wi' a full pantry an' plenty o' beer an' gin. So, they'll be inna place fulla food 'n drink, plenty coal fer a fire, an' th' *last* think they gonna wanta do is look thet gift 'orse in 'is mouth. If Oi know boys, an' Oi do, they'll stuff thesselves an drink till they fall over, an' wake up t'do it summore."

"And by that time, we'll have the girls." It seemed a sound plan. He'd had a look at the flat upstairs; it was on the same plan as this one, and furnished in a rudimentary fashion, with one big bed in the room that corresponded to his, and two smaller beds in what would have been Alf's room and his study. "You take the coach out before we do all this and pick up a few kitchen things, and lots of blankets. And curtains. We should make sure the windows have curtains over them. You'll know better than me what the boys will need to keep them satisfied."

Alf nodded. "Once I git 'em, we c'n make a try next day fer three girls. If we on'y get one, we'll give th' thing the girl an' one uv the lads. Oi'll tell th' one Oi pick Oi'm takin' 'im t'Marster's 'ouse." Alf certainly seemed to have taken the bit between his teeth on this, and Alexandre was disinclined to discourage him.

"I . . . think that's a good plan, Alf," he said, finally. "If we can take the third girl before the first and second are discovered to be missing—that will make it all immensely easier." He considered the times he had run into American girls in the shops and dressmakers around the hotels they frequented. They were often alone. They were bold. They were fearless—never having learned to fear anything. All that would work against them. Yes, this might work. This might well work.

And meanwhile, he wanted to take Alf's prescription of getting as much of a bottle of brandy inside him as possible and then going back to bed.

"Wait," he said, and fumbled a nice packet of folded banknotes out of his pocket. "You'll need money; you'll be doing a lot of moving around, and later, you'll have to buy those things for the flat upstairs. While you are scouting, you should take cabs or 'buses if you need them. We shouldn't let the coach be seen before the day. Someone might recognize it—a doorman, or a shopgirl. And you'll want luncheon, tea, dinner, and beer at least."

"Roight yew are, guv," Alf saluted him with two fingers to his forehead. Then he bustled out, and a few minutes later, the front door closed and the flat was silent.

After a while, Alexandre got up and went to the kitchen. He found it cleaned up with not so much as a dirty saucer in the sink. Alf had already tidied everything away—it occurred to him that for a fellow with such a low background, he was surprisingly fastidious.

Or maybe it's because of the low background. Maybe he was sick of living in squalor by the time he was old enough to leave home. He already knew from tidbits that Alf had dropped that his father was a drunk and his mother a slattern. Not a whore—but someone who literally never swept anything so the floors of the single rooms in which they lived consisted of dirt and bits of trash pounded down by feet into layers of grime.

Alexandre found the half-open bottle of brandy in the pantry with the rest of the liquor, cut himself two thick slices of bread, buttered them well, and ate them. Long experience had taught him that if he was going to drink to get *drunk,* he needed to cushion his stomach first. Then, with the blanket still draped over his shoulders, he took a glass and the bottle and sought his room.

The fire was going well; he put coal on it to make sure it kept going while he slept.

But before he got ready to climb into bed, he opened the drawer full of magical supplies in his bureau and got The Book. Because right now . . . he didn't want to sleep unless he had some protection.

I don't think my standard protective magic is going to work against that . . . thing. But written after the summoning spell in The Book . . . he thought he remembered some sort of protective spell. Which would make sense; whoever had written the book out surely had a way of protecting himself from the thing he had summoned. *I was just in so much of a hurry for power . . . I never even considered what I woke up might pose any danger to me.*

Half averting his eyes, he flipped past the summoning spell, and then when he reached the next section, he began to read, carefully. And with a feeling of hope, he knew he had found what he was looking for. *Yes! Here it is.*

It was, as such things went, fairly standard, with just a couple of small tweaks to it—tweaks, he suspected, that had to do with *this* particular entity. Normally such things used holy water, or at least water the magician himself had blessed. This used heavily salted water, red paint into which a couple of herbs, ground fine, had been mixed, and a couple of precious oils. And he had everything he needed in that drawer, because after he'd made his first copy of The Book, he'd gone out and bought every last ingredient listed in it. Now he was inexpressibly glad he had done so.

He pulled the head of the bed a little farther away from the wall so he could make a circle all the way around it, picked up the rugs for the same reason, and went to work. He washed down the floor with the salted water and let it dry, made the circle in the red paint, an inner circle in the two oils, and painted certain glyphs in the four cardinal points of the compass, and more on the door to his room, on the hearth, and on the windowsills. Fortunately the paint was a quick-drying variety, and quite permanent—he'd consulted one of his artist friends on such things a very long time ago, and now his caution was paying off handsomely. Only when he was finished did he undress, get back into his nightshirt, and step over the still-drying circle to climb into bed.

It might have been all in his mind, but once he was *in* the circle he felt a sense of profound relief. As his body warmed up in the bed and the brandy he was sipping gradually relaxed his muscles, he felt the tension draining out of him. Finally he felt . . . not safe, precisely, but at least *safer*.

When he found himself starting to nod off, he put the bottle on his bedside table, drained the last of the brandy in the glass, filled it with water and drank that, and slid down into his bed. And finally slept.

When he woke again, it was late afternoon, and he could tell by the chill in the air and the silence in the flat that Alf wasn't back yet. That was fine, actually. It meant Alf really was taking this with the deathly seriousness it required, and was being as thorough as only Alf could be.

The paint was quite dry by this time, so according to The Book, his protections were now complete and solid. He got out of bed just long enough to build up the fires in his bedroom, the study, and Alf's bedroom. When he had washed off the coal dust in the kitchen, he made himself some cold ham sandwiches and took them and a bottle of beer back to the safety of his bed. He lit the oil lamp next to his bed and climbed in. Once there, he read more in The Book—trying to figure out just what it was that the entity wanted, and what it was going to do when he satisfied its need for victims.

He didn't find much. Only one passage. *He who serves the Master faithfully and well shall himself become the Master.*

But nothing more than that. No indication of what that meant, if the "Master" was the entity, or if it was a classical Master of the Elemental sort and the "he who serves" would be an apprentice, or . . . well, it wasn't clear what was meant, exactly. The Book *did* seem to assume you were at least an Elemental Magician, because it gave specific means of excluding creatures of all four Elements from the area of the conjuration. And it said this was to keep "spies" away.

Obviously whoever had written The Book knew very well what the entity was going to ask for, and that this sort of thing was likely to bring a White Lodge or the equivalent down on the caster's head.

He'd followed those instructions to the letter, and had taken pains of his own to make sure there weren't any snoops around. When he'd set up the magic chamber in the basement in the first place, long before he'd found The Book, he'd sealed it against intruders. The last thing he'd wanted, even back then, was for the local Masters to find out some of the things he'd been up to. He'd played about a bit with sex magic and performed some animal sacrifices, and both those things were frowned on by the prudish White Lodge. Now he was glad he had taken those precautions. He doubted that even the most powerful of the Masters would be able to sense what was going on past all the shields and barriers he'd layered, one over the other. The outermost one was a very clever thing he'd learned from Alf's former employer—a shield that made it look quite literally as if there was nothing there, hiding all the other shields beneath it.

It was well past dark when Alf came in; by that time, he was up and dressed again, and had moved his researches to his study, which was the first place Alf went to look for him.

"One more day o' scoutin' guv," Alf said with satisfaction, "Oi'll take th' coach out t' pick up wut we needs fer th' upstairs flat i' th' mornin'."

"Then you deserve a fine supper, old man," he replied with great satisfaction. It was amazing what a change in attitude a decent sleep could give you. "Let's raid those hampers."

Alf all but licked his chops.

It was just after luncheon. Alf had "hired" *five* boys, all of them now sleeping away in the upstairs flat, after having stuffed themselves with food, none of them inclined to poke their noses out the door. Alf had told them, in the darkest of warning tones, that this was a test by their new Master—that if they didn't stay in the flat until they were called for, they'd be dismissed on the spot and thrown straight out the door into the snow. None of them wanted to risk it. This was probably the first time any of them had been able to eat until they were full in years. It was definitely the first time they'd slept warm since last summer. *The condemned do get a last hearty meal,* he reminded himself with grim humor.

"Although what we are going to do with *five* boys, I have no idea," he told the mirror as he dressed for his foray into American abduction.

I do.

His hands froze in the process of tying his bowtie. He glanced frantically down at his feet—sure enough, he was standing *outside* the circle of protection on the floor. And now, it seemed the entity could reach out of the basement to read his mind as well as speak to him whenever it chose. This . . . was . . . terrifying.

But he swallowed his fear, and instead asked aloud, "What do you want us to do with the two extras?"

Bring them downstairs to me now. Then I will be able to help you control the three witnesses as you take them.

"Right," he gulped, and finished his preparations in a hurry.

Alf was waiting in the kitchen, dressed in his coachman's "uniform," which consisted of a top hat and a black frock coat. He looked up and immediately read trouble in Alexandre's expression.

But before he could ask what was wrong, Alexandre told him, in hushed, tense tones.

"The thing in the basement wants two of the boys right now. It says if we give them to it, it will be able to help us control the girls."

He had expected Alf to be alarmed, or annoyed, or a combination of both, but Alf stroked his chin thoughtfully. "So. The thing c'n talk t'ye hupstairs. An' hit sez hit c'n 'elp yew control th' girls, all three uv 'em. Tha's new, too. So we feeds hit, hit gets stronger."

"So it would seem," Alexandre replied, resisting the urge to pluck at his tie or his sleeves out of sheer nerves.

"Look, guv, th' big prollem wit' th' plan terday was keepin' the girls we got unner control. An naow th' thing says hit c'n take care'a that." He nodded. "I don' see a prollem. In fact that solves our prollem."

Bring me two of the five. I will hold the three. The mage merely needs to meet their eyes.

Alf's eyes widened for a moment. "Did yew 'ear that?"

Alexandre nodded.

Alf let out a puff of breath. "Huh." Then he stood up. "Guess Oi better fetch them boys."

Ten minutes later, they were on their way, Alexandre in the coach and Alf on the box. Alf had handled the boys himself; he told the other three that the Master had come

to take the two strongest to his country house. They'd been
too sleep-fuddled, all of them, to do anything other than
take the words in as Alf roused the two oldest and strongest
and led them down the outside stair to the back door. By
the time he got them to the basement door, they had figured
out that something wasn't right, but at that point, his iron
grip on their upper arms prevented them from escaping,
and once the heavy basement door swung shut, no one
could have heard their cursing. And, being boys, they didn't
think to shout for help; instead, they tried to kick him.

When one of them connected with Alf's shin, they were
about halfway down the stairs. With a curse of his own, Alf
had thrown them both down the stairs. They landed within
two feet of the void in the floor, and before either of them
could scramble to his feet, the temperature in the basement
dropped, the void had become a pillar, and the pillar had
grown tentacles and pulled them in.

They didn't even get a chance to scream.

And that was that. Alf and Alexandre headed for the
coach. If the other boys gathered enough of their wits to
look outside, they would have seen the two men heading for
the vehicle, and they'd have assumed their erstwhile companions were already in the coach. They were probably too
ignorant to be aware that servants would never have been
permitted to ride inside—or if they actually *did* somehow
know that, they'd think that being allowed inside was a
mark of their new Master's "softness," all of a piece with the
warm, comfortable beds, plenty of coal for the fires, the
abundant food, and the run of a six-room flat that included
an indoor bathroom.

He knew what to look for, having observed Americans,
and their women in particular, in the past. He didn't want
the extremely wealthy, the ones who had brought daughters
over looking for husbands with important titles and large
estates. He wanted the ones who were the equivalent of the
English girls he'd been taking—wealthy parvenus. And he
knew exactly what they looked like, or more accurately,
dressed like. In clothing that was visibly expensive, at least
marginally in bad taste . . . and visibly a copy of something

out of a ladies' magazine, made by a local American seamstress. That was partly why they came here—for new wardrobes.

The hotels that Alexandre had chosen were each at a considerable distance from one another. Should one of the girls' families realize she was gone and raise a hue and cry, he wanted to be sure the other two hotels were far enough away that the alarm did not reach to that neighborhood.

The first hotel he had selected was the Langham, a block or so from Regent's Park. There were plenty of exclusive shops on Oxford Street nearby, and American girls, he was told, were accustomed to walking miles in the course of the day. And, of course, Liberty of London was a mere three-tenths of a mile from the door of the hotel. Unlike the truly wealthy girls, who came back to London as often as every year for their new wardrobes, these girls got *one* trip to London, Rome, and Paris. After that, they would have to depend on their local seamstresses again to copy their London and Paris gowns. So a trip to Liberty of London was a necessity—they would travel home with a steamer trunk full of the laces, ribbons and trims they couldn't get in San Francisco, or Kansas City, or Chicago.

And as it happened, he was able to use that little tidbit almost immediately. From the lobby of the Langham, he picked out a lively looking young lady, marked the over-abundant profusion of pink ostrich plumes on her hat, and followed the plumes to Oxford Street. Once there, he window-shopped, keeping an eye on her as she made several purchases, then followed her into a haberdashery, just in time to hear a clerk say ". . . but the best place for that is Liberty's."

"Liberty's? I've heard of that, and I need to go visit," she said in somewhat nasal tones and that curiously flat American accent. "How can I get there?"

Before the clerk could reply, he sidled up to her. "Beg pardon for intruding, miss, but my carriage is just around the corner, and I myself was planning on shopping at Liberty's. I would be happy to offer you a ride there and back, if you feel comfortable accepting one from a stranger."

And the moment she looked into his face, he felt it. The cold, quiet hand of the entity, reaching out through him, as it had outside the theater.

"I'd be delighted," she said, and blinked in surprise, as if that had not been what she intended to say at all. But it was too late; he extended his arm, she took it, and the entity assumed complete control of her. They strolled to the lane where Alf had parked the coach; he assisted her inside and into the rear-facing seat.

And there she stayed. As still as if she was already one of those mindless dolls the entity called a "witness." *I have her. Obtain the next,* the thing said in his head.

The Berkeley was the next hotel, in Knightsbridge, just off Hyde Park. This one was even easier. He followed a horsey-looking young woman who was clearly on her way for a walk in the Park. "Pardon me, miss, but I think you dropped this," he called out, extending a filmy, lacy hand-kerchief to her—she met his eyes, and took the hand-kerchief, and his arm, and they walked mere feet to the coach, where she joined the first, who was sitting like a statue on the far side of the seat. The new girl took a seat next to her, and sat there, still as a stone. Except for her eyes, which were full of terror. He glanced at the first girl. Her eyes, too were wide with fear. He couldn't help but smile. This was going splendidly.

The last hotel was the farthest from the other two, the Great Eastern. Once again, he waited in the lobby, perusing a newspaper, until he heard a very loud young lady asking the desk clerk if there were ". . . any interesting old churches around." The clerk directed her to the nearby St. Botolph's and off she went, with an impressive and athletic stride.

He followed, and arrived just in time to be witness to her voluble disappointment. "Say!" she was telling the rector, "This's no nicer than the First Presbyterian in Denver! I thought England was supposed to be *thick* with fancy churches!"

He strolled up to the two as the ancient rector sputtered a little in indignation, plainly at a loss for words. "If I might be so bold, young miss, my carriage is nearby and I was just on my way to St. Paul's Cathedral. I'm sure you must have heard of that—"

"Say!" she replied, turning to him. "You just bet I have!"

"Then allow me to offer you the comfort of my carriage, so you need not avail yourself of a hansom," he said warmly, meeting her eyes.

And before the rector could interject anything, she had all but seized his arm and was hauling *him* out the door, chattering loudly about how *nice* English gentlemen were. Or she chattered until she was well outside, at which point she shut up in the middle of her sentence. He had never been more grateful for silence in all his life. Within five minutes, she was on the seat next to him, as statue-like as the other two girls.

"We'll have to drive around until it gets dark," he said aloud, when they were well away from the hotel, getting further from the possibility of discovery with every passing minute.

I am aware, the thing said in his mind. *This will be of no difficulty.*

Following Alf's plan, they crossed the Thames on Tower Bridge and, now well out of any range of hue and cry, joined the slow-moving traffic as they headed toward Battersea. It had been about teatime when he had acquired the third girl, and by the time they arrived in the lane behind the flat, it was dusk.

He and Alf hurried all three of them inside and down into the basement, and arranged them in a circle around the void in the floor. Then he and Alf brought the three remaining boys down as far as the kitchen. Once there, Alf fed them brandy mixed with cherry juice until they were tipsy, then half led, half carried them down into the basement, arranging them with the girls. They couldn't even stand up at that point, and sat on the floor, staring about them with bemusement, while the girls wept silently, tears pouring down their otherwise expressionless faces.

The entity did something different this time; the void became a pillar of darkness, as usual, but the pillar suddenly expanded outward, engulfing them all at once, and contracted just as suddenly, leaving only a single pink ostrich plume on the floor.

Alexandre waited patiently; he'd left his heavy winter coat on, but it didn't help much; the basement was so cold that by the time the three girls came shuffling out of the pillar, one after another, he could scarcely feel his toes. He glanced at Alf.

"Naow back in th' coach," Alf said, "Quick, afore someone notices hit's been standin' there awhile."

They had to physically guide each of the girls, leaving one in the kitchen while they took the first two out to the coach. And Alf had a good plan; a flawless plan, in fact.

They drove into Battersea Park; the road was heavily used, even in winter, and even in winter there was enough activity around the bandstand that it would be impossible for anyone to tell their tracks from anyone else's. They left the three girls standing passively inside the shelter of the bandstand. Then Alf brought the things he'd piled on top of the coach while Alexandre had been inside waiting for the entity to finish what it was doing—a huge amount of wood, a tin of paraffin oil, and a lot of rags. He and Alexandre made a bonfire with paraffin-soaked rags in the center, then he left a long wick leading into the rags and lit it. They ran for the coach. They were well away, and actually out in traffic, when the flame finally met the rags, and there was soon a bonfire merrily ablaze, attracting attention from all over.

And, of course, rather than drive *away,* they did what everyone else was doing—drove *toward* the bonfire. They were by no means the first people there—and the first to arrive soon discovered the three girls standing there like wax dolls. By the time Alexandre got out of the carriage and approached the bandstand, police had arrived.

"What's going on?" he asked, and got several confused answers. Some people thought the girls had made the fire "as a lark." Others were sure the girls had boyfriends or brothers waiting in hiding who had started it. Seeing the police taking the three away only cemented this in the minds of the onlookers. Alexandre went back to the coach, in time to be intercepted by a constable.

"'Scuze me, sir," the man said diffidently. "Is there any chance you saw anyone larking about here before we arrived?"

"I'm afraid not," Alexandre replied, apologetically. "My man and I were on Battersea Park Road when we saw the flames. By the time we were in the park, there was—" he gestured at the crowd, "—all this. I wish I could help, but we really didn't see anything, not even someone running away."

The constable sighed, and pulled on the rim of his helmet. "Thenkew very much, sir. That'll be all."

Alexandre didn't look at Alf; he knew he'd be unable to suppress a snicker if he did. Instead he swung back up into his seat. "'Ome?" asked Alf.

"Definitely. It has been a long day for both of us," he replied. "You, especially."

"Yew c'n say that agin, guv," Alf sighed, and touched the whip to the horse, who moved off, leaving behind the chaos and mystery that they and they alone had the key to.

15

"*THREE* of them!" Sherlock snarled. "And left in the bandstand in Battersea Park! It's as if he is mocking me." He came to the end of the rug, turned, and paced back toward the hearth. Sahib's study was full of tension right now, but the normally controlled Holmes was producing enough tension all by himself for two men. Grey and Neville's heads swiveled solemnly, following him as he paced.

Nan nodded in somber agreement. It was extremely rare for anyone to see Holmes lose his temper, but he certainly had for at least this brief moment. Within minutes, however, he regained his usual calm. Outwardly, anyway. He had been here with Sahib when Nan and Sarah had arrived, and he had been pacing even then. "Have you learned anything?" she asked carefully.

"My theory that the chemicals used to turn humans into *zombies* was at work here is incorrect," he replied. "I learned that much from the three newest victims. Our foe made the fundamental mistake of releasing his captives in such a way that the police found them almost immediately, and I, of course, was summoned soon after. I was able to test all three of them for blowfish toxin, which is, according to my researches, the most common way to create such slaves. I was also able to examine them for nearly every other toxin known to me. I then checked all three of them for puncture marks in case some agent unknown to me had been introduced by needle, and I was able to employ gastric lavage, to check for any residue still remaining in the stomach. There were no puncture marks anywhere on them, and there was nothing out of the ordinary in their stomachs." He frowned. "I am now forced to consider, Watson, that you are correct. That these women were rendered mindless by magic."

The last word was pronounced in tones of extreme distaste. Nan actually felt some sympathy for him. Magic irked Holmes. It violated his sense of a properly ordered world, in which everything could eventually be reduced to scientific principles. He didn't mind psychic powers, because to him those were merely abilities akin to any other sense. In his shoes, she would have been irked too.

Everyone involved in the case had gathered together at the Harton School—even Puck, which was why this meeting was taking place in the Harton School in the first place. Puck today looked like a man of indeterminate age—not young, but not middle-aged either, unless that middle-aged man was very fit and had "ageless" features. He had been introduced as "Robin," with no last name, and as a colleague of John Watson's—which was technically true. Holmes probably assumed Puck was a member of Alderscroft's White Lodge.

They were all in Sahib's study once again, disposed in various chairs and the two sofas, with Agansing, Selim and Karamjit leaning against the bookcases with folded arms and Holmes striding restlessly back and forth in the center of the group.

The three sets of parents—all American; was that significant?—had been absolutely hysterical when they discovered the condition their daughters were in. Fortunately for Holmes' ability to conduct his investigation—particularly the parts about "examining them for puncture marks" and "gastric lavage"—the various parents had not been located until late in the day following the incident in Battersea Park. Their insistence on having the young women whisked away to "the best facility in London!" would have severely hampered his ability to pump their stomachs and strip them naked to examine them for wounds.

So now all six of the victims were together. And no one was any closer to finding out what had happened to them and if it could be fixed—much less locating and apprehending the one who had done this to them.

"Did you find any clues as to the perpetrator's identity?" Watson asked, as if he was reading Nan's mind.

Holmes frowned again and momentarily stopped pacing. "What I found ... was another thing that I cannot account for. All three of them had traces of ... well, I would call it 'soil' under other circumstances ... on the hems and other parts of their outer clothing, and on their gloves, as if they had all fallen to their hands and knees at some point. I assume this was during their captivity because I cannot imagine girls like these wearing dirty gloves. It is like no 'soil' I have ever taken a sample of, certainly no soil in London, and ... soil, even in its wintry, frozen state, is still alive with insect eggs, spores, pollen, organic material, microscopic life. There was organic matter I could not identify, but this 'soil' was utterly sterile. I couldn't even grow microbes from it."

John Watson blinked. "Is that even possible?"

"Until this moment, I would have said no," Holmes replied. "So once again, I am reduced to ... conceding to the possibility that magic was involved."

"You are aware, good sir, of the theory of other worlds that lie alongside ours?" Puck spoke up for the first time, riveting Holmes' attention on him. "That *would* be an explanation for the soil. If these young women had been flung through a door into a world parallel in time and space to ours. A sterile world from which life has been purged...."

"Are you suggesting that a passageway from our world to that was opened up, and these women were thrust through it? To—suffer whatever it was that turned them into mindless dolls, then be thrust back *into* our world?" Holmes demanded. "Once, perhaps, but *six times?*"

"I am suggesting that, yes," Puck agreed. "But I suggest also that it was by the agency of someone living in *this* world, and that it was done for some purpose we have not yet divined. Hence, six victims so far."

Holmes ran a hand through his hair, absently. "It sounds uncommonly as if you are describing a deal with the Devil."

"*The* Devil, no. *A* devil of sorts, perhaps...." Puck shrugged. "It would take a great deal of effort to open such a doorway; even more effort than it takes to abduct six young women right off the open streets. Taken all together, it is clear that the perpetrator had enough to gain to make all this effort worth his while. You seldom make a misstep when you follow a path suggested by greed and gain."

"But what would this—putative devil have to gain?" Holmes demanded. "What could induce it to agree to this bargain?"

"Presumably whatever it took that now means these young women are mindless." Puck cocked his head to one side. "They once had something. Now they don't. You may call that thing whatever you wish."

Holmes growled a little, then shrugged himself.

"I am already accepting that someone opened a magical hole in the universe," he admitted, begrudgingly. "I might as well accept that something purloined—what? Their souls?"

"It's enough to use for a premise, Holmes," Mary Watson pointed out. "You can always discard whatever parts of it you discover don't match the facts, but it does give us a place to start. A few moments ago we didn't even have that."

Well, that's not entirely true, Nan thought, *because that is the premise that the rest of us had been operating on.* But it was good that now Holmes was at least willing to consider it.

"The student becomes the master," Holmes replied, with a dry chuckle. "You are right to remind me of my own method. Very well then. What do we have?"

"Battersea," said Nan. "Every single one of these girls has been found in Battersea. That can't be a coincidence. The perpetrator must be doing his work there, or on the outskirts of it."

"And he is clever enough to have taken his victims from

places quite distant *from* it." Holmes regarded a map they had attached to one of the bookcases, with red marks indicating roughly where the girls were from and blue where they had been found. "I suggest that the reason the three were found together in the park is that the park is the most public place in the borough that is *also* the most deserted on a winter evening. He had three to dispose of at once. For some reason, he *wants* them found. I cannot otherwise account for all three of them being taken to that spot, and a bonfire being set to draw attention to the very place where they were left standing."

"The other three showed signs that they had walked for quite some time before being discovered," John Watson observed. "Their clothing and boots were caked with snow—and they kept walking when accosted until they were physically stopped. They probably could have kept walking for hours."

"So we can assume the first three were—wound up and let go in the direction of discovery, like clockwork toys," Holmes agreed. "If he had *not* wanted them found, the Thames borders Battersea, and it would have been simple to point them in the direction of the shore and order them to walk." He clasped his hands behind his back and pondered. Nan suspected that if he had been at home in his flat, there would have been more bullets decorating the area above the mantle. "We cannot search every blasted room, house, and flat in Battersea, however."

"I have had a search out for traces of magic where I know no magician lives," Puck said. "I can narrow that search to Battersea, and it does not require physically searching each dwelling to look for such things."

"Then—" Holmes began, when Sarah shrieked.

They all turned to see she was pointing at the door to the study and quickly looked in that direction, expecting something horrific to be coming in the door.

But worse, she was pointing to where the door *had been*. Because the door was almost certainly gone now, and in its place was a door-shaped area of utter blackness, like the darkness of the void between the stars itself.

Instinctively they all leapt to their feet and backed away from it. And just in time, for a moment later, the void erupted with tentacles, tentacles that flailed into the space where living humans had just been.

In the next moment, Nan felt the Celtic Warrior Woman erupt from her slumber deep within her. Anger, rather than fear, filled her. She raised her head and screamed defiance at whatever was trying to reach them, unsurprised to discover her gown had turned into a short checkered tunic and leather trousers, that her feet and legs were wrapped in crude leather boots, and that there was a bronze sword in her hand. With a matching scream of defiance, Neville launched himself from his perch and landed on her shoulder, now the size of an eagle.

Behind her Selim uttered a bloodcurdling war cry in which the name of Allah figured prominently; in the next moment he, Agansing, and Karamjit were beside her, their own swords in hand.

As the tentacles continued to flail, the four of them charged.

They could scarcely have missed if they had tried; there were plenty of targets, and the main concern Nan had—beneath the Warrior's white-hot rage—was not to hit the other three by accident. With one stroke, she lopped off three squirming tentacles. She had braced herself, expecting some reaction, a hideous scream, mental or physical—but there was nothing. Just silence, and the amputated tentacles vanished into mist.

Abruptly the rest of the monster, or monsters, withdrew, and the void began to shrink.

That was when Puck leapt past her and thrust a green, glowing staff, sprouting vines and vividly emerald leaves, into the blackness. "I'll hold the door!" he shouted. "Go! You'll never get a better chance to cut this thing off at the root!"

Nan didn't hesitate, and neither did Selim. Side by side the two of them vaulted into the darkness, with Neville clinging to her shoulder.

They emerged under a cold, starless sky, landing on

ground that felt like ashes. Faint, sourceless light seemed to come from that sky; just enough to see by to keep from stumbling into things, not enough to see far, or clearly. With a glance at each other, they moved out of the way, just in time for the rest to come through.

And *half* of Puck. He planted his glowing staff in the barren soil; it lit up the night like a beacon. "I'll have to stay here to hold the door," he said, grimly. "This is not my world, and I have little power here. But I will stay as long as any of you remain."

Nan tore her eyes away from him and took in her surroundings—and recognized them in an instant. The shattered buildings—the skeletal trees—the cold wind moaning among the branches—

"This is—" she exclaimed.

"The same place as Amelia's visions," Memsa'b finished for her, grimly. "Well, now at least we know it is a real place, and not some presentiment of a diabolical future."

Memsa'b too had transformed; she sported a scandalously short Grecian tunic and carried a spear. Like Nan's bronze sword, it gave off a faint light. Sahib had taken on the aspect of a medieval knight—Selim, Agansing, and Karamjit were all enhanced versions of their everyday selves, chiefly with more bits of armor. Sarah, Sherlock, John, and Mary remained as they had been, except that Grey was the size of a very large hawk.

Sherlock stared at them all incredulously. But he did not permit their transformation to hold his attention for long. The first thing he did, once he tore his eyes away from them, was to stoop and scoop up a bit of the soil they were standing on, feeling it carefully, holding it to his nose and sniffing it, tasting it.

"Is this what I think it is?" John Watson asked his friend.

"Without making exact tests, I would say this earth is identical to that which I removed from the clothing of the latest victims, yes," Holmes replied. "I wish I had a fighting stick, or my revolver."

"Come over here and lay your hand on my staff," Puck ordered. Not even questioning him, Holmes did as he was told. A moment later one of the vines straightened, thickened, then broke off, dropping to Holmes' feet. He bent and snatched it up. "This will do admirably," he said. "Thank you."

"I'd like one of those," John said. "And so would Mary and Sarah." Soon everyone who wasn't already armed at least had a weapon. Nan hoped, coming as they did from Puck's staff, the sticks might also have some magic to them that would work against whatever lived here.

"Sherlock, does this look like London to you?" Mary Watson asked. "It does to me."

"It looks enough like London to me," John added, "Though I'll be damned if I know where."

Nan looked around her at the broken buildings and shivered. Many of the buildings were without roofs. And the dim light coming in through the glassless windows made the broken walls look like stacks of gargantuan skulls.

"I'm not surprised neither of you recognize this place," Holmes replied. "You haven't had much cause to visit the Royal Courts of Justice, or consult a barrister. It's Temple. I fancy in our world we're not far from the Blackfriar Bridge. I—" he coughed. "I suppose you magicians can create a light?"

"Only two of us are magicians, Sherlock," John chided him. "But yes, I can. I don't think it advisable, however. A light will make us exceedingly visible to anything hunting in these ruins. Those tentacles came from *something*, and I would rather not attract the whole beast."

With a start, Nan glanced down at her glowing sword and, with a thought, extinguished the light. The others did the same—all but Puck, for obvious reasons. If they were going to venture into these ruins, they were going to need a beacon to guide them back to the door.

"Whatever you mean to do, do it quickly," Puck urged. "That thing might be back at any moment, and I doubt it's going to ask me to tea."

"We should scout, Sahib," Karamjit said. "But I do not believe we should separate."

"Holmes, there is a former patient of John's who has

been having visions of this place," Nan said in a low voice, when Sherlock looked as if he disagreed with that idea. "With my ability to read minds, I was able to share in those visions. These ruins might *look* empty, but they hold things that were hunting human beings in the ones I saw. I think Karamjit is right. And I think there is no doubt that whatever is *here* is the thing that has been behind the abductions. I believe it somehow discovered we were getting closer to finding its agent in our world and chose to act, to attempt to finish us before we discovered anything else."

"Very well, then," Sherlock agreed reluctantly. "We could cover twice the ground if we split up into two parties, but I will yield to your superior information. My only question to you is this—London is vast. Its counterpart is probably just as vast. Where do you propose we should look?"

Nan stared at the others, who all mirrored her indecision. And they might have stood there for some time, had they not heard a heartrending cry, and the sound of snarls coming toward them. Instinctively, the ones with weapons formed a line of protection in front of the ones who had next to nothing—which, to his chagrin, included John Watson. They hadn't time to do more than that when the quarry burst into view, scrambling over the rubble of a completely ruined building. Human, certainly. Moved by a joint humane impulse, Nan shouted, "Over here!" at the same time as John created a light over his head.

The man was clutching his chest as he stumbled toward them, and the closer he got to them, the more it was apparent that this was a man from *their* world, an elderly man, gray-haired, dressed in the tattered remains of what had once been a conservative suit. He fell at their feet, exhausted and bleeding, just as his pursuers flung themselves over the top of the hill of rubble, stopped and stared at them, John's light making their eyes reflect a hellish red.

Or perhaps their eyes were *glowing* a hellish red.

If one had crossed a pariah dog with a spider and covered the whole with mangy black fur, added a barbed tail, and inserted teeth that were so long they couldn't actually close their mouths, that was something like the horrors that

Nan saw all too clearly. There were ten to fifteen of them—they wove in and around each other, so it was hard to tell their exact number—and they snarled and slavered as they stared at their erstwhile victim.

"Would that I had a torch," Selim said, as John and Mary pulled the man behind the defensive line. "I would burn those unholy things until there was nothing but ash."

"I think we should remedy that, before we go a step further," Sherlock said grimly. He looked about, and added, with a little more doubt, "If we can find something to burn, that is."

He was right. There was nothing like a branch or a piece of wood anywhere around them.

As if their voices had awakened fear in the things, their heads came up and they turned tail and vanished, back over the hill of debris. So they were safe from attack. *For now, anyway.*

Nan was not inclined to let her guard down, and the Celtic Warrior absolutely *forbade* the very idea, so she, Selim, and Karamjit kept a watchful eye, weapons out, while Agansing joined the others in tending to the stranger.

"Escape . . . if you can," he gasped, as John worked feverishly over him. "Do not tarry. This . . . place is a charnel house."

"Who are you?" Holmes asked urgently. "How did you come here?"

"Fensworth," the man replied faintly. "Arthur Fensworth. I . . . don't know . . . how I came here."

Haltingly, a few words at a time, with his voice growing weaker by the moment, Arthur Fensworth told them what little of his story there was to tell. "I fell through my own door," he croaked. "I found myself here. At first, I thought I must have suffered a fit, and was lying in the snow, hallucinating."

He had spent his first day wandering, and when he got desperately thirsty, drinking from water caught in little pockets in broken-down walls. He had recognized the area, being a solicitor. He had even found where the rooms of a barrister friend would have been and hid there, drinking stagnant water from a broken cistern, sleeping in the rubble inside the remains of a wardrobe. He searched the ruins for food, growing ever more desperate. Then his hunger grew too great to bear.

"And then . . . I heard the call," he said. "It was the creature that rules this hell. I followed the call. It ended in the broken dome of St. Paul's. There were others like me: women, children. Not many. The thing fed us, strips of meat in piles on the floor. We ate like dogs. I think . . ." He broke down then. "I think it might have been human flesh. I was hungry . . . so hungry . . ." He wept, then, meager tears etching their way through the dirt on his face, and Nan turned away, not wanting to stare at the poor old man in a moment of such terrible weakness. "Then it drove us out with its creatures. I swore not to eat again, but . . . I was so hungry . . ."

He was silent for a moment, then began to cough wetly. Alarmed, Nan glanced back at him. There was a trickle of blood coming from his mouth. Then he coughed again, and brought up several great clots of blood, turning his head to cough it into the dust.

She looked at John, who looked up at her, and sadly shook his head.

Fensworth groaned in pain, coughed once more, gasped "Save yourselves. This place is death," and died.

John Watson laid the old man gently down, took out his handkerchief, and covered his face. He and Mary stood up; he brushed off his trousers and Mary shook out her skirts. Nan felt as if she *ought* to be sad, but she couldn't seem to manage anything but rage or fear. Was this place meddling with their emotions? Or was it just that the poor man was a complete stranger and, right now, they were in a situation of great peril without a lot of emotion to spare for anyone else?

Poor old man. What did he ever do to deserve a death like this?

"Jolly old place this is, what?" John said sardonically. "Brilliant for holidays."

Sherlock looked about, trying to orient himself. "Unless I miss my guess, this version of St. Paul's is over there." He pointed. "The streets seem passable, barring opposition. We have four swords, a spear, and fighting sticks among us. Will you magicians be of any use?"

"Limited," Mary replied sadly. "Our power is mostly in our Elementals, and—" she shivered. "There's nothing *I* know that I can sense, and I don't think I would dare to try to call whatever passes for an Air Elemental here."

"We're not limited," Memsa'b and Sahib said together, and glanced at each other. "And you can see the rest of our troupe is no weaker here than at home," Sahib added.

"Wish I had my revolver," John muttered. "I almost dropped it in my pocket before we left, but I didn't."

"The longer we stand here, the more likely opposition will form," Karamjit pointed out, with inescapable logic.

"Our turbaned friend is right," Holmes proclaimed. "Regardless of who is responsible for abducting the victims on our side of that door, the thing he is feeding is *here*. Cut that off, and we end this." He looked each of them in the eyes. "If you are ready, we go."

"Do," urged Puck. "The longer we stay here, the worse our peril."

With Selim and Karamjit in the lead, Nan and Holmes flanking, and Agansing and Sarah bringing up the rear, they moved out. "Fly?" suggested Neville, still on Nan's shoulder. She glanced up at the starless sky, and shook her head.

"We don't know what's up there," she pointed out. "It could be bigger and much meaner than you. I don't want to risk you or Grey."

"Rrrr," he agreed. When Nan glanced back at Sarah, Grey bobbed her own agreement.

The were limited in what they could see by the amount of light cast by the orb floating over John's head. Nan was just as glad. What was visible was bad enough.

The streets themselves were strewn with the rubble of utter destruction. Broken buildings hemmed them in on both sides, and they often had to climb over loose drifts of shattered brick and stone, but what was even more unnerving were the remnants of what looked like ordinary life. Furniture, kitchen things, even toys mingled with the rubble—and it appeared that the only plant-like material surviving was a sort of fungus that blotched these articles of everyday living, crept down the walls, and hung in grisly festoons from dead tree branches. Holmes tried wrapping some of that around a chair leg and setting it on fire, but all it did was emit a choking smoke, not create the torch he was hoping for. While there probably were rags of fabric here and there, the torn curtains they could see were well out of reach, and it seemed imprudent to hunt for bits of cloth when they could be ambushed at any moment.

There was a strange, bitter smell in the cold air that Nan could not identify. Just out of range of their light, they could hear skittering sounds in the wreckage, and occasionally see the red gleam of an eye. Those "hounds" were almost certainly following them, and possibly other things as well. Her heart was in her throat, and she almost wished something would attack, because the tension was nearly unbearable.

It was a good thing that Holmes had some idea where he was going, because Nan was disoriented and lost within minutes. Only by looking back and seeing the steady, healthy green glow of Puck's beacon was she able to keep herself oriented at least to their escape route. The light shone even above the wrecked buildings, which eased one of her fears—that they'd get separated and be unable to find their way back. That green light must have been how Fensworth found them in the first place.

As they drew nearer to "St. Paul's," or whatever you would call this hellish analog, she realized two things. First, she was actually able to make out the shattered dome against the dark sky by the fact that it glowed, faintly, like foxfire. And second, that the skittering now surrounded them on all sides, and had been joined by faint snarls, panting, and chittering noises. Fear rose in her, overwhelming the Celtic Warrior for a moment, and leaving her feeling very small and very frightened. Then she took a long, deep breath between one step and the next, and the Warrior came surging back.

"We seem to have an escort," Holmes said dryly. "I would give a great deal for one of those modern Maxim guns."

Nan kept her grip on her sword firm, but not a clench. The Celtic Warrior did not recognize any of those sounds out there, but she also did not flinch from them. She had been, in the deep past and another lifetime, a warrior not pledged against the common foes of other tribes or even Romans. She had fought monsters, directed by the Druidic leaders of her clan. This was nothing new to her, even if it was to Nan.

The nearer they drew to St. Paul's, the closer those creatures out in the dark came. Now they began darting into and out of the light, growling or snapping, and making *sure* the humans could see them.

"I believe we are being herded," Sahib said, in a conversational tone. "I have seen this in India, when our enemies wished to drive us in a particular direction."

"And I in Afghanistan," replied John Watson tightly. "We have lost any element of surprise, if we ever had one."

They turned a corner and came into full view of the wreckage that was this world's version of St. Paul's Cathedral, Christopher Wren's masterpiece. If it had not been for the surroundings, it would have been beautiful still in its ruin. The elegant lines of the building had been shattered by something impossibly powerful—Nan could not imagine *what* could have brought such a monumental work down.

The two towers at the front were nothing but drifts of rubble. The great dome had been cracked unevenly off, as if someone had shattered a soft-boiled egg with the bowl of a spoon. The whole was covered in a thicket of black, ropy, leafless vine. That was, perhaps, the most unnerving part. The stems near the ground had to be the size of three or four tree-trunks put together! She had seen monstrous trees and vines in Africa, but nothing like this! Where had this thing come from, and how had it come to cover the face of St. Paul's as if it was trying to strangle the building?

There was a center path up the steps to the entrance; that path was clear of rubble and vine. Unnervingly clear, actually, since it was obvious that it was used regularly. And standing on the mounds of rubble on either side were . . . horrors.

Shoulder to shoulder, with ranks behind them, were hybrid monsters—the spider-dogs they had already seen, enormous naked, flightless birds with the heads of lizards, rats the size of mastiffs with wolf-heads, ape-like creatures, and things Nan couldn't even really make her mind understand. And what was most unnerving about them . . . was their utter silence. Not a snarl. Not a squeak.

No one spoke. It was clear now they had made an enormous mistake and completely underestimated their unknown foe, but it was too late to turn back. Even the Celtic Warrior within Nan was cowed, and as for Nan—she was petrified. Neville huddled down on her shoulder, making himself as small as he could, his eyes darting everywhere.

They entered the gaping holes where the doors should have been and walked into the nave. The roof was intact here, although the huge columns on either side were chipped and cracked. The aisles to either side were filled with rubble, but the nave itself was clear. The checkered marble floor was a ruin, the tiles shattered or buckled, the few intact stretches caked in mud. At the end of the nave, beneath where the apex of the dome would have been— was something. Another huge pile of rubble, of course, but there was something large sitting on it, as if it was a throne, and the entire thing, rubble pile, creature, and all, glowed like foxfire.

Inside was only silence, a silence so profound that it made Nan's ears strain to try and hear *anything* other than the sounds of their own footsteps.

They paused and looked at one another, but no one said anything. What was there to say? That they were trapped? That it was quite likely none of them were going to get back to Puck alive? That coming here had been the biggest mistake any of them could have made? That they were going to vanish from the face of the earth, and *if they were lucky* they would die here—and if they were not, their soulless bodies would be spit out and they'd join those unfortunate girls in the hospital?

I won't believe that, Nan thought to herself and set her chin, warring within herself against the terror that threatened to take her over, body and soul. There had to be a way out of this.

But right now, it looked like the only way was forward. So forward they went.

With every step they took, the creature sitting on the pile of rubble grew clearer. Or at least, the long robes and hood it had draped itself in grew clearer. The shape beneath the robe, not so much, although Nan fancied she saw movement in places under it where there would be no movement if the thing was actually humanoid. It was roughly ten feet tall, and sitting about ten more feet above the floor.

"You may stop there," it said, when they were about twenty feet away. It had a curious voice—absolutely expressionless, and impossible to describe as male or female. Loud without sounding loud. It had no accent at all, as far as she could tell. "We have allowed you to come this far without devouring you, because We wish you to carry a message to your world."

They said nothing. The oppressive silence filled the space beneath the shattered dome. Nan lowered her mental shields slightly and reached tentatively for Sherlock's mind.

Only to find he was thinking one fierce thought at her. *You are the strongest telepath. Tell the rest to say nothing. We will get more information out of this creature if we give it nothing to react to.*

Quickly, she did as she had been told, passing on to Sherlock the fact that everyone knew as soon as she was done. Immediately his mind became occupied with a chess problem—the tactic she had shared with him of how a non-telepath could shield his mind from telepathic probes. She took her cue from him, and immediately put up the strongest protections she had.

When the creature spoke again, there was just a touch of annoyance in its otherwise neutral voice. "We are soon to enter your world. When We do, it will be well if you do not resist."

Although (at least for Nan) the temptation to shout defiance at the thing was overwhelming, no one uttered so much as a sigh.

Its voice rose a little. "Those who do resist will be torn apart by Our minions. Those who do not will live. The pure will serve in Our Communion, and We will grow strong, until We conquer all of your world."

That . . . was a very odd thing to say. The pure will serve in "Our Communion"? What on earth does that mean?

"We *will* conquer your world!" the creature said, its tone now distinctly shrill. "We *will* have the victory that has been denied Us! We *will* feed on your terror and despair, and grow mighty! All this shall come to pass! *All this shall come to pass!*" It had risen from its seat, and towered over them — and what was inside the arms of its robe were definitely *not* anything like human arms. No human arms moved that . . . bonelessly.

"Go!" the thing shrieked in fury, in tones that hurt Nan's ears. *"Go now! Return to your world and bear Our message, those of you that survive the passage!"*

"Don't run," Sherlock said quietly.

16

THEY walked, quickly and steadily, back down the nave to the exit. Nan could *feel* the thing's fury behind her. Somehow the fact that they had not reacted to it had sent it into a blind rage. And the fact that now they were not pelting as fast as they could for the exit had enraged it further. That, and that alone, was what was keeping her from disobeying Sherlock and racing for Puck and the passage out as fast as she could run.

When they reached the exit, Sherlock held out his hand, and they all paused. Nan had expected that the monsters would have clogged the path down the stairs—but no. They were still arranged up on the hills of rubble, snarling and slavering, but making no move to charge them.

"If we run, we become prey," Sherlock said quietly. "As long as we show no fear, they may leave us alone out of fear themselves."

"Like jackals or pariah dogs," murmured John, and Karamjit, Selim and Agansing all nodded in agreement. "They're used to chasing things that run away from them. When they encounter something that doesn't do that, they can't think how to handle it. A couple of them may gather up enough courage to rush us. Be ready for that, kill them as quickly as you can. That will make the rest even more cautious."

"Mary and Sarah, I would like you in the middle of the group," Sherlock said. "The main attacks will come from the side. Nan, I would like you and Agansing on the left and Karamjit and Selim on the right. Sahib Harton and I will lead, John and Memsa'b Harton, put your backs to Mary and guard the rear. We will proceed slowly in this fashion until we are past the gantlet of enemies, if that seems to be a good strategy to you, John."

"I was just an Army Surgeon," John replied with a shrug. "Agansing? Karamjit? Selim?"

"Letting go the fact that it will force you to walk backward, this is a sound strategy," Karamjit agreed, and drew his sword, which never left his side. For his part, Agansing drew his two Gurkha long knives, the curved *Kukri* knives that were nearly as long as a sword. Selim nodded and drew his saber.

They formed up. "I have changed my mind about using my power. I'm going to see if there is anything here I can control," Mary said in an undertone. "But don't worry, I have no intention of doing anything that will bring yet more trouble down on us. I'm just going to . . . well, try and carefully feel things out. I can do that while we are moving, easily."

"If you find something friendly, don't hesitate to call it," John advised. He got a firm grip on his stick—or rather, club, since that was what it resembled rather than Holmes' singlestick. "We can use all the help we can get."

Nan wished there was some way to tell Puck the danger they were in. He would surely be able to send them some aid from "their" side of the portal, if only he knew they needed it.

They made a few tentative steps down the staircase. By the time they reached the bottom of it, they were moving more confidently, as a single body. "Stand as if you are absolutely ready to fight back, but don't challenge them," Holmes advised, as they slowly edged their way down the middle of the street between the two mounds of rubble.

There was a strange, dry, bitter-green scent in the air. It was cold—but not as cold, Nan thought, as "their" London. Somehow Memsa'b seemed unaffected by the chill even though her tunic left arms and legs bare. A half-seen mob of creatures crowded the top of the hills of rubble on either side of them. They didn't make much noise—nothing seemed to make much noise in this place, actually. There was some angry chittering, snarls, growls, and the scuffling of clawed feet on slippery rubble, but other than that—nothing.

Nan edged sideways with the rest of them and wished she could see the amorphous mass clearly. John's light was not helping much. There was something more unnerving about a moving mound in which the occasional eye reflected back the light from that meager orb, like a will-o'-the-wisp over John's head, than there would have been in seeing a horde of monsters.

Her stomach and throat were clenched tightly with fear. She held her sword two-handed, her gaze flickering above, to the rear, then ahead of them. How long was it going to take them to get to the portal this way? Longer, surely, than it had to get here in the first place.

"Curse this," John muttered. "Sherlock, unless you tell me not to, I am putting up a better light. I can't take much more of not being able to see these things clearly."

"It's probably better if you do that," Holmes admitted. "We'll be able to move faster too. Make it as bright as you can; with luck it will blind any of them that can hurl things at us."

John needed no further encouragement. He muttered something under his breath, and a few moments later, a miniature sun blossomed over their heads, flooding the area with light.

Some of the creatures on the tops of the ridges squalled and slid down the back of the rubble pile, avoiding the light, like cockroaches or mice scuttling for cover. But others stood there, half-paralyzed, blinking in the unexpected brightness. These were all the half-seen creatures from before, squinting and looking stunned. Nan felt her fear ease just a little. "We'll move a little faster," Holmes muttered quietly. "We'll take advantage of their being stunned." And suiting actions to words, he did pick up the pace.

And for a while, Nan began to hope that the light alone would keep the monsters at bay. It looked as if most of them were about the size of a mastiff—if they attacked one at a time, she thought the group could deal with them handily, but if they rushed in a pack . . .

The rubble-mounds slowly decreased in size, which unfortunately brought the monsters nearer. A glance to the rear told Nan that there would be no escape back toward St. Paul's—as if that had ever been an option—because the things had closed ranks and filled the street behind them. Now they were darting in and out of the ruined buildings on either side of the street, still unnervingly silent. Then they turned a corner, and the dim, beautiful green glow of Puck's staff shone at the end of the street, showing that he was still there, and the portal was still held open.

That was when the first of the beasts got enough courage to make a rush for them.

Without John's little sun, they'd have had no warning. Even with it, there wasn't much warning; just sudden tension in one of the wolf-headed things, and then it was hurtling toward Nan as Neville erupted in an earsplitting scream. The scream shocked it just as it reached their group, and the Celtic Warrior's reflexes did the rest. In the next instant the head of the creature was rolling toward the others across the rubble, and the body tumbled tail-over-blood-spurting-neck into a pile of wrecked furnishings.

She heard Selim shout something in his own language, and John cursing, but there was no time to take any of that in, because one of the spider-things was racing toward her and Agansing was fending off a second, chopping at the too-many-legs striking at him.

She swung at a black, hairy leg ending in a wicked claw or talon that arced down at her; she manage to cut off the end of it, but another whacked at the sword as she was recovering from the stroke and, to her horror, sent it hurtling straight up into the air as Agansing finished his spider and carved up hers.

No!

But the weight was off her shoulder and Neville had launched himself after the blade, intercepting it just as it reached the top of its arc and clamping his beak on it firmly. Before she could blink, he landed heavily back on her shoulder, proffering the sword. She snatched it back just in time to intercept another spider. She kept a tighter grip on her sword this time; out of the corner of her eye she caught Agansing's technique, and copied it as best she could with her single blade.

Sweat plastered her hair to her head and ran down the back of her neck. The monsters had lost their fear of the light, and the only things to their advantage were that the creatures didn't attack like a pack would, in a coordinated fashion, and that at least half of them were stopping to feast on the remains of the ones the humans had killed. In fact, some were running off with pieces in their maws, and others were fighting over the grisly remains.

But there seemed no end to the things. And that green beacon of safety seemed just as far away as ever. She was too frantically busy to think about fear, and yet fear knotted up her insides regardless. Her arms and legs felt as if her bones were made of lead, and she panted with effort. *I don't think—we can keep this up.*

Her arm ached horribly. Neville snapped and stabbed at the things with his enormous, razor-sharp beak—in the case of the spider-things, seizing a leg, and with a vicious twist of his head, snapping it right off. In the case of everything else, stabbing out eyes when he could, and leaving deep, bleeding gashes when he couldn't. But even he was wearying. She wanted to check on everyone else, and she didn't dare take her eyes off the monsters for so much as a single glance. They were still moving forward, but at one hard-fought pace at a time. She was pretty sure she had been hit, but the things had some sort of venom that numbed where they struck, so she couldn't *feel* the pain of her wounds. That might be the most dangerous thing of all. They could bleed to death from a hundred wounds and never realize what was happening until it was too late.

Suddenly, Mary Watson called out something in a high, clear voice. Again, Nan didn't understand the words, but they were clearly not meant for her.

There was a low, muttering growl overhead, and all of the monsters froze, looking up in startlement and fearful silence.

"Hold on to each other!" Mary called, "Birds, take shelter with the girls!" and Neville suddenly shrunk to his normal size. Nan had just time enough to grab him from her shoulder and tuck him inside her tunic, then link arms with Agansing and John Watson, when the tempest struck.

A wild, fierce wind dropped down out of the dark sky, nearly sucking the breath from her lungs. She heard Selim gasp, but had no time to think about what might have made him utter that sound. The whirlwind buffeted them and came close to knocking them down—but that was nothing to what it was doing to the monsters.

As the little sun hung serene and unchanged above John's head, not moving an inch from its position, the brilliant illumination showed that outside their huddled group, braced against the tempest, the wind roared around them in a clockwise circle, and two feet outside their group it was ten times stronger. It picked up the spiders and carried them up into the starless sky as they shrieked in terror; it sent the rest of the creatures tumbling about head over heels as they tried in vain to hold on to the rubble or the more solid bits of wreckage standing up in the rubble. Neville tried to bury himself in her armpit as the circle of wind expanded and howled with a voice like a great, thundering church organ. As it grew, the area in which they stood grew calm, an "eye" of uncannily still air, like that of a typhoon. And once the wind had established that "eye," it strengthened yet again, and Nan could scarcely believe her eyes as she watched it sending monsters smashing into the rubble and the sides of buildings. The vortex kept expanding until it was hundreds of yards wide. Nan stared at the whirlwind surrounding them in utter fascination—and as she looked up at the top of it, she thought for a moment that she saw a huge, fierce eye made of wisps of cloud and light and darkness looking down at her out of it. Fierce—but somehow, she was not afraid of it. Then it vanished, and she wondered if it had just been a trick of the light or of her imagination.

The last of the monsters was scoured from the rubble, and the moment that happened, as quickly as it had spun up, the tempest stopped. The wind dropped to nothing; a few bits of debris, mostly sticks ripped from the dead trees, or possibly detached spider legs, fell straight down out of the air, clattering onto the piles of scattered bricks and stones. The profound silence that followed made her ears ring.

"Run," said Sherlock, sounding uncannily calm. "*Now.*"

They ran. Karamjit supported Selim, who seemed to have fared the worst in the fight. They stumbled from weariness. Nan's breath burned in her lungs. Her side was on fire, and her numb fingers could barely keep hold of her sword, but they ran. And they kept as tightly together as they had been during the fight. Now fear flooded over her, giving her a last reserve of strength to keep running. There was only room in her mind for watching the road lest she fall over something. They ran toward that wonderful green glow, and just as Nan was sure she couldn't run any more, she looked up to see the portal a mere ten yards away, with Puck still holding it open. They flung themselves through; Nan and John were the last through; she landed on her knees on the carpet of the blessedly warm and familiar study, and Puck pulled himself and his staff back.

As soon as he did that, the Celtic Warrior faded, and she was only Nan again. Her sword vanished. Her clothing reverted to her jacket and skirt, in somewhat battered and torn condition. Neville squirmed out of her jacket, jumped down to the floor, and sneezed.

The portal closed with an audible *snap*. She felt blood trickling down the side of her face from a wound in her scalp she hadn't felt, and suddenly turned in panic to the others. Were *they* all right?

Just as she turned, "Selim!" cried Memsa'b rolling a prone Selim over on his back, and there was blood all over the front of his coat, soaking through it. John went to his knees beside Selim, tearing open his coat and shirt to show a gash in his stomach that was pumping out blood so fast—too fast—

Nan uttered a cry of despair.

"Move, Doctor," Puck snapped, and shoved Watson aside without waiting for him to obey. Kneeling beside Selim, his eyes closed in concentration, he held his staff crosswise over the wound, stretching the length of Selim's body.

A brilliant burst of green light erupted from the staff. Half-blinded, Nan looked away and shielded her eyes for a moment. The light was so intense she could see it right through her eyelids! But her panic cut off as if someone had blown out a lamp; for a moment she smelled flowers and thought she heard birdsong, and the cut on her head—all her aches and pains—faded away.

The light died, and she opened her eyes, and when she looked back at Puck and Selim—

Puck stood up at that moment, and stepped back, grounding his staff on the carpet, expression both stern and exalted. *Like a . . . a defending angel,* Nan thought, a little dazed. *Like St. George, or the Archangel Michael.* And there was no sign of Selim's wound, except for the blood caking his clothing.

"Great Scott," Watson breathed.

"I am the Oldest Old One in all England," Puck said. "And I will not let a fellow warrior fall to those—things. Not while there is life in me. But—" he continued, with a lifted brow. "He will still need you, Doctor. I cannot replace the blood he lost, and you must tend him for fever and watch him for infection."

Memsa'b looked up at him with Selim's hand in hers, and tears coursing down her face. "You have saved the life of our dear friend. I can never repay—"

"Fiddlesticks," Puck interrupted, looking like the old Puck again, losing that exalted look. "Let there be no talk of repayment. Get him to his bed and return, for what there *must* be talk of is what happened, and what must happen next."

Staff was summoned. Selim was taken to bed. The rest of them—except for Puck, who remained in the study—dispersed briefly to their rooms. Neville and Grey were exhausted and subdued—and very cold, so Nan and Sarah tucked them into their sable muffs to warm up.

That was when Nan started to shiver. She looked over at Sarah and realized her friend was shivering, too. "I'm chilled to the bone," she said aloud. "I think we all are."

Sarah draped a couple of blankets over chairs by the fire. "Nan, there's blood in your hair," she said, looking at Nan in shock. Nan put a hand up to her head, and it came away sticky.

"I can't feel any wounds," she said. "But I know I had one—" She looked down at her arms and pulled her skirt up to look at her legs. Her stockings were slashed to ribbons, and the sleeves of her jacket were cut in three places. "I think Puck must have healed all of us, not just Selim."

She cleaned up where the wound had been. They bundled themselves into warm, clean clothing, draped themselves in the blankets, picked up the muffs and headed back to the study, where they found pots of hot tea and curry and rice waiting. The others must have been just as cold as they were, for everyone turned up draped in blankets or shawls. And they were all as hungry as tigers, even Puck. Without any regard for manners, one and all, they practically inhaled the food, and then sat nursing mugs of hot, sugared tea in their hands.

"I think we had best get what we remember down on paper immediately," Sherlock advised. "Once we have that . . . we must see what we can make of it."

"I'll take notes," Memsa'b volunteered.

"We'll ward the room," John Watson said, grimly. "I'll be damned if I want another hole into hell opening up here again." He and Mary did incomprehensible things around the edge of the room while Memsa'b gathered up a notebook and pencil and sat down at Sahib's desk where the lamp was.

One by one, they went through everything they could drag out of their exhausted memories. When they were finished, they all sat in silence for a very long time.

Finally Nan spoke up. "If it's coming here . . . why hasn't it come already?" she asked into the quiet. "It can open those portals—so why hasn't it just come through one?"

"Likely because it can't," Puck spoke up at last. "These things have rules, though I'll wager Holmes doesn't believe that. It can reach in here briefly, take prey and drag it back, but it can't just *come* here. It has to be *invited*. And invited in a particular way."

"A magic ceremony of some kind—" John Watson hazarded, and Puck nodded.

Since this was completely out of Nan's purview, she half listened with one ear, with Neville in his muff, cradled in her lap, while trying to put together both sides of the puzzle— the abductions, and the pronouncement from that thing in the other world. King? Priest? A little of both. It had talked about *Our Communion,* and said that "the pure" would enter into it. But it spoke about this "Communion" as if it already existed. So what could it be? And *why* had it had girls taken from here then sent back mindless? If all it had wanted to do was rip their souls out of them, why send them back? If she had learned anything from John and Mary about magic, it was that magic was costly in terms of energy, and making a door between two worlds must have been *fantastically* costly. So why send them back?

And there was something about "the pure" that kept nagging at her. The thing had taken Arthur Fensworth, and had not removed his soul. Could it have been taking other people all along? Fensworth had spoken of seeing other humans. Had Amelia's visions been a view into that other world right at the time when those people were taken? And if so, why had they not had their souls taken? Why had they been left to scavenge and hide in the ruins? What was the difference between Arthur Fensworth and those girls? It couldn't have been that he was male; he had said he had seen women and children coming to "feed." It had to be something else. . . .

Was it that they were "pure" and he was not?

Her eyes widened. "John," she said, slowly, into a pause in the other discussion. "The girls at the hospital—are they all virgins?"

John Watson looked at her for a moment, mouth agape, ears reddening. "Ah . . . I . . . er . . . I cannot speak for the three newest, but . . . ah . . . yes, the first three are. . . ." He couldn't bring himself to say the word.

"Well, *I* can speak for the other three, since I examined them closely," said Holmes, without a hint of embarrassment. "They were."

"That *thing* back there . . . it talked about how the 'pure' would become part of its 'Communion.' And that's certainly one difference between them and Arthur Fensworth." She raised an eyebrow. "Also between them and those other people he saw in the ruins, coming to feed."

"By Jove," John Watson said. "I think you might be right. But . . . why?" Then he shook his head. "Never mind that. There's six of them. It said it was 'about' to come across into our world. That means it can't yet . . ." He turned to Puck. "*You* said it has to be invited, probably with a magic ceremony. Magic ceremonies often need odd numbers of participants; three, five, seven, nine or thirteen. What if he can control these girls on *this* side? They could invite him!"

"So . . . the obvious thing would be to separate them," Nan pointed out. But Holmes shook his head.

"If he can control them, all he needs to do is open one of those portals wherever they are, call them across, and make another anywhere he wants to put them," Sherlock pointed out. "*He* doesn't care if he drops them down on the Downs in midwinter and they die of exposure, as long as they invite him across before they drop dead." He shook his head. "If we want any warning before he crosses, if we want any control over *where* he crosses, we need to have them together." His lips compressed together into a tight line.

"Sherlock," Nan said slowly, thinking about those terrible mobs of monsters that had nearly killed them all. "You

are talking as if we have any chance at actually stopping
them when they come over. We barely made it out of there
alive, and we nearly lost Selim—and they weren't trying to
stop us, not really. That thing intended for some of us, at
least, to escape; it said as much. So what are we supposed to
oppose it with?"

"The White Lodge—" John began, then dropped his
head in his hands. "—won't be of much use. Not against an
army. Except for Fire, and perhaps Earth, our Elementals
are not well suited to combat."

Sherlock got an odd expression on his face, one that Nan
couldn't read. "We keep saying 'him' and 'it.' What if that
thing is . . . a queen?"

John blinked at him. "You mean like Her Majesty?" he
asked, looking confused.

"No. Like a queen bee," Holmes corrected. "Or an ant.
That thing's behavior—it seems to control all those creatures over there without any obvious means of communica-
tion. We are surmising it can control the girls as well. That
it spoke of taking the 'pure' into a kind of hive mind suggests more queen-like behavior. Watson, what happens
when a queen ant decides to take over another queen's
nest? Never mind, you probably don't know. She sends in
her warriors and kills the other queen, then enslaves the
rest of the nest." He paused. "So what do you think will
happen when this queen discovers there is another queen
on this island? I think we only saw a handful of the thing's
warrior ants tonight. And I suspect that queen can hatch
out as many as she needs to. If she establishes a foothold
here—the first thing she will do, as soon as she learns of a
rival's existence, will be to eliminate that rival."

"She's probably hatching out more monsters right now,"
Mary Watson agreed, despondently. "She's very close to
making her invasion—and that might be why we weren't
overwhelmed by monsters as soon as we appeared. Why
hatch out a hungry horde until you need them?"

"How in the name of God are we supposed to stop
them?" Sarah asked.

"I . . . don't know," Sahib replied.

Gloom settled over the entire party. Neville crept out of his sable muff and into Nan's lap, huddling there like a cat and making unhappy muttering noises while she stroked him. She glanced over at Sarah and saw that Grey was doing the same thing.

"I don't suppose Lord Alderscroft would be of any use in acquiring a few troops and a Maxim gun or two, would he?" Sahib asked. "There will be a limit to how large a portal that thing can create. If we can destroy enough of them, we may be able to stop them until magicians can destroy the portal."

"Until it moves the girls and makes a portal where we can't find it," Sarah pointed out, bleakly. "And if we . . . if we were to murder the girls, it would just create more of them where we can't find them."

John shook his head, though whether that was denying that the girls should be killed or at the impossibility of stopping the thing from creating more of the "Communion," Nan could not tell. "Alderscroft is not the problem with getting Maxim guns and troops. Explain to me how we are to frame this for the government! How do we convince them this is a genuine threat? This is the greatest Empire on Earth, and our armies have faced vast hordes of enemies— now tell me how we convince them that a paltry couple of hundred monsters and a thing that can siphon souls away is any kind of a threat that the White Lodge cannot handle? Because I believe it is, down in my bones, but I am *blamed* if I can think of a way to convince anyone else!"

Nan petted Neville and tried to make her mind quiet while it persisted in running in frantic circles like a cornered mouse. But all she could think of was that John was right. She was sure they could convince Alderscroft, and *he* could summon the White Lodge, but the White Lodge was composed of magicians who normally set their powers against purely magical threats. When faced with a horde of those monsters pouring through a portal they could not close, what would they do?

She had the sinking feeling they would either try to stand their ground and be slaughtered, or flee and be slaughtered.

If such formidable fighters as Selim, Agansing, Karamjit, and *she* had barely escaped with their lives when the creatures were not truly *trying* to kill them, a disorganized lot of gentlemen would be cut down out of hand.

"We need real fighters," she said aloud. "With *guns*. I don't think that thing has ever seen a gun. Didn't you just suggest there is a limit on the size of a portal that can be made?" She looked over at Puck, who shrugged and spoke for the first time since they'd all sat down.

"I don't know," he admitted. "But it does stand to reason. Making one takes a mort of power, and the bigger it is, the more power it takes. There has to be a limit."

"So if we could convince *someone* that we need soldiers and guns . . . the thing can only send through so many at a time. Right?" Now she looked to Agansing and Karamjit.

"It would be like forcing our enemies to come through a narrow mountain pass," Agansing agreed. "This is a good strategy. A very few men with guns have held off tremendous forces in this way before now."

"And meanwhile, the White Lodge can be figuring out how to close and seal the portal?" Now she turned to John and Mary.

"I should think so," John said slowly. "But . . . we need those soldiers and guns in the first place."

But Sherlock had gotten a new expression of determination on his face. "If you can convince Alderscroft, I can virtually guarantee he has some way to get the assistance of conventional forces. And I will talk to my brother. The threat to Her Majesty will get his attention as nothing else will. John, Mary, I think you and I need to travel back to London, posthaste."

"Nan!" Sarah said, suddenly. "I just thought of something! Surely Amelia can give us some warning if the thing is on the move!"

Nan wanted to hit herself in the head. Why hadn't *she* thought of that? "I should think so, especially if Memsa'b and I work with her."

"Alderscroft and I will have the girls moved to some place on the property where they will be safe, but which will also provide us with a more defensible position," John said after a moment. "Damn shame it's not summer—we could put them in a tent in the middle of a field somewhere."

"If you move them too far, the thing might be able to tell," Mary pointed out. "And then there is the chance it would abandon the group it has already created and start a new one."

Holmes nodded. "We should not underestimate this thing. There is no harm in overestimating its cleverness, but—well, you see my point."

"I'll muster what I can," Puck said, looking determined. "You have it right, John Watson; my folk are not warlike. But we will not surrender this island Logres! If this thing succeeds—well, it won't, that's all. It won't."

Agansing and Karamjit exchanged a look. "There are preparations we can make," said Karamjit.

"Memsa'b and Sarah and I will work with Amelia," Nan added. "We can telegraph Alderscroft if anything changes before you muster us all at the hospital." Neville interrupted her with an imperious *quork,* and she looked down at him. "Or I can send Neville. That's probably faster."

"Right, then, I think we all have our tasks." Sherlock rose, and the rest of them rose with him. His face was set in grim determination. "As our young friend has said, they shall not have our island. And there's the end to it."

17

ALEXANDRE dreamed. In his dreams lately, no matter what they were about, he was always cold. He had tried putting a warming brick in his bed, he had tried piling on more blankets, but he was always cold.

Most of the time, they were not easy dreams.

Tonight . . . while it was not an easy dream, at least it started out as being satisfying. He dreamed that he was beating his father with a riding crop, as he had so often longed to do, humiliating the man, chaining him to a doghouse in his best suit, and forcing him to eat out of a dish on the ground. *"There!"* he was shouting. *"Call on Jesus, old man. Go ahead! Call on him! See if Jesus will save you!"*

And then, just as the bastard broke into helpless tears, he sensed something behind him. A wave of the too-familiar cold washed over him. The sky turned dark, and the air became thin and hard to breathe—then he turned to see—It.

Behind him in the ground was that hole into nowhere. The deep, black void, which immediately became a pillar as soon as he turned, and as he stared at it in horror, it grew a hundred tentacles and seized him, and dragged him screaming toward it, and in his mind the words burned. *Bring Us another! Bring it to Us now! Bring it! Bring it!*

He started up out of his dream in a cold sweat, only to discover, to his continuing horror, that part of it, at least, was *not* a dream. *It* was somehow still here. The voice still echoed in his head. *We need another! Now! Get it for Us now!*

This isn't possible. I just fed it! "You—you gave me seven days—" he objected, speaking into the chill darkness of his room, aware only that there was something horribly, terribly *wrong* with his bedroom door. It was ... darker than it should be; there was just a black rectangle that soaked up all the light from the fire and reflected nothing. As if there wasn't a door there anymore. "You can't ask this!" he continued, his voice rising in panic. "You gave me seven days! For Godsake, I gave you *six at once!* You gave me seven days!"

And that has changed! We need the pure one and the food NOW!

And then the freezing temperatures of his bedroom abruptly warmed, the darkness where his bedroom door had been vanished, and the door returned. He found he was gasping for breath, his heart racing in panic.

And Alf was pounding on the closed bedroom door. "Guv! *Guv!* Yew oil roight?"

He was still too paralyzed with terror to move; fortunately, Alf was not. The doorknob rattled, as Alf tried it, then the door slammed open. "Guv! Oi 'eard yew yellin', an' th' damn door wouldn' open—"

"It was here," Alexandre panted. "The thing. From the basement. It was here, in my room, I don't know *how* it was here, I don't know how it got out of the basement, but it was *here.* It isn't happy, Alf! It told me it wants its next victims now!"

"Bloody 'ell," Alf muttered, looked around in the light from the coal fire, spied the little ladder-back chair Alexandre sometimes used to drape his coats over at the end of the day, and helped himself to it. He sat down on it backward, with his arms over the top of it, and shook his head. "Cain't be done, guv. Impossible. Last snatch was too much, coppers took notice and took it 'ard, an' papers got aholt of it. Acrost th' river's ballyhooin' 'bout it in all the papers. Heard tell the 'Murican Ambassydor's yellin' at the PM. Battersea's crawlin' wi' coppers. Guv, *Sherlock bloody 'Olmes* was there! In Battersea! Crawlin' all over where we left them gels. Ain't safe t'grab a gel from anywhere in Lunnon, with or without thet thing's 'elp."

"Oh God," Alexandre moaned, burying his face in his hands. "What am I going to do? *It got into my room!* If it can go there, it can probably go anywhere! Even if we cut and run, it can probably find us!"

"Likely," Alf agreed, completely calm. "Likely it's got yer scent. I've knowed that t' 'appen with magical beasties. It'll foller yew no matter where ye run. Yew could prolly cross th' Channel an' it'd find yew."

He . . . didn't say "us." He said "you." The bottom dropped out of his world as he understood that Alf—very correctly— was pointing out that *he* was the only one tied to the entity. He and he alone had summoned it. He and he alone had brought it the sacrifices it had asked for. He'd thought this would mean he and he alone would be rewarded when it was happy. He had not thought about the other side of that coin, that if he failed to please this thing, he and he alone was going to pay the price.

Alf, however, had obviously thought this out more thoroughly than he had. Was Alf about to abandon him, cut and run?

"Lemme think on this a minnit," Alf continued, calmly, and Alexandre nearly wept with relief, understanding that Alf was not about to leave him. At least, not yet. Alf put his chin down on his crossed arms on top of the chair, and pondered. Finally he straightened up again. "Oi cain't get ye a virgin ternight, an prolly not termorrow, but yew 'member I tol' yew I c'ld git one from thet madame I know? Reckon, Oi c'n git one in four days, at most. An' Oi c'n 'ire another boy."

"I remember," Alexandre said, feeling hope again. "Do you think she'd have one now? Is there any chance we can get one tomorrow?"

Alf made a face. "She pretty much always 'as one, but

it'll cost, cost yew dear, 'pending on 'ow 'andsome th' gel is. Look, guv, thet's dangerous. Pretty gel, she'll hev bin looked over a *lot.* Lotta men'll hev been lookin' t'pay fer th' privilege. *Yew* know."

Indeed he did, having paid quite a high price for the "privilege" a few times in the past.

"So if th' gel goes missin' then turns up i' th' paper? Lotta men'll recognize th' pichure. They'll know where she come from, an' they likely won't be shy 'bout tellin' that 'Olmes 'bout it, though they'd not tell th' coppers. An' th' madame ain't gonna be shy about tellin' th' coppers 'bout us to stay outa trouble."

"Damn," he swore under his breath. Alf was right.

"But that's a pretty one. One she's already got in th' 'ouse. Thing is, she c'n *get* another one easy, one that ain't 'andsome, nor suited for th' trade, an' she won't give two pins if the gel shows up in the papers, or in the river fer thet matter. So she ain't gonna say nothin' t' nobody." Alf tipped him a wink. "Thet thing on'y cares if it's a virgin, don't care if the gel's so ugly yew need ter put a bag on 'er 'ead. So that's 'alf the prollem solved. Other 'alf's gettin' rid of 'er. An' I gotter ideer 'bout that, too."

"Let's hear it," Alexandre said, clutching his blankets to his chest to stop his shivering. But he was feeling comforted. Alf clearly knew what he was doing, and had been able to think of a good plan. Surely he had just as good a plan for getting rid of the wench once the entity was done with her.

But Alf's next words shocked him to the core. He grinned. "We takes 'er t' coppers oursel's."

"What?" Alexandre was only able to get that single word out around his shock. "You can't—"

Alf held up a hand, cutting him off. "Oi said, 'ear me out. We takes 'er t' coppers oursel's. This's in *all* th' papers naow. Oi'll pick up one, when oi go talk t'madame. Madame'll wrap 'er up nice'n'tidy drugged fer us, an' we brings 'er 'ere in the coach. The thing takes 'er an' spits 'er out. We dresses 'er up pretty, then calls a cab. We goes t'Battersea Perlice Station, all right'n'proper, wi' th' wench *an'* th' paper. *Was comin' 'ome from thee-ayter, an' there she was in th' middle of road,* you sez. *Loik in paper, see 'ere,* you sez. *Yessir, we did,* I sez, all respekfull." He winked. "An' if they ask you *Wut thee-ayter,* yew 'em an' 'aw an' then tells 'em your moosic 'all. An they'll grin an' wink an' think yer a roight ol' dawg. An' even if Sherlock Bloody 'Olmes comes along later an asks at the 'all if yew was there, yew *know* wut they'll say."

"I've heard them say it with my own ears," Alexandre admitted. "That they don't ask for bloody names at the door and it's not their bloody job to memorize every customer's face."

"Heg-zactly. Ain't *nobody* gonna suspect yer." Alf cackled. "Woi should they? Didn't yer bring th' gel along loik a good liddle gennlemun? Ain't yew got a good repewtation? Doin' yer doody an' all thet muck. Yew'll get a pat on th' back an' sent 'ome, thet's what'll 'appen. An' if Sherlock Bloody 'Olmes comes along askin' where we found 'er, Oi'll give 'im a good answer an' 'e c'n go do 'is bloody detectin' there."

And, in fact, once his heart stopped pounding like a steam piston, he realized Alf was absolutely right. No one would suspect him, any more than they'd be suspecting anyone else in this street. He'd be commended for being a good citizen and sent away. And if Sherlock Holmes did turn up, why, there would be nothing connecting them to the girl.

"Alf . . . you are a genius," he said fervently. "What time is it?"

"Not tew late fer me t'hev a talk wit' th'madame," Alf assured him. "But yew better go down an' let thet thing know it ain't gonna get nuthin' *naow,* an' if't gets rid'a yew, it ain't gonna get nuthin' *ever,* 'cause it don't got *my* scent an' Oi ain't gonna play no games with somethin' what et my boss, Oi'm gonna leg it outa 'ere an' lock the 'ouse up behind me. Naow lemme get dressed proper fer visitin' th' 'Ouse."

Alf left, and shaking in every limb, Alexandre pulled on trousers, a dressing gown, and slippers—and went to the strongbox in his bureau. Loyalty like Alf's needed to be rewarded immediately, so they *both* knew the consequences of both desertion and continued loyalty. He counted out ten golden guineas—he had no fear that Alf would have any trouble making use of a coin that large, for he had done so before, just not quite so many—and opened the door to find Alf pulling on an overcoat in the hall.

"Here," he said, holding the heavy gold coins out where the hall light would catch their glow. "This is just for your cab fare out and back, and you keep all the rest for yourself. I'll expect to pay the madame separately. And accordingly."

Alf's eyes gleamed, but he tugged on his hat brim. "Thenks, guv. I 'spect we're *both* clever fellers, eh?"

"I certainly hope so, because I am about to test my cleverness against that . . . thing." He squared his shoulders and swallowed. "Let's just see how clever I am."

Resolutely, he lit the lamp waiting on the hall table, opened the basement door, and if he didn't exactly *march* down the stairs, at least he didn't tiptoe, either. *Better open with my strongest cards,* he decided as he reached the bottom. He stood just out of tentacle reach (or so he hoped) and barked at the dark void in the floor, "You there! I have something to say to you!"

Nothing. *Well, at least it didn't strike me down for insolence . . . yet.* He didn't venture any nearer, but he raised his voice, and *thought* at it as hard as he could, "I said, you there! If you want any more sacrifices, you had better come out of that hole right now because we need to have a chat! You are in *no* position to be demanding any—"

He bit off the last word as the pillar of darkness suddenly loomed up, larger than ever, out of the hole. And there was something both hostile and edgy about it, although he could not have said what told him that if his life had depended on it. At least it didn't sprout tentacles—or at least, not yet.

We told you—

"I know damned well what you told me," he snapped. "And you're not going to bloody well *get* it! You think virgins are lying about in the street for me to pick up? That last little delivery has sent the police crawling everywhere, looking for the abductor now! I'm of no damned mind to get myself hauled off and thrown in a cell because *you* are impatient to get your last 'pure one'!"

There was a long—a very long—pause.

. . . what are Police?

"People that can and will *lock* me up and brick up this house, leaving you to starve alone until the end of time, my friend!" he snapped. "There are a *lot* more of them than you imagine, I promise you! They can seal this place up so you *can never get out.*" Unless they called on the White Lodge, that probably wasn't true—but the odds had certainly changed, and they might. Now that Sherlock Holmes was on the case, they might! God only knew the kinds of resources that devil had at his disposal. He could probably have tracked the coach back *here* just from the cuts and dents in the wheels if the streets hadn't been frozen as hard as rocks!

He *felt* something cold and alien crawling through his mind at that point . . . and this time, rather than being paralyzed, he thought, fiercely, about the worst possible outcome he could imagine. Holmes *finding* him. Being dragged off in a Black Maria and thrown into prison and hung. The White Lodge turning up and performing a ceremony of the sort he could only create out of imagination, full of clergymen and Elementals and lights and pure power, and sealing the house away inside something like a glass egg, only made of power.

He felt the thing withdraw from his mind. And there was silence for a very long time.

We need the final sacrifice, he heard, finally, and it was not his imagination, the voice was much subdued. *We must have the final sacrifice, so that We may come fully into this world. There will be reward for you. Much reward. You will be a Great Master, greater than those in your mind. But to do that We must have the last pure one, or we will not have the power.*

Well now, that was more like it. "I'll get the sacrifices, but to do so without risk will take several days," he said, stiffly. "You'll have to wait. It shouldn't take the full seven days, but it simply cannot be *now.* It's not possible."

He could sense that the thing was not happy, that it was very angry, in fact, but it had to accept what he had told it. *Very well,* it said. And the pillar collapsed down into the floor again.

"Oi'm orf," said Alf from the top of the stairs. And Alexandre was left to go back up to his room, where he lay in bed, eyes wide open, until Alf returned. Only then could he manage to close his eyes and try to sleep.

But his dreams were not pleasant.

Nan and Amelia were in Memsa'b's office, with Neville sitting on the back of Nan's chair. It was . . . surreal, actually. She was completely aware of that whole other world, separated from her own by what seemed like the thinnest of veils. She knew that at any moment, with little to no warning, that world could break in on hers, with a terrible, potentially very powerful enemy pouring through that break to try and turn London into a copy of that world. She had fought off the denizens of that world herself; one of her best friends lay wounded and had nearly died.

And yet, here she was, with Holmes, sitting in Memsa'b's study, drinking tea and nibbling cakes with Amelia—who was describing in more detail what it was like to have her visions, quite as if those visions were merely frightening and unpleasant, rather than the harbingers of potential doom. She could hardly believe Amelia's calm; the girl was almost a different person from the one she had first met.

"It's like a door, opening and shutting again," Amelia explained. "Now that I have . . . some experience at this, I can tell you that I can *feel* when it is about to open, and ready myself. It's not immediate, the vision doesn't immediately follow the sensation. The vision comes perhaps ten minutes later, but no more than that."

Holmes looked to Nan, who shrugged. "I would think, given what I have watched John and Mary do, that opening the portal into this world takes some preparation. That might be what Amelia is sensing."

Sherlock nodded, and Amelia continued. "Memsa'b and I have been taking notes, and I have been drawing pictures. They aren't very good," she added shyly, handing them to Holmes who examined them closely, then passed them to Nan.

"You are too modest," Holmes said. "They are quite good. And they are certainly identical to that place in which we found ourselves last night."

Though she had only used a pencil, Nan thought that Amelia had caught the essence of the place perfectly. The dead trees, like skeletal hands clawing at the sky, the broken buildings like piles of empty-eyed skulls. There were hints of creatures lurking in the ruins, but nothing easy to identify.

"Yes, I thought that was you in the first vision I had last night," Amelia said, matter-of-factly. "I recognized everyone except you, Mr. Holmes. I actually had two visions last night. The one where you entered that strange world while a wonderful creature with a glowing staff kept the entrance open for you, and another, later." She bit her lip, and paled. "I saw you enter, and arm yourselves, then I saw that poor old man run to you and die. Then you all went further into that world, and I couldn't follow. I can't seem to move past that entry-point in my visions. I was in the vision until you all returned, supporting poor Selim, and then after you came back through, the vision ended."

"You said you had a second vision, later?" Holmes prompted.

Amelia nodded. "Not very much later, either. I had just awakened from the first and was about to call for Memsa'b when the second began. It did not last very long, but by the time it happened, something had already carried the body of the old man off. Other than that, it was quiet. When it ended, and I awakened again, there was a great deal of bustle going on outside my room. I opened the door, learned from one of the ayahs coming by in the hall that Selim had been hurt, and decided to wait to tell Memsa'b about the visions until things settled down again. So I took notes and drew some pictures and went back to sleep." She settled the pile of pencil drawings carefully back inside a portfolio and looked expectantly at Holmes.

Yes, Amelia was certainly a very different young woman than the one who had been in that hospital, Nan reflected. Now that she knew she wasn't going mad—that, in fact, what she was seeing was important—she was showing a great deal of composure and even bravery in the face of having to endure those horrific visions of hers. Nan wasn't at all sure *she* would be able to sit here and speak calmly if her nights were interrupted without warning by visions of that terrible world into which they had thrust themselves a night ago.

A very great deal had happened in less than twenty-four hours. Much more than Nan would have ever dreamed could happen.

Sherlock had spoken with his brother, and Watson with Lord Alderscroft. It was Alderscroft who had gone to the director of the hospital and arranged to move the soulless girls to a concert hall. Nan marveled that the place even *had* such a thing in it, but then the patients were, for the most part, of the sort of class that was used to being entertained. And, she supposed, it made the lives of those who had been incarcerated against their will there a little more bearable.

Events were certainly on the move—*had* moved, much faster than Nan would have expected. At first light John and Mary had taken the coach into London, and apparently it had been easier to convince Alderscroft that things were perilous than any of them would have predicted.

Somewhat to Holmes' bemusement, the Hartons' amazement, and her astonishment . . . it turned out there *was* a very special platoon of Her Majesty's Army that was kept at the ready to deal with . . . "unnatural situations," as Alderscroft had called it. These were all men who had, at some point in their military careers, dealt successfully with "incidents" of the supernatural. They were well trained, sharp, and again, as Alderscroft put it, "not easily rattled." Based in London and at the call of Alderscroft, they were already deployed to the hospital, where pairs of them were to guard the girls day and night.

Alderscroft must have invoked Her Majesty's name to get all this done, Nan reflected. *I cannot imagine that doctor allowing part of his hospital to be taken over by a platoon of soldiers otherwise.* And he must have invoked some sort of Special Privilege to keep the man quiet about it so that he would ask no questions.

I wonder if that was Lord A's work, or Holmes' brother's? It could have been either or both, working together, as she knew now they often did; moving a small group of very special troops and presenting the doctor with an order with the Royal Seal on it would have been well within Alderscroft's powers, but Holmes' brother actually had the ear of Her Majesty and could probably manage it quicker.

Alas, to Holmes' disappointment, there was no Maxim gun to be had on such short notice, but on his recommendation, one had been called for, and if this stretched on for very much longer, it might well arrive before the Unhallowed Queen opened her portal to conquer this world.

Enhanced magical wardings had been placed all around the School, by Puck himself. That was why Karamjit and Agansing were there at the hospital now, rather than here. As it happened, two of those special soldiers had been Sikhs, and one a Gurkha, and they were the very men the Hartons' servants had intended to attempt to recruit themselves! According to a letter carried to her this evening by Neville, there had been great surprise all around when the acquaintances learned that Agansing and Karamjit were in the employ of *"pukka jaadoogar"* like their own commander, Alderscroft. And Agansing and Karamjit had been quite chagrined to discover there actually was a platoon that held men like themselves, as adept in battling supernatural evils as they were the more mundane evils that men were only too capable of producing.

Puck was nowhere around, but Nan was not at all concerned; he could be summoned in an instant, either by Roan here, or Durwin, who had moved himself to the hospital, where he had established himself with an eye to being helpful to the soldiers. The rules that governed hob behavior were very much suspended for now, by Robin's own decree.

"What's the point of these rules, if they keep us from defending our own home?" he had said. *"And if I can't break the rules I set, then who can?"*

Holmes interrupted her thoughts. "It seems to me that we have good, sound evidence pointing to you being sensitive to these portals opening, Miss Amelia," he said. "There is no reason to think that the being did not open a second one last night, after the first had closed. It probably wanted to contact its ally in our London, to prepare him for the imminent invasion. Was there any difference in the strength of the visions?"

"Oh, yes," Amelia nodded decisively. "The first one was much clearer, much stronger than all the rest have been. The others were much the same in strength."

"A good argument for all the other portals being some physical distance away from you, then." Holmes looked at his own notes, and added another.

It was too bad that they couldn't delay the thing for a while by separating the girls, or merely keep the seventh away from the rest. But John Watson had rightly pointed out that if they delayed for longer than usual in bringing the last girl to the rest, the thing would likely grow impatient, snatch away *all* of them, and work its spell in some remote place where it could do as it pleased. They had decided that as soon as the last girl was located, they could delay as much as two days, but not more.

Holmes continued to ask questions about minute details of Amelia's visions; she answered him as best she could, although too often her answer had to be "I don't know." Nevertheless he did not seem unsatisfied with her performance. Finally he thanked her. "What are you doing with yourself?" he asked, out of what seemed to be pure curiosity. "It would be better to occupy your mind somehow, and try not to fret yourself too much—"

Amelia smiled faintly at him. "I am going about my day, Mr. Holmes, which at the moment consists of helping to teach some of the children here, and taking classes in things my parents forbade me to learn. I enjoy being here; quite frankly, it is much more pleasant here than it ever was at home. There is very little that I can do to combat this terrible creature should it break through to our world. So I am doing what I can to prevent it, and meanwhile living my life. Either you will stop this thing, and any time I spent wasted in huddling in my room in fear will have been wasted, or you will not, and wiser heads than I will instruct me on what next I can do. The longer I am here at the Harton School, the more I realize how little freedom life under my father's rule allowed me. I am not going to permit fear and uncertainty to rob me of what I have only just won."

She raised her head high as she said this and looked Holmes straight in the eyes. He nodded.

"Well said, Miss Amelia. God willing, we shall finish this creature, and you may continue to enjoy the freedom you have here." He sketched a little salute to her; she bobbed a suggestion of a curtsey, and went on her way, head held high.

"If you and Sarah and that girl are examples of the kinds of women Isabelle Harton is turning out of her school, England is in safe hands," he said to Nan. "Now . . . let us put our heads together and see what we can adduce from all the clues in these visions."

Alexandre was bitterly unhappy at the moment. Alf's initial interview with the madame had been inconclusive.

"She's gotta virgin in th' 'Ouse, but it ain't one yew want," he'd reported to Alexandre when he got in. "Too many gents 'as seen 'er an is biddin' on 'er. I seen 'er m'self." He'd smacked his lips. "Blimey, she's a looker. 'Ore-'ouse born'n'raised, so she knows wut's wut, too." He shook his head. "Price's gonna go 'igh, 'Ouse of Lords 'igh, an' plenty of gents'll wanta know 'oo she goes to. But Madame says she'll think on't, an' Oi'm t'come back termorrer." Then he'd yawned hugely and gone to bed.

Alexandre had pinned all his hopes on Alf coming back with word of success, if not in possession of a girl. His heart and courage had plummeted. And he was, frankly, too nervy and too upset to stay in the flat after that.

So Alexandre had gone out. He couldn't bear to stay in the house with *that* thing so clearly able to get at him whenever it chose. But wherever he went that day, fear followed. He could not enjoy his food, or the performers at his music hall, or even the discovery of several gems at the bookstore. He slunk back to the flat, feeling exhausted, unsatisfied . . . and laboring under a weight of dull fear that prodded him with muted pain, like pebbles in his shoes that he could not rid himself of.

When he slumped into the kitchen where his man was, Alf took one look at him and went to the pantry, returning with a bottle of clear liquid. He poured a small glass full and set it down in front of Alexandre. "Drink thet," he ordered. "All at once."

Alexandre tossed it down—and nearly choked. As he gasped for breath, Alf put a glass of water in his hand, which he tossed down. "What . . . was . . . that?" he asked, still gasping. His eyes watered. His throat and gut felt as if he had just swallowed fire, but whatever it was, he could already tell it was going to make him drunk in a very little while.

"'Omemade stuff," Alf said. "Somethin' Oi make. Oi gotta liddle still. Don' usually drink't when yew got so much better tipple, but it's got its uses. Don' need it much, but . . . when yew need it, yew need it."

It must have been nearly two hundred proof. He felt the pure alcohol going straight to his brain, fuzzing things out a little. Forcing relaxation on him. Taking the edge off his fear.

"Naow yer ready t'sit'n listen," Alf said. "Talked t' Madame Maude. She's got th' virgin auction on th' boil, *but* Oi did some fancy talkin' an' made some promises, an' she decided she hain't about t' miss out on prime money fer sorry goods what she c'n git fer free, so she's makin' time fer us. She reckons t' git a gel from a work'ouse she knows. 'S run boi a lotta Bible pounders, they keeps the gels separate from the lads, an' dragons at th' door t'keep 'em apart. Uglier a gel is, more like she' a virgin, but Maude'll inspect on th' prem'ses t'make sure. She hain't astin' no questions, an' she wants five guineas."

"Five guineas, versus having to face that *thing* without a virgin for it?" He shuddered. "That's no contest. When?"

"She'll 'ave the gel tomorrer. Oi tol 'er yew wasn't fussy 'bout th' face, but yer partiklar 'bout bein' clean an' lookin' loik a lady. She'll 'ave her good'n'sleepy an' dressed up posh. Oi' got a lad t'day an' put 'im upstairs. 'E's on t'out-side of 'nuff beer t'put 'im t'bed, an' when 'e wakes up, 'e'll be thinkin' more 'bout all the food 'e c'n eat than anythin' else." Alf patted his shoulder. "Easy-peasy nice an' breezy, guv. This tiome next week, ye'll be laughin' an' in clover."

Alexandre tried not to shudder.

He went to his bedroom with great reluctance and took a brandy bottle with him. If this devil's brew Alf had given him wore off, he wanted to renew the haze. This might not be the best way of dealing with the entity, but he'd *tried* keeping it out with the magic that was in the same book as the summoning spell, and that hadn't worked—

Or had it? It might have been able to speak to him—and it might have been able to transform his bedroom door—but the protective circle hadn't reached to the door, just around the bed. And it hadn't crossed that.

He undressed quickly and pulled on the nightshirt. If the protective circle *did* work, he wanted to be inside it as soon as he could get there.

He began to feel a little better. By the time he had climbed into his bed, he had begun to relax enough that he actually was able to fall asleep.

Alf left for the whorehouse a little before dark in the coach. Alex waited impatiently for him to return by the back door. They had both agreed to continue to take the utmost cau-tion in making sure the neighbors saw nothing, and the very last thing they needed at this point was for some busybody to see a well-dressed girl half carried into the house. The house was utterly silent, except for the slow ticking of the eight-day clock. He was tempted to drink the brandy bottle dry, but nursed his drink, sipping it carefully, just enough to keep the edge off his anxiety.

It was moon-dark, so all he saw of the coach when it finally arrived was a dark shape against the snow. But when he made out a figure coming up the path to the door, he knew his long wait was finally over, and he flung it open immediately.

In the light streaming out of the door, Alf looked like—an ordinary servant bringing in a bundle. He heaved a tremendous sigh of relief. Alf had been cautious—tremendously cautious. There was a roll of what looked like carpet over his shoulder. Presumably the girl was inside it. He found himself giggling, as he recalled how Cleopatra had had herself smuggled in to Julius Caesar in the same fashion. Well, he was no Caesar, and he already knew the girl in the carpet was no Cleopatra either.

Alf thudded up the stairs into the kitchen, and Alexandre closed the door behind him and made sure the curtains were closed on the kitchen windows as Alf stopped next to the table.

Alf slowly slid his burden off his shoulder. " 'Elp me 'old 'er hup, guv," Alf said, and Alexandre steadied the roll upright while Alf unwound the carpet from its contents, catching the swaying girl by her shoulders and keeping her standing. Her eyes were half-closed, and she didn't seem even remotely aware of her surroundings.

The girl revealed was scrupulously clean, scrubbed right down to her fingernails, which were neatly trimmed. Her hair was washed, her ears had been cleaned. That was a detail that he hadn't considered, but he was very glad either Alf or the madame had. She was dressed "posh," as Alf would say—wearing a brown wool gown that would not have looked out of place on a girl of his own social set, a cream silk waist, and good leather boots. Her hair had been pulled back into a severe knot at the base of her neck, and she smelled faintly of lavender.

As for her face . . . she was very, very plain. Horse-faced, he'd have said; her upper teeth protruded over her lower

ones, her chin was receded, her nose was large and flat, and
her eyes small. But there were plenty of girls in his social set
and higher who were just as plain. She would not stand out
as an oddity among the other six.

"She's perfect," he said aloud. "Worth every penny."

Alf nodded with satisfaction. "Think yew c'n git 'er
downstairs by yerself?"

She was quite light—judging by the thin wrist bones, she
hadn't been fed all that well in the workhouse. And again . . .
that was not necessarily an anomaly. He knew girls who
were even thinner. He lifted her, and felt a good corset under that dress. The Madame seemed to have covered every
possible detail. She had certainly earned her guineas. "Easily. Can you get the boy by yourself?"

Alf snorted. "Jest a tap on th' 'ead an' 'e'll be dreamin'.
Leave th' door open. Oi'll be roight down."

The feeling of relief he experienced as he carried the girl
down the stairs was the most profound emotion he had ever
felt in his life. He was almost giddy with it, as he laid the girl
down beside the void in the floor, and stepped back.

Five minutes later, Alf joined him, and laid the boy
down beside the girl. The boy looked to be another workhouse or hiring hall acquisition. Thin, poorly dressed, about
thirteen. And probably he'd been guzzling beer and stuffing himself and dreaming of what he could steal from his
"new employers."

"Oi'll jest leave ye to it," Alf said, and went back up the
stairs.

But he hadn't gotten more than halfway up when the
void suddenly erupted into a pillar, the pillar exploded with
tentacles, and the tentacles seized the two victims and
dragged them into the darkness. The pillar alone remained.

Alexandre let out his breath. "Now . . . we wait."

18

ALF had always considered himself a practical man, and one of the things about being a practical man was constantly weighing loyalty against . . . circumstances. So far, he had never had circumstances outweigh loyalty, but this situation might change all that.

He sat in the kitchen, nursing brandies. He had fallen in with magicians quite by accident. One had plucked him out of the workhouse at the advanced age of eight, and at that moment, *anything* would have been better than the life of hard, unforgiving labor in the mills that he seemed to be destined for. He had learned the value of loyalty when his first master had generously rewarded it—and harshly punished disloyalty. A mere Elemental Magician, he had a benign relationship with his Elementals, if a criminal one. He was a professional gambler, and had a small flock of sylphs who thought it highly amusing to tilt dice in his favor,and whisper the cards in each of his opponents' hands. He never used his own cards or dice, and thus, though he was often accused of cheating, nothing whatsoever could be proved. And the White Lodge either saw no reason to chastise him, or never knew about him—probably the latter.

His first master retired—and old as he was, was probably dead by now—and his second master hired him. This one . . . was one where the weighing of loyalty began. Another mere "magician," he was . . . a grifter. He always had a scheme going, and thanks to his magic, he generally pulled them off. But he had had a terrible weakness. Not content with visiting whorehouses, as Alf had learned to do, he had to use his powers to convince others to have sex with him: male, female, it didn't matter. It was one thing when he "seduced" victims of the working class. It was quite another when he decided to set his gaze higher. That was how he had gotten into trouble and how he had found himself on a small smuggling ship being taken across the channel—the trip arranged by Alf. Luckily almost none of the victims remembered Alf, or loyalty would definitely have been outweighed by circumstance.

As it was, he'd had his eye on Harcourt, who was in his then-current master's circle of disreputable magicians, and who, in fact, had been one of his master's chief protégés. So he had passed seamlessly from one good master to another who, like his first, rewarded loyalty very generously.

But generosity was far outweighed by the possibility of being eaten by some mystical monster. If that was where this was going . . . Alf decided, between the second and third brandy, that it might be time to pack up his things and find someone new. And possibly go straight to the White Lodge and let them know about the "rum goings-on."

One hour passed. Then two. Then three. From time to time he went out to check on the horse, make sure it was still warm and comfortable under the blanket he'd thrown over it, make sure no one had noticed and meddled with the coach. And three hours were more than enough time to wait. Something should have happened by now. The last girls had been spit out by the monster within a quarter hour. And if something had gone wrong. . . .

Alf made his way back down the stairs to find Alexandre still sitting, waiting, just out of reach of the pillar of darkness. "Somethin' th' matter, guv?" he asked, cautiously. In his opinion, Alexandre couldn't hold a candle to his last two masters when it came to magic. It seemed to him that most of what had been happening was all due to sheer accident on Alexandre's part, an accidental success that whatever lived on the other side of that blackness was only too happy to take advantage of.

"I ... don't know," Alexandre admitted. "It hasn't rejected the girl, but it hasn't sent her back, either." Alexandre looked over his shoulder at Alf, and Alf could see that his face was pale and drawn with anxiety. He moved a step back up on the staircase.

"Mebbe they was both virgins, an' th' thin's tryin ter make up its mind." Alf was beginning to get a very uneasy feeling about this. The same sort of uneasy feeling he'd had when his previous employer began engaging in riskier and riskier behavior. The same sort of uneasy feeling he'd had ... well, many, many times in the past, when he'd escaped danger by the skin of his teeth. He backed his way further up the stairs, quietly, to the point where he could just see the young man. If this thing couldn't see him, maybe it wouldn't realize he was there.

Then he heard it, and shuddered at the coldness of it. The voice in his head. Presumably Alexandre heard it too.

Are you prepared for your reward? Are you prepared to become a part of the Great Masters?

Alexandre bolted to his feet with excitement, while Alf's nerves practically sizzled with the conviction that something was very, very wrong. Alexandre was about to make a terrible, terrible mistake. *He* wasn't the one in control here. And Alf had the feeling that this was the culmination of a very carefully thought-out plan on the part of that—thing. "Yes!" he shouted. "Yes! I—"

Then you shall have what you desire.

And before Alf could move a muscle, the pillar erupted with those hideous, black, boneless tentacles, dozens of them. They seized Alexandre, and before he could even gasp, they dragged him into the pillar, quick as you could say "knife."

And then there was nothing left in the basement but the pillar. Alf froze, hoping the monster couldn't "see" him. For two long, breathless minutes, nothing happened. Alf knew it was two minutes, because he counted the ticks of the clock in the flat above.

And then the shape of the pillar changed a little. It bulged on Alf's side. The girl staggered out of the bulge, and then dropped bonelessly to the floor.

The pillar collapsed, as he had seen it do before. But this time, *not* into a dark hole in the middle of the basement floor. It collapsed, and kept collapsing, growing smaller and smaller until finally, there was nothing left. Not the void. Not the painted diagrams on the floor. Not the stone altar that had been there. Nothing but a scoured flagstone floor, an overturned chair, an oil lamp, and the breathing body of the mindless girl. Whatever the thing was . . . it was gone. Presumably it had what it wanted, and there was no more reason for it to keep a foothold here.

Alf let out the breath he had been holding, and sat himself down on the staircase, thinking.

The thing was *gone*. He knew his magic, and it wasn't going to come back through the basement anymore. The patterns that Alexandre—probably now his *late* master—had painted on the floor were what had anchored its portal here, and since it had erased them as it left, it had no more use for this basement. Whatever it had wanted, it had gotten, and now it had decamped to elsewhere, taking Alexandre with it. Which technically left Alf without an employer, and homeless. . . .

. . . except . . .

He wasn't homeless, not really. And he didn't actually need an employer now. He'd been able to forge Alexandre's name for years; he'd been practicing doing so on the chance that one day he might *have* to, the life of a magician being uncertain and all. For instance, what if Alexandre had gone and blinded himself? Or what if his hands were set on fire? Or what if he was laid up in bed, unconscious, for a long time? Alf knew where the blank cheques were. He knew where the stash of banknotes and the stack of gold guineas were. Alexandre had no notion he knew all these things, of course, and had Alexandre remained the sane and generous employer he'd been, Alf would never have made any use of this talent for forgery or his knowledge of where the hidden money was.

As for being able to pass the cheques, that was simple. He'd been taking cheques to the bank to cash for Alexandre for years. He could continue doing so, with the forged cheques, as long as he didn't start exceeding proper expenses without a damn good reason. He could continue to pay for the horse and coach, the household expenses, and whatever entertainment he cared to have.

The house was paid for. He could live here as long as he cared to, no one would know Alexandre wasn't here.

As for income, Alexandre's monthly stipend would continue to be deposited every quarter, as regular as clockwork, and Alf could draw cheques on it. As he understood these things, Alexandre had actually been living on the interest of a much larger sum, and as long as that "principal sum" was not touched, no one at the bank or the solicitor would care. Expenses would, in fact, be halved. If—not likely, but if—the solicitors came to have a look 'round, he could say the guv was out, which would technically be true. And meanwhile, he could be tucking half the expense money in his drawer, just in case the day came he had to cut and run for it. Bloody hell, if he felt like it, he could pick up some odd work with that coach and horse for a little more ready.

There was his old woman's house of course. Papers would have to be signed in person by the guv if it was sold, and that could be a problem . . . all right, he'd go through Alexandre's letters, and carefully copy out the right phrases suggesting to the solicitors that so valuable a property should be rented, not sold, and leave it to them to make the arrangements. Then there wouldn't be papers to sign, and there would be *more* income, income he could draw on by slowly, gradually, increasing the size of the cheques he was writing.

He felt a slow smile spreading over his face. This wasn't bad. This wasn't bad at all. Just one little inconvenient thing to be rid of, and then—well, then it would be time to celebrate his new independence and freedom.

He went to the prone body of the mindless girl and got her to her feet and up the stairs. No point in that elaborate ruse to take her to the police station now—what would be the point of it? He just made sure she was warmly dressed, with a folded blanket draped over her by way of a coat or a shawl, secured in place with a few rough stitches in the front and under the arms, and led her out to the road in front of the house, pointing her the way she should go. "Start walkin'. An' keep walkin' until somebody stops yew," he said, and obediently, she did just that. He was amazed that she didn't shuffle along, like some of the loonies or lads full gone with drink he'd seen. She walked pretty normally, all things considered.

He retreated to the front door immediately. Around him, all the houses were dark; it wasn't likely anyone had noticed him sending her on her way. Then he went back inside the house, locked up, went out the back door, and headed for the coach. The uneasy feeling was quite, quite gone. Time to put the horse to bed. Time to get a ride to where he could get a cab. Time to celebrate his new freedom, wealth, and independence. He grinned, and kept grinning, all the way to the stable. He'd wondered what the guv's posh bed felt like; he'd had to make do with an old straw tick on a foundation of rope, while the guv had a wool mattress, proper springs, and a featherbed over all, in a bed big enough for four.

"There ye go, ol' man," he said aloud to the horse, as he drove it to its stable. "Thi's 'ow bein' loyal gits yew rewards. Nice 'ot mash fer yew, nice 'ot toddy an' a even 'otter gel fer me."

The horse picked up its pace, which seemed to indicate it agreed with his sentiments.

He chuckled, clinked the money in his pocket, and grinned all the way to the stable.

Nan woke out of a fitful sleep to find that Amelia was shaking her arm. She came completely awake, immediately; habit from years of living with her slut of a mother, when being too slow to wake up could mean being slapped awake or worse. In the dim light from the coal fire, she saw Amelia was kneeling at the side of her bed. "Nan," the girl said urgently. "I'm about to have a vision—"

This might be the one we're waiting for. But she couldn't take the chance on Amelia being taken by the vision while she was sitting out there on the cold carpet. "Get into my bed," Nan ordered, throwing back the covers and vacating her place so that Amelia could fill it. The girl obeyed her, and it was just as well that Nan had not wasted time trying to get her back to her proper place, because she was no sooner comfortable than she went rigid, her eyes got that fixed, entranced look about them, and Nan knew that a vision had overtaken her.

Thoroughly used to this by now, Nan wrapped herself in a warm dressing gown, sat down on the edge of the bed, allowed herself to drop into a light trance with one hand on Amelia's, and joined her mind to the girl's. There was a moment of disorientation, and then she seemed to be falling through blackness until she emerged into a place that, unlike when she had been there in person, shone with a dim, spectral radiance outlining everything.

That certainly would have been helpful when we were actually there.

Amelia was already waiting for her there, in that world where darkness seemed to be eternal and everything was in ruins. It was the same, too-familiar, lifeless landscape: skeletal trees clawing at the starless sky, broken ruins, rubble-strewn road pocked with holes and studded with the shattered detritus of everyday living. Only *this* time the landscape was not unpopulated. Two of the spider-things were scuttling away, with something carried between them. It looked like the lifeless body of a male human, though man or boy, Nan couldn't tell. Was it a new victim, dragged inside by those black tentacles when Amelia sensed the portal opening? Was it someone who had been here a while, who had finally lost his battle to survive?

There was another change; an air of tense expectation. *Something* had changed, charging the very air with antici-

pation. *Something* new and different was about to happen.
There were glimpses of more creatures in the distance,
though what those creatures were, it was too dark and too
distant to tell. Still there was more activity and more movement than Nan had ever seen in any of these visions before,
and that suggested something had stirred the monsters of
this world into activity.

Then, abruptly, Nan felt the two of them ejected from
the vision, without warning, and so forcefully that when she
came to herself again, she was sitting on the floor beside the
bed, rather than on the edge of it, as if the shock had made
her lose her balance and fall. Amelia stirred, and met her
eyes.

"It has found the last victim it needed," she said, softly,
but with certainty. And she shivered with the cold that always overcame her after these episodes.

"You stay where you are, get warm, and rest. I'll send the
messages. *Roan!*" she called, and the little hob literally appeared in front of the fire, popping into existence as if he
had materialized himself. Though, it was entirely possible
he had just become visible. She'd had the feeling he was
following her around, mounting a guard over her and Amelia at night—if he'd been human, that would have been un-
settling, but given he was an Elemental, the thought was
actually comforting.

"Tell the others at the hospital that we think the creature
has gotten its seventh girl, please," she said. Roan saluted
without speaking, and vanished. Nan took a moment more
to find her slippers and rewrap her dressing gown, and ran
to the room Sahib and Memsa'b shared. She tapped urgently at the door.

"A moment," came Sahib's muffled voice, and it really
wasn't more than a moment before the door opened and
Sahib poked his head around the edge of it. He looked as if
he had already guessed what brought her, and his words
confirmed it.

"It's got the last girl?" he asked, although it sounded
more like a statement than a question. She nodded, and he
closed the door again, wasting no words. They all knew

their parts in this. They must have gone over the plan a dozen times before they separated, with Nan and Sarah and the birds staying at the school with Memsa'b and Sahib, and the rest basing their excursions out of the hospital. What the doctor made of all of this, she couldn't say, but he didn't have much choice in the matter. A Royal Command was a Royal Command.

She went back to her room to find Roan waiting on the hearth. "They've been told at the hospital. Yon big thinker was there, so he knows too. And I woke the Air and Water Masters and the Great Fire Master and told them." He peered at her, anxiously. "There anything more I can do?"

"Not tonight," she assured him. "When you see us leave for the hospital in the morning. . . ." she paused, and then went down on her knees beside him. "Roan, you are a hob, and your kind are not made for fighting. You and Durwin are free now. Unless the Oldest Old One has orders for you, I don't see any reason why you must stay where the danger is."

Roan drew himself up to his full height, such as it was. "And I see every reason, Daughter of Eve," he replied, stoutly. "You lot be fighting to keep *us* safe from these beasties, as much as yourself. Unless the Oldest Old One sends us away or gives us a task, we'll be there." He clapped a hand on the hilt of a tiny sword he now wore at his waist. "You have my sword."

A number of impulses moved through her; she picked the one that would allow him the most dignity. "Then I accept, on behalf of all of us. When we go to battle, I will be honored to have you at my side."

He stood even straighter, gave her a salute he must have learned from the soldiers, and disappeared.

She stood up again, gathered her dressing gown around her, and went back to bed. There was nothing more any of them could do until daylight.

Holmes joined them at the hospital at about teatime. As expected, the police in Battersea had called him in, but it

had been very shortly after Amelia had had her vision,
rather than the first thing in the morning. Evidently they
were so rattled at the Battersea constabulary that they
chose to call in Holmes immediately rather than waiting.
The new girl had been found by a cabby on his way to his
home in Battersea; by now all the cabbies knew to be looking out for girls wandering the streets in a daze.

They had met in the large room where the girls were
being kept in a row of beds installed for the circumstances.
Holmes had been waiting there, in front of the fire at the
opposite end of the chamber from the girls, when the contingent from the school arrived.

"This one is different, very different," Holmes said, with
what sounded oddly like satisfaction. "I believe our unknown foe has grown desperate. All the other girls were in
their mid to late teens. This child is *barely* thirteen. The others were girls of middle or upper class. And we were meant
to think this girl was the same; superficially, this girl was
dressed in fine garments no working class girl would ever
dream of owning, much less wear, and she was immacu-
lately groomed."

"But obviously, Holmes, you found something different,"
Watson stated. Holmes grinned. "Let me guess. She was
malnourished, her skin, hair and teeth showed the effects of
an insufficient diet. And she had calluses no girl of good
standing would ever display."

Holmes tipped an imaginary hat to his partner. "Quite
so. It was obvious on removing her shoes and stockings that
fine, well-fitted shoes were something she didn't wear at all;
her feet showed the signs of being blistered and healed
many times, as if by poor-fitting shoes or wooden clogs of
the sort worn in workhouses, and she had chilblains. Her
hands showed the distinctive calluses and cuts derived from
oakum-picking, that is, unraveling old ropes into their fi-
bers. I have never seen marks of this sort outside of a workhouse."

The large concert hall space was rather too large to heat
effectively; they were all huddled around the fireplace at
one end; Nan and Sarah were draped in their second-best

plain wool cloaks with quilted lining, with blankets over the top and the birds on their laps underneath. Grey and Neville's heads poked out through the openings in the front. "So the girl is from the workhouse? Was she a virgin?" Nan asked bluntly. As she could have predicted, John Watson blushed. Sherlock, however, answered her straightforward question just as bluntly.

"She was, which tells me there are not many workhouses in London that she could have come from. There are only two or three that maintain such strict separation of the sexes that girls past puberty retain their virginity for very long." He paused. "She was . . . very plain. Which probably aided her in keeping that condition."

"Do you think all that was meant to deceive the monster?" Sarah asked curiously.

Holmes shook his head. "Not at all. I think it was meant to deceive *us,* so that although her origin was unknown, we would assume she was of the same social standing as the rest of the girls and bring her here. Our foe must have been desperate enough to go to the effort of obtaining a workhouse girl, and by doing so, he left a trail I may be able to follow back to him once we have eliminated the greater threat. So, the main question now is, when do we want her brought here? Because the moment she joins the rest, our time begins to run out. I sensed a great impatience in that monster when we confronted it. I think it will be no time at all before it makes its move once the seventh girl is here."

He looked around the circle of faces; besides all the original group who had ventured into that strange world, only the leaders of the new combatants were here, representing their people. Lord Alderscroft for the White Lodge, or those of the White Lodge who had any sort of magic that could be considered a weapon. Sergeant Frederick Black for the platoon of soldiers. Memsa'b stood for a circle of psychics she had managed to gather—none of them was as strong as Nan, so they would work together, while she worked alone. Robin—well, Robin was bringing Elementals, or so Nan assumed, but he had said with a bit of a grim look that they were not Elementals that anyone here would recognize. If circumstances had been less fraught, she would have been wildly curious about that. As it was, she just hoped that whatever they were, they were going to be fierce enough.

Sarah ... Sarah had been going about these past few days with an abstracted look on her face, and Nan assumed it was because she was communing with spirits. Whether or not spirits could be of any help—well, Nan had no idea. They certainly had been useful against the Lorelei, but the thing they faced now was a lot tougher than a single woman, however magical she was, and it was bringing with it an army.

"I think we're all ready, sir," said the Sergeant. "We ain't going to get any readier for more waitin'."

Holmes nodded. "Then I'll go and bring her myself in the morning. You all know the plan. The rest of you, get sleep, a good meal, and be ready to face this thing once I arrive with her."

He got up and left, and all the rest except Nan and Sarah dispersed.

The room they were in looked more like a ballroom, or the banqueting hall at Hampton Court Palace, than a concert hall. Perhaps it had been intended to serve all of these functions when the hospital had been built. It was one single, large room, wooden paneled and floored in oak, about three stories tall, with the windows all in the upper half of the walls. So at least the drafts weren't bad. It was much longer than it was wide, with a fireplace and two doors at either end. The girls were lying in their beds on the other side of the hall, uncannily silent, like unmoving lumps of blankets. They were absolutely, mechanically obedient to even quite complicated commands. Three times a day, a nurse went to each in turn, ordered her out of bed, walked her around the room, ordered her to eat and drink, then walked her to the water closet to do whatever it was she needed to do. Then the girl was ordered back into bed, and the nurse moved on to the next. The whole procedure took three hours, about thirty minutes for each girl. It was ... very uncomfortable for Nan to watch. The whole thing made her queasy. The empty eyes haunted her dreams. The sounds they made, walking on the wooden floor in their slippers, were so mechanical that they could have been giant puppets rather than girls. The only thing that made *any* difference in their behavior was giving them morphine, which made their bodies sleep.

"I've been talking to the ghosts here," Sarah said, interrupting her thoughts.

"There's ghosts here?" Nan replied, surprised. "I would have thought this place was too new for ghosts."

"The doctor also accepts wealthy people who are going to die," her friend said, matter-of-factly. "It has mostly been people with consumption, but there was one gentleman who contracted some sort of strange sickness in Egypt, and a couple who did the same in India, and some from the Boer War. They are all former officers. They are actually eager to help. They . . . they think they are confined to earth for some dereliction of duty, and if they can discharge their obligations by defending England here and now, they'll be free to move on."

Oh—what stuff and nonsense! "You did tell them that's not true, right?" Nan demanded.

Grey sighed. "Stubborn," she said.

"Grey is right. Their minds are completely made up. If they believe it that truly, there is nothing I can do to convince them otherwise. At least," she added thoughtfully, "Not with so little time to work with. However, that means I have a small army of spirits that are helping me. They all confirm that the girls are soulless. This . . . disturbs them, even more than it disturbs us. And it has confirmed in them the desire to find out just what happened to those souls."

"Is that going to help us?" Nan asked doubtfully.

"It won't hurt," Sarah pointed out. "We really need to know *how* the thing does that, and they'll be in the best position to tell us that before it happens to one of us. And, I hope, warn us in time to save us from such a fate!"

Robin, who was, as usual of late, looking like a completely ordinary young man of the "country yeoman" sort, wandered up to them. Nan noticed that even after being "within housen" for days now, he still smelled pleasantly of ferns, moss, and a faint hint of pine. He looked grim. "The question I have, which I am going to put to you young ladies, since you have been witness to it in action, is this. I have many of the older, more dangerous Earth Elementals at my disposal now, like trolls—though I have been careful to pick the ones that have never tasted human flesh, so I can direct them against the monsters that will come. But this may be a battle in which we need *everything*. Do I call the Wild Hunt?"

Nan looked up at him, and so did Neville. "What is your concern?" she asked him. "I know they are dangerous, and I know they can affect spirits as well has the living. But what about them has you worried?"

"The Hunt is . . . neither good nor evil, and *I* do not control it, though I can summon it. It answers only to the Huntsman. *He* determines who or what is fair prey. Normally, on the rare occasions when I've summoned it, there is been someone obviously very wicked that needs to be dealt with. But this time. . . ." He shook his head. "*Is* that monster wicked? Are its subjects?"

"Robin, it's been ripping souls out of innocent girls!" Sarah replied, in a scandalized tone of voice. "It tried to kill us! It's certainly been killing other people!"

"Yes, but . . . by the standards of the world it is in, that might not be wicked. That might just be survival. And I don't know what the Huntsman will think of that." He looked helplessly from Nan to Sarah and back again. "And as if that isn't bad enough, some of the people here have probably done things in their lives that the Huntsman would deem sufficiently wicked to make *them* prey. What if he turns on us rather than on the monster and its minions?"

And Neville made a rude sound at him. Astonished, Robin looked down at the black-feathered head poking out of the front of Nan's cloak. "And what exactly does that mean, bird of ill omen?" he demanded.

"Monster wins, Huntsman dies. Stupid," Neville replied, and made another rude noise, expressing with tone rather than words just what at idiot he thought Robin was. "Huntsman is not stupid!"

Robin stood there with his jaw working back and forth for a very long moment. "I hate to admit that I have been bested by a bird, but you are right," he said at last. "This is the Huntsman's world as well. I think I'll be safe in summoning him."

"You're overthinking," Sarah said in a kindly tone of voice. "I'm not surprised; this is probably the longest you've spent among the Sons of Adam and the Daughters of Eve in a very, very long time. We're contaminating you with our prevarication and indecision."

He shook himself not unlike a dog. "Brrrr. I think you are. After this, I am going to take a very long time among the wild sheep of the Orkneys. And I am not sure *that* will be far enough to get my mind set back where it belongs."

Let's just all get through this alive, please, was Nan's only thought.

Morning light streamed through the high windows in the hall. The fireplaces here were fed with wood, not coal, and the pleasant scent of woodsmoke flavored everything. The soldiers were set up against the walls along both sides of the room, rifles at the ready, ammunition piled beside each of them. Some special ammunition, too: all of it had been blessed by their chaplain, and some of it was dipped in silver. Memsa'b and Sahib fronted a small group of psychical workers in one corner. A handful of magicians, including John and Mary and fronted by Lord Alderscroft, waited in the opposite corner—that would be the members of the White Lodge who were capable of offensive magic, most of which were Fire Masters like Alderscroft himself. Nan and Sarah stood with the psychics. They were dressed for action, Sarah in a divided skirt and boiled-wool jacket, with leather guards on her forearms, Nan in men's riding jodhpurs, stout boots, and a heavy leather vest over a tunic of boiled wool.

Sherlock led the seventh girl into the room with the others. "Stand there," he told her, positioning her in the midst of their beds. Then he moved to the fireplace behind their beds.

A hush fell over the room. No one moved.

The silence held for so long that for a moment Nan was afraid that nothing was going to happen. That they had been mistaken, that the seven girls had *nothing* to do with the creature's intentions, and that it would cross—or had already crossed—somewhere else and its invasion had already begun.

But then, abruptly, she felt the temperature drop, and her breath puffed out in clouds in the suddenly frigid air.

She didn't need to see the other six girls rising from their beds and joining the seventh to know that her fears had been wrong. The thing was coming, and coming *now*.

19

THE girls all suddenly rose from their prone positions at exactly the same moment. As one, they swung their legs over the sides of their beds, and the soldiers tightened their grips on their rifles. As one, they stood up and began walking until they converged on the new one. With a strangely sinuous motion, eerily reminiscent of the writing of tentacles, they entwined their arms until they were bound in a tight circle. They tilted their heads back, opened their mouths, and began to chant.

Monotonous, identical no matter which throat it was coming from, and utterly unintelligible syllables emerged from them in a kind of drone. There was *nothing* about the guttural chant that was even remotely familiar to Nan.

But it certainly had an effect on the Celtic Warrior—and on Grey and Neville. She felt a primal rage engulf her— *some* incarnation of the past recognized those words—and in a flash, she was wearing her bronze armor, woolen tunic and trews, and carrying her glowing bronze sword and a small round wooden shield strapped to her arm so she could still use her sword two-handed at need. And Neville was now the size of an eagle, with Grey the size of a huge hawk. This time, instead of staying with the girls, they both flew up to the rafters. Nan placed herself between the group of psychics and the chanting girls; Memsa'b in her short Grecian tunic and with her spear and Sahib in his medieval armor and with his sword both moved to flank her. And flanking them were Agansing and Karamjit, a wedge of protection in front of people who were ill-equipped to defend themselves.

On the other side of the room, Lord Alderscroft and half of the magicians with him held out hands that were engulfed in flame while fire in the form of lizards climbed over their shoulders or wove patterns around their feet. John Watson's form of offense was more mundane; he had a shotgun and a double bandolier of shells. Nan couldn't see Mary from where she stood, but she knew that Mary was a fine shot with a rifle and probably had one in her hands.

A black void formed between the chanting girls and the assembled defenders. It doubled in size every few seconds, until it stood nearly a story tall.

And then the monsters poured through it, and with them the strange, bitter wind of that other world. Dozens of them. Not just the things Nan had seen before, but other creatures, things that in the chaos she barely got a chance to look at, much less identify. She only knew that she was fighting for her life and the lives of those behind her as the things hurled themselves at their line. She heard the steady *crack* of rifles and the voice of the Sergeant, calmly, calling out orders. But mostly she saw horrifying, hideous things flinging themselves at her, trying to disembowel her with claws and talons, shred her with fangs, crush her with powerful jaws, sting her with barbed tails. The stench of these things was overpowering, bitter, sour, *poisonous.* She didn't remember that from the other world—but maybe that had been because they had all been in the open then and were in the confines of four walls now.

Neville and Grey dove at the things from above, shoving off from the beams where they perched, plummeting to hammer at a head or rip at a limb with their powerful beaks, and flapping back up to safety before the monsters could retaliate.

And *none* of it was enough. The monsters kept pouring in, two for every one that was cut down. The only limit to how many could pour in seemed to be the size of the portal and the size of the room itself. Nan and the others were pushed back into the corner—she couldn't tell what was happening to the others, but the sharp *cracks* of the rifle volleys were growing more ragged, and the only thing she could see of Alderscroft and his group were the occasional gouts of flame rising above the heads of the beasts.

Where's Puck? she wondered frantically, as she hewed and hacked at the beasts two-handed, her arms aching, spattered from head to toe with gore. Roan should have alerted him the moment Sherlock brought the seventh girl to the hall. So where was he? *Did he desert us after all?*

But just as that horrible thought crossed her mind, the two doors in the middle of the wall to her left burst open, unleashing an army of things most children would have recognized from fairy books on the horde of monsters.

There were trolls, eight feet tall and looking as if they were made of stone, wielding huge clubs. There were giants even taller, who could barely make it through doors that were themselves ten feet tall. There was something Nan would have been willing to swear was a "small" dragon, and plenty more of the fiery salamanders. There were a half dozen tall warriors too, with faces the color of clay, armored in antique style and carrying thick bronze blades. There were creatures she *didn't* recognize; they almost seemed to be composed of rags and sticks, with a horse-skull where the head should have been. But despite their apparent fragility, when those heads came down and rose again, it was usually with a limb between their teeth.

Nan heard an unholy battle howl from somewhere near her waist, glanced down, and saw Durwin and Roan making good on their promise of defending her and Sarah, with little round wooden shields to protect them and swords that glowed like Nan's own.

As short as the hobs were, the monsters generally didn't notice them until it was too late, and one or the other had gotten up underneath their target and chopped a leg nearly in half or executed a perfect gutting strike.

As for Robin—she got glimpses of him bareback atop what appeared to be an enormous black stallion. She knew better than to think it was anything of the sort, of course. A *pooka,* most likely. He was flanked on either side by two more of the beasts, which fought viciously, lashing out with all four feet and snapping flesh and bone with their teeth. And flanking *them* were creatures that looked to be half man, half tree; as tall as the trolls, with hair and beard of leaves, clothing of bark, and rough skin that seemed half skin and half bark. The creatures seemed impervious to stings, bites or claws, and waded into the monsters, tearing them apart with their bare hands. *Green Men!* She'd never seen one, only heard of them, mostly in the Arthurian tale of Gawaine and the Green Knight.

And yet . . . the monsters still kept coming.

Nan struck, and struck, and struck until her arm felt like lead and her breath burned in her throat. She longed for a chance to rest, but the never-ending torrent of monsters gave her no chance. And just when she was certain things could not get worse, the strange chant of the seven girls rose several notes and took on a tone of urgency.

She looked up from the struggle in front of her for a moment . . . and was sorry she had.

The Queen herself had appeared, slithering through the open portal.

The hood of its robe had been cast back, and its eyeless face was in full view. It was the color of rancid butter; its head was covered with a nest of ever-moving tendrils, like wire-thin worms. Where its eyes should have been were shallow pits; it had no nose, either, just two slits in the middle of its face. In place of a mouth, there was a round, lipless orifice ringed by needle-like teeth, like that of a lamprey.

It moved with a curious gliding motion, and what emerged from the sleeves of its robe were not arms. Just as Nan had guessed, what served it for upper appendages, and probably lower ones too, were something very like tentacles.

A thing with a head like a skinned panther charged at her, and Nan was forced to take her attention off the Queen. When she looked again, it had not moved; it seemed to be surveying the battlefield. Looking for what? Nan couldn't imagine.

But that was when she noticed it was surrounded by an almost-invisible bubble. Like the shields against magic she had seen the Elemental Masters produce—except that *this* shield, as evidenced by the sparks when bullets struck it, was impervious to physical attack.

Oh no—how can we counter that?

It appeared it was not sharing its protection with its underlings, but that was the only bright spot in this increasingly hopeless fight. She wanted to try and back out of combat to see if her mental powers could be used as a weapon, but she couldn't do *that* without putting people behind her at risk.

Superficially this was a stalemate. In actuality they were going to lose unless something changed in their favor. The enemy had an ever-renewing source of monsters. They only had those who had assembled here.

In desperation, Nan reached out to the only person who *might* be able to come up with an idea at this point.

She sought for, and found, Holmes' mind. He had exhausted all the ammunition for his revolver and had resorted to his singlestick. *We have to shut the portal!* she thought as hard as she could at him. And then a thing with giant, razor-sharp crab-like pincers lunged for her, and she spent the next couple of minutes dueling with it for her life.

It was Roan who finally dispatched the beast from underneath; as it collapsed, she glanced up again to see the creature's shield momentarily drop, as it lashed out a tentacle to ensnare Grey. *"Grey!"* she screamed in warning—not that she could have been heard over the riot—but Grey was smarter than that, and dodged up into the ceiling where it couldn't reach her as Neville dove in and slashed at the extended tentacle with his beak in passing. He scored a hit too, severing the tip right off. The creature uttered a piercing, keening cry of pain, which redoubled as a handful of bullets struck it. The shield snapped up again immediately, and the monster howled its rage and pain.

So, you can *be hurt!* Evidently some of the soldiers had seen that as well, for a ragged cheer came up from along the walls.

But being wounded only infuriated the thing more. It howled, which seemed to have the effect of redoubling the other monsters' fury. That was when Karamjit's guard dropped for a split second. He was hit badly, collapsed, and was pulled back to safety by the psychics behind him—and a moment later, Agansing was knocked unconscious and likewise rescued.

They're doing it. They're wearing us down. Taking us out of the fight one at a time.

We can't win this. . . .

Despair flooded over her for a moment. Then her resolve hardened. *Then we'll end it like the three hundred Spartans.*

But just as she steeled herself for a mad rush at the monsters, the strange high-pitched chanting, which had carried right over the sound of the fighting, faltered.

And the monsters paused for a moment; every gaze, whether friend or foe, turned toward the sheltered area behind the Queen Monster where the seven girls had been chanting.

One girl sagged in the arms of the rest. Next to her, Holmes was jabbing a hypodermic needle into the neck of the next, while Puck waited beside him on the huge black "horse," standing guard so no one could touch him. Neither the Queen monster nor her minions seemed to understand what he was doing, nor how to counter it.

It was over in moments; the last girl collapsed and Puck pulled Holmes up onto the back of the *pooka*—for that was obviously what it was now that Nan got good look at it—and the three of them executed an impossible leap that brought them to the side of the room and the line of soldiers there.

And the void vanished.

With a hellish screech, the Monster Queen sent her minions hurtling back into battle while she turned her attention to the prostrate girls. But Holmes must have given them an enormous dose of morphia or some similar drug; no effort the Queen expended revived them for more than a second. Furious now, the Queen turned back to those opposed to her, just as Sarah caught Nan's attention with a frantic wave.

Nan fended off four of the legs of a spider-thing and opened her mind to her friend's. *Busy!*

The spirits say that the girls' souls are in the Queen.

So?

They're still alive *in the Queen. Otherwise their bodies would be dead, too.*

Nan snatched Roan out of the jaws of something like a crocodile covered in hair and blinded it with a slash across its eyes so that it went blundering into the mob, snapping at friend and foe alike. She knew what Sarah was saying: kill the Queen, free the girls' souls, and they might return to their proper bodies.

Or might not. Right now, the Queen was the least of their worries, even if they could figure out some way to bring that shield down. And right now, even though reinforcements were no longer pouring through the portal every minute, the odds were still not in their favor. *Well, ask your spirits if they can pry the girls away from the Queen. That might weaken her.*

She had no more time to spare for Sarah; they had already lost Agansing and Karamjit, and that only left five fighters to guard the psychics. One of *those* was down, too. How many soldiers had they lost? And what about the magicians on the other side of this mob? How were they faring? The Queen might not have her reinforcements, but she could still win this battle, and once they were all out of her way, she could probably reopen the portal herself—or wait for the girls to revive—or turn seven of the patients or staff here at the hospital into more of her soulless minions. There had to be at least seven of them who were virgins.

The Queen suddenly uttered a piercing cry that did not sound like a command, but Nan's attention was captured by the sound of a horn on the other side of the room, where she had last seen Holmes and Puck.

It was the call of no ordinary horn. It held in it the lonely howl of a single wolf searching for his pack, the wail of a fury looking for vengeance, and the triumphant cry of a victorious elk. It made the hair go up on the back of Nan's neck, and the small part of her that was not already terrified by the situation they were in gibbered with horror and demanded that she drop everything and hide.

Because something as dreadful as the Monster Queen had been called, and would without a doubt answer.

For Robin Goodfellow, Oldest of Old Things in all England, had summoned the Wild Hunt, and when one such as Robin calls, that which is called invariably answers.

The last time he had called it in her presence, she and Sarah had been children, and he had ordered them to close their eyes as it arrived. She had no such luxury today; with body weary and aching, wounded, and sweat-soaked, she had no choice but to keep fighting. But there was no doubt when the Hunt arrived.

The light in the room dimmed, the walls seemed to thin, then disappear, and they were all somehow standing, still fighting, in a snow-buried, mist-covered meadow. Nan somehow understood this was an echo of the meadow that had been here long before the hospital had been built. Confused now, the monsters spread out, and the Queen reared up to her full height, screaming unintelligible commands at them.

And then, breaking through the mist, came the Hunt in full cry.

First came the hounds—black as velvet with fiery eyes, they circled the monsters and humans alike, bellowing and baying in tones that made Nan want to clap her hands over her ears and sink to the ground lest she go mad. Then came twenty riders and their leader, all on horses as black as the hounds with similar eyes; they also circled the group and halted before Puck. Puck's mount bowed before the one-eyed leader, and Puck saluted him.

The fighting had completely stopped. The monsters appeared to have no idea who to attack, and the Queen seemed struck dumb.

In fact . . . they weren't moving at all. And neither were most of their friends.

That was when she realized that she couldn't move either.

No, she realized. *None of us can move. The Huntsman has frozen us in place. This is his ground, and he can command us and everything on it.*

"Oldest of Old Things," said the leader, in a voice like something coming from a tomb. "What is this that has come into our England?"

"It is Death," Puck replied steadily.

"It is Wickedness," Holmes stated, looking up fearlessly into the eye of the Huntsman.

"It doesn't belong here!" cried Nan from where she stood, whatever passed for the blood of these things running down her sword and dripping onto the ground. *At least we can talk!* "Huntsman, will you hunt? Will you drive these things out, or send them to their fate?"

The Huntsman looked over the heads of all the creatures between himself and her, and she sensed she was being weighed and measured, and if she could have shivered, she would have. "And will you Hunt beside me until I release you, Battle Maiden?"

Sarah gasped. "No—" whispered Memsa'b. Nan knew why. Since that day one summer when the Huntsman had claimed a murderous ghost as his prey, she had studied the Hunt, and she knew all about it. If you promised the Huntsman you would Hunt with him until he released you—you might hunt for an hour, or a year, or . . . well, there were those in his Hunting Pack who had not been released in centuries.

But if this was what it was going to take—

"I will," she said, raising her chin as Neville flew to her and landed on her shoulder.

"I Hunt too!" the raven declared, and the Huntsman laughed.

"Well said! Hunters!" he called, making his horse rear and prance. "Bring the lady a steed!"

She found that she could move again. Behind her, she heard Sarah whimpering. One of the riders trotted out of the pack, leading a riderless horse. Nan mounted into the saddle and settled her sword in her hand. "I'm ready," she declared.

"Then *we fight!*"

The monsters unfroze. The Queen let out another one of her hellish screams, not at all disturbed by the change in her surroundings. And the black horse leapt, and carried Nan into the heart of the fighting.

No longer confined to the space between the four walls of the hall at the hospital, both sides spread out, and the fighting broke into little groups. *Now* the psychics could come into their own; now that they could see targets clearly, they could concentrate on one whose opponent was faring badly, wrest control of the creature from the Queen for a crucial moment, and give the human a fighting chance. The soldiers had exhausted their ammunition and were laying about themselves with bayonets and swords, often helped by one or more of the Hunters. Nan was surrounded on all sides, but the horse, whether it was demon or spirit or merely another form of Elemental, was as much of a fighter as she, and laid about itself skillfully with hooves and teeth. The Hounds of the Hunt did their share too; fearsome as they were, they were no match for the monsters one-on-one, but they could harry and distract, and so they did, like dogs keeping a great boar at bay while human hunters moved in with rifles and spears.

She lost all track of time, lost track of everything except the next monster to be cut down. Until suddenly, unexpectedly, she chopped the head off a thing like a stick insect with huge, venomous jaws, to find there *were* no more foes. Or at least, there were none in her immediate vicinity.

The Huntsman appeared at her side, out of nowhere. "So Battle Maiden, can you throw a spear?" He offered her something that looked more like a javelin than a spear; she took it and hefted it, and nodded. "Then yonder is the author of all this trouble." He pointed at the Queen, still protected by row after row of her monsters.

Nan shook her head. "She's protected," she protested.

"Not from this." The Huntsman raised the eyebrow over the eye not covered by a patch. "But it is my daughter's and no man can wield it, only one who is willing to give all for her fellows can give it strength, and only the true-hearted can send it to the mark."

Doubt struck her, as she balanced the spear in her hand. *Was* she "true-hearted"? And what would using this weapon of the Huntsman's cost her? This was a "fairy gift"—but did it come with a hidden price? What did his words cover? What had he *not* told her? True, it might kill the Queen, but would it cost Nan her own life? Or would it doom her to ride with the Hunt forever?

It doesn't matter what it costs me if our world is safe again, she decided. *This has to end now.* And she hurled the spear with all her might.

It flashed like a bolt of black lightning across the distance between her and the Queen. It pierced the barrier that protected the Queen with a sound like the tearing of the world in two.

And it buried itself in the Queen's chest so deeply it protruded from her back.

Everything, and everyone, froze.

The Queen opened her mouth as if to shriek, but all that came out was a gurgling cry. She wavered in place for a moment, then, bonelessly, she collapsed to the ground and did not move again.

Her monsters shrieked in a thousand different voices; shrieked in panic, and tried to flee. But the Hounds were ready, and so were the Hunters, and while the humans fell to their knees in exhaustion, or leaned against one another, they hunted down and slew every last one of them.

When the final monster had been pounded into the ground by the hooves of one of the horses, the Hunt gathered itself around the Huntsman and Nan. Outside that circle waited Puck, Sarah, the Watsons, and Holmes, all of them staring numbly at her, none of them daring to move or speak.

I never thought I would see Sherlock Holmes speechless.

"A good Hunt," the Huntsman said, with satisfaction. "A good kill. And now, Battle Maiden, what shall we do with *you?*"

Her heart pounded with fear, and she was afraid that if she did not keep control of herself she would burst into tears. But she had made the promise, and she had known what she was doing. She would have to honor it. "Whatever you will," she said, steadily. "I vowed to Hunt with you until you released me. I'd like Neville to stay with me, though, if he wants to."

"Hurrrr," said Neville, raising all his feathers, making it very clear they'd have to pry his talons off her shoulder and bundle him off in a basket before he'd leave her.

The Huntsman laughed. "And what would I do with *another* raven? My own are trouble enough. Give me back my horse, Nan Killian, and go with your friends in peace. It was a privilege to see you fight."

Feeling lightheaded with relief, she dismounted. And no sooner had she set both feet on the ground than the meadow faded, then the Hunt faded, and last of all, the Huntsman faded away, leaving them all standing in the decimated concert hall.

The place was an absolute wreck. Piled high with the bodies of the monsters and their Queen, bullet holes riddled the walls, and there was nothing left of the furnishings, sparse as they had been, that was bigger than a finger. And Nan looked around, and suddenly realized that, although there were many wounded or injured, *no one had died*.

She sat down abruptly where she was, as Sarah picked her way around the edge of the room to get to where the seven girls were still lying in their tangle of bodies. Nan was wearing the ordinary men's clothing—riding jodhpurs, a heavy woolen tunic, boots, and a helmet borrowed from the soldiers—that she had been wearing before her transformation. Sarah, too, was back to her divided skirt and jacket. And Neville and Grey were their normal sizes. They both flew down from the rafters, Grey going straight to Sarah's shoulder. Neville landed in a clear spot, hopped over to her and begged for a lap. She made room for him, stroking him, too exhausted to feel any relief.

How in the name of God Almighty are we going to explain all . . . this?

"How," apparently, was a very special group of people under the aegis of Mycroft Holmes, who swept in as soon as it was clear that it was safe to do so, whisked everyone away, and repeatedly told them all that "everything would be taken care of." At that point, Nan didn't care. Someone took care of her wounds—wounds she hadn't even realized she'd taken. Someone else got her clothing to replace what she was wearing—now irreparably ruined with whatever hideously smelling ichor passed for blood in the monsters. Someone helped her into a carriage with Neville under her salvaged cloak, and soon the rest of the Harton School contingent joined her there, and with everyone too exhausted and numb to speak, the carriage rolled away. She—and Neville—were asleep before they arrived. She had vague memories of being guided to her room and her bed, with Neville electing to nestle down into the bedclothes as if he was in a nest rather than taking his usual perch. And by the time she woke up again, it was teatime the next day.

Sarah's bed and Grey's perch were empty. Seeing she was awake, Neville stood up, roused all his feathers, and looked at her expectantly.

"Eat!" he demanded.

Her stomach growled in answer, and she threw on the first clothing that came to hand, put Neville on her shoulder, and went in search of everyone.

The first place she checked was Memsa'b's drawing room, which turned out to be the right guess. The air was full of the agreeable smell of curry, both fireplaces were lit and roaring, and the room was full of people. Sarah looked to be halfway through an enormous plate of curry on a tray in her lap, Grey was eyes-deep in a cup of chopped vegetables, and there was another cup of bloody bits of meat waiting for Neville. He leapt from her shoulder to his perch and set to it, while one of the servants made sure Nan was supplied with the same curry Sarah was eating on a tray of her own. There was also beer, and although she wasn't much of a drinker, she felt strongly in need of it.

"What happened?" she asked, then started stuffing herself. She felt as hollow as an empty vase, and as if she would never get enough to eat.

"We have no idea what happened at the hospital, except that Mycroft sent us a message saying that 'thanks to Sarah' the seven girls are awake and no longer mindless." Memsa'b frowned. "I cannot think that being part of that hideous Queen is going to have done their minds any good, however."

"I believe my brother is being rather too sanguine on that subject," Holmes drawled from the darkest corner of the room. "But the young women are now under his aegis and not ours, and he has made it very clear we are not to enquire after them, or their welfare. The same, I am told, goes for the remains of the creatures we fought. In fact, we are ordered by my brother never to speak of this to anyone except among ourselves. Tedious of him."

Nan looked over at Sarah, who shrugged. "The girls' souls were released when the Queen died, and I helped them back into their bodies, but I won't speak for their sanity after this. Of course, they were one and all fairly unimaginative girls, and if they are sufficiently strong-willed, they may be able to convince themselves it was all a fever dream. I hope so," she added. "There is nothing that any of them did to deserve this. They are absolutely the purest of victims in this situation. What they *do* deserve is the right to have the sort of life that they want."

"What about Karamjit, Agansing and Selim?" Nan asked anxiously, certain now that Sarah was fine. Grey showed no anxiety whatsoever, and whatever fright Nan had given her friend, she knew that Sarah knew she could not have acted otherwise.

"Selim is much better—" began Sahib.

"Selim can speak for himself, Sahib." Nan became aware that there were three cots placed over near the second fireplace in the spacious drawing room, each one containing one of the three warriors that had fought with them. Selim was propped up on his own elbow, the other two on piles of pillows. "Selim is very much aware of his mortality and that he is no longer as young as he once was. And very grateful that Allah forgave his hubris and allows him to tarry awhile before attempting the gates of Paradise."

"'Tis about time, you old fool," Karamjit mock-grumbled. "I have been telling you this thing for years."

"A Gurkha does not know age—" began Agansing, who was interrupted by Karamjit flinging a cushion at his head.

"To make a long story short, we were never at the hospital, there was never any battle with an otherworldly creature, and the young ladies we were investigating were the victims of some unknown disease that caused a brain fever," Sahib said.

"That may be so, but I am going to endeavor to trace that last girl to whatever workhouse she came from, and from there, to whoever it was who purchased her indenture as a servant," Holmes said firmly. "If there is an agent out there who caused this once, it could happen again."

Sarah looked up from her now-empty plate, and said, somberly, "Yes, it could. And we should be on the watch and on our guard for just such a thing."

"I am going to be guardedly optimistic," John Watson replied. "Historically, those who have allied themselves with such creatures are generally rewarded by being devoured or destroyed themselves. I suspect that is the fate of our unknown collaborator with evil."

"I hope you are right," said Memsa'b. "We called in a great many favors that we may not have at our disposal another time."

"I hope there is *never* another time," Mary Watson said fervently. "I would be very happy dealing in smaller crises. A werewolf outbreak, perhaps, or a plague of vampires."

"Oh *come* now, Mary, you certainly aren't going to gull me into believing those mythological beings are real," Holmes scoffed.

"Oh?" Mary turned to give Holmes the sort of stare one gives a particularly stupid child. "And what about the Green Men you saw with your own eyes? And the salamanders. And the *trolls?* For someone who claims—"

"Children, children, don't fight," Sahib said indulgently. "Take up that particular argument somewhere other than our drawing room, please."

Mary sniffed. Holmes shrugged. "I will admit," he said at last, "That being involved in this superstitious farradiddle does make for more interesting cases."

"Oh *please*—" Mary said, but was interrupted by the entrance of one of the servants.

"There are three young men with letters of introduction to you, Sahib," he said diffidently. "Shall I show them in?"

Sahib looked baffled, and so did Memsa'b. Nan could not help but notice, however, that Selim, Karamjit, and Agansing were looking . . . conspiratorial.

So she was not terribly surprised to see that the three young men in question—not *terribly* young after all, certainly in their late twenties or early thirties—were dressed, respectively, in the native costumes of the Gurkha, the Sikh and the Indian Moslem, all modified to suit the bitter winter weather.

All three bowed stiffly to Sahib when they were brought before him. The Sikh seemed to be their spokesperson, and he began to open his mouth, when Karamjit interrupted him, "Sahib Harton, may I introduce our nephews. After due consultation with their elders, we have selected these three youngsters to train as our replacements in your service, and we beg you to accept them immediately."

Nan was not sure which of the four were the more astonished, Sahib Harton, or the three young men, who apparently had been unaware that their uncles were *lying down* in the presence of their employer. All four mouths fell open, and all four faces had such comical expressions that the entire room broke up with laughter.

Selim held his midsection as the laughter ended, looking still amused, but pained. "Please to be refraining from making such faces again for some time. I fear I may have torn stitches."

Sahib finally recovered. "You are certainly hired, and you will certainly begin learning your duties as soon as your uncles are able to instruct you," he said, and turned to the servant. "Mustafa, please see to it that these gentlemen get rooms next to their uncles, and something to eat, and help them take their belongings to their new quarters. I am sure they are fatigued by the journey and will want to rest. We'll let them get settled and used to our School before their uncles start putting them through their paces."

The young men followed the servant out, and Sahib turned on Karamjit. "What do you mean by this, old friend? You are surely not leaving us—"

"Nothing of the sort," Karamjit replied, interrupting. "But we are getting no younger, and if you and Memsa'b keep having adventures of this sort, we will certainly *need* some younger bodies to absorb the punishment while we convey orders from behind some sturdy wall. That is all. We fully intend to grow ancient, wrinkled and withered in your service, forcing you in the end to hire ayahs for all three of us."

Agansing snickered, and Selim held his side again. Then Karamjit turned to Holmes.

"And you, good sir, if you are going to keep entangling yourself with the Hartons' affairs, I advise you to begin training a replacement of your own. Their lives tend to be . . . interesting."

Grey laughed, and Neville made a rude noise. "Interesting!" Grey exclaimed. "Verrrrry interesting!"

But Holmes only smiled.

MERCEDES LACKEY

The Dragon Jousters

JOUST
978-0-7564-0153-4

ALTA
978-0-7564-0257-3

SANCTUARY
978-0-7564-0341-3

AERIE
978-0-7564-0426-0

"A must-read for dragon lovers in particular and for fantasy fans in general." —*Publishers Weekly*

"It's fun to see a different spin on dragons...and as usual Lackey makes it all compelling."—*Locus*

To Order Call: 1-800-788-6262
www.dawbooks.com

DAW 141